invisible REPUBLIC

CREATED BY **GABRIEL HARDMAN & CORINNA BECHKO**

WRITTEN BY	**GABRIEL HARDMAN & CORINNA BECHKO**
ART BY	**GABRIEL HARDMAN**
COLORS BY	**JORDAN BOYD**
LETTERING—ISSUE 10	**SIMON BOWLAND**
DESIGN BY	**DYLAN TODD**
EDITORIAL ASSISTANCE BY	**BRENDA SCOTT ROYCE**

INVISIBLE REPUBLIC, VOLUME 02.

COPYRIGHT 2016 GABRIEL HARDMAN & CORINNA BECHKO.

FIRST PRINTING. JULY 2016.

ISBN : 978-1-63215-658-7

Published by Image Comics, Inc. Office of publication: 2001 Center Street, 6th Floor, Berkeley, CA 94704. © 2016 Gabriel Hardman & Corinna Bechko. Image Comics® and its logos are registered trademarks of Image Comics, Inc.

Originally published in single magazine form as INVISIBLE REPUBLIC #6-10.

Printed in the USA.

For information regarding the CPSIA on this printed material call: 203-595-3636 and provide reference # RICH – 696511

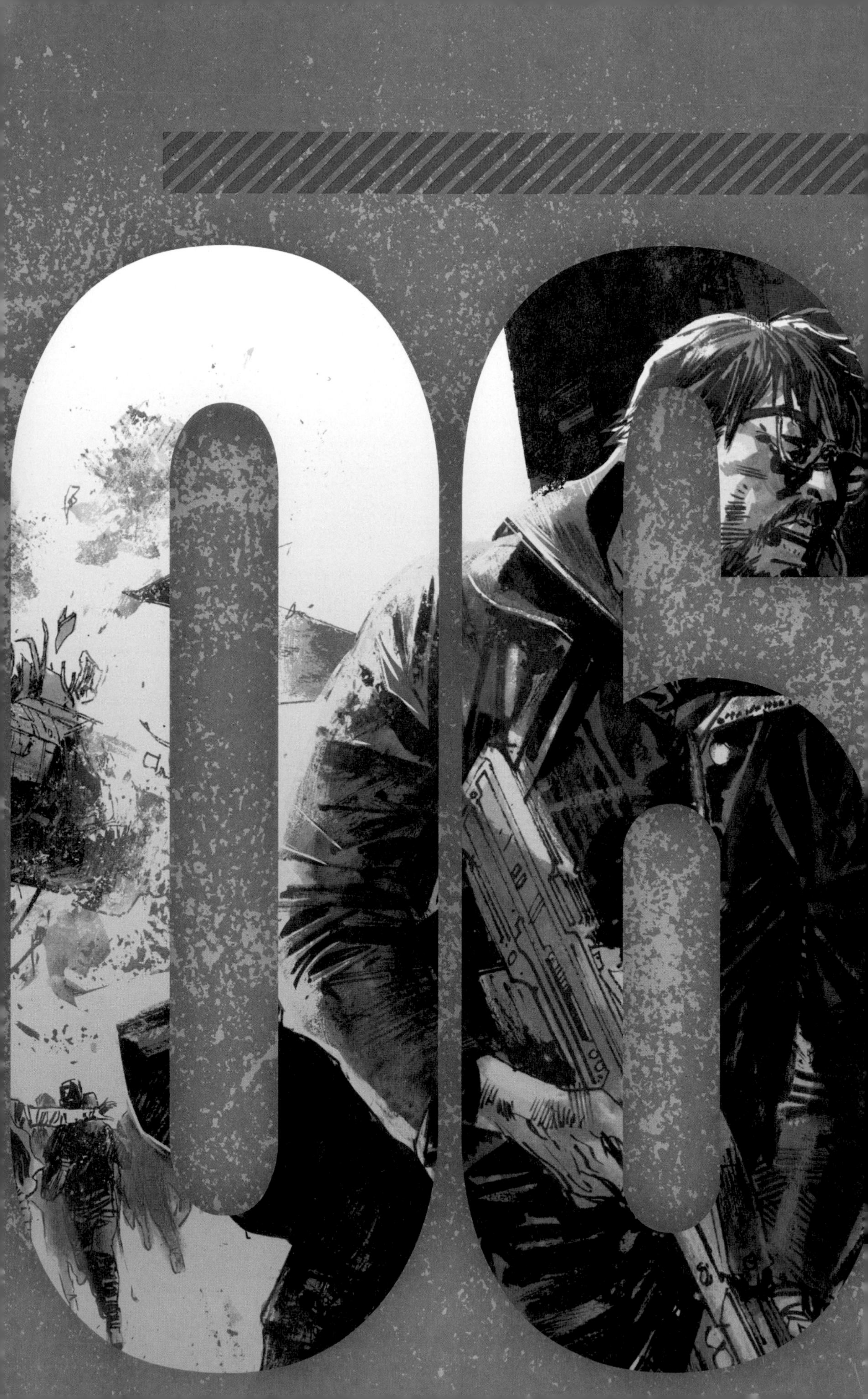
06

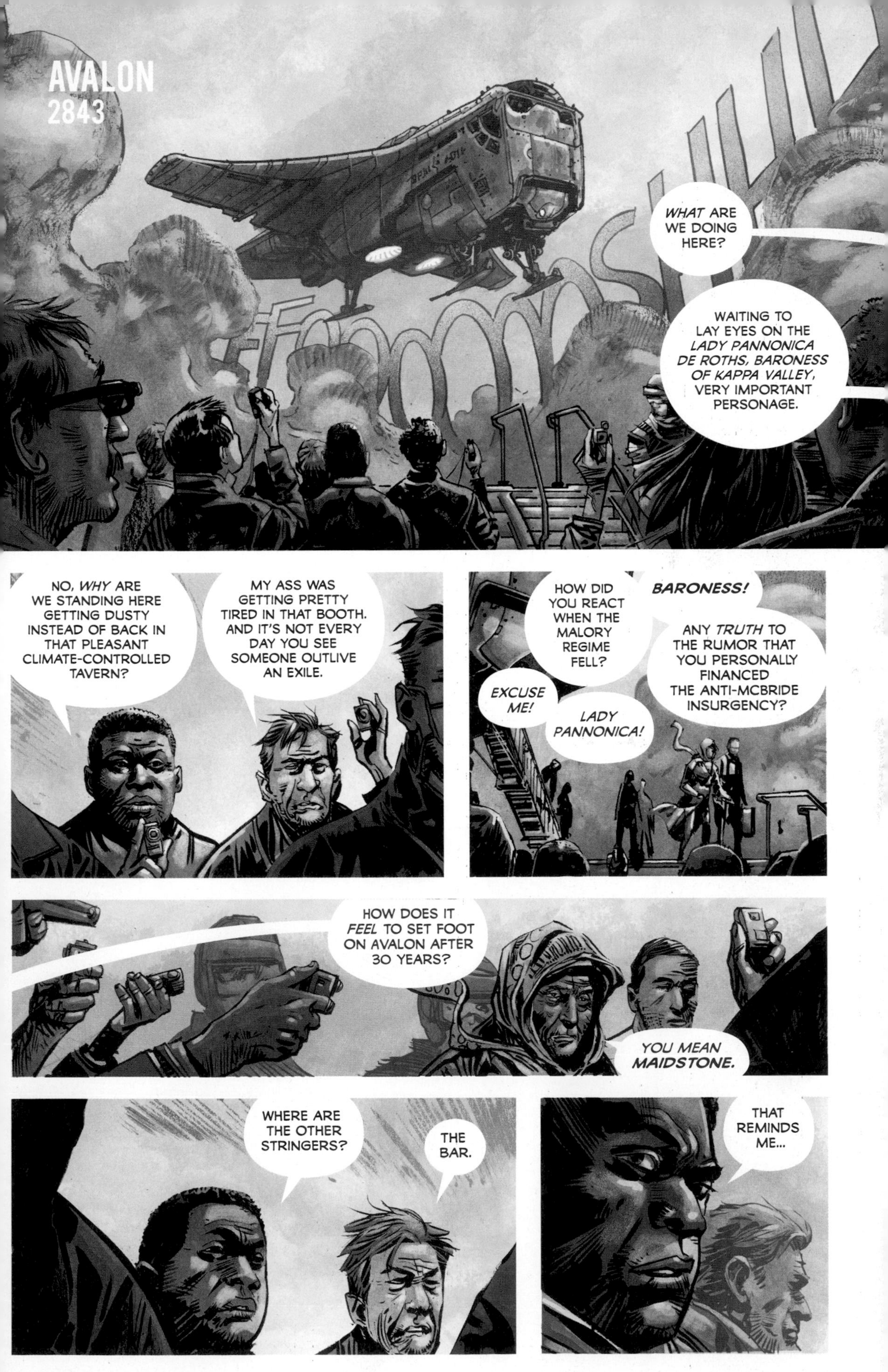
AVALON
2843
WHAT ARE WE DOING HERE?
WAITING TO LAY EYES ON THE LADY PANNONICA DE ROTHS, BARONESS OF KAPPA VALLEY, VERY IMPORTANT PERSONAGE.
NO, WHY ARE WE STANDING HERE GETTING DUSTY INSTEAD OF BACK IN THAT PLEASANT CLIMATE-CONTROLLED TAVERN?
MY ASS WAS GETTING PRETTY TIRED IN THAT BOOTH. AND IT'S NOT EVERY DAY YOU SEE SOMEONE OUTLIVE AN EXILE.
HOW DID YOU REACT WHEN THE MALORY REGIME FELL?
BARONESS!
ANY TRUTH TO THE RUMOR THAT YOU PERSONALLY FINANCED THE ANTI-MCBRIDE INSURGENCY?
EXCUSE ME!
LADY PANNONICA!
HOW DOES IT FEEL TO SET FOOT ON AVALON AFTER 30 YEARS?
YOU MEAN MAIDSTONE.
WHERE ARE THE OTHER STRINGERS?
THE BAR.
THAT REMINDS ME...

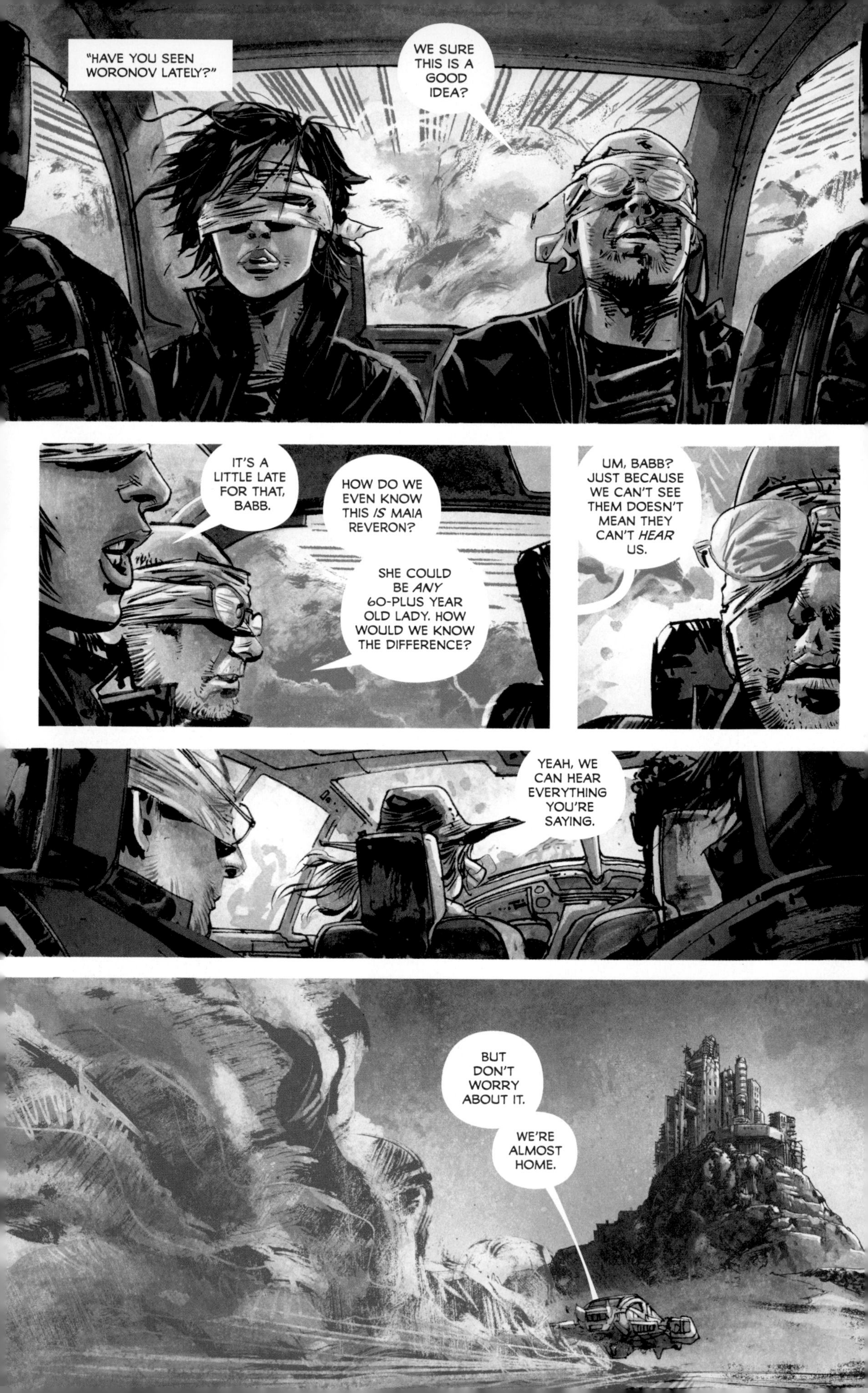
"HAVE YOU SEEN WORONOV LATELY?"
WE SURE THIS IS A GOOD IDEA?
IT'S A LITTLE LATE FOR THAT, BABB.
HOW DO WE EVEN KNOW THIS *IS* MAIA REVERON?
SHE COULD BE *ANY* 60-PLUS YEAR OLD LADY. HOW WOULD WE KNOW THE DIFFERENCE?
UM, BABB? JUST BECAUSE WE CAN'T SEE THEM DOESN'T MEAN THEY CAN'T *HEAR* US.
YEAH, WE CAN HEAR EVERYTHING YOU'RE SAYING.
BUT DON'T WORRY ABOUT IT.
WE'RE ALMOST HOME.

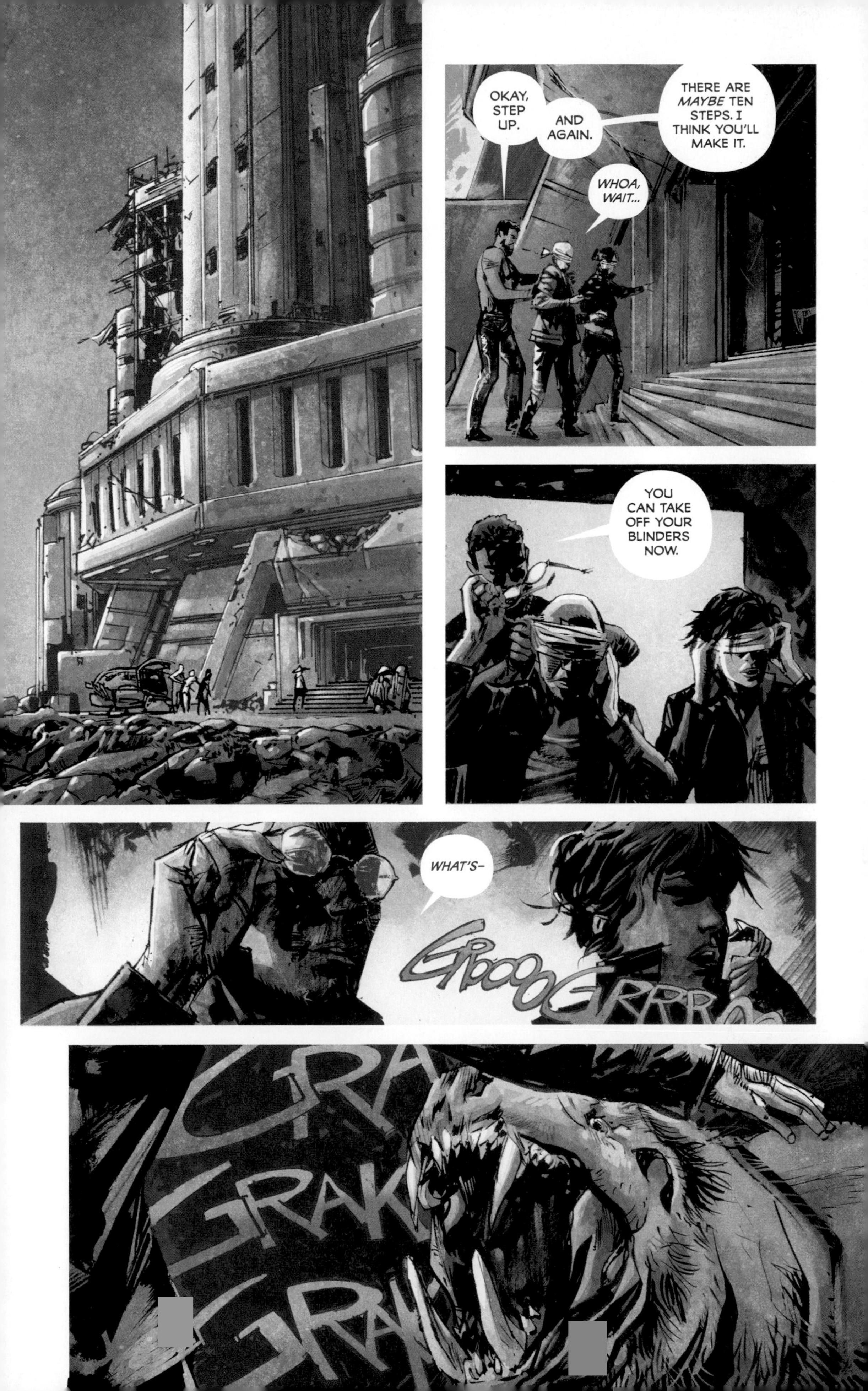
OKAY, STEP UP.
AND AGAIN.
THERE ARE *MAYBE* TEN STEPS. I THINK YOU'LL MAKE IT.
WHOA, WAIT...
YOU CAN TAKE OFF YOUR BLINDERS NOW.
WHAT'S-
GRA
GRAK
GRA

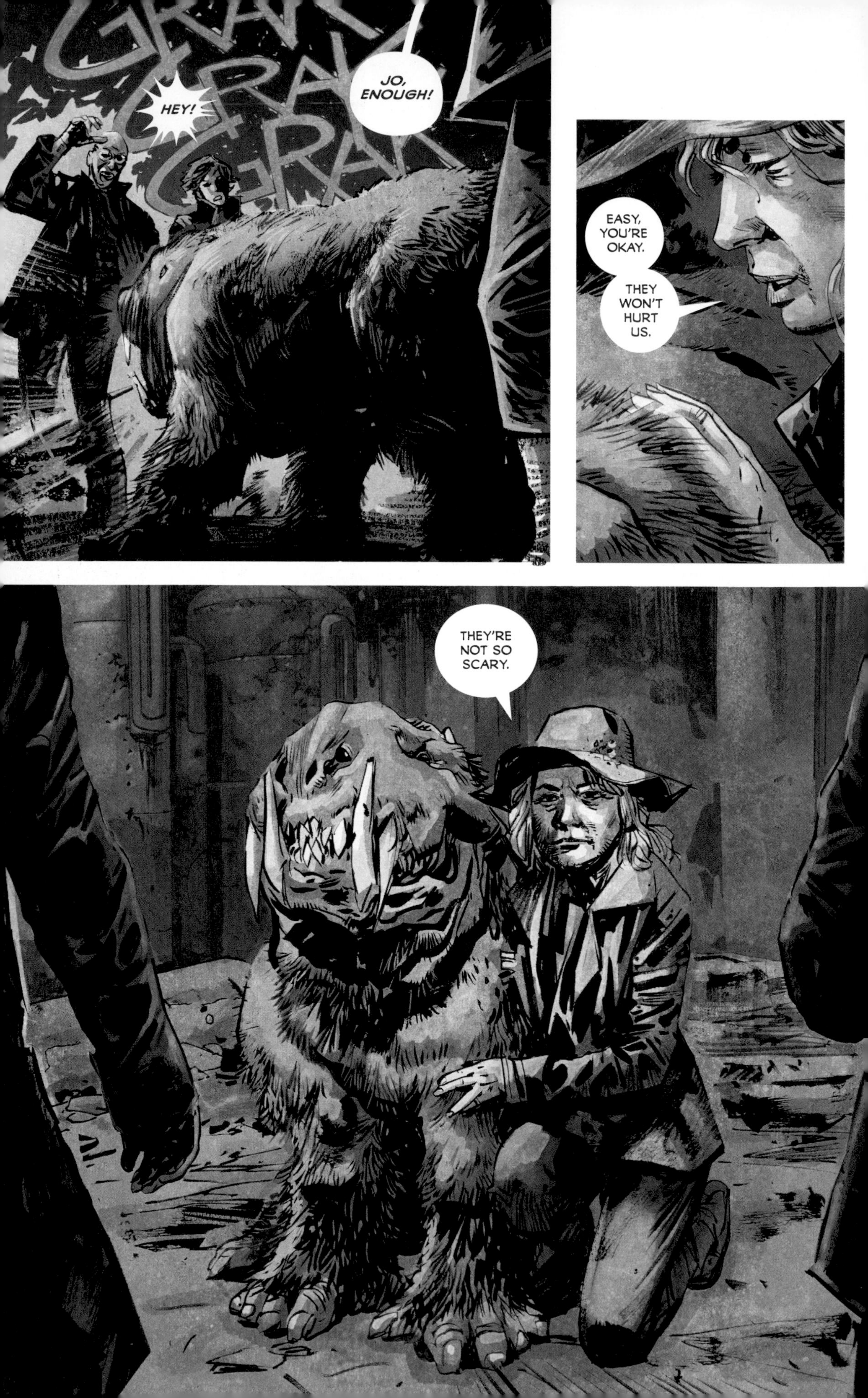
HEY!
JO, ENOUGH!
EASY, YOU'RE OKAY.
THEY WON'T HURT US.
THEY'RE NOT SO SCARY.

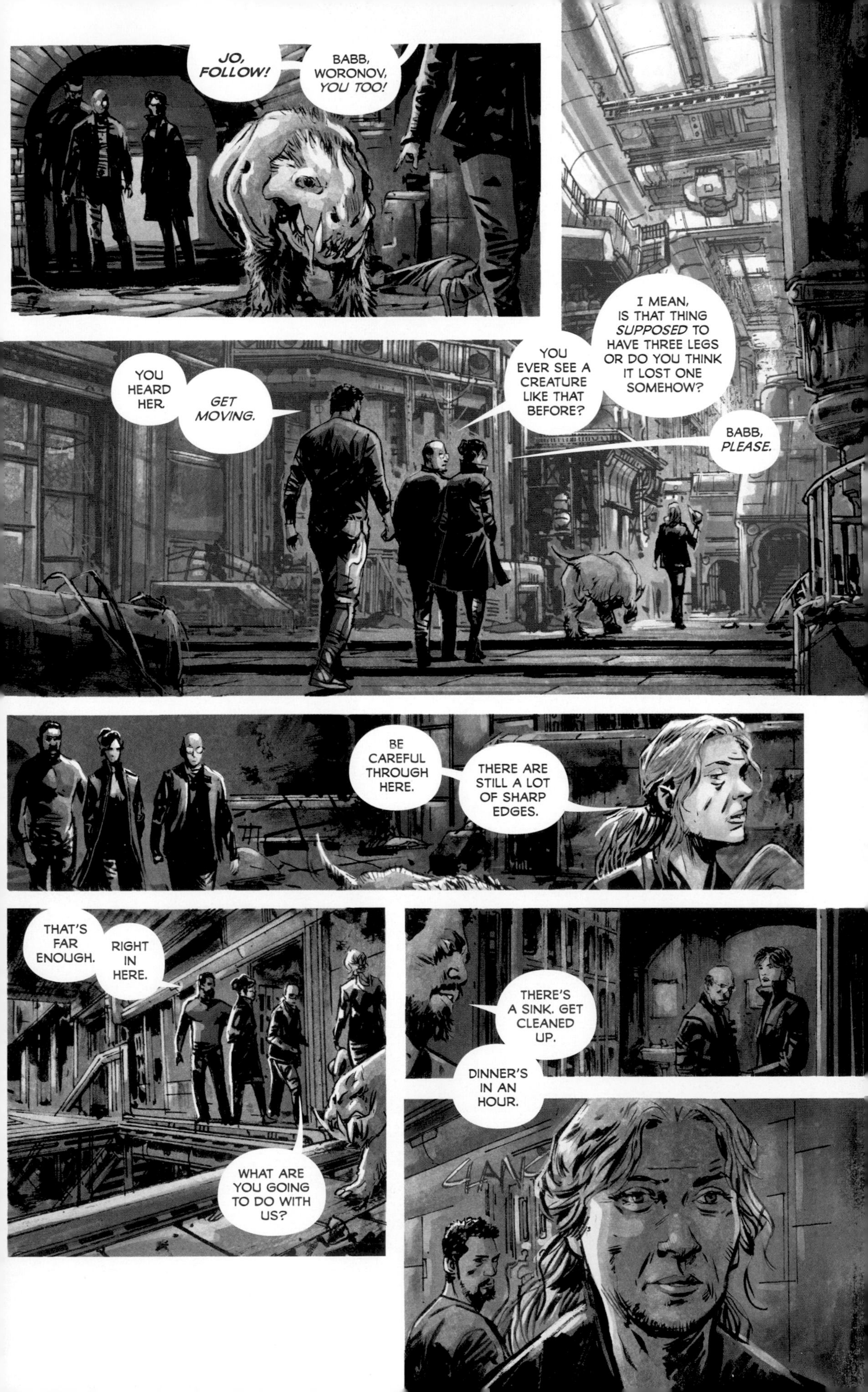
JO, FOLLOW!
BABB, WORONOV, YOU TOO!
YOU HEARD HER.
GET MOVING.
YOU EVER SEE A CREATURE LIKE THAT BEFORE?
I MEAN, IS THAT THING SUPPOSED TO HAVE THREE LEGS OR DO YOU THINK IT LOST ONE SOMEHOW?
BABB, PLEASE.
BE CAREFUL THROUGH HERE.
THERE ARE STILL A LOT OF SHARP EDGES.
THAT'S FAR ENOUGH.
RIGHT IN HERE.
WHAT ARE YOU GOING TO DO WITH US?
THERE'S A SINK. GET CLEANED UP.
DINNER'S IN AN HOUR.
CLANK

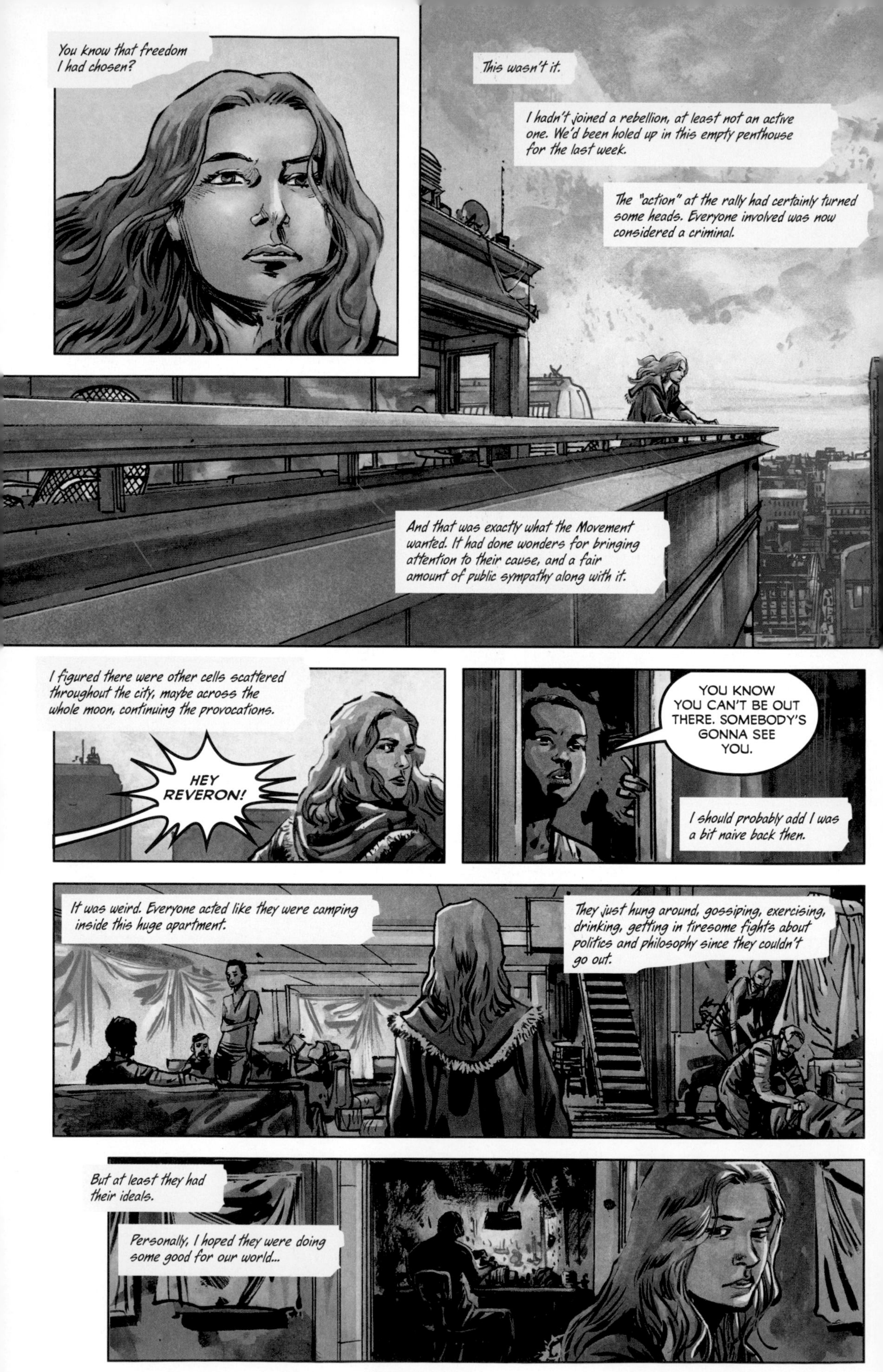
You know that freedom I had chosen?
This wasn't it.
I hadn't joined a rebellion, at least not an active one. We'd been holed up in this empty penthouse for the last week.
The "action" at the rally had certainly turned some heads. Everyone involved was now considered a criminal.
And that was exactly what the Movement wanted. It had done wonders for bringing attention to their cause, and a fair amount of public sympathy along with it.
I figured there were other cells scattered throughout the city, maybe across the whole moon, continuing the provocations.
HEY REVERON!
YOU KNOW YOU CAN'T BE OUT THERE. SOMEBODY'S GONNA SEE YOU.
I should probably add I was a bit naive back then.
It was weird. Everyone acted like they were camping inside this huge apartment.
They just hung around, gossiping, exercising, drinking, getting in tiresome fights about politics and philosophy since they couldn't go out.
But at least they had their ideals.
Personally, I hoped they were doing some good for our world...

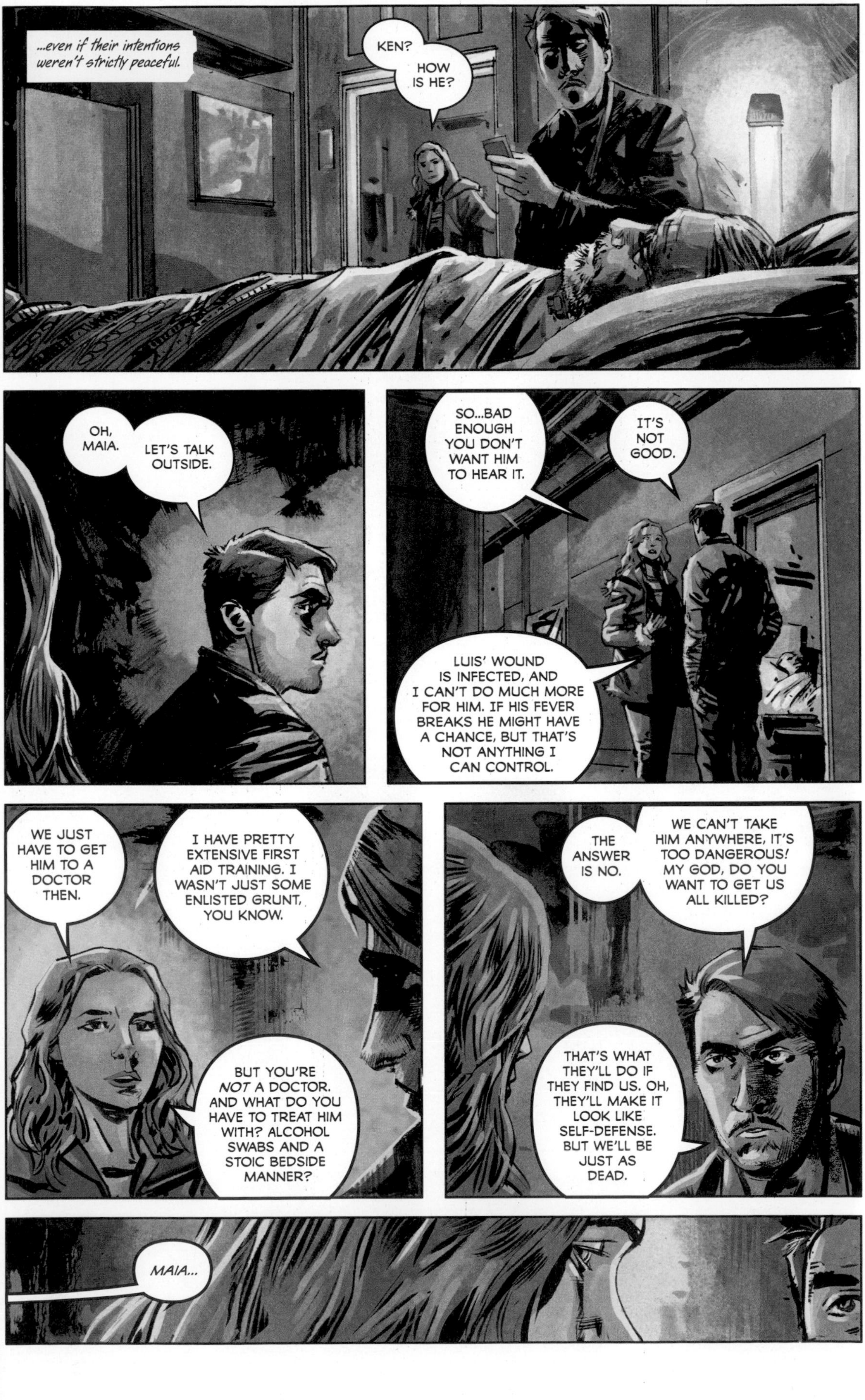
...even if their intentions weren't strictly peaceful.
KEN?
HOW IS HE?
OH, MAIA.
LET'S TALK OUTSIDE.
SO...BAD ENOUGH YOU DON'T WANT HIM TO HEAR IT.
IT'S NOT GOOD.
LUIS' WOUND IS INFECTED, AND I CAN'T DO MUCH MORE FOR HIM. IF HIS FEVER BREAKS HE MIGHT HAVE A CHANCE, BUT THAT'S NOT ANYTHING I CAN CONTROL.
WE JUST HAVE TO GET HIM TO A DOCTOR THEN.
I HAVE PRETTY EXTENSIVE FIRST AID TRAINING. I WASN'T JUST SOME ENLISTED GRUNT, YOU KNOW.
BUT YOU'RE *NOT* A DOCTOR. AND WHAT DO YOU HAVE TO TREAT HIM WITH? ALCOHOL SWABS AND A STOIC BEDSIDE MANNER?
THE ANSWER IS NO.
WE CAN'T TAKE HIM ANYWHERE, IT'S TOO DANGEROUS! MY GOD, DO YOU WANT TO GET US ALL KILLED?
THAT'S WHAT THEY'LL DO IF THEY FIND US. OH, THEY'LL MAKE IT LOOK LIKE SELF-DEFENSE. BUT WE'LL BE JUST AS DEAD.
MAIA...

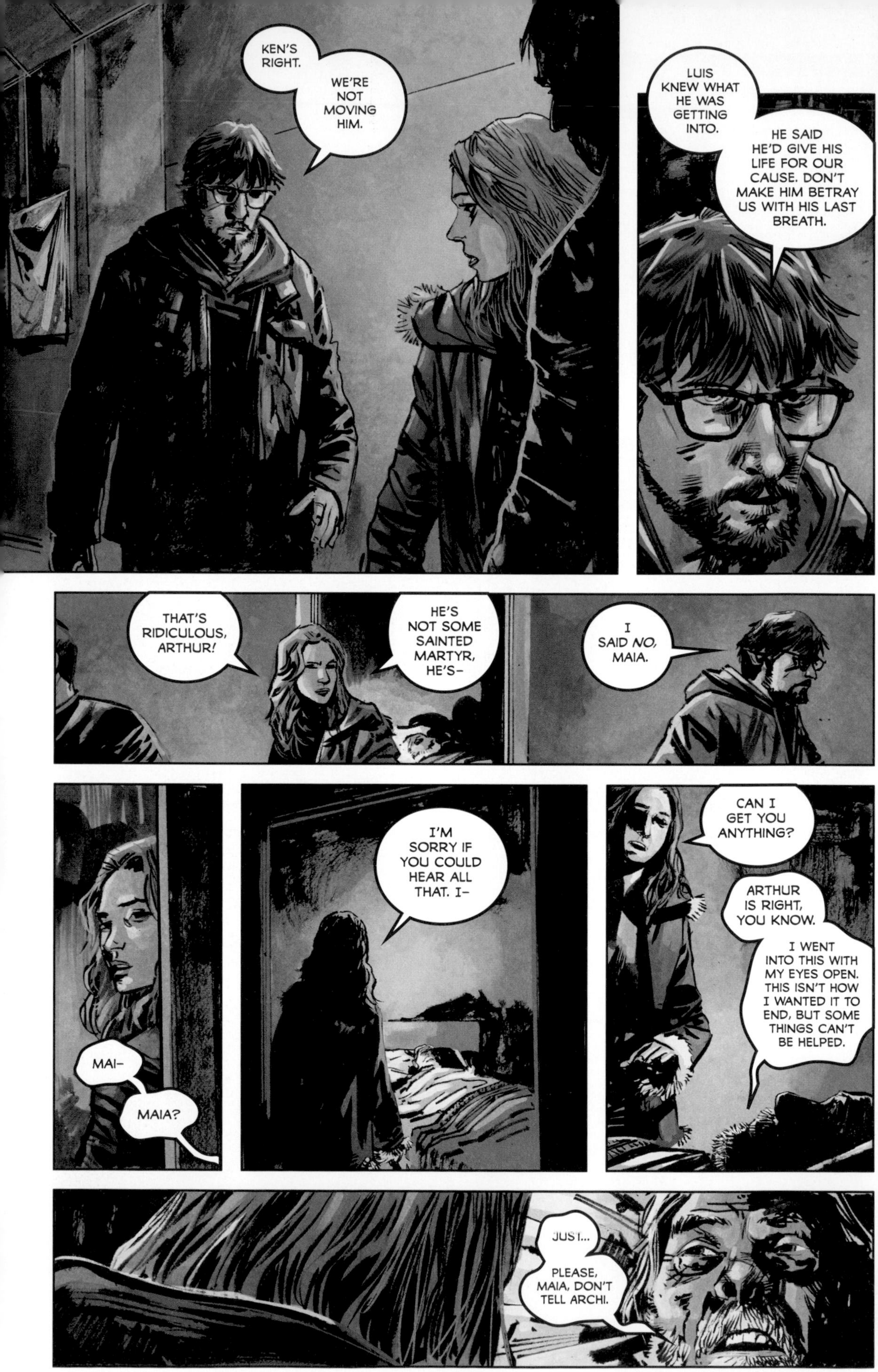
KEN'S RIGHT.
WE'RE NOT MOVING HIM.
LUIS KNEW WHAT HE WAS GETTING INTO.
HE SAID HE'D GIVE HIS LIFE FOR OUR CAUSE. DON'T MAKE HIM BETRAY US WITH HIS LAST BREATH.
THAT'S RIDICULOUS, ARTHUR!
HE'S NOT SOME SAINTED MARTYR, HE'S–
I SAID *NO,* MAIA.
MAI–
MAIA?
I'M SORRY IF YOU COULD HEAR ALL THAT. I–
CAN I GET YOU ANYTHING?
ARTHUR IS RIGHT, YOU KNOW.
I WENT INTO THIS WITH MY EYES OPEN. THIS ISN'T HOW I WANTED IT TO END, BUT SOME THINGS CAN'T BE HELPED.
JUST...
PLEASE, MAIA, DON'T TELL ARCHI.

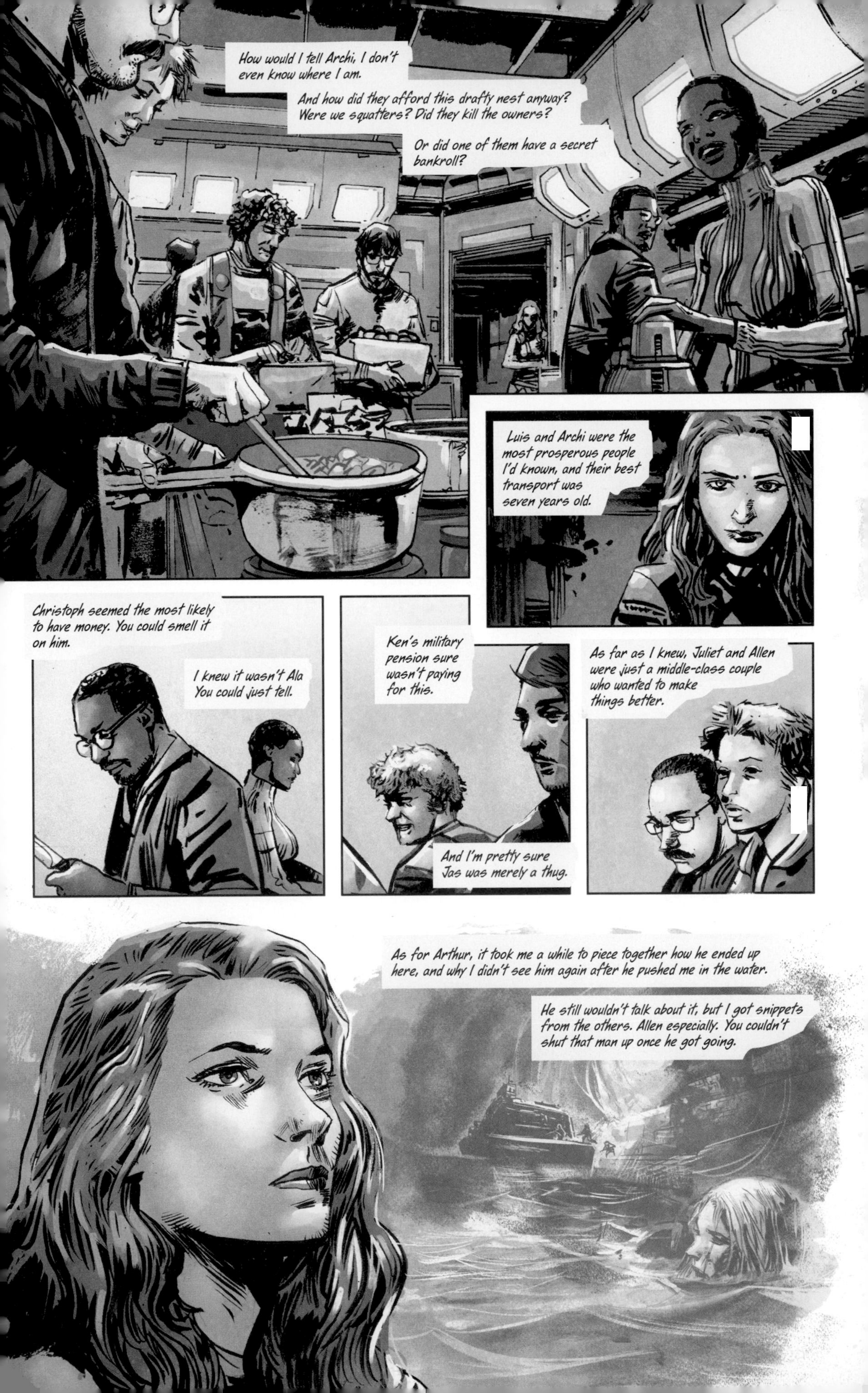
How would I tell Archi, I don't even know where I am.
And how did they afford this drafty nest anyway? Were we squatters? Did they kill the owners?
Or did one of them have a secret bankroll?
Luis and Archi were the most prosperous people I'd known, and their best transport was seven years old.
Christoph seemed the most likely to have money. You could smell it on him.
I knew it wasn't Ala
You could just tell.
Ken's military pension sure wasn't paying for this.
And I'm pretty sure Jas was merely a thug.
As far as I knew, Juliet and Allen were just a middle-class couple who wanted to make things better.
As for Arthur, it took me a while to piece together how he ended up here, and why I didn't see him again after he pushed me in the water.
He still wouldn't talk about it, but I got snippets from the others. Allen especially. You couldn't shut that man up once he got going.

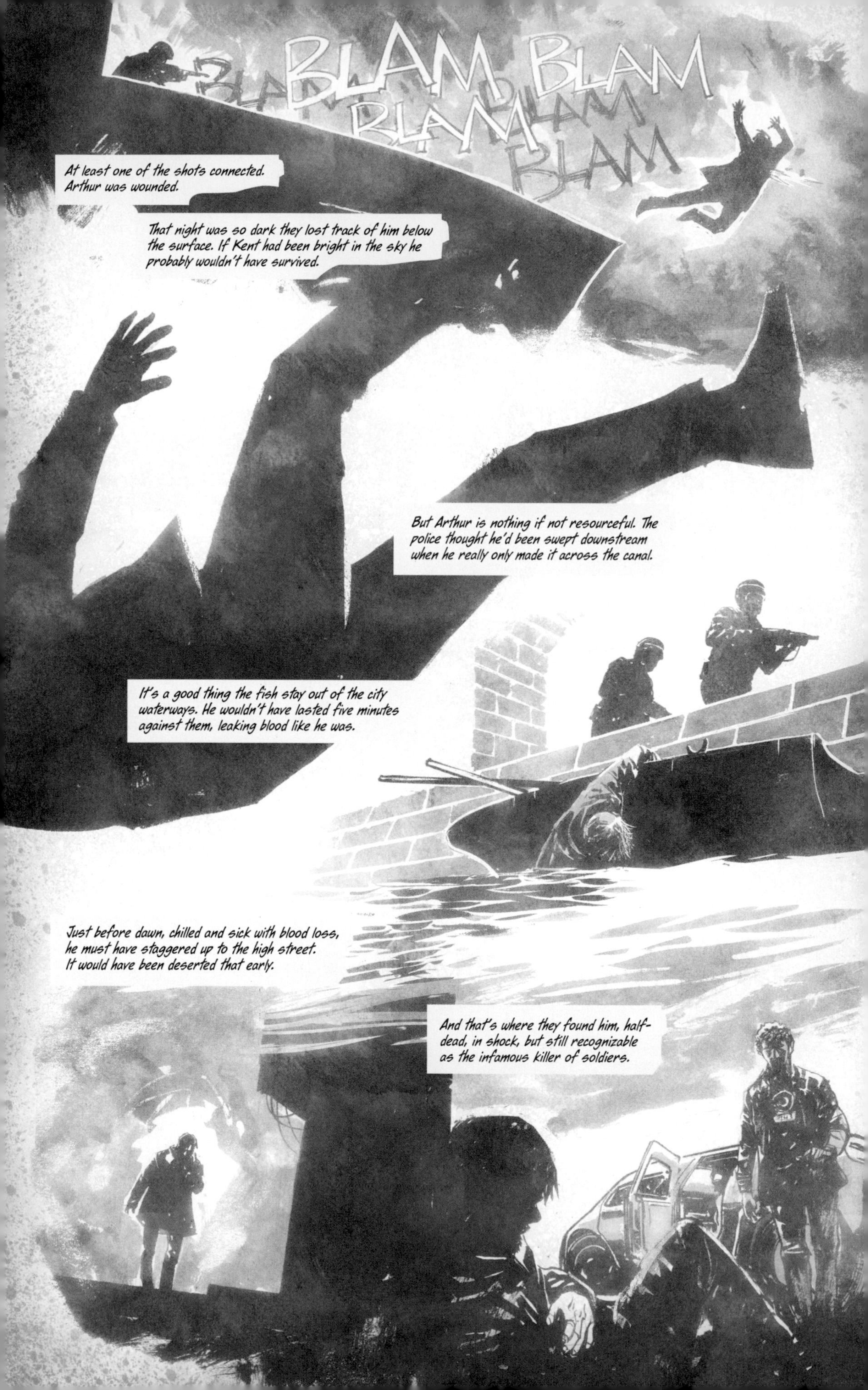
BLAM BLAM BLAM BLAM BLAM BLAM BLAM
At least one of the shots connected. Arthur was wounded.
That night was so dark they lost track of him below the surface. If Kent had been bright in the sky he probably wouldn't have survived.
But Arthur is nothing if not resourceful. The police thought he'd been swept downstream when he really only made it across the canal.
It's a good thing the fish stay out of the city waterways. He wouldn't have lasted five minutes against them, leaking blood like he was.
Just before dawn, chilled and sick with blood loss, he must have staggered up to the high street. It would have been deserted that early.
And that's where they found him, half-dead, in shock, but still recognizable as the infamous killer of soldiers.

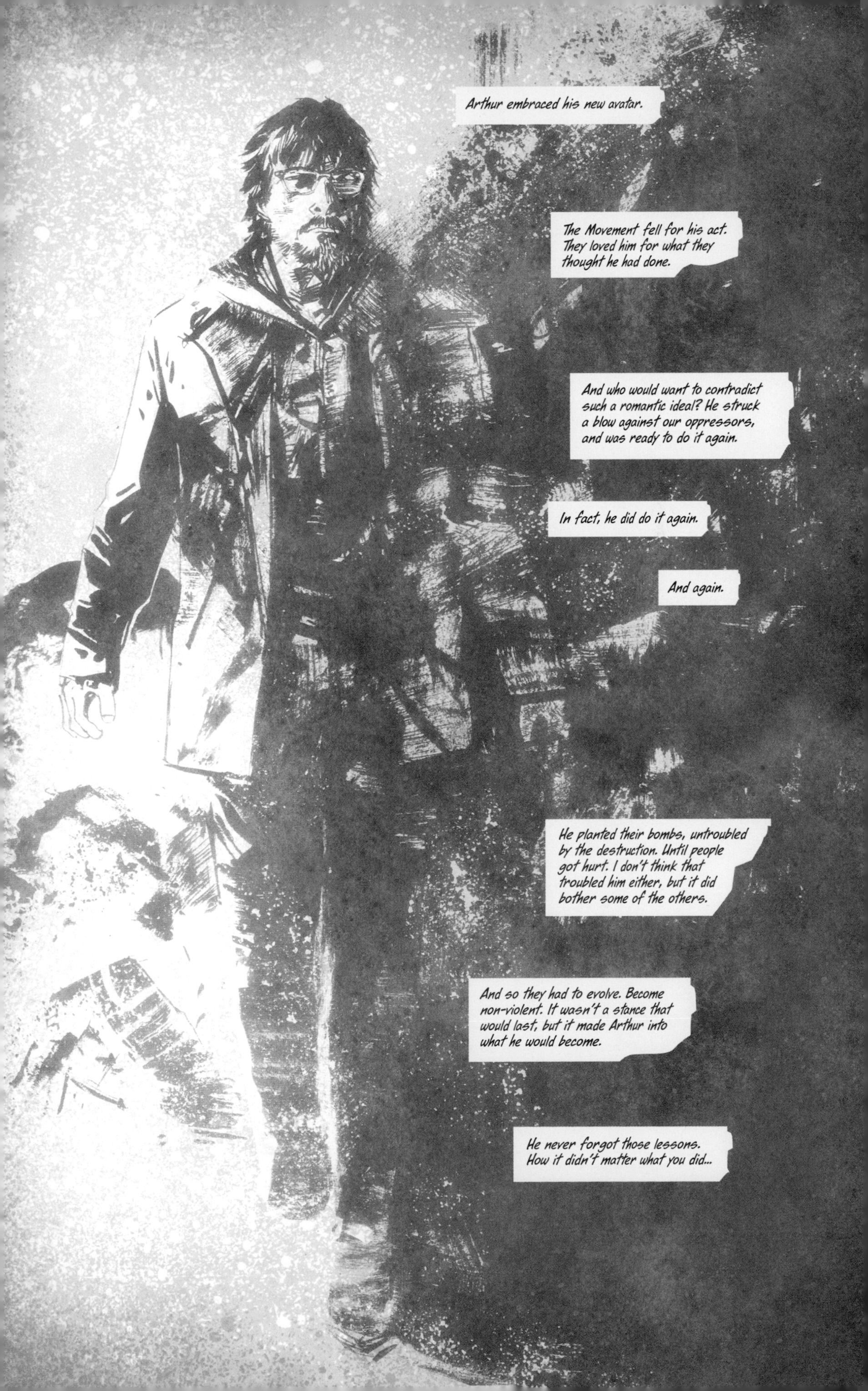
Arthur embraced his new avatar.
The Movement fell for his act. They loved him for what they thought he had done.
And who would want to contradict such a romantic ideal? He struck a blow against our oppressors, and was ready to do it again.
In fact, he did do it again.
And again.
He planted their bombs, untroubled by the destruction. Until people got hurt. I don't think that troubled him either, but it did bother some of the others.
And so they had to evolve. Become non-violent. It wasn't a stance that would last, but it made Arthur into what he would become.
He never forgot those lessons. How it didn't matter what you did...

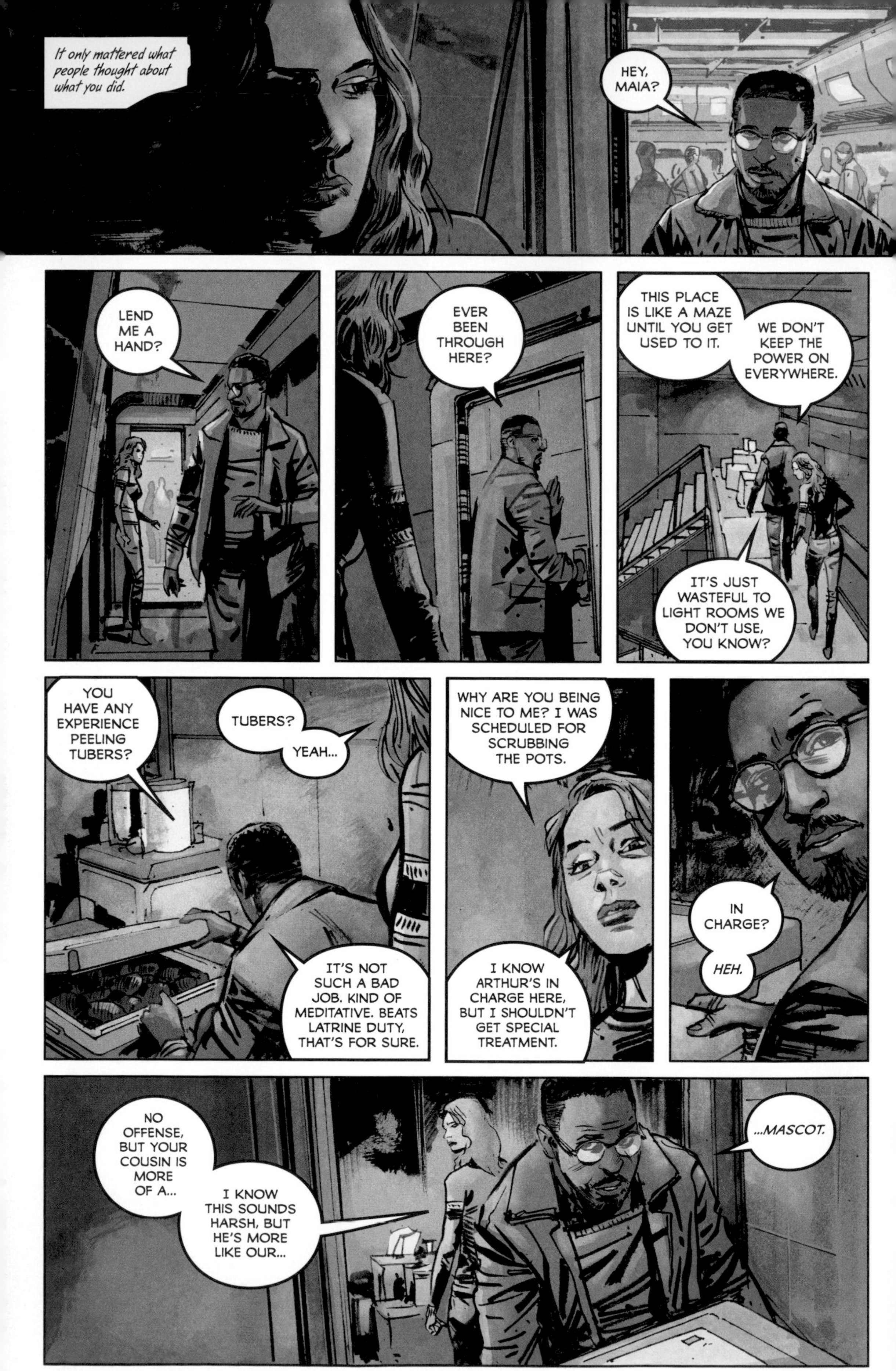
It only mattered what people thought about what you did.
HEY, MAIA?
LEND ME A HAND?
EVER BEEN THROUGH HERE?
THIS PLACE IS LIKE A MAZE UNTIL YOU GET USED TO IT.
WE DON'T KEEP THE POWER ON EVERYWHERE.
IT'S JUST WASTEFUL TO LIGHT ROOMS WE DON'T USE, YOU KNOW?
YOU HAVE ANY EXPERIENCE PEELING TUBERS?
TUBERS?
YEAH...
IT'S NOT SUCH A BAD JOB. KIND OF MEDITATIVE. BEATS LATRINE DUTY, THAT'S FOR SURE.
WHY ARE YOU BEING NICE TO ME? I WAS SCHEDULED FOR SCRUBBING THE POTS.
I KNOW ARTHUR'S IN CHARGE HERE, BUT I SHOULDN'T GET SPECIAL TREATMENT.
IN CHARGE?
HEH.
NO OFFENSE, BUT YOUR COUSIN IS MORE OF A...
I KNOW THIS SOUNDS HARSH, BUT HE'S MORE LIKE OUR...
...MASCOT.

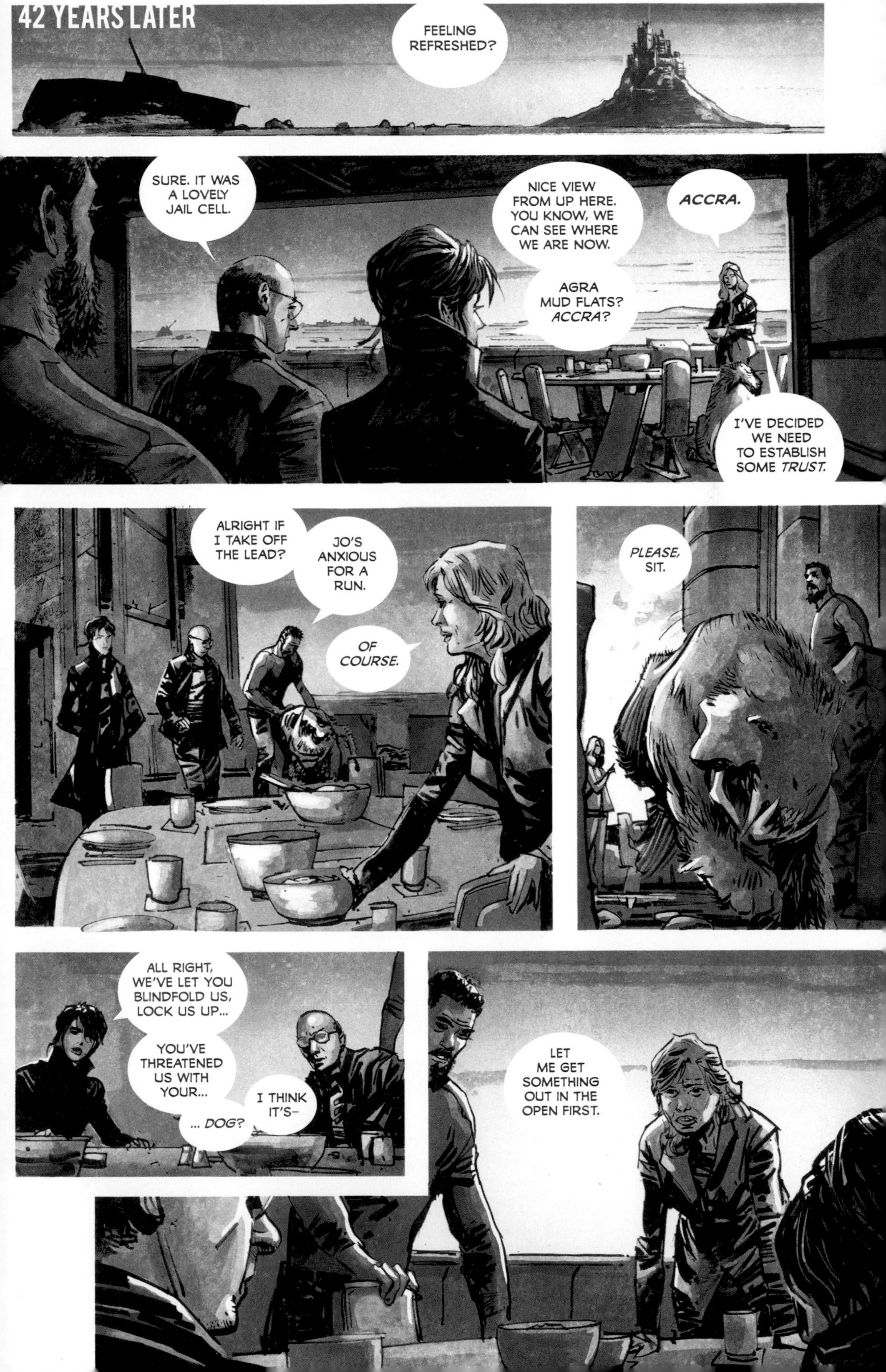
42 YEARS LATER
FEELING REFRESHED?
SURE. IT WAS A LOVELY JAIL CELL.
NICE VIEW FROM UP HERE. YOU KNOW, WE CAN SEE WHERE WE ARE NOW.
AGRA MUD FLATS? *ACCRA?*
ACCRA.
I'VE DECIDED WE NEED TO ESTABLISH SOME *TRUST.*
ALRIGHT IF I TAKE OFF THE LEAD?
JO'S ANXIOUS FOR A RUN.
OF COURSE.
PLEASE, SIT.
ALL RIGHT, WE'VE LET YOU BLINDFOLD US, LOCK US UP...
YOU'VE THREATENED US WITH YOUR...
... *DOG?*
I THINK IT'S–
LET ME GET SOMETHING OUT IN THE OPEN FIRST.

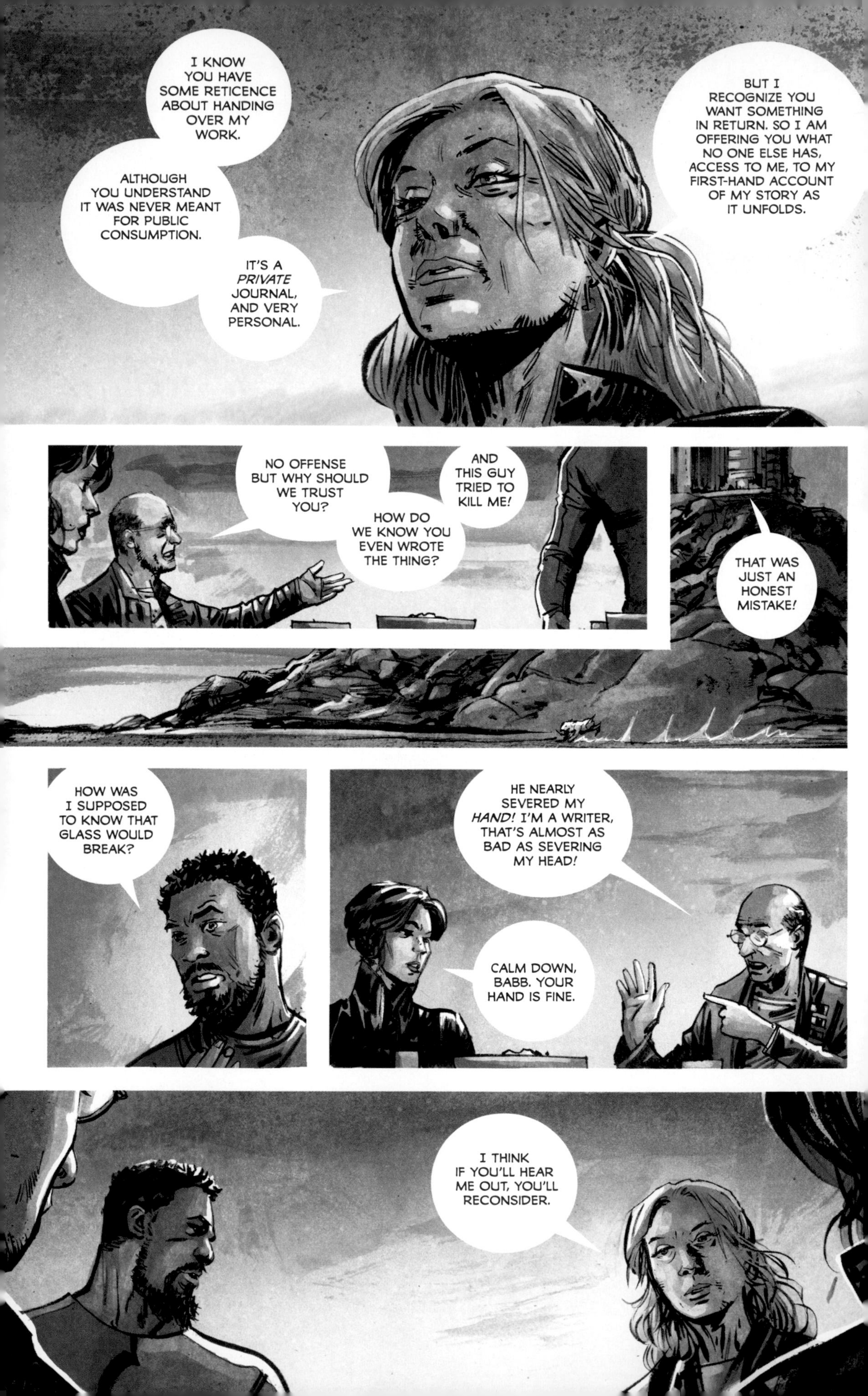
I KNOW YOU HAVE SOME RETICENCE ABOUT HANDING OVER MY WORK.
ALTHOUGH YOU UNDERSTAND IT WAS NEVER MEANT FOR PUBLIC CONSUMPTION.
IT'S A *PRIVATE* JOURNAL, AND VERY PERSONAL.
BUT I RECOGNIZE YOU WANT SOMETHING IN RETURN. SO I AM OFFERING YOU WHAT NO ONE ELSE HAS, ACCESS TO ME, TO MY FIRST-HAND ACCOUNT OF MY STORY AS IT UNFOLDS.
NO OFFENSE BUT WHY SHOULD WE TRUST YOU?
HOW DO WE KNOW YOU EVEN WROTE THE THING?
AND THIS GUY TRIED TO KILL ME!
THAT WAS JUST AN HONEST MISTAKE!
HOW WAS I SUPPOSED TO KNOW THAT GLASS WOULD BREAK?
HE NEARLY SEVERED MY *HAND!* I'M A WRITER, THAT'S ALMOST AS BAD AS SEVERING MY HEAD!
CALM DOWN, BABB. YOUR HAND IS FINE.
I THINK IF YOU'LL HEAR ME OUT, YOU'LL RECONSIDER.

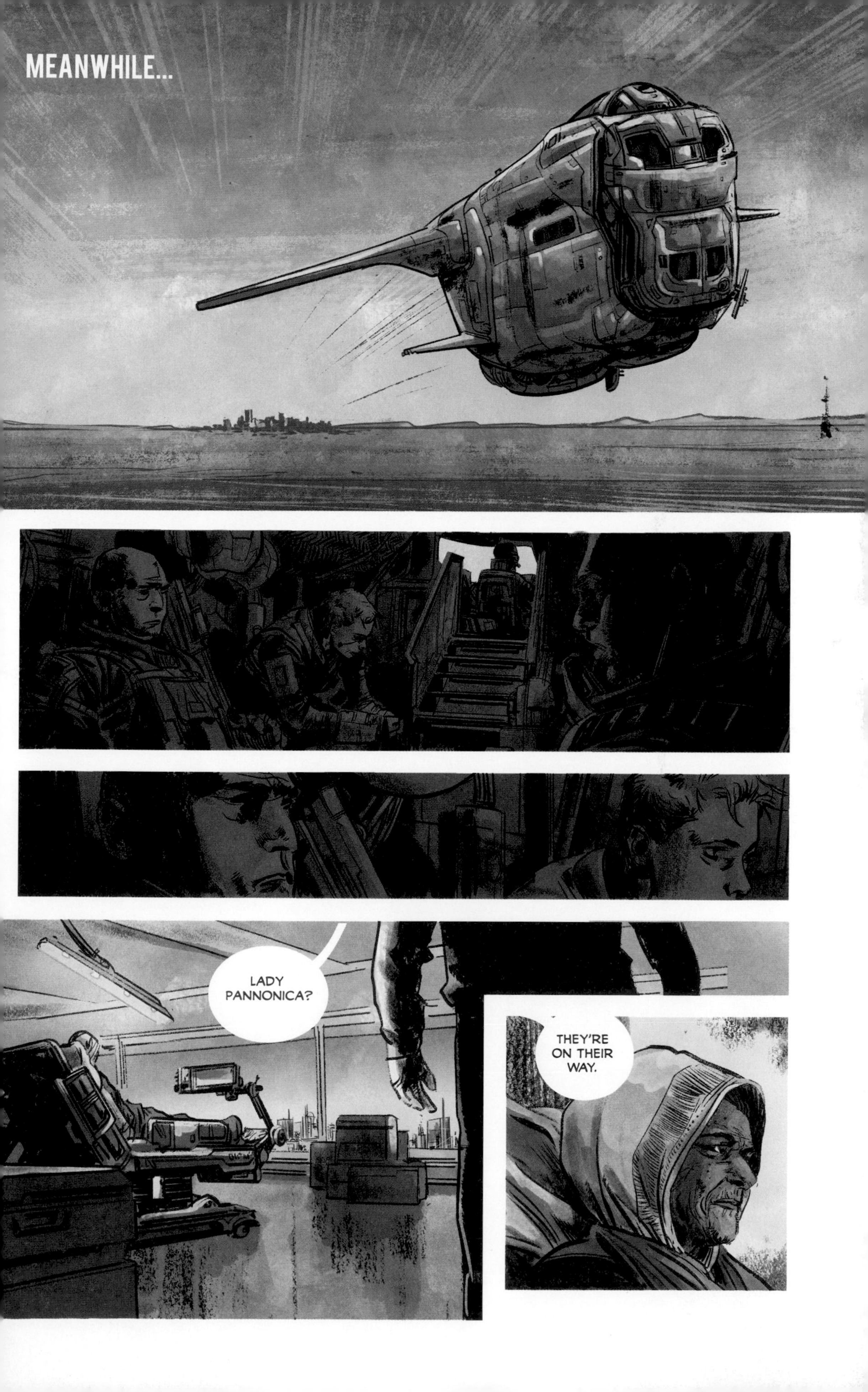
MEANWHILE...
LADY PANNONICA?
THEY'RE ON THEIR WAY.

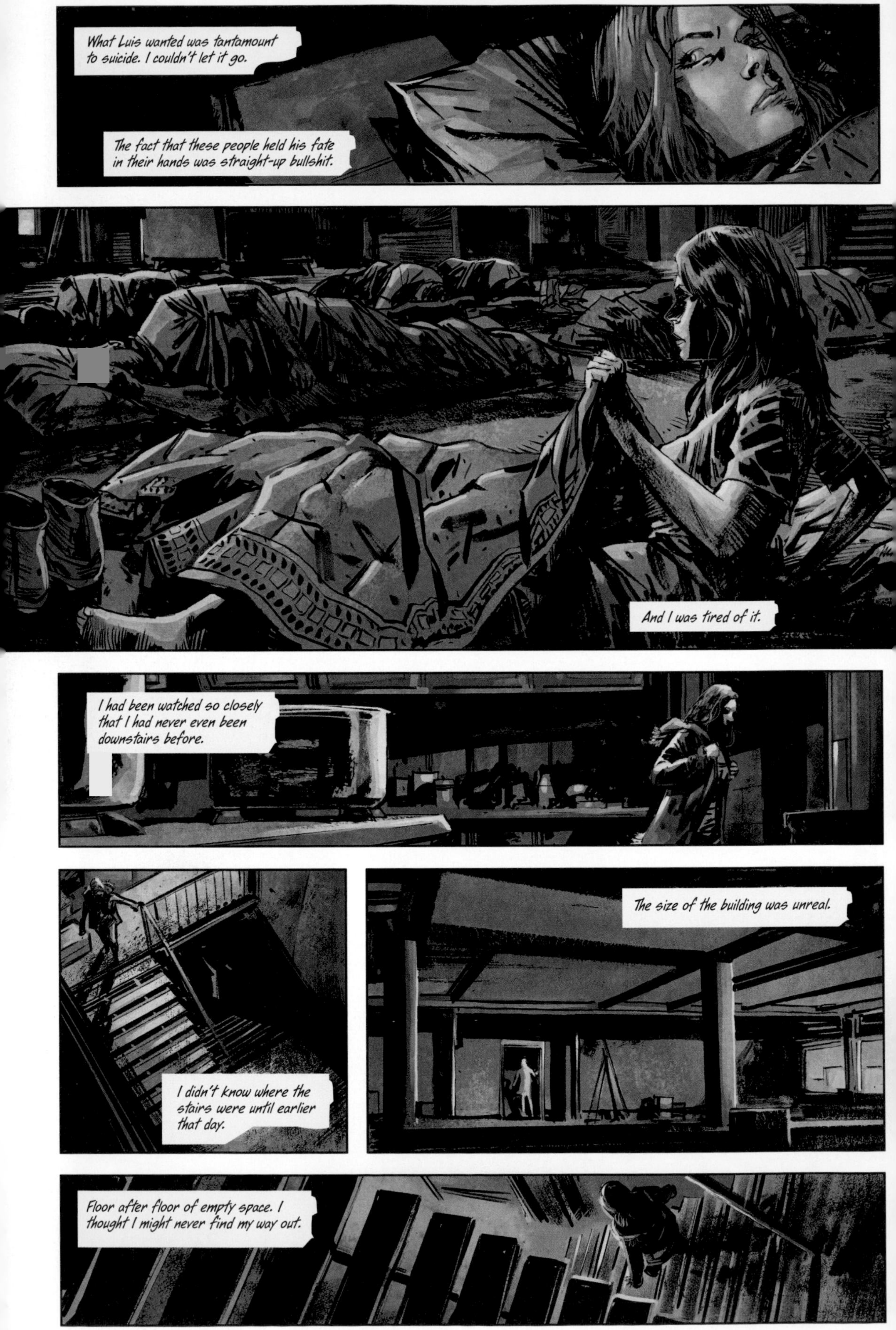
What Luis wanted was tantamount to suicide. I couldn't let it go.
The fact that these people held his fate in their hands was straight-up bullshit.
And I was tired of it.
I had been watched so closely that I had never even been downstairs before.
I didn't know where the stairs were until earlier that day.
The size of the building was unreal.
Floor after floor of empty space. I thought I might never find my way out.

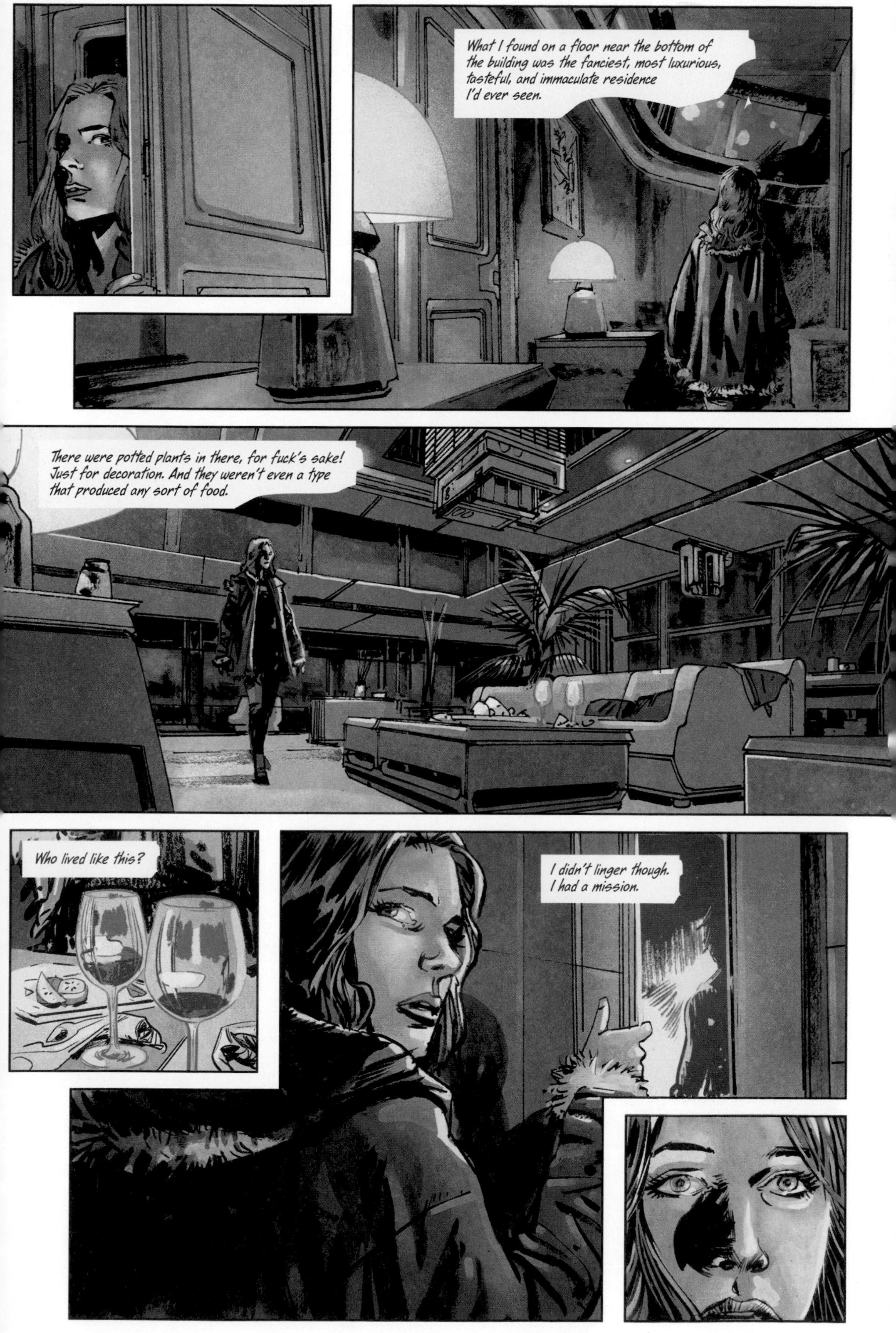
What I found on a floor near the bottom of the building was the fanciest, most luxurious, tasteful, and immaculate residence I'd ever seen.
There were potted plants in there, for fuck's sake! Just for decoration. And they weren't even a type that produced any sort of food.
Who lived like this?
I didn't linger though. I had a mission.

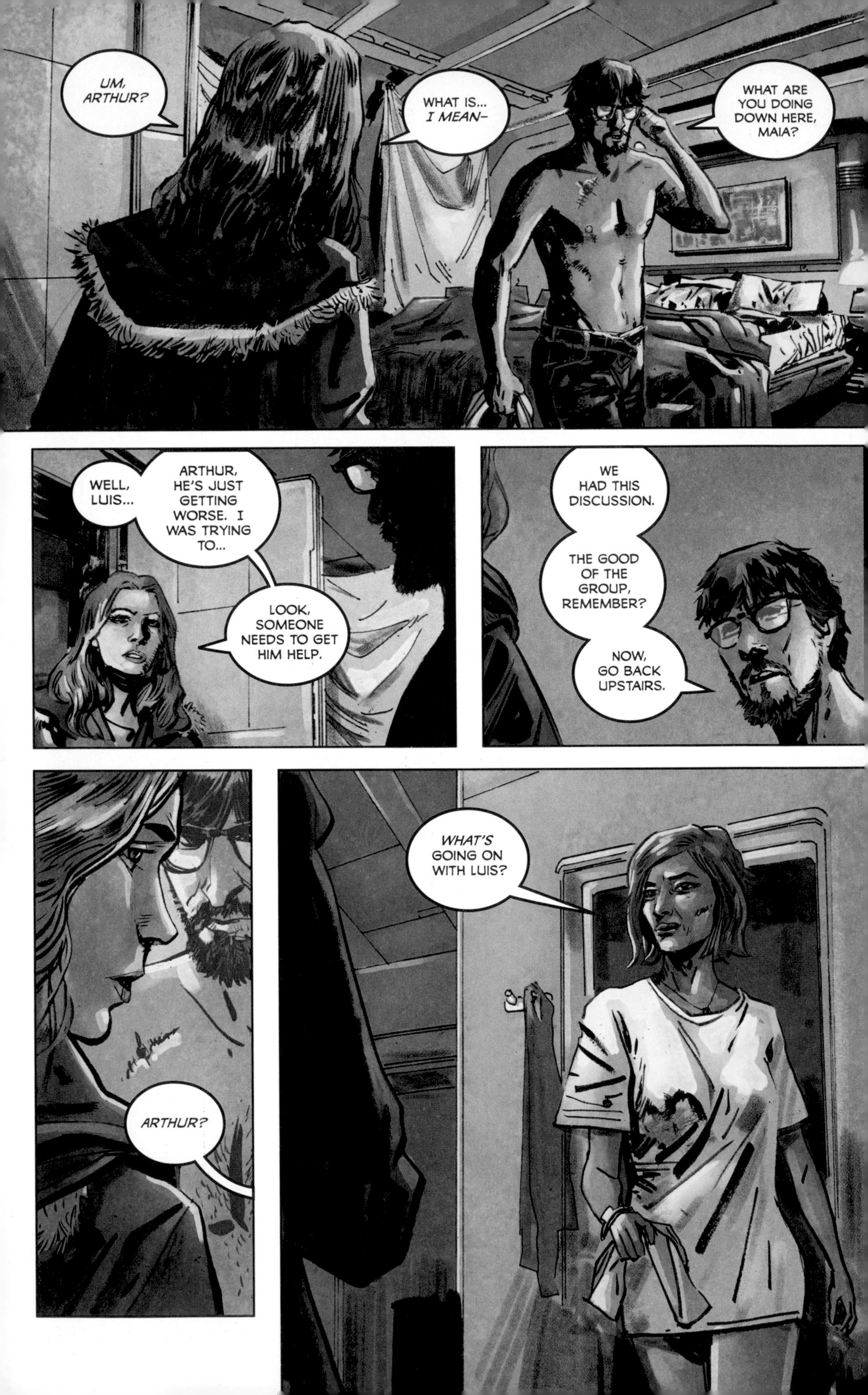
UM, ARTHUR?
WHAT IS... I MEAN–
WHAT ARE YOU DOING DOWN HERE, MAIA?
WELL, LUIS...
ARTHUR, HE'S JUST GETTING WORSE. I WAS TRYING TO...
LOOK, SOMEONE NEEDS TO GET HIM HELP.
WE HAD THIS DISCUSSION.
THE GOOD OF THE GROUP, REMEMBER?
NOW, GO BACK UPSTAIRS.
ARTHUR?
WHAT'S GOING ON WITH LUIS?

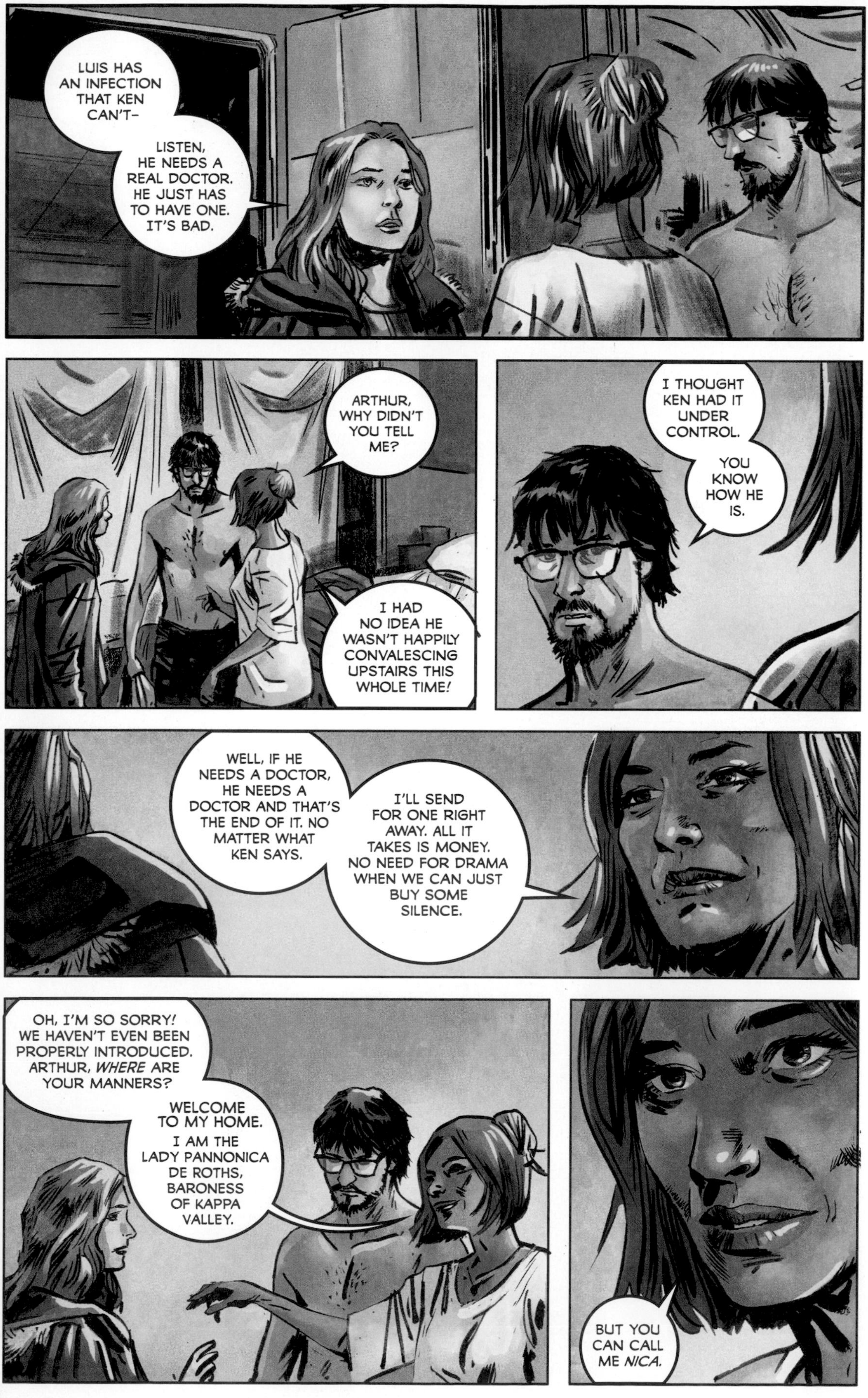
LUIS HAS AN INFECTION THAT KEN CAN'T–
LISTEN, HE NEEDS A REAL DOCTOR. HE JUST HAS TO HAVE ONE. IT'S BAD.
ARTHUR, WHY DIDN'T YOU TELL ME?
I HAD NO IDEA HE WASN'T HAPPILY CONVALESCING UPSTAIRS THIS WHOLE TIME!
I THOUGHT KEN HAD IT UNDER CONTROL.
YOU KNOW HOW HE IS.
WELL, IF HE NEEDS A DOCTOR, HE NEEDS A DOCTOR AND THAT'S THE END OF IT. NO MATTER WHAT KEN SAYS.
I'LL SEND FOR ONE RIGHT AWAY. ALL IT TAKES IS MONEY. NO NEED FOR DRAMA WHEN WE CAN JUST BUY SOME SILENCE.
OH, I'M SO SORRY! WE HAVEN'T EVEN BEEN PROPERLY INTRODUCED. ARTHUR, *WHERE* ARE YOUR MANNERS?
WELCOME TO MY HOME.
I AM THE LADY PANNONICA DE ROTHS, BARONESS OF KAPPA VALLEY.
BUT YOU CAN CALL ME *NICA*.

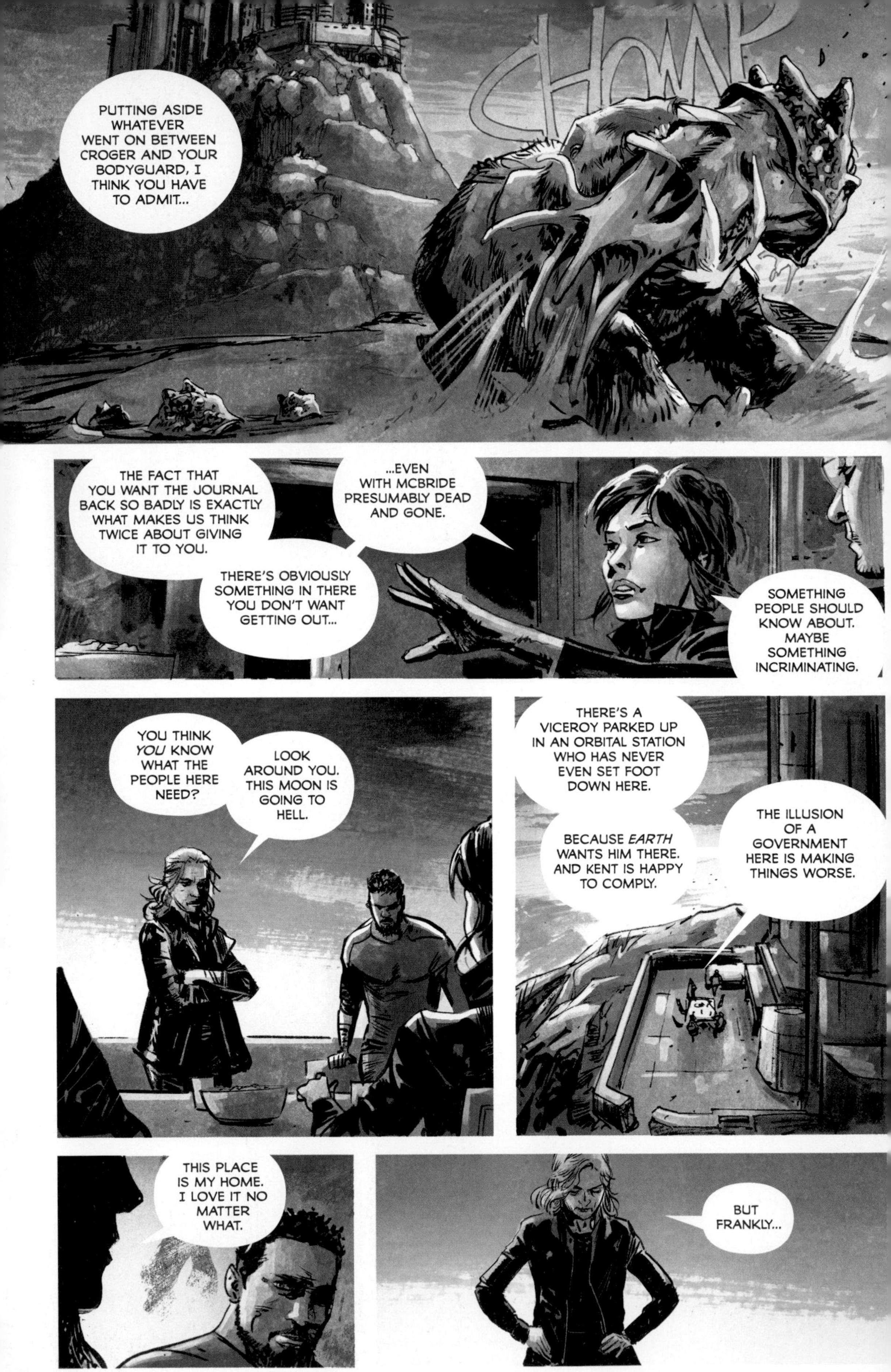
PUTTING ASIDE WHATEVER WENT ON BETWEEN CROGER AND YOUR BODYGUARD, I THINK YOU HAVE TO ADMIT...
CHOMP
THE FACT THAT YOU WANT THE JOURNAL BACK SO BADLY IS EXACTLY WHAT MAKES US THINK TWICE ABOUT GIVING IT TO YOU.
...EVEN WITH MCBRIDE PRESUMABLY DEAD AND GONE.
THERE'S OBVIOUSLY SOMETHING IN THERE YOU DON'T WANT GETTING OUT...
SOMETHING PEOPLE SHOULD KNOW ABOUT. MAYBE SOMETHING INCRIMINATING.
YOU THINK *YOU* KNOW WHAT THE PEOPLE HERE NEED?
LOOK AROUND YOU. THIS MOON IS GOING TO HELL.
THERE'S A VICEROY PARKED UP IN AN ORBITAL STATION WHO HAS NEVER EVEN SET FOOT DOWN HERE.
BECAUSE *EARTH* WANTS HIM THERE. AND KENT IS HAPPY TO COMPLY.
THE ILLUSION OF A GOVERNMENT HERE IS MAKING THINGS WORSE.
THIS PLACE IS MY HOME. I LOVE IT NO MATTER WHAT.
BUT FRANKLY...

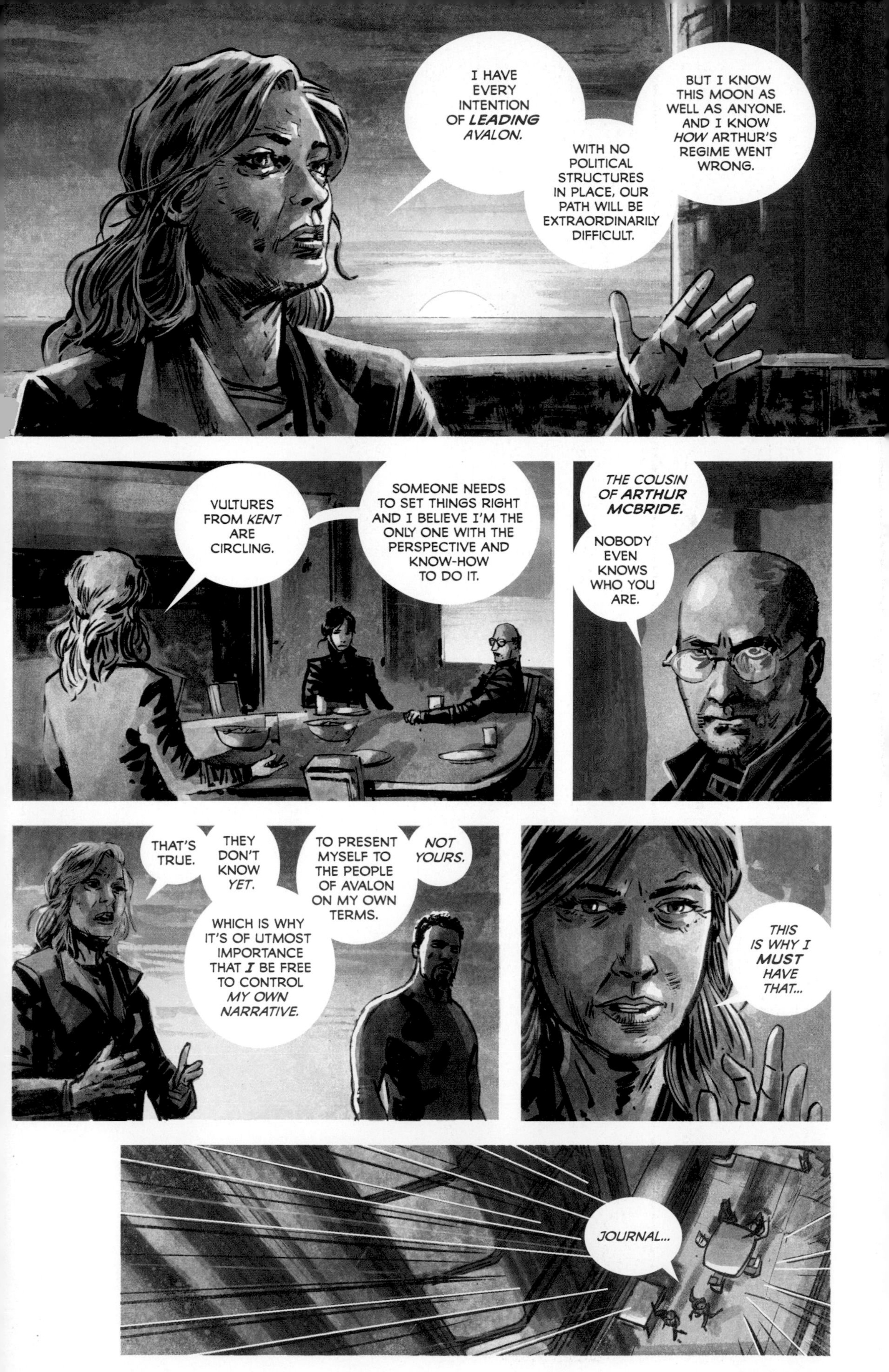
I HAVE EVERY INTENTION OF *LEADING AVALON.*
WITH NO POLITICAL STRUCTURES IN PLACE, OUR PATH WILL BE EXTRAORDINARILY DIFFICULT.
BUT I KNOW THIS MOON AS WELL AS ANYONE. AND I KNOW *HOW* ARTHUR'S REGIME WENT WRONG.
VULTURES FROM *KENT* ARE CIRCLING.
SOMEONE NEEDS TO SET THINGS RIGHT AND I BELIEVE I'M THE ONLY ONE WITH THE PERSPECTIVE AND KNOW-HOW TO DO IT.
*THE COUSIN OF **ARTHUR MCBRIDE.***
NOBODY EVEN KNOWS WHO YOU ARE.
THAT'S TRUE.
THEY DON'T KNOW *YET.*
WHICH IS WHY IT'S OF UTMOST IMPORTANCE THAT *I* BE FREE TO CONTROL *MY OWN NARRATIVE.*
TO PRESENT MYSELF TO THE PEOPLE OF AVALON ON MY OWN TERMS.
NOT YOURS.
*THIS IS WHY I **MUST** HAVE THAT...*
JOURNAL...

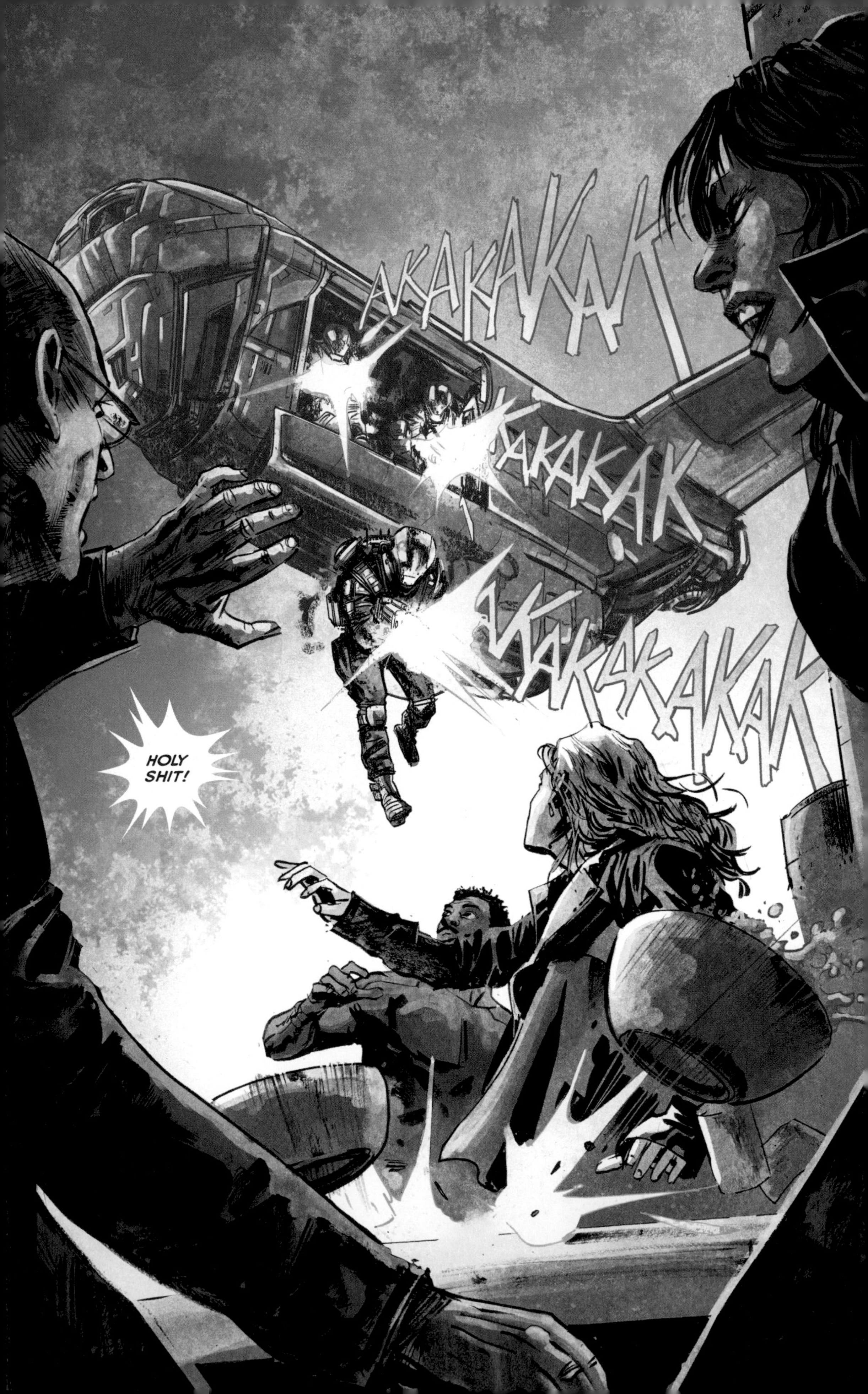
AKAKAKAKAK
KAKAKAK
KAKAKAKAKAK
HOLY SHIT!

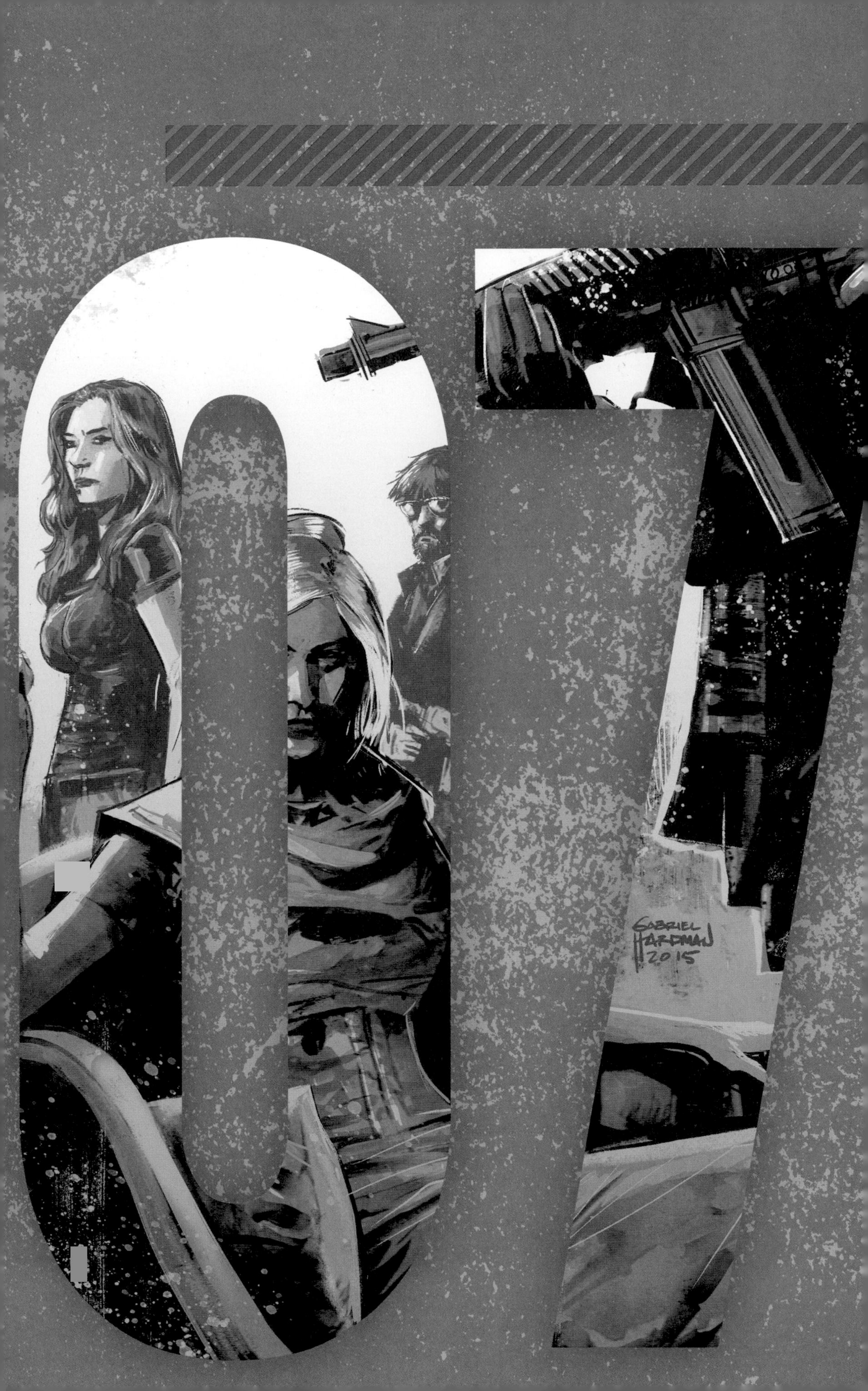
GABRIEL HARDMAN 2015

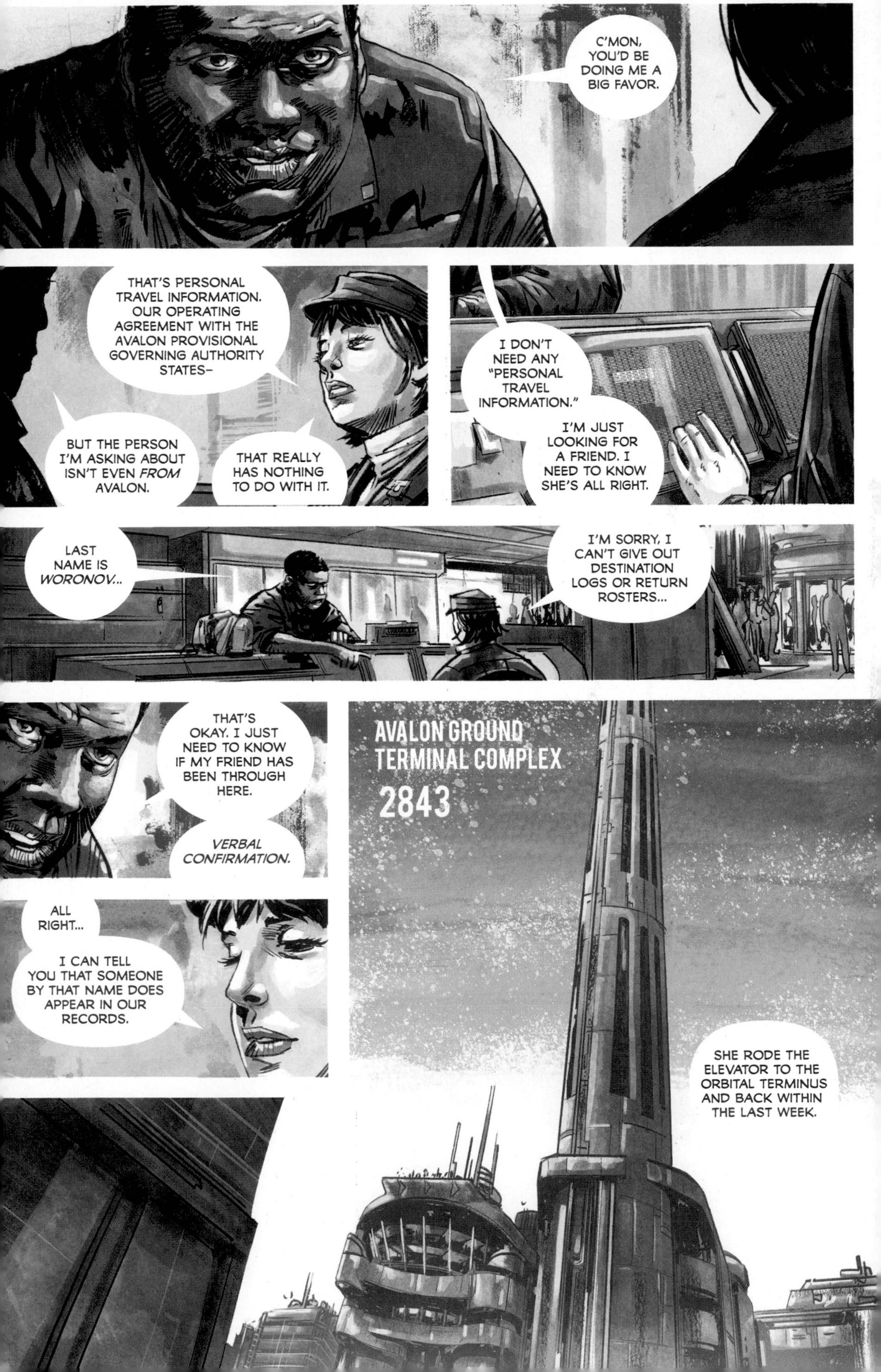
C'MON, YOU'D BE DOING ME A BIG FAVOR.
THAT'S PERSONAL TRAVEL INFORMATION. OUR OPERATING AGREEMENT WITH THE AVALON PROVISIONAL GOVERNING AUTHORITY STATES–
BUT THE PERSON I'M ASKING ABOUT ISN'T EVEN *FROM* AVALON.
THAT REALLY HAS NOTHING TO DO WITH IT.
I DON'T NEED ANY "PERSONAL TRAVEL INFORMATION."
I'M JUST LOOKING FOR A FRIEND. I NEED TO KNOW SHE'S ALL RIGHT.
LAST NAME IS *WORONOV*...
I'M SORRY, I CAN'T GIVE OUT DESTINATION LOGS OR RETURN ROSTERS...
THAT'S OKAY. I JUST NEED TO KNOW IF MY FRIEND HAS BEEN THROUGH HERE.
VERBAL CONFIRMATION.
ALL RIGHT...
I CAN TELL YOU THAT SOMEONE BY THAT NAME DOES APPEAR IN OUR RECORDS.
AVALON GROUND TERMINAL COMPLEX
2843
SHE RODE THE ELEVATOR TO THE ORBITAL TERMINUS AND BACK WITHIN THE LAST WEEK.

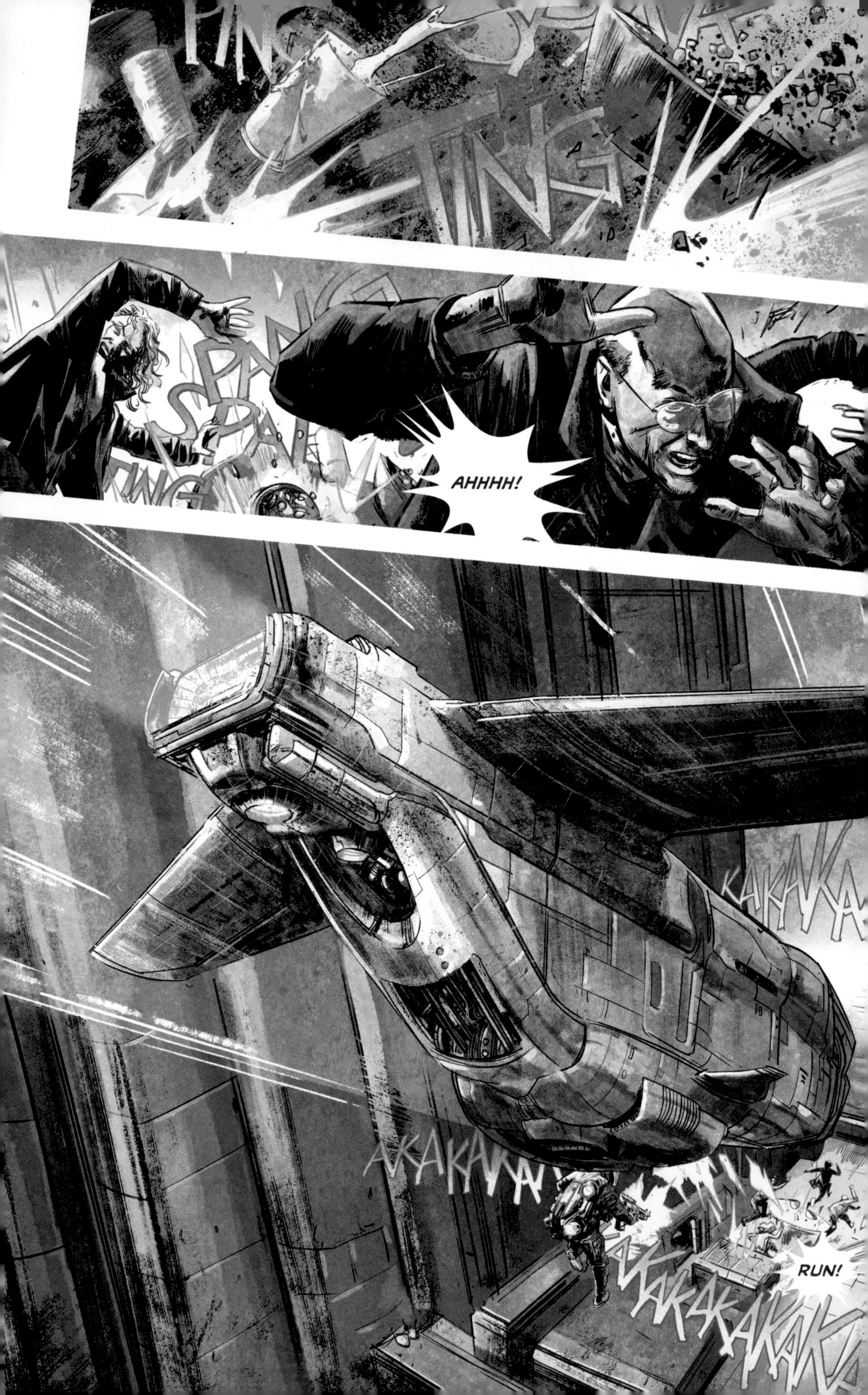
PING
TING
PANG
SPANG
TING
AHHHH!
KAKAKA
AKAKAKAKA
KAKAKAKAKA
RUN!

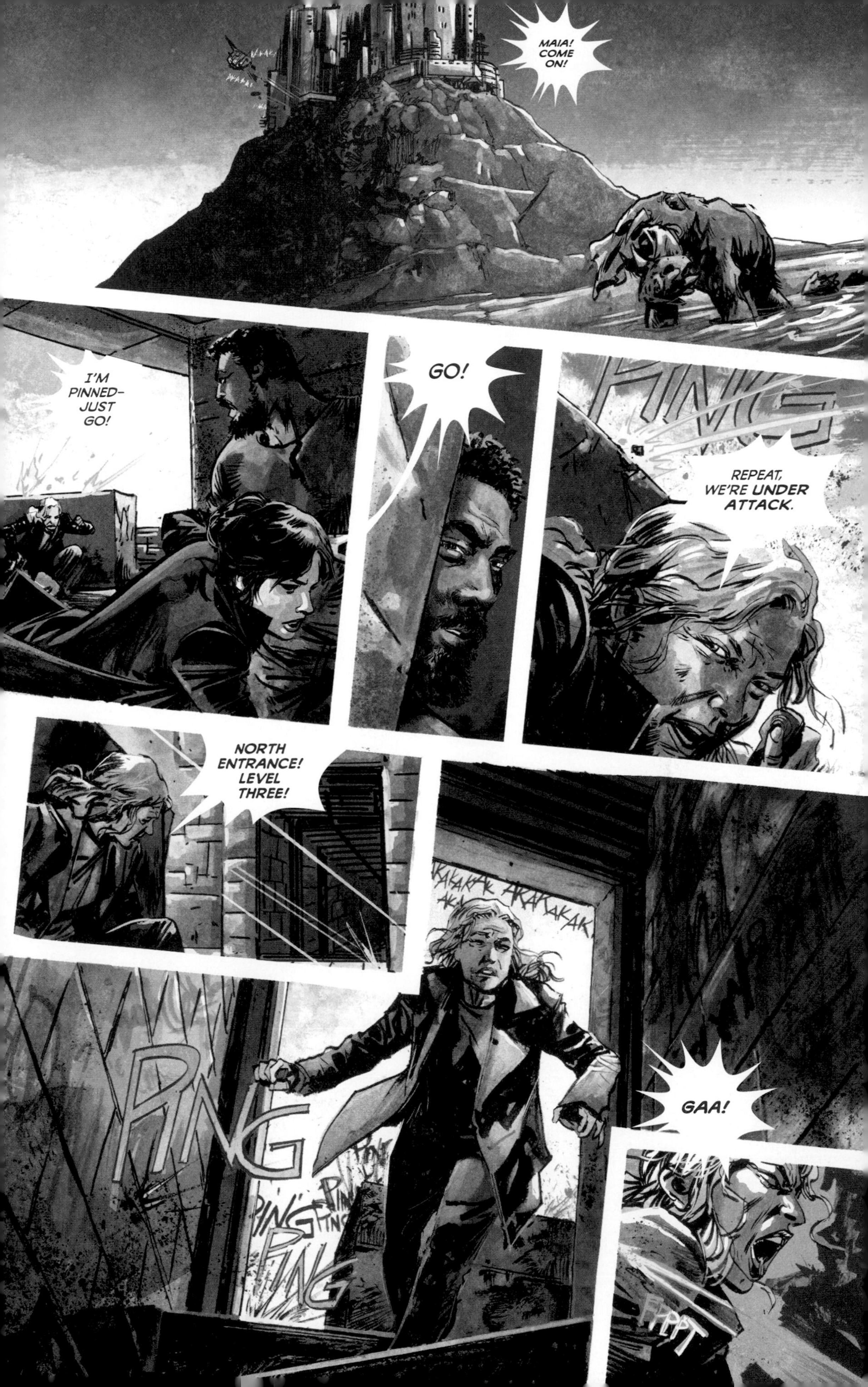
AKAKAK
AKAKAK
MAIA! COME ON!
I'M PINNED– JUST GO!
GO!
PING
REPEAT, WE'RE **UNDER ATTACK**.
NORTH ENTRANCE! LEVEL THREE!
AKAKAKAK AKAKAKAKAK
PING
PING
PING
PING
PING
GAA!
FFFPPT

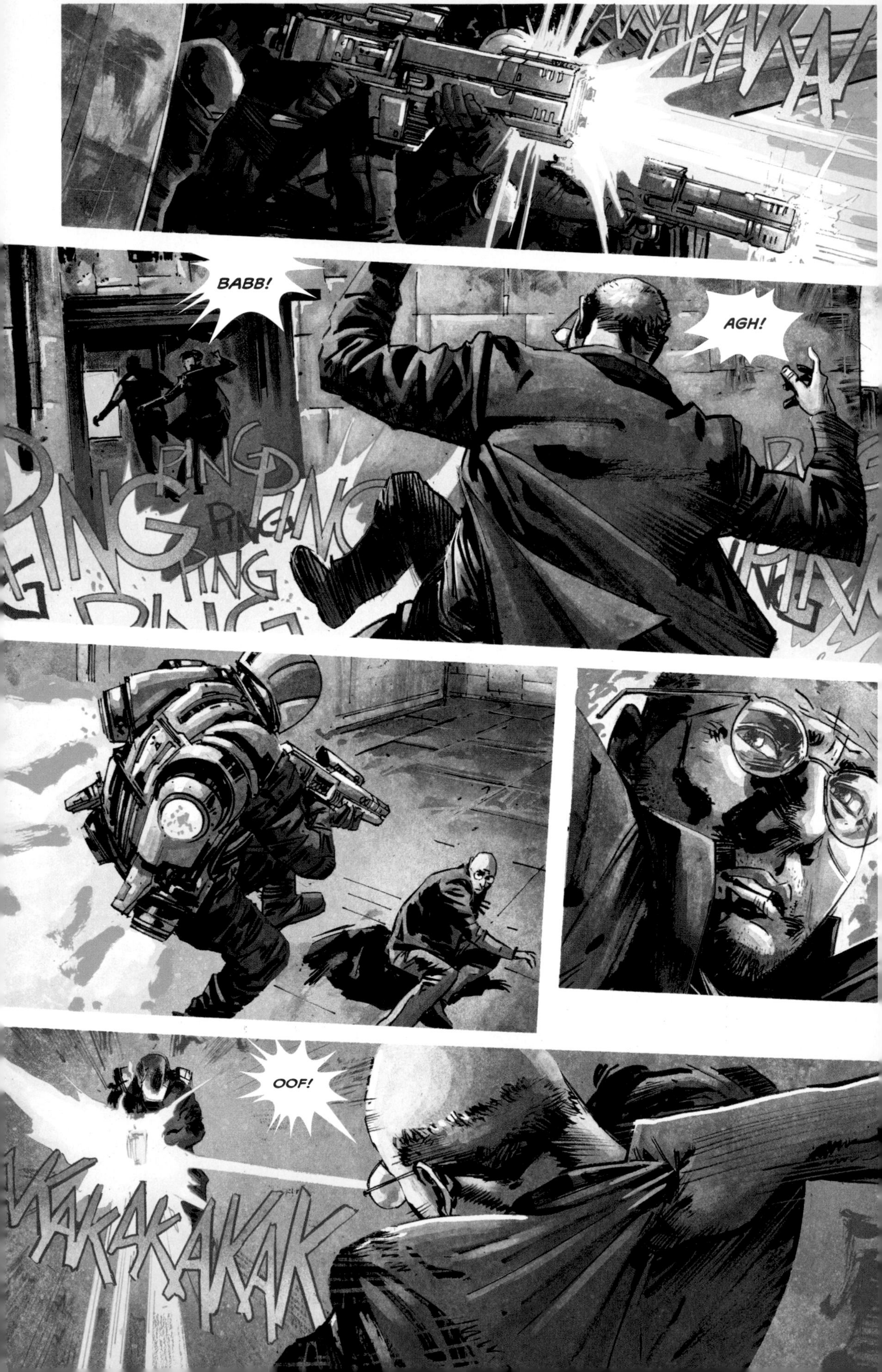
BABB!
AGH!
PING PING PING PING
OOF!

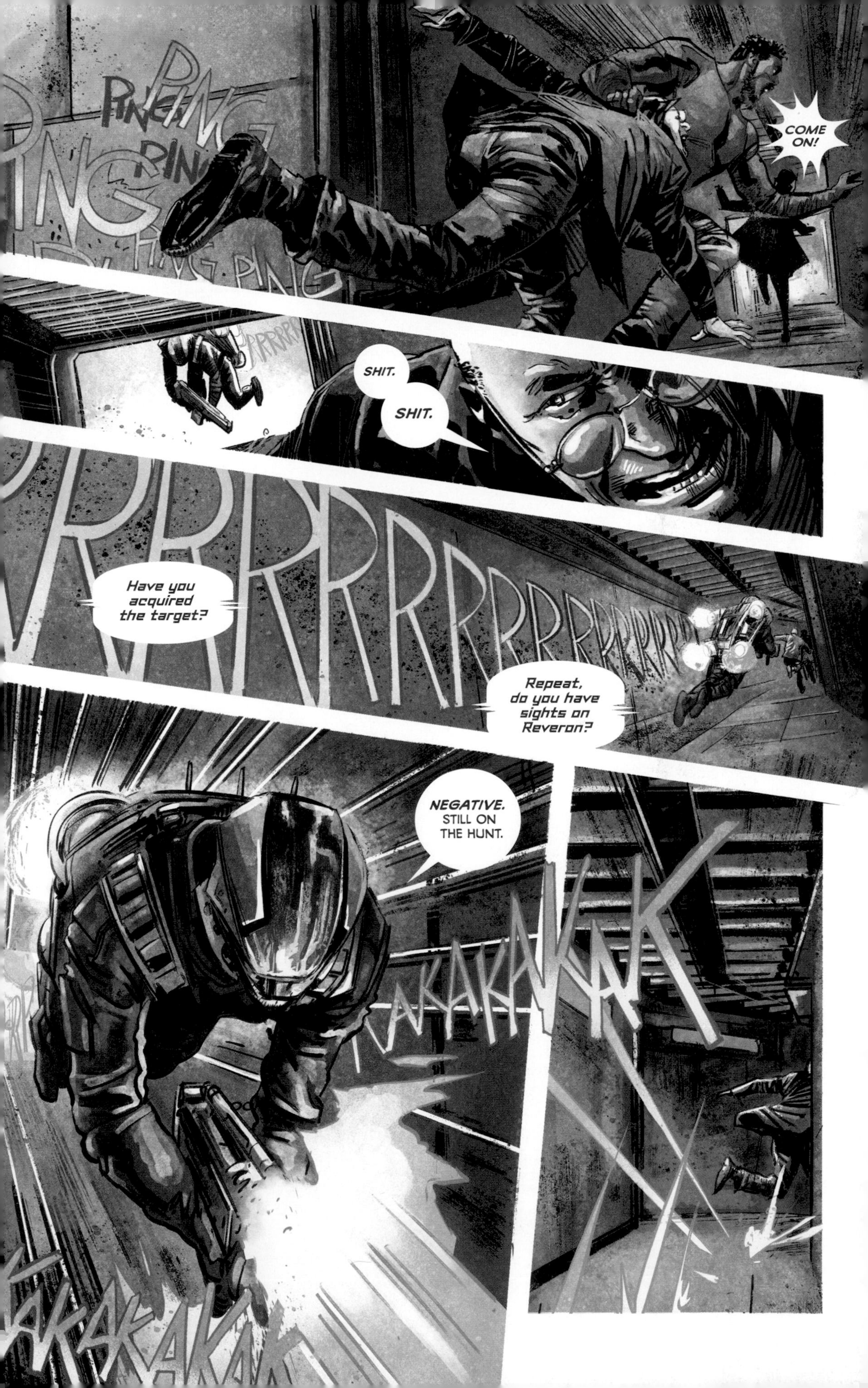
PING
PING PING
PING
PING
PING PING PING
COME ON!
RRRRR
SHIT.
SHIT.
RRRRRRRRRRRRRRRRR
Have you acquired the target?
Repeat, do you have sights on Reveron?
NEGATIVE. STILL ON THE HUNT.
KAKAKAKAKAK
KAKAKAKAK

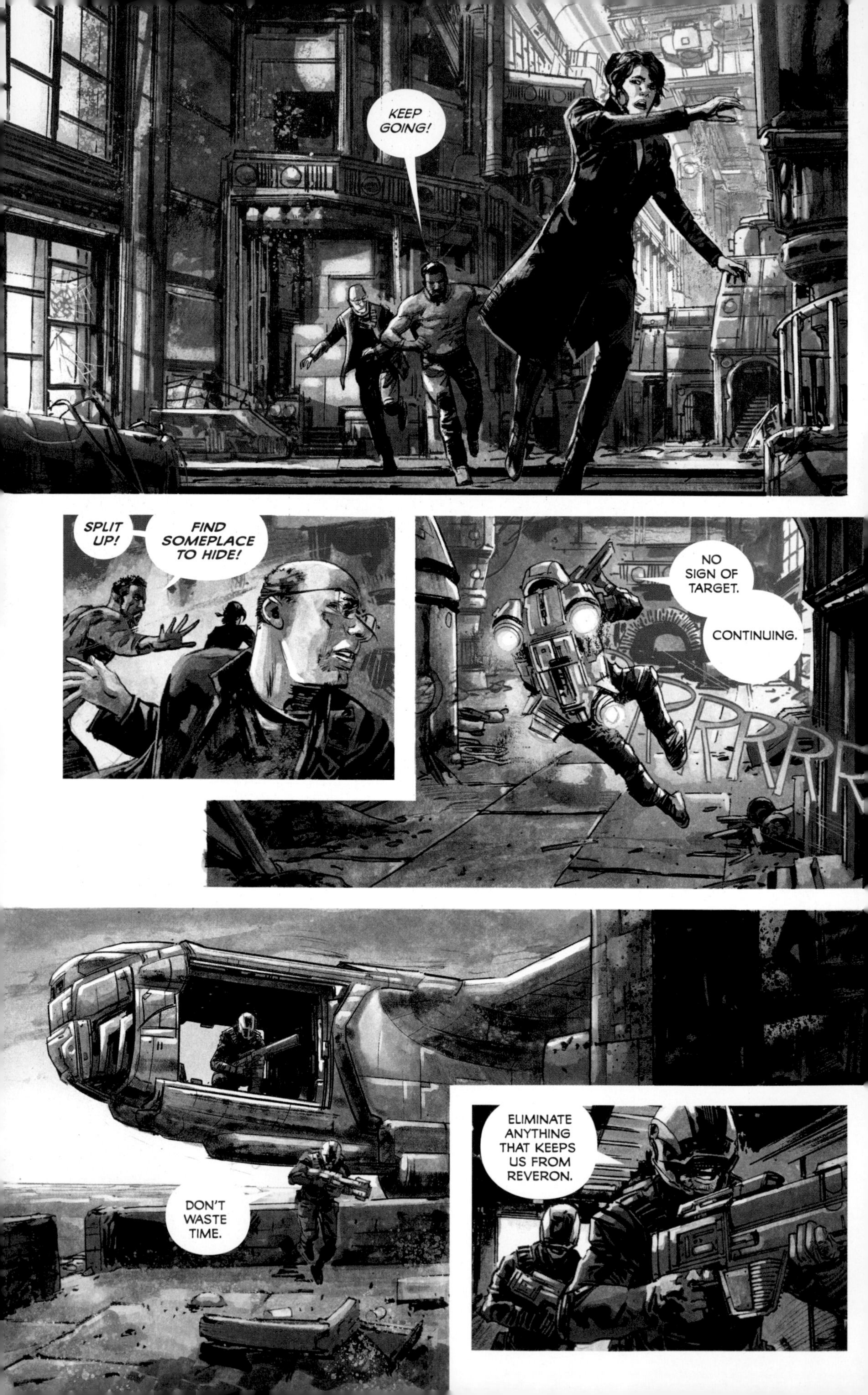
KEEP GOING!
SPLIT UP!
FIND SOMEPLACE TO HIDE!
NO SIGN OF TARGET.
CONTINUING.
RRRRRRR
DON'T WASTE TIME.
ELIMINATE ANYTHING THAT KEEPS US FROM REVERON.

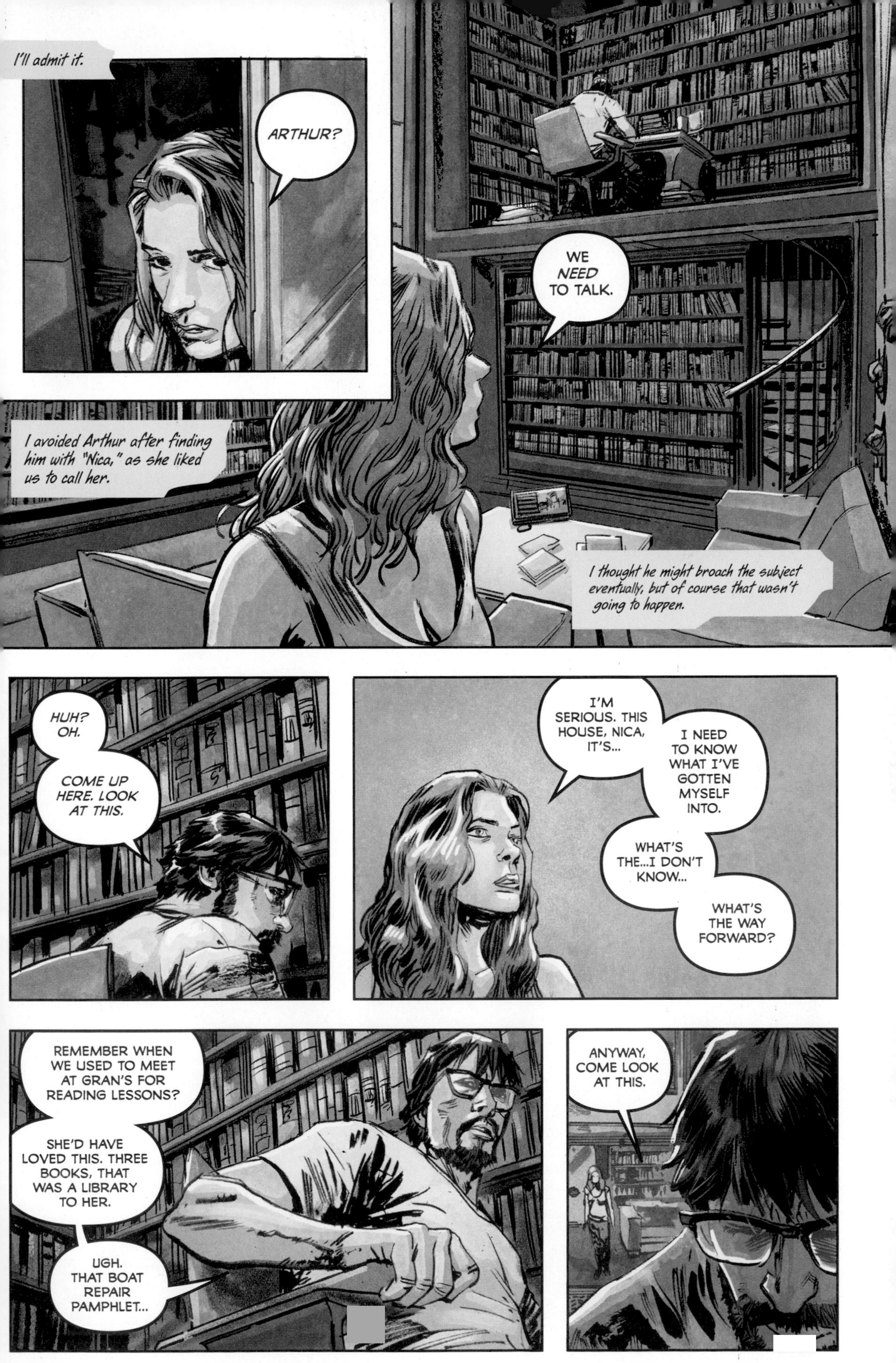

I'll admit it.
ARTHUR?
WE NEED TO TALK.
I avoided Arthur after finding him with "Nica," as she liked us to call her.
I thought he might broach the subject eventually, but of course that wasn't going to happen.
HUH? OH.
COME UP HERE. LOOK AT THIS.
I'M SERIOUS. THIS HOUSE, NICA, IT'S...
I NEED TO KNOW WHAT I'VE GOTTEN MYSELF INTO.
WHAT'S THE...I DON'T KNOW...
WHAT'S THE WAY FORWARD?
REMEMBER WHEN WE USED TO MEET AT GRAN'S FOR READING LESSONS?
SHE'D HAVE LOVED THIS. THREE BOOKS, THAT WAS A LIBRARY TO HER.
UGH. THAT BOAT REPAIR PAMPHLET...
ANYWAY, COME LOOK AT THIS.

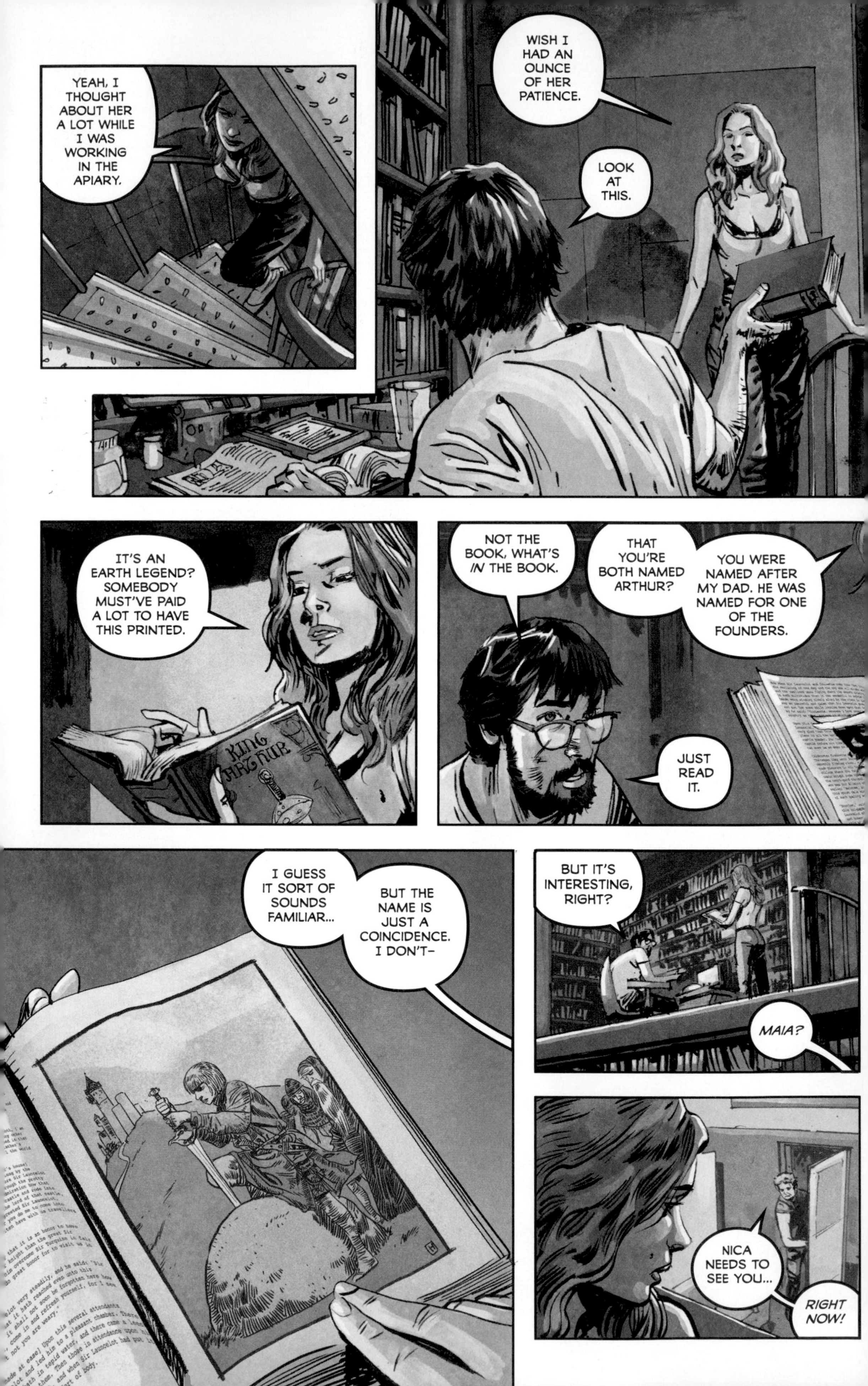
YEAH, I THOUGHT ABOUT HER A LOT WHILE I WAS WORKING IN THE APIARY.
WISH I HAD AN OUNCE OF HER PATIENCE.
LOOK AT THIS.
IT'S AN EARTH LEGEND? SOMEBODY MUST'VE PAID A LOT TO HAVE THIS PRINTED.
NOT THE BOOK, WHAT'S *IN* THE BOOK.
THAT YOU'RE BOTH NAMED ARTHUR?
YOU WERE NAMED AFTER MY DAD. HE WAS NAMED FOR ONE OF THE FOUNDERS.
KING ARTHUR
JUST READ IT.
I GUESS IT SORT OF SOUNDS FAMILIAR...
BUT THE NAME IS JUST A COINCIDENCE. I DON'T–
BUT IT'S INTERESTING, RIGHT?
MAIA?
NICA NEEDS TO SEE YOU...
RIGHT NOW!

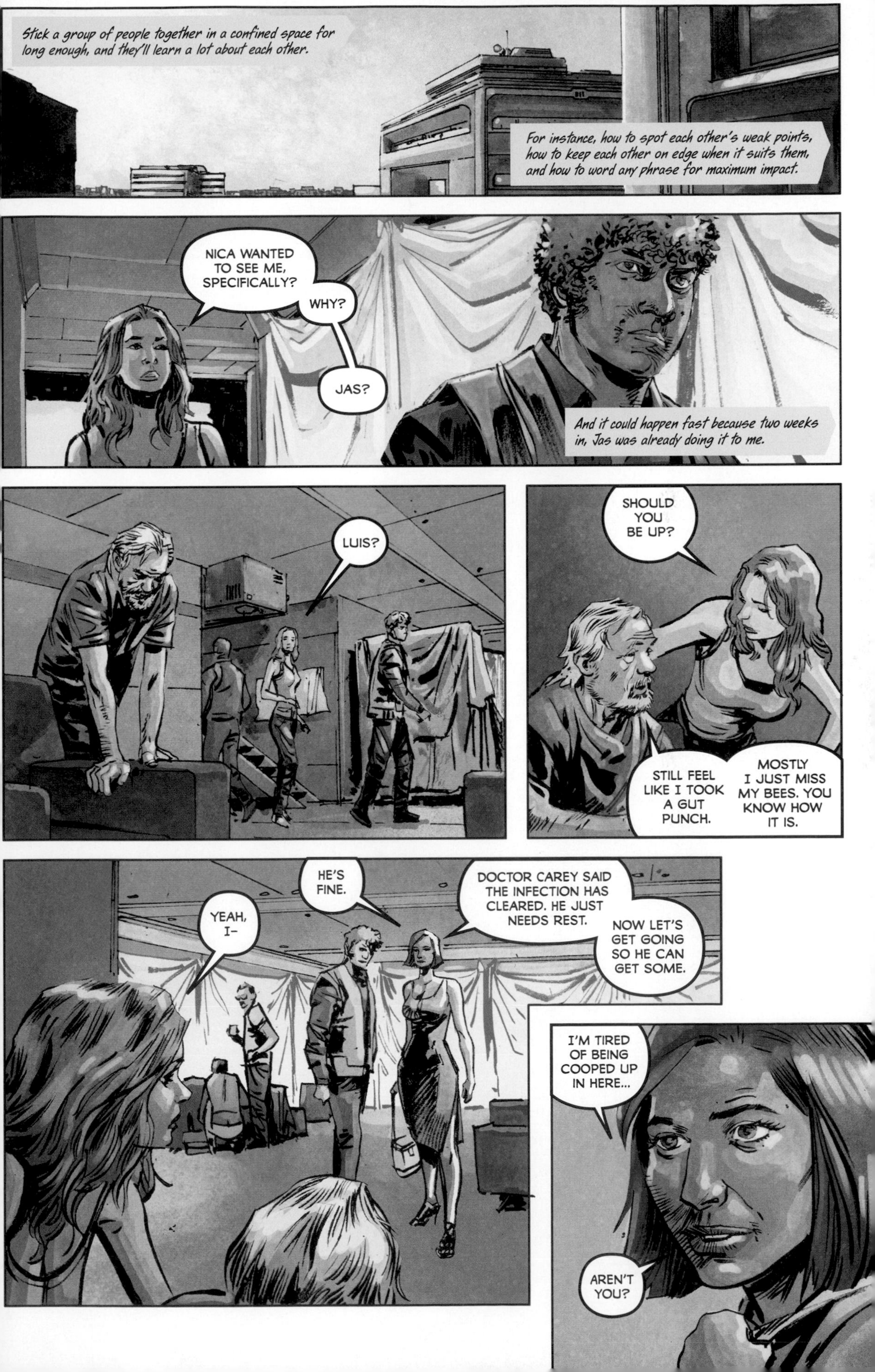

Stick a group of people together in a confined space for long enough, and they'll learn a lot about each other.
For instance, how to spot each other's weak points, how to keep each other on edge when it suits them, and how to word any phrase for maximum impact.
NICA WANTED TO SEE ME, SPECIFICALLY?
WHY?
JAS?
And it could happen fast because two weeks in, Jas was already doing it to me.
LUIS?
SHOULD YOU BE UP?
STILL FEEL LIKE I TOOK A GUT PUNCH.
MOSTLY I JUST MISS MY BEES. YOU KNOW HOW IT IS.
YEAH, I–
HE'S FINE.
DOCTOR CAREY SAID THE INFECTION HAS CLEARED. HE JUST NEEDS REST.
NOW LET'S GET GOING SO HE CAN GET SOME.
I'M TIRED OF BEING COOPED UP IN HERE...
AREN'T YOU?

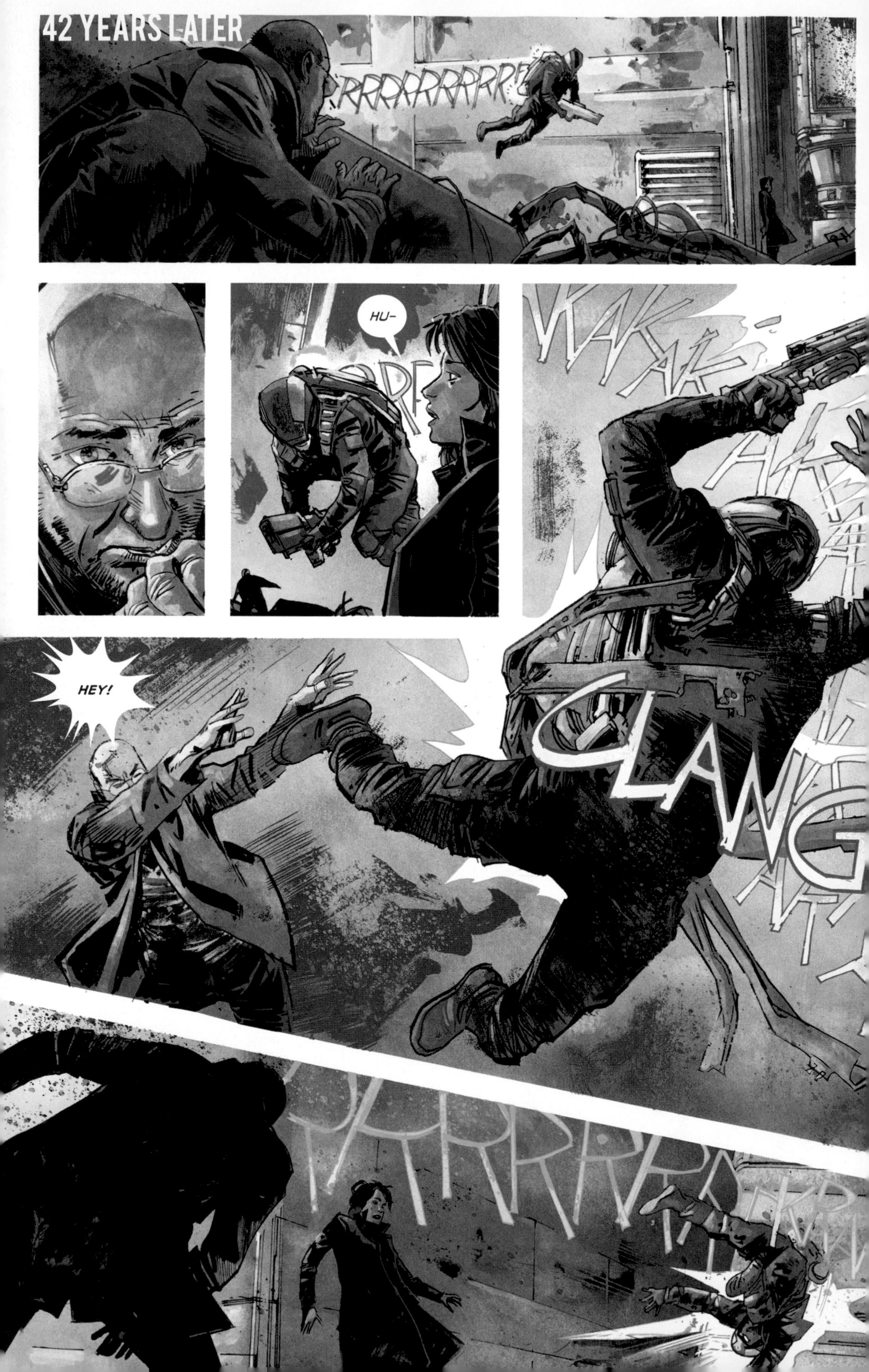
42 YEARS LATER
HU–
HEY!
CLANG

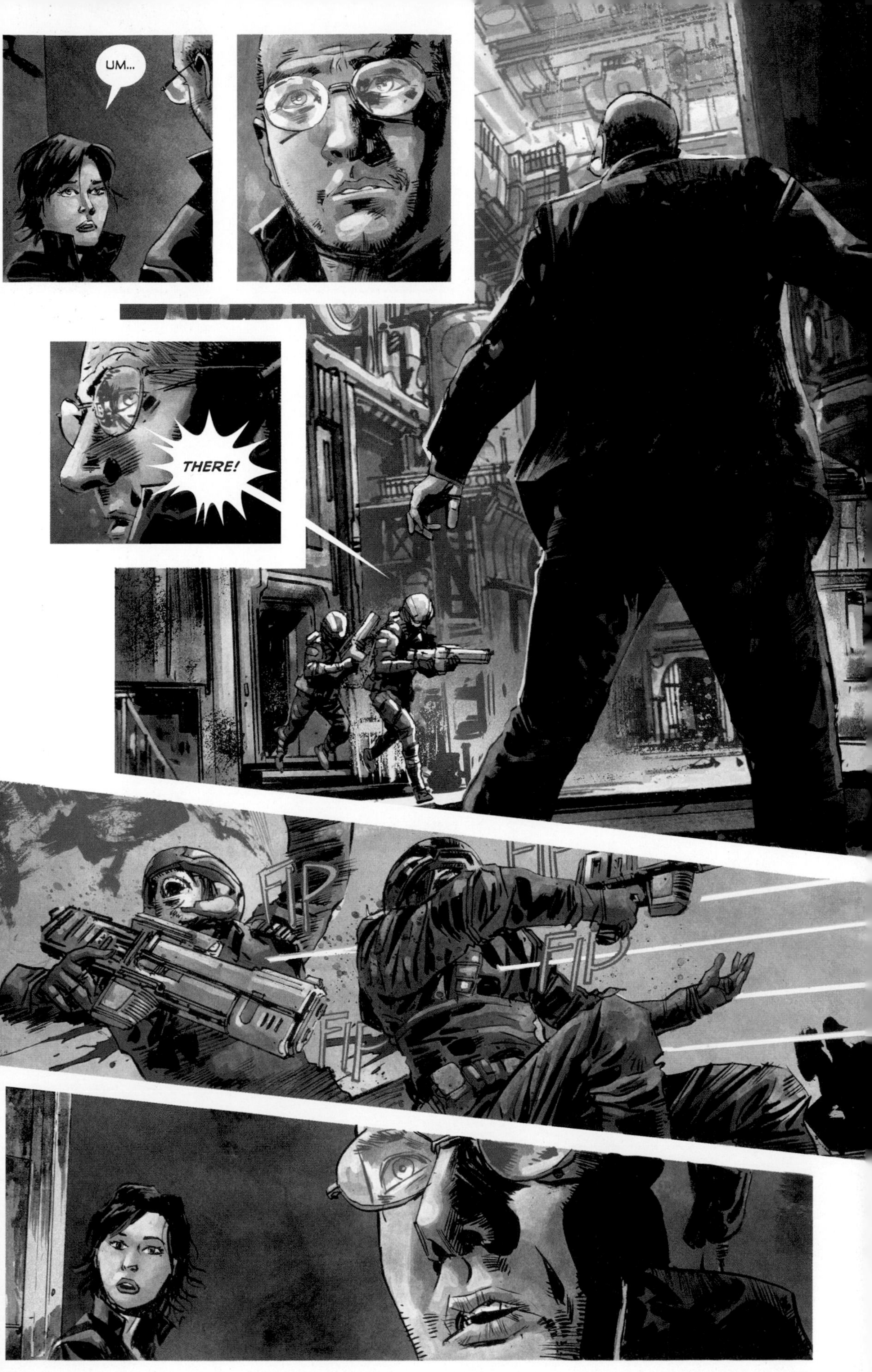
UM...
THERE!
FIP
FIP
FIP
FIP

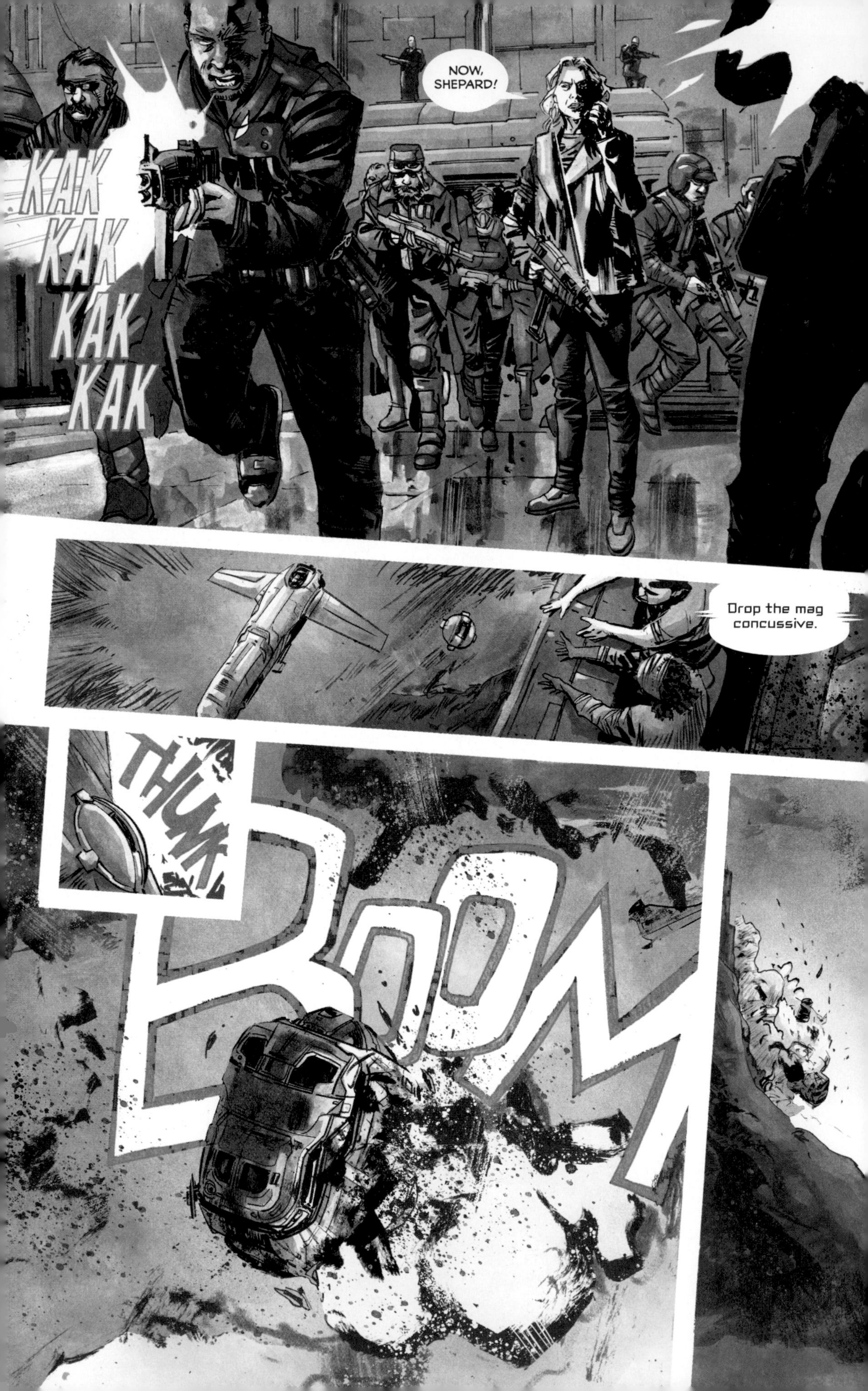
NOW, SHEPARD!
KAK KAK KAK KAK
Drop the mag concussive.
THUNK!
BOOM

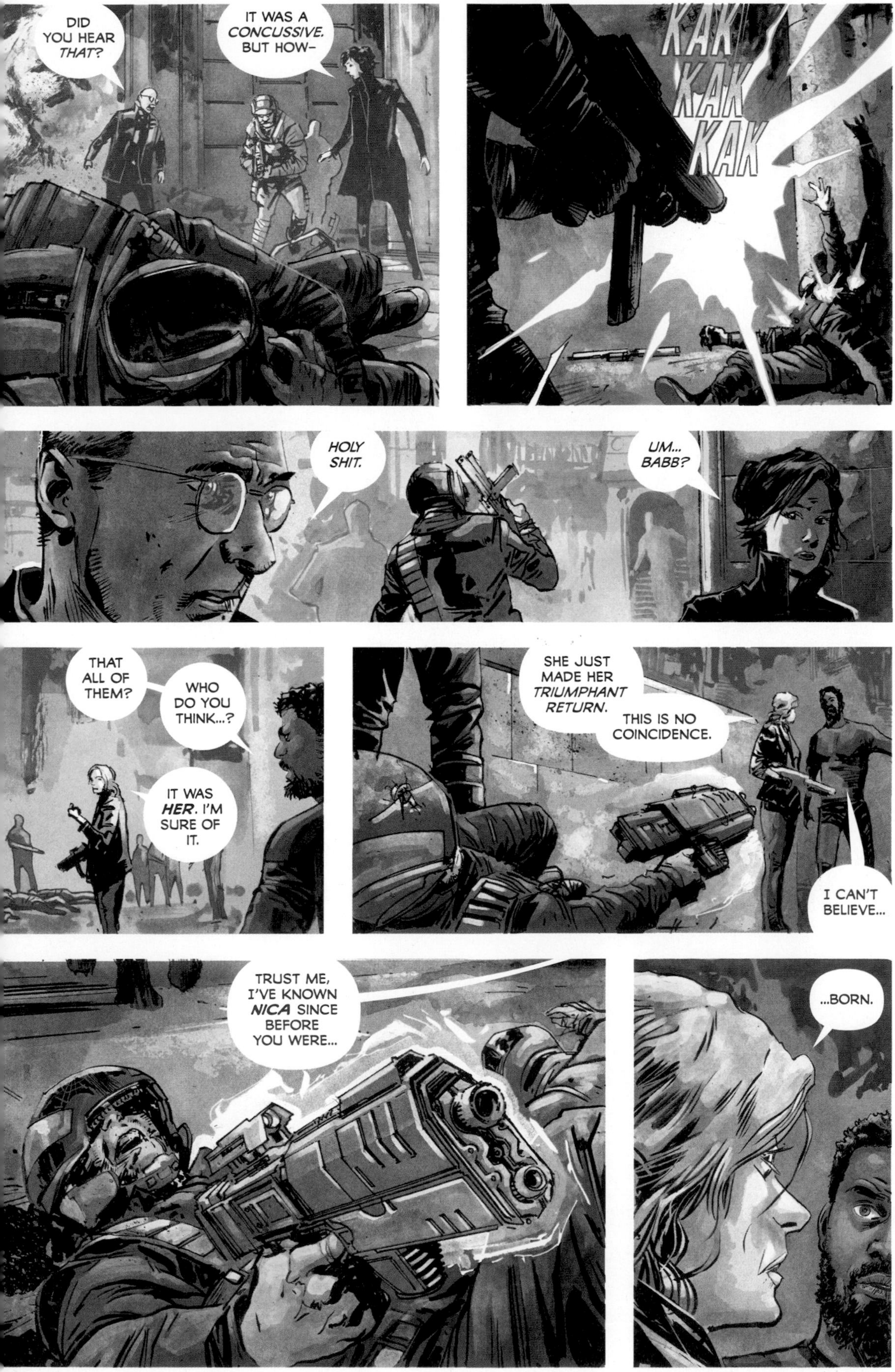
DID YOU HEAR *THAT?*
IT WAS A *CONCUSSIVE.* BUT HOW–
KAK KAK KAK
HOLY SHIT.
UM... BABB?
THAT ALL OF THEM?
WHO DO YOU THINK...?
IT WAS ***HER***. I'M SURE OF IT.
SHE JUST MADE HER *TRIUMPHANT RETURN*.
THIS IS NO COINCIDENCE.
I CAN'T BELIEVE...
TRUST ME, I'VE KNOWN ***NICA*** SINCE BEFORE YOU WERE...
...BORN.

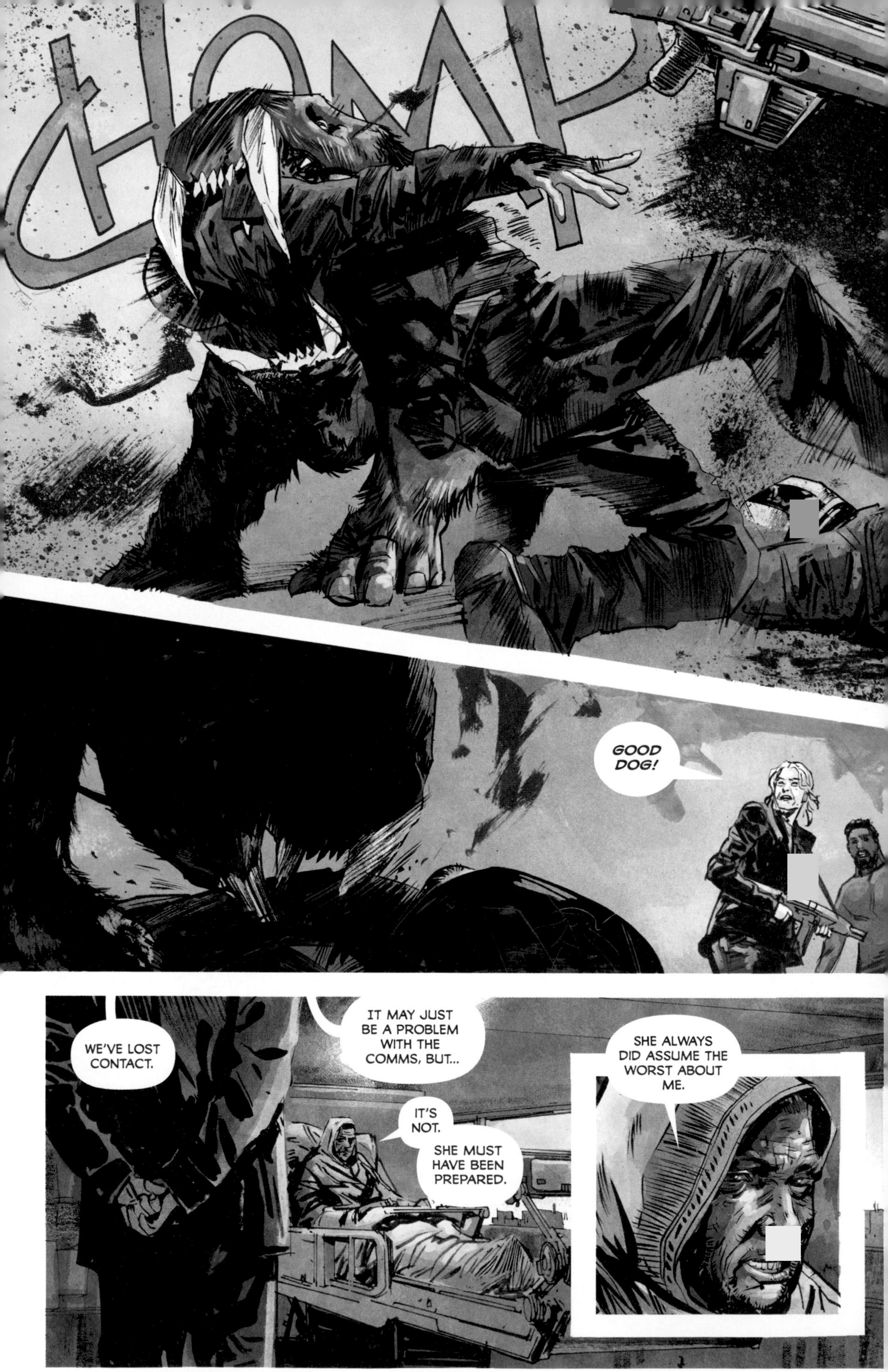
CHOMP
GOOD DOG!
WE'VE LOST CONTACT.
IT MAY JUST BE A PROBLEM WITH THE COMMS, BUT...
IT'S NOT.
SHE MUST HAVE BEEN PREPARED.
SHE ALWAYS DID ASSUME THE WORST ABOUT ME.

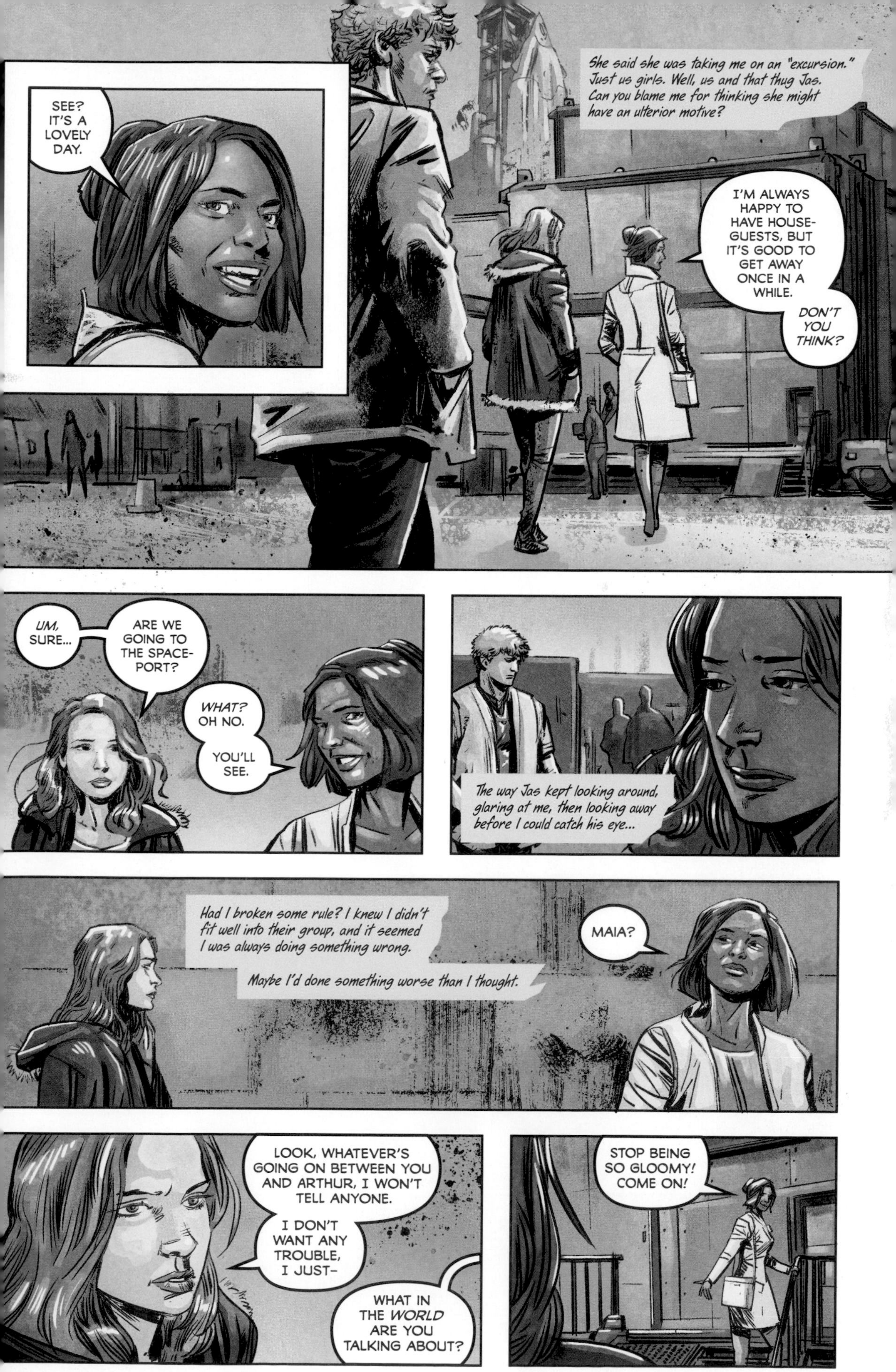
SEE? IT'S A LOVELY DAY.
She said she was taking me on an "excursion." Just us girls. Well, us and that thug Jas. Can you blame me for thinking she might have an ulterior motive?
I'M ALWAYS HAPPY TO HAVE HOUSE-GUESTS, BUT IT'S GOOD TO GET AWAY ONCE IN A WHILE.
DON'T YOU THINK?
UM, SURE...
ARE WE GOING TO THE SPACE-PORT?
WHAT? OH NO.
YOU'LL SEE.
The way Jas kept looking around, glaring at me, then looking away before I could catch his eye...
Had I broken some rule? I knew I didn't fit well into their group, and it seemed I was always doing something wrong.
Maybe I'd done something worse than I thought.
MAIA?
LOOK, WHATEVER'S GOING ON BETWEEN YOU AND ARTHUR, I WON'T TELL ANYONE.
I DON'T WANT ANY TROUBLE, I JUST-
WHAT IN THE WORLD ARE YOU TALKING ABOUT?
STOP BEING SO GLOOMY! COME ON!

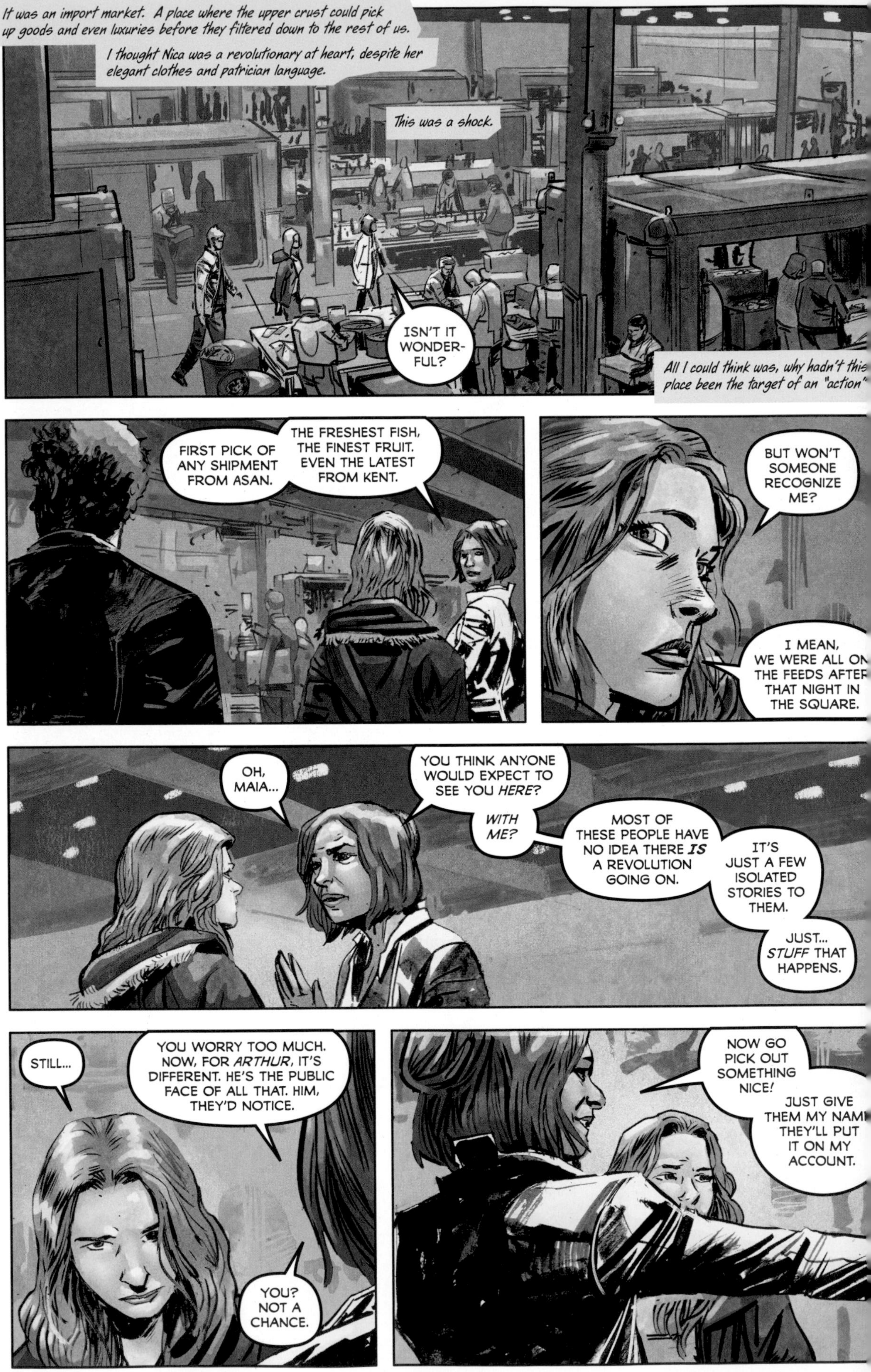
It was an import market. A place where the upper crust could pick up goods and even luxuries before they filtered down to the rest of us.
I thought Nica was a revolutionary at heart, despite her elegant clothes and patrician language.
This was a shock.
ISN'T IT WONDERFUL?
All I could think was, why hadn't this place been the target of an "action"
FIRST PICK OF ANY SHIPMENT FROM ASAN.
THE FRESHEST FISH, THE FINEST FRUIT. EVEN THE LATEST FROM KENT.
BUT WON'T SOMEONE RECOGNIZE ME?
I MEAN, WE WERE ALL ON THE FEEDS AFTER THAT NIGHT IN THE SQUARE.
OH, MAIA...
YOU THINK ANYONE WOULD EXPECT TO SEE YOU *HERE*?
WITH ME?
MOST OF THESE PEOPLE HAVE NO IDEA THERE ***IS*** A REVOLUTION GOING ON.
IT'S JUST A FEW ISOLATED STORIES TO THEM.
JUST... *STUFF* THAT HAPPENS.
STILL...
YOU WORRY TOO MUCH. NOW, FOR *ARTHUR*, IT'S DIFFERENT. HE'S THE PUBLIC FACE OF ALL THAT. HIM, THEY'D NOTICE.
YOU? NOT A CHANCE.
NOW GO PICK OUT SOMETHING NICE!
JUST GIVE THEM MY NAM THEY'LL PUT IT ON MY ACCOUNT.

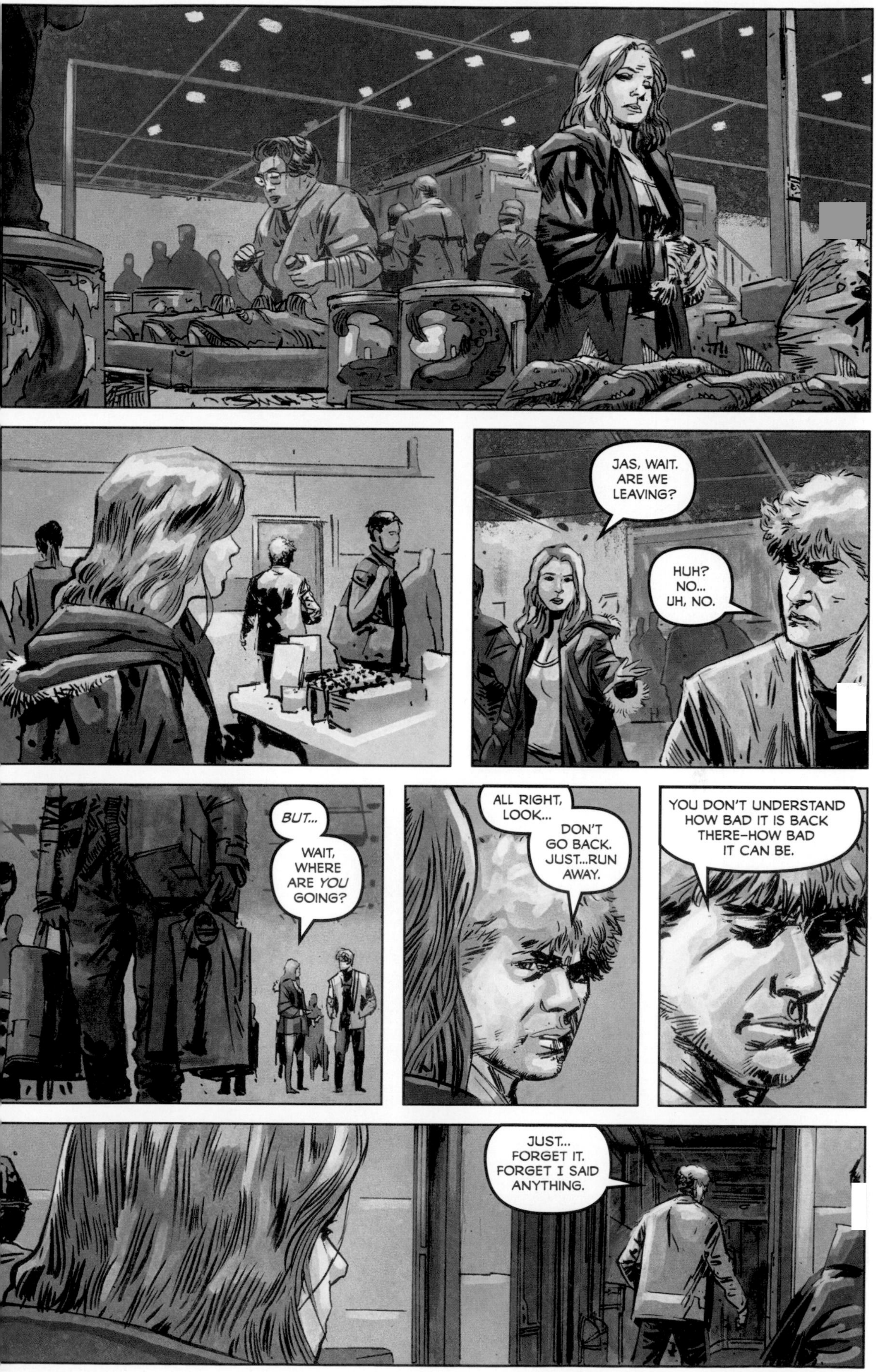
JAS, WAIT. ARE WE LEAVING?
HUH? NO... UH, NO.
BUT...
WAIT, WHERE ARE *YOU* GOING?
ALL RIGHT, LOOK...
DON'T GO BACK. JUST...RUN AWAY.
YOU DON'T UNDERSTAND HOW BAD IT IS BACK THERE–HOW BAD IT CAN BE.
JUST... FORGET IT. FORGET I SAID ANYTHING.

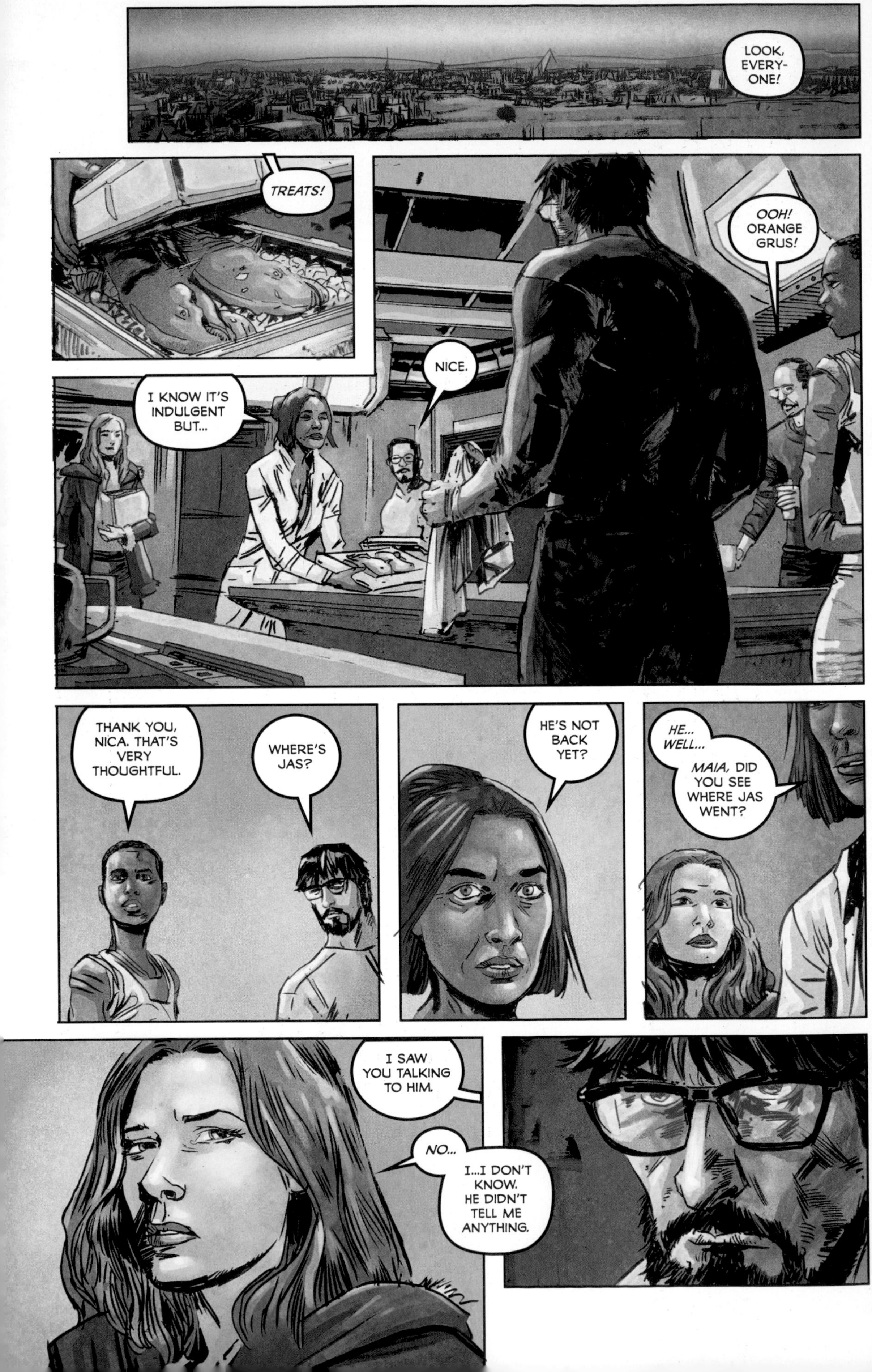
LOOK, EVERY-ONE!
TREATS!
OOH! ORANGE GRUS!
NICE.
I KNOW IT'S INDULGENT BUT...
THANK YOU, NICA. THAT'S VERY THOUGHTFUL.
WHERE'S JAS?
HE'S NOT BACK YET?
HE... WELL...
MAIA, DID YOU SEE WHERE JAS WENT?
I SAW YOU TALKING TO HIM.
NO...
I...I DON'T KNOW. HE DIDN'T TELL ME ANYTHING.

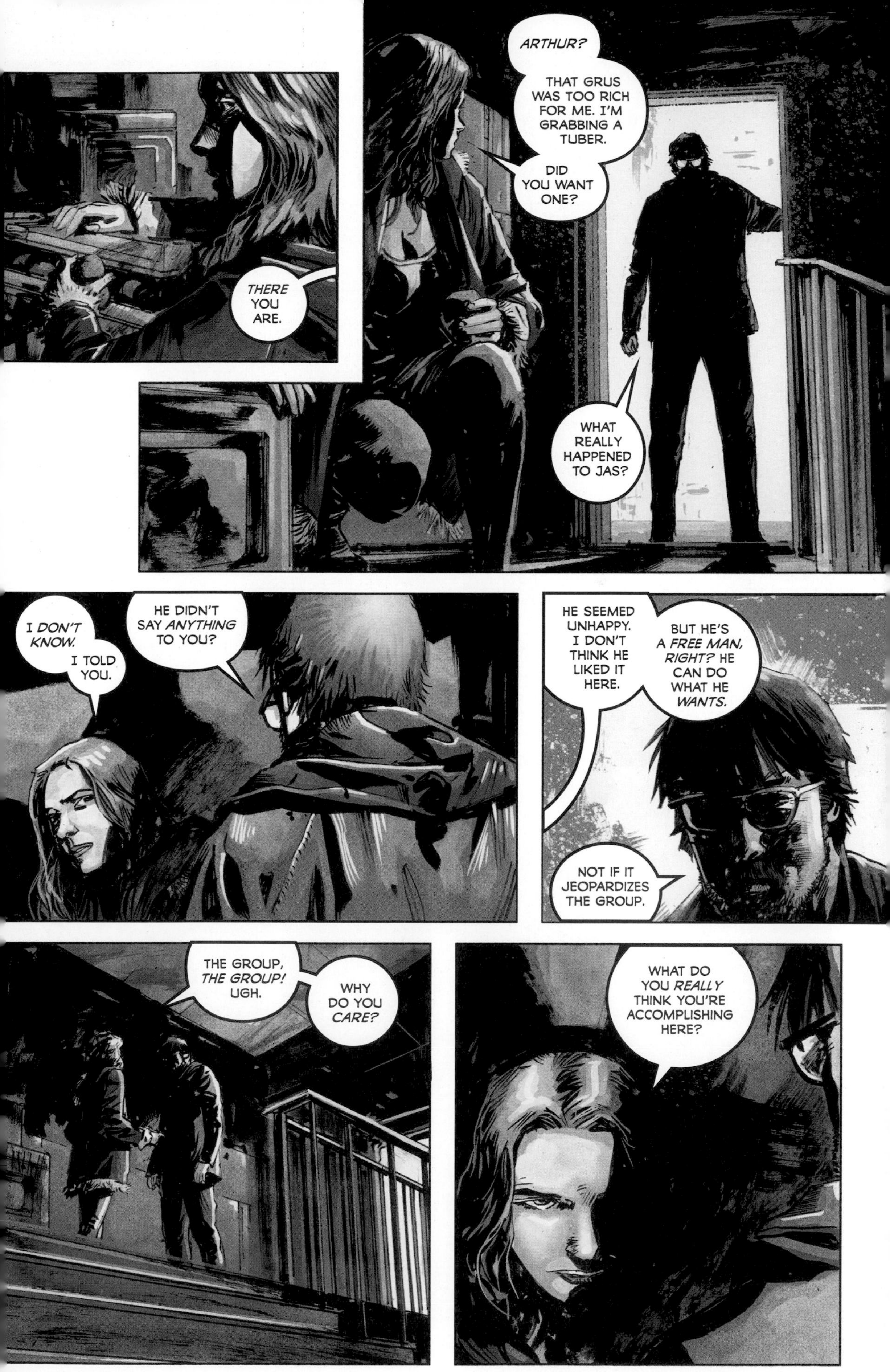
THERE YOU ARE.
ARTHUR?
THAT GRUS WAS TOO RICH FOR ME. I'M GRABBING A TUBER.
DID YOU WANT ONE?
WHAT REALLY HAPPENED TO JAS?
I DON'T KNOW.
I TOLD YOU.
HE DIDN'T SAY ANYTHING TO YOU?
HE SEEMED UNHAPPY. I DON'T THINK HE LIKED IT HERE.
BUT HE'S A FREE MAN, RIGHT? HE CAN DO WHAT HE WANTS.
NOT IF IT JEOPARDIZES THE GROUP.
THE GROUP, THE GROUP! UGH.
WHY DO YOU CARE?
WHAT DO YOU REALLY THINK YOU'RE ACCOMPLISHING HERE?

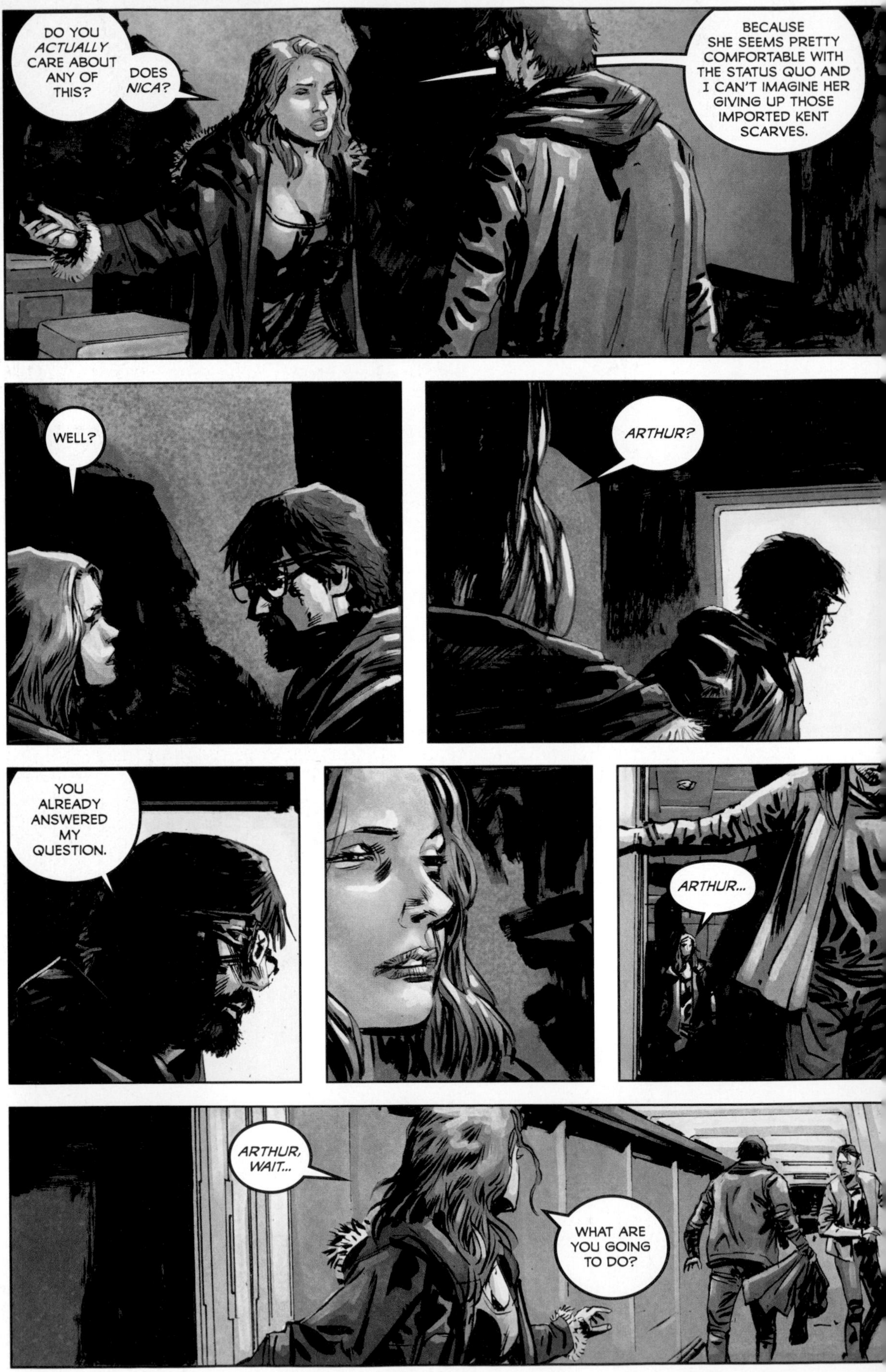
DO YOU *ACTUALLY* CARE ABOUT ANY OF THIS?
DOES *NICA?*
BECAUSE SHE SEEMS PRETTY COMFORTABLE WITH THE STATUS QUO AND I CAN'T IMAGINE HER GIVING UP THOSE IMPORTED KENT SCARVES.
WELL?
ARTHUR?
YOU ALREADY ANSWERED MY QUESTION.
ARTHUR...
ARTHUR, WAIT...
WHAT ARE YOU GOING TO DO?

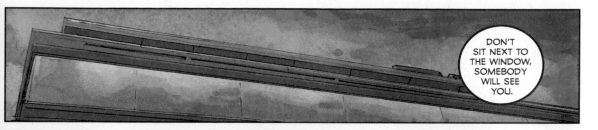

DON'T SIT NEXT TO THE WINDOW, SOMEBODY WILL SEE YOU.

WHAT?

LOOK CHRISTOPH, I'M JUST—

I WAS JOKING.

IT'S NIGHT, NOBODY CAN SEE YOU.

I GUESS THINGS ARE A LITTLE TENSE FOR IRONY.

SORRY. I DIDN'T...

YEAH.

NOT A LOT OF LAUGHS IN A REVOLUTION, I SUPPOSE.

WHAT REVOLUTION? WE JUST SIT AROUND THIS MANSION ALL DAY.

HEH.

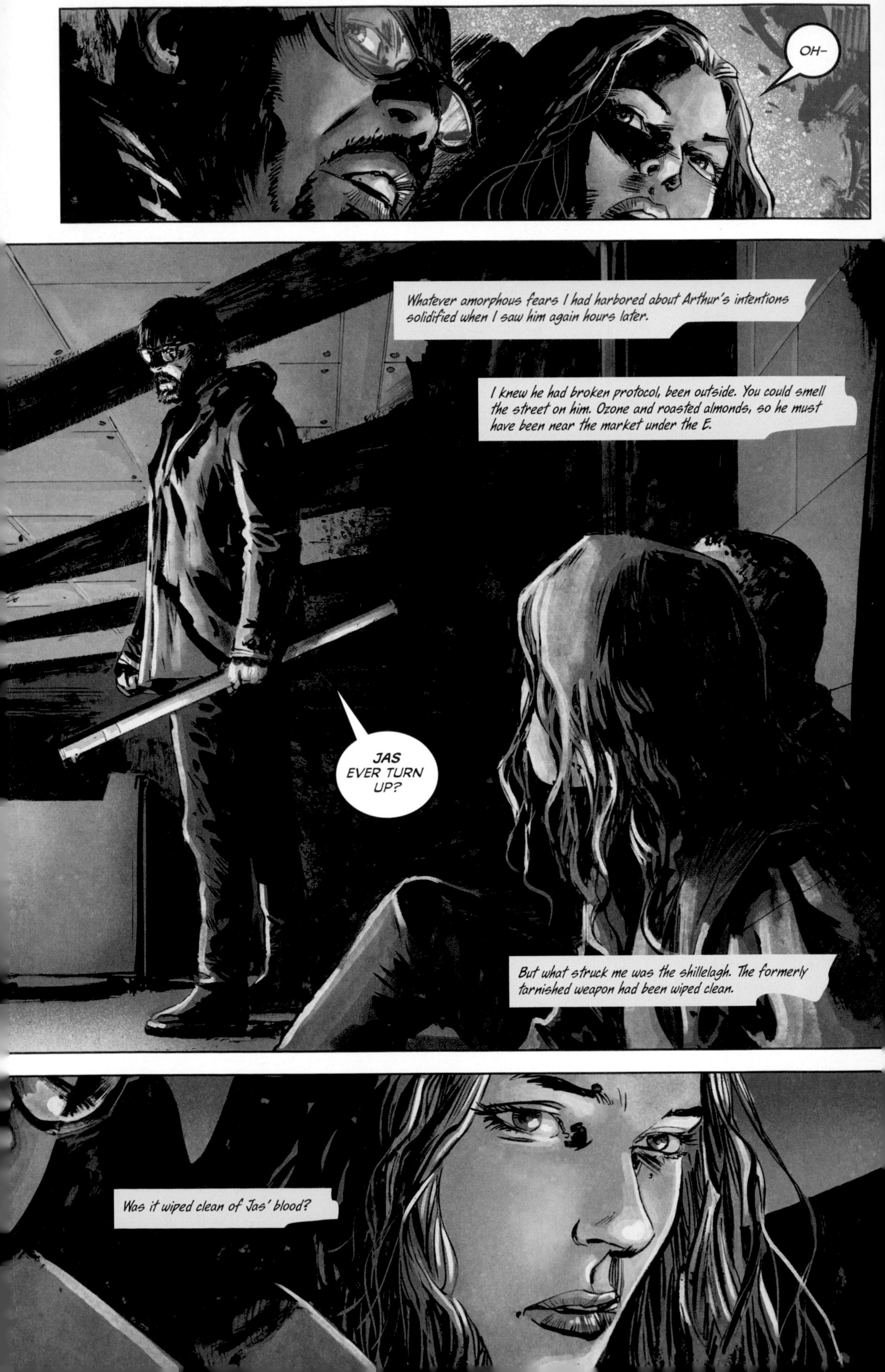
OH-
Whatever amorphous fears I had harbored about Arthur's intentions solidified when I saw him again hours later.
I knew he had broken protocol, been outside. You could smell the street on him. Ozone and roasted almonds, so he must have been near the market under the E.
JAS EVER TURN UP?
But what struck me was the shillelagh. The formerly tarnished weapon had been wiped clean.
Was it wiped clean of Jas' blood?

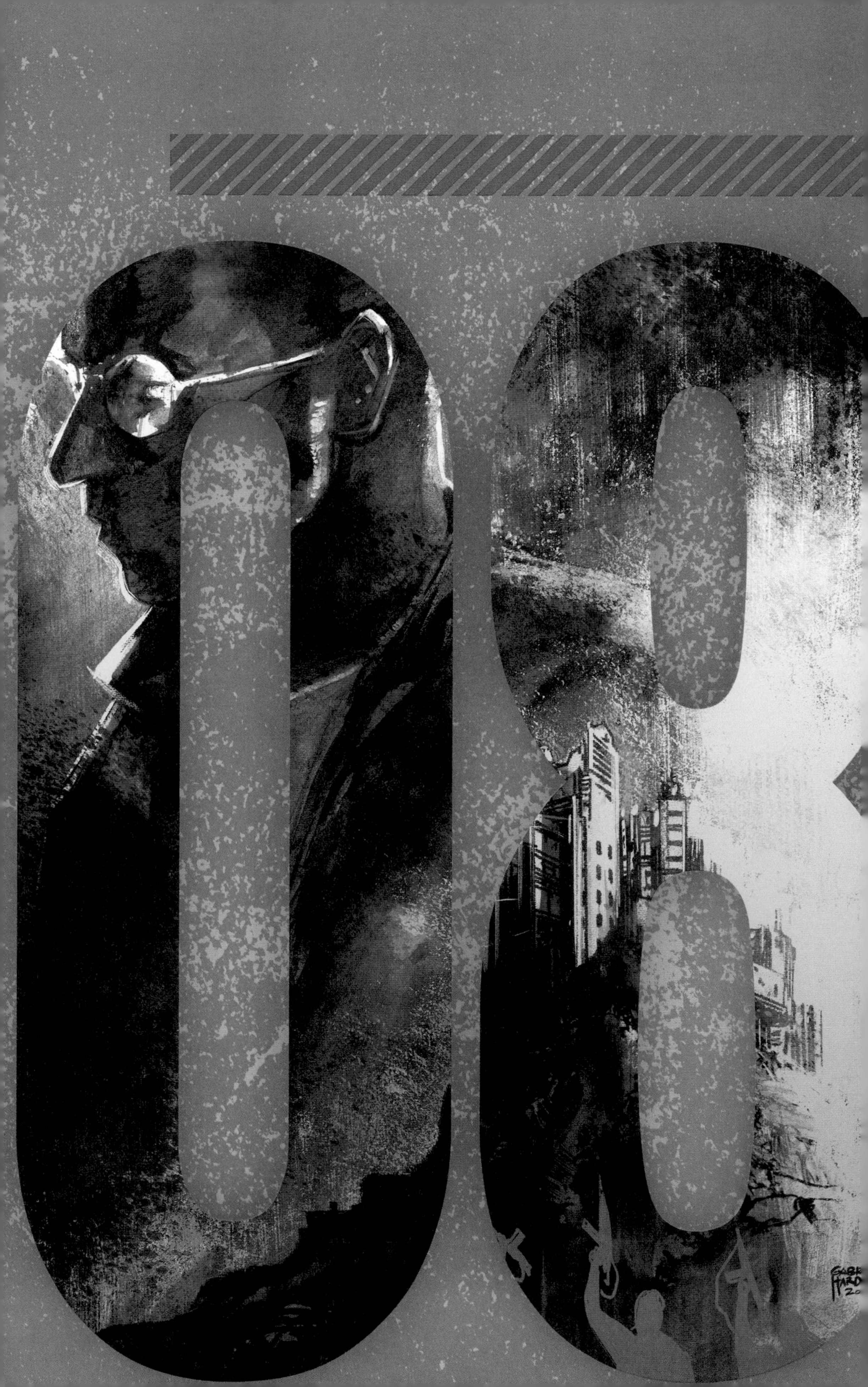
08

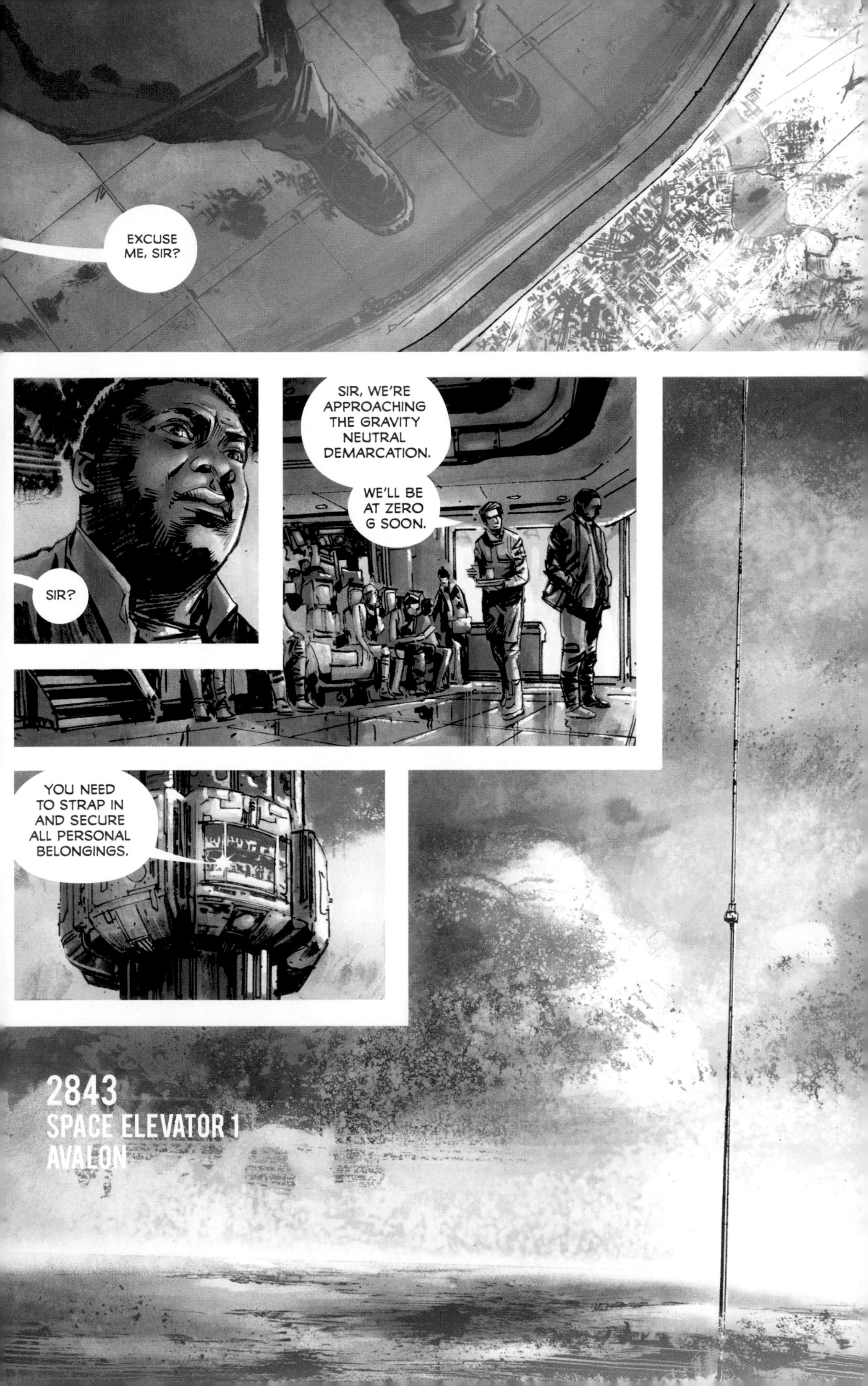
EXCUSE ME, SIR?
SIR?
SIR, WE'RE APPROACHING THE GRAVITY NEUTRAL DEMARCATION.
WE'LL BE AT ZERO G SOON.
YOU NEED TO STRAP IN AND SECURE ALL PERSONAL BELONGINGS.
2843
SPACE ELEVATOR 1
AVALON

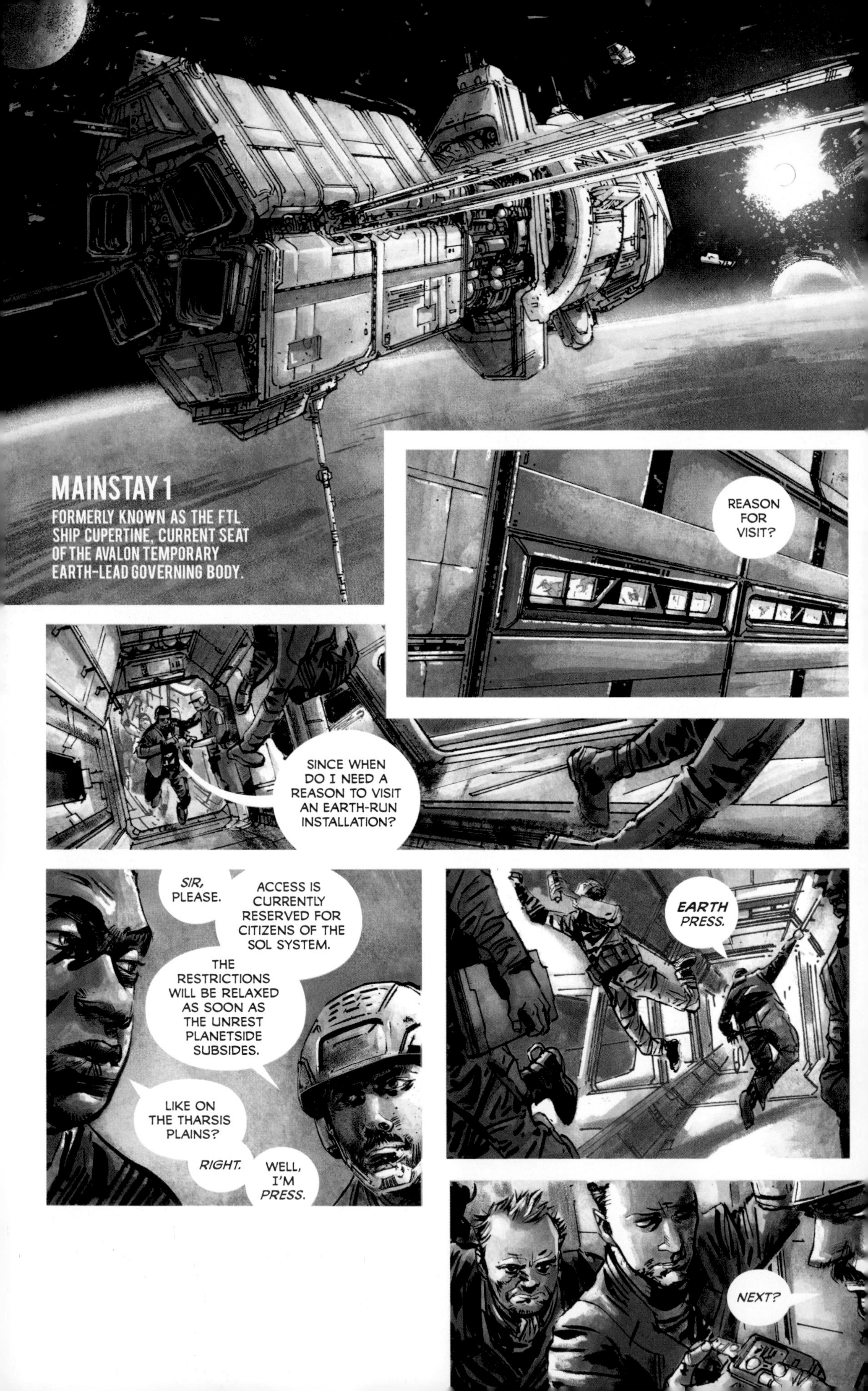
MAINSTAY 1
FORMERLY KNOWN AS THE FTL SHIP CUPERTINE, CURRENT SEAT OF THE AVALON TEMPORARY EARTH-LEAD GOVERNING BODY.
REASON FOR VISIT?
SINCE WHEN DO I NEED A REASON TO VISIT AN EARTH-RUN INSTALLATION?
SIR, PLEASE.
ACCESS IS CURRENTLY RESERVED FOR CITIZENS OF THE SOL SYSTEM.
THE RESTRICTIONS WILL BE RELAXED AS SOON AS THE UNREST PLANETSIDE SUBSIDES.
LIKE ON THE THARSIS PLAINS?
RIGHT.
WELL, I'M PRESS.
EARTH PRESS.
NEXT?

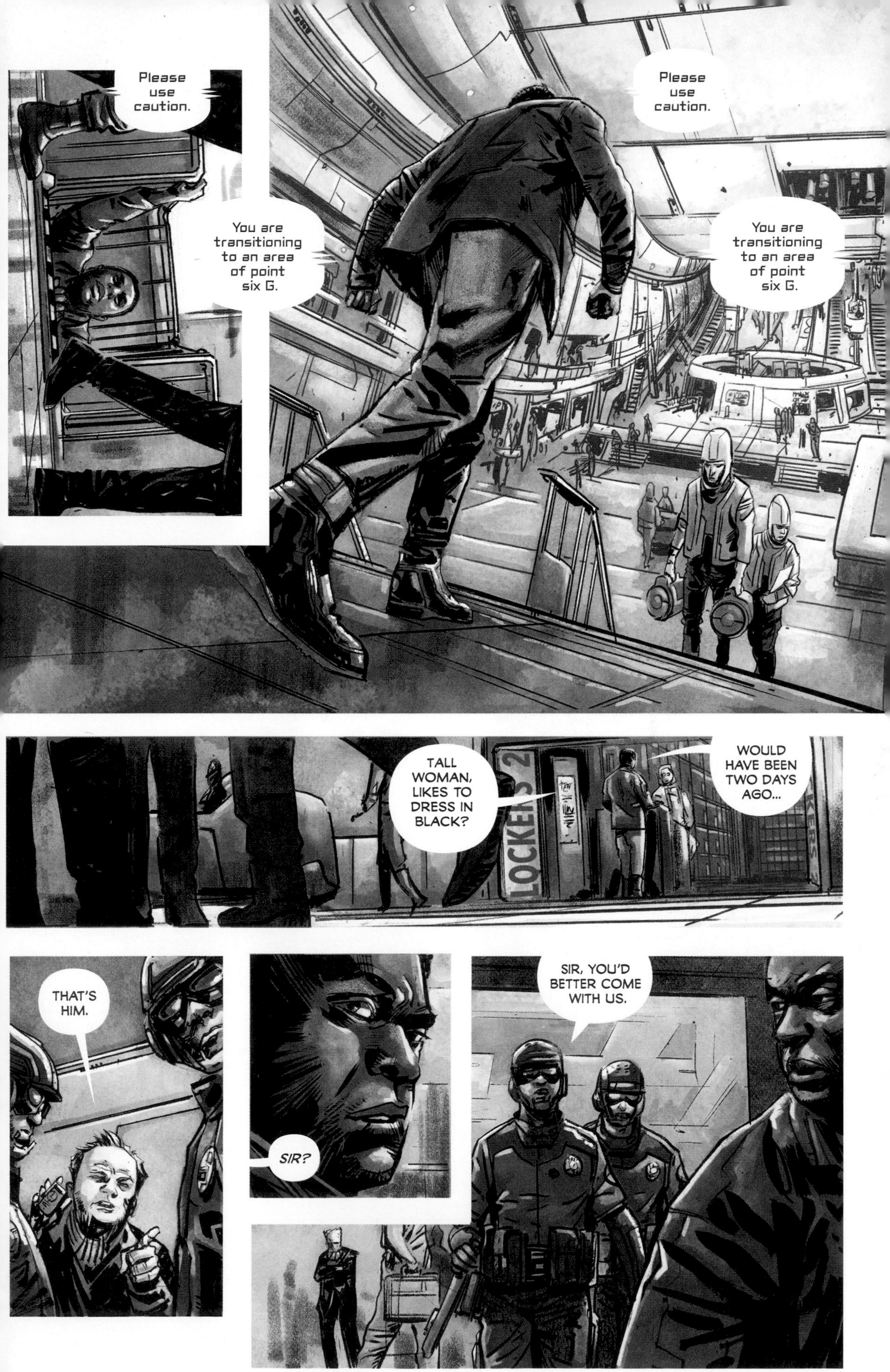
Please use caution.
You are transitioning to an area of point six G.
Please use caution.
You are transitioning to an area of point six G.
TALL WOMAN, LIKES TO DRESS IN BLACK?
WOULD HAVE BEEN TWO DAYS AGO...
LOCKERS 2
THAT'S HIM.
SIR?
SIR, YOU'D BETTER COME WITH US.

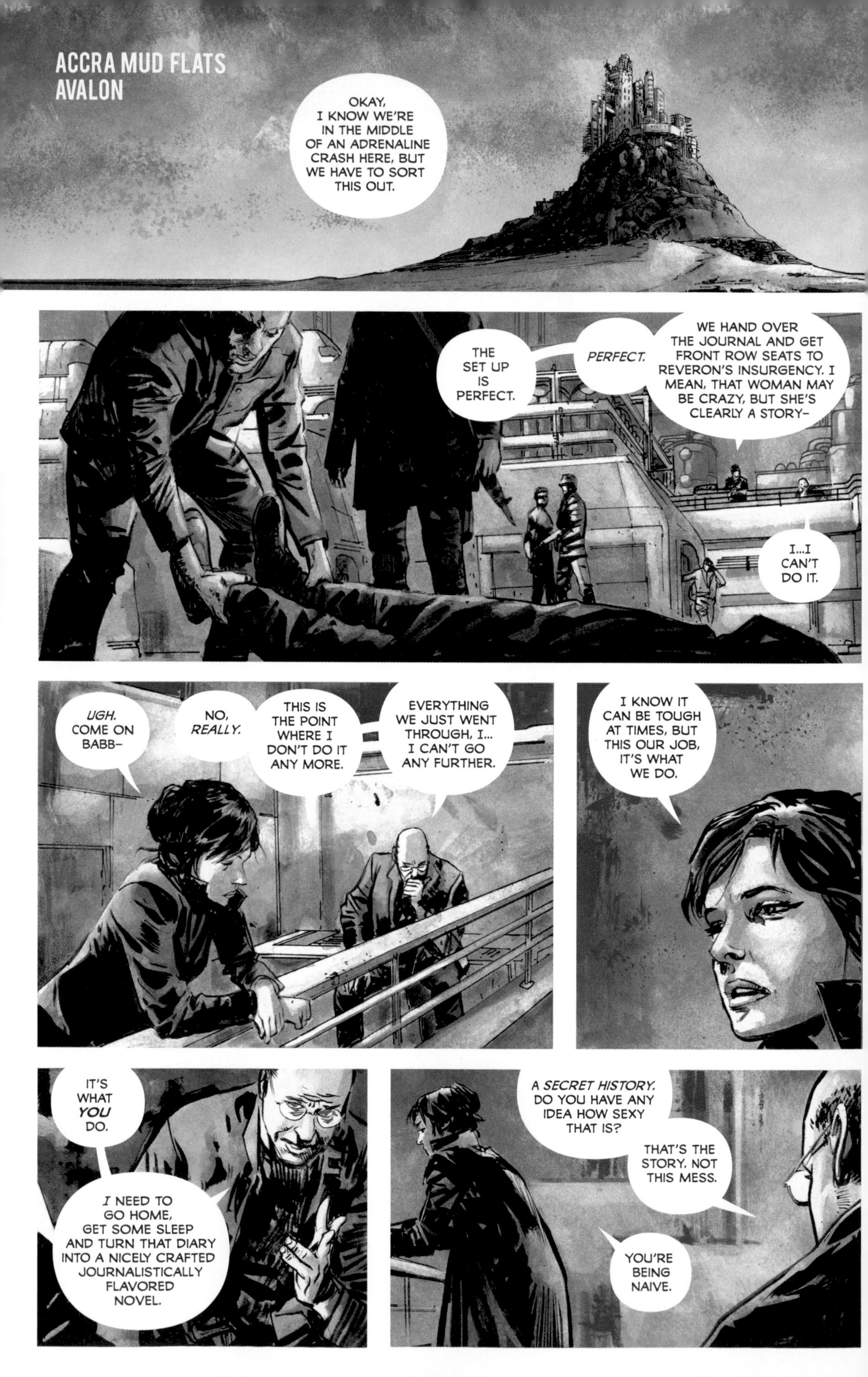
ACCRA MUD FLATS
AVALON
OKAY, I KNOW WE'RE IN THE MIDDLE OF AN ADRENALINE CRASH HERE, BUT WE HAVE TO SORT THIS OUT.
THE SET UP IS PERFECT.
PERFECT.
WE HAND OVER THE JOURNAL AND GET FRONT ROW SEATS TO REVERON'S INSURGENCY. I MEAN, THAT WOMAN MAY BE CRAZY, BUT SHE'S CLEARLY A STORY–
I...I CAN'T DO IT.
UGH. COME ON BABB–
NO, *REALLY.*
THIS IS THE POINT WHERE I DON'T DO IT ANY MORE.
EVERYTHING WE JUST WENT THROUGH, I... I CAN'T GO ANY FURTHER.
I KNOW IT CAN BE TOUGH AT TIMES, BUT THIS OUR JOB, IT'S WHAT WE DO.
IT'S WHAT ***YOU*** DO.
I NEED TO GO HOME, GET SOME SLEEP AND TURN THAT DIARY INTO A NICELY CRAFTED JOURNALISTICALLY FLAVORED NOVEL.
A *SECRET HISTORY.* DO YOU HAVE ANY IDEA HOW SEXY THAT IS?
THAT'S THE STORY. NOT THIS MESS.
YOU'RE BEING NAIVE.

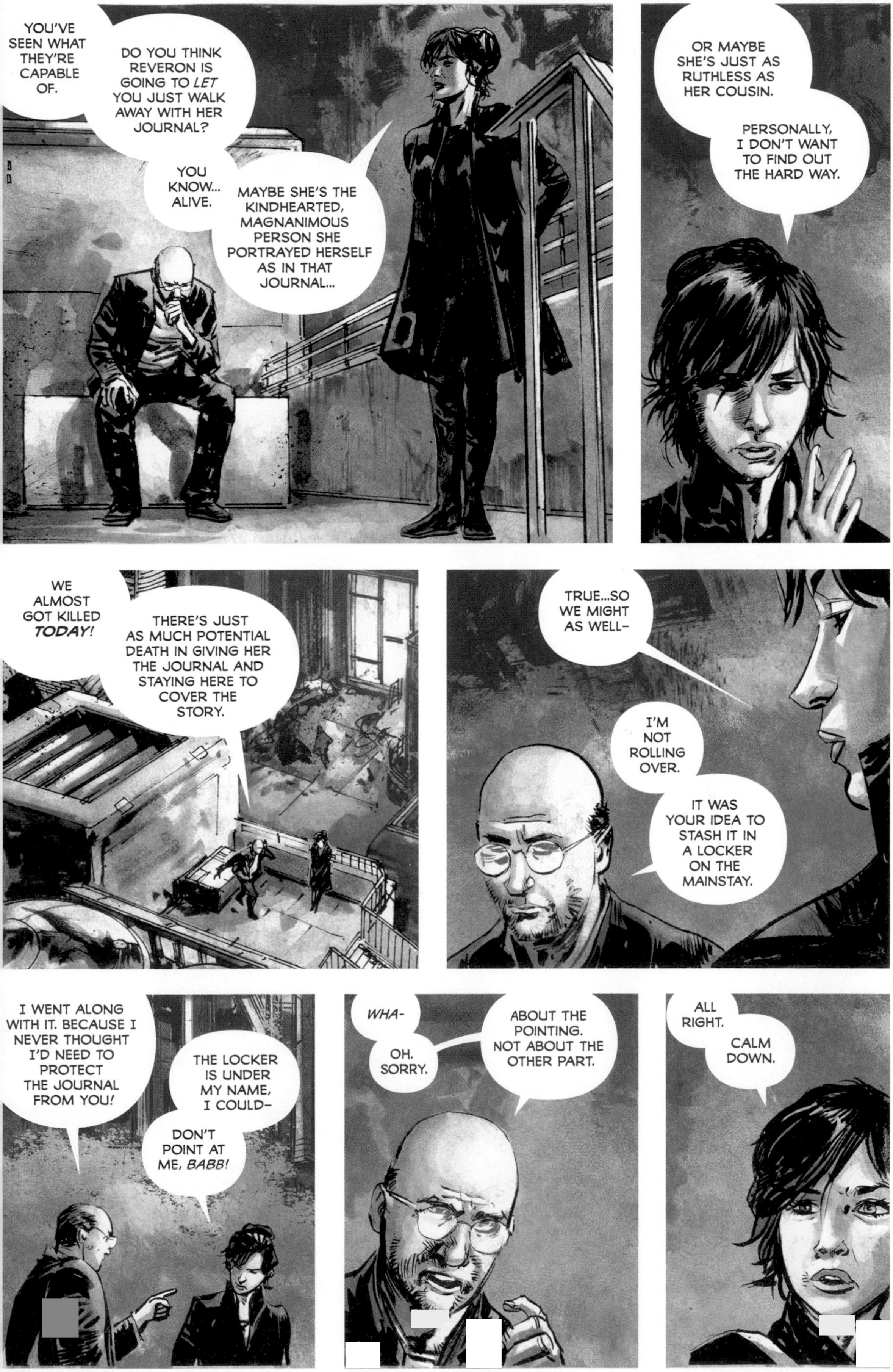
YOU'VE SEEN WHAT THEY'RE CAPABLE OF.
DO YOU THINK REVERON IS GOING TO *LET* YOU JUST WALK AWAY WITH HER JOURNAL?
YOU KNOW... ALIVE.
MAYBE SHE'S THE KINDHEARTED, MAGNANIMOUS PERSON SHE PORTRAYED HERSELF AS IN THAT JOURNAL...
OR MAYBE SHE'S JUST AS RUTHLESS AS HER COUSIN.
PERSONALLY, I DON'T WANT TO FIND OUT THE HARD WAY.
WE ALMOST GOT KILLED ***TODAY***!
THERE'S JUST AS MUCH POTENTIAL DEATH IN GIVING HER THE JOURNAL AND STAYING HERE TO COVER THE STORY.
TRUE...SO WE MIGHT AS WELL–
I'M NOT ROLLING OVER.
IT WAS YOUR IDEA TO STASH IT IN A LOCKER ON THE MAINSTAY.
I WENT ALONG WITH IT. BECAUSE I NEVER THOUGHT I'D NEED TO PROTECT THE JOURNAL FROM YOU!
THE LOCKER IS UNDER MY NAME, I COULD–
DON'T POINT AT ME, *BABB!*
WHA-
OH. SORRY.
ABOUT THE POINTING. NOT ABOUT THE OTHER PART.
ALL RIGHT.
CALM DOWN.

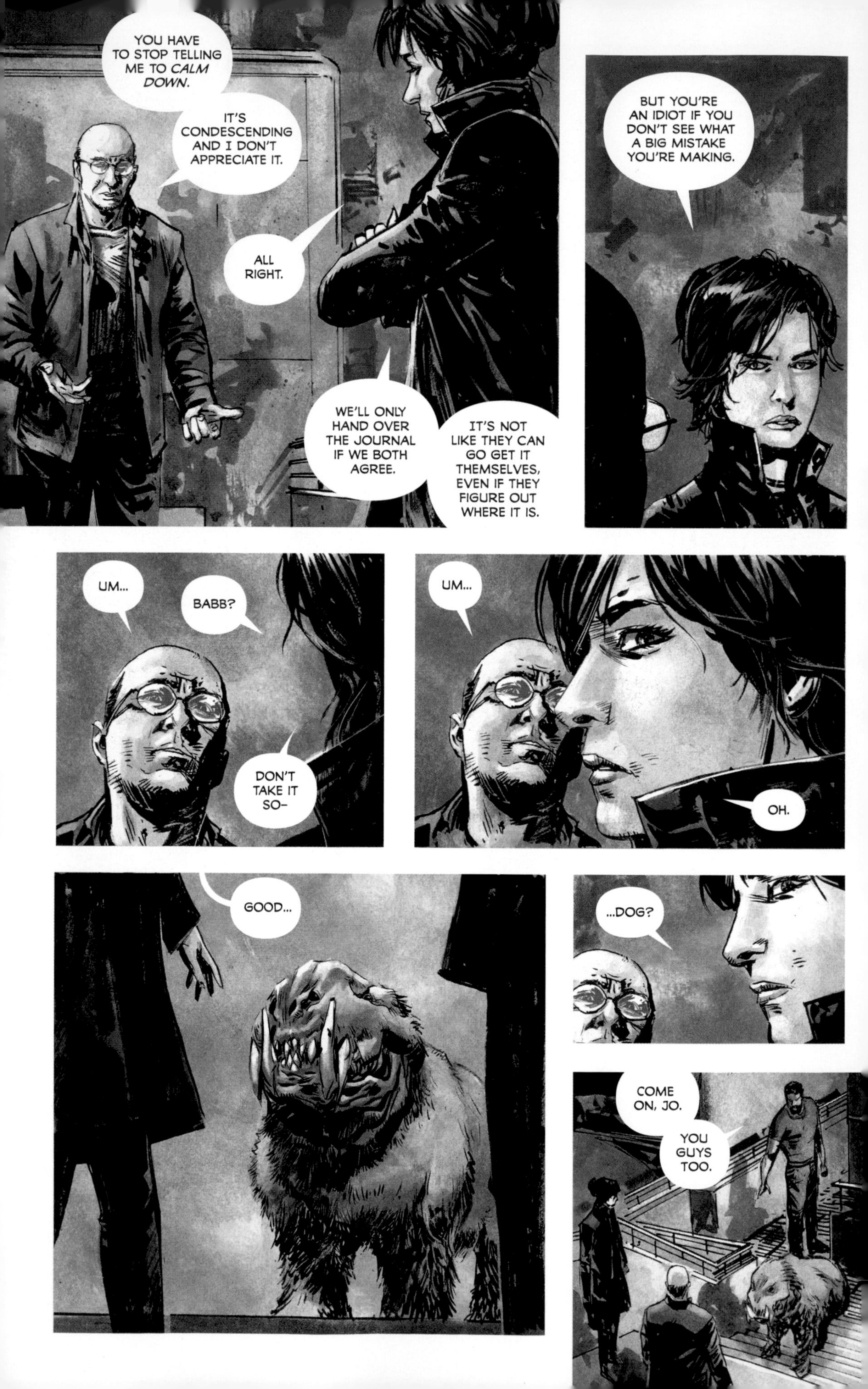
YOU HAVE TO STOP TELLING ME TO *CALM DOWN*.
IT'S CONDESCENDING AND I DON'T APPRECIATE IT.
ALL RIGHT.
WE'LL ONLY HAND OVER THE JOURNAL IF WE BOTH AGREE.
IT'S NOT LIKE THEY CAN GO GET IT THEMSELVES, EVEN IF THEY FIGURE OUT WHERE IT IS.
BUT YOU'RE AN IDIOT IF YOU DON'T SEE WHAT A BIG MISTAKE YOU'RE MAKING.
UM...
BABB?
DON'T TAKE IT SO–
UM...
OH.
GOOD...
...DOG?
COME ON, JO.
YOU GUYS TOO.

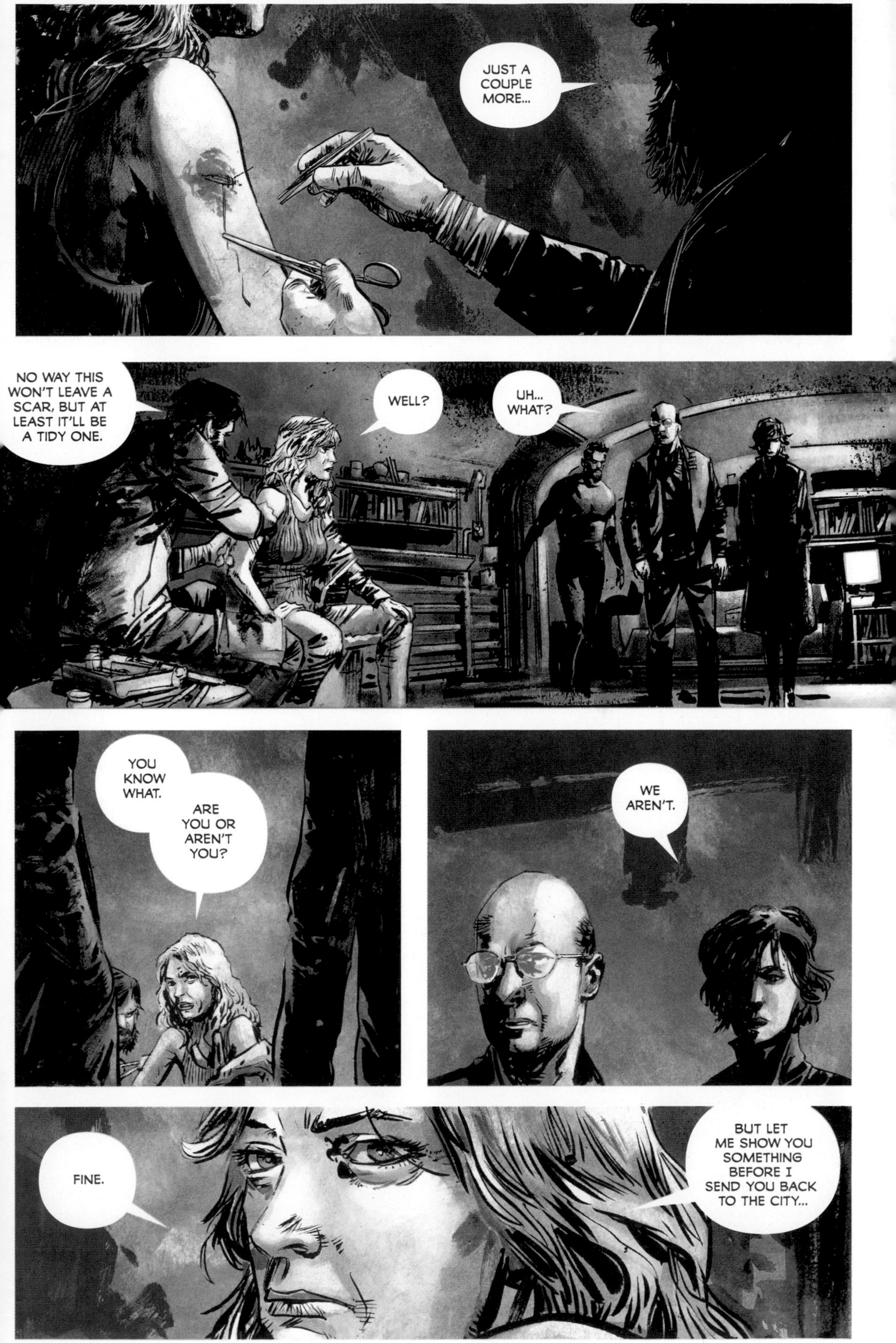
JUST A COUPLE MORE...
NO WAY THIS WON'T LEAVE A SCAR, BUT AT LEAST IT'LL BE A TIDY ONE.
WELL?
UH... WHAT?
YOU KNOW WHAT.
ARE YOU OR AREN'T YOU?
WE AREN'T.
FINE.
BUT LET ME SHOW YOU SOMETHING BEFORE I SEND YOU BACK TO THE CITY...

Jas never returned.

Things got worse.

OKAY, ALLEN, YOU'RE UP. *CRITICISM, SELF-CRITICISM!*

UM, YEAH. OKAY.

SO, SELF-CRITICISM...

I THINK I COULD BE MORE *COMMITTED.* THERE ARE TIMES I LET MY MIND WANDER AWAY FROM THE CAUSE. IT'S NOT FAIR TO ANY OF US IF I'M NOT GIVING MY ALL.

AND...CRITICISM. UM...JULIET SAID THIS TO ME YESTERDAY, AND I AGREE WITH HER. I THINK WE SOMETIMES, AS A GROUP, ARE TOO COMPLACENT.

GOOD POINTS, ALLEN. THANK YOU. ALRIGHT, MAIA.

THAT'S IT?

WHAT'S THE POINT OF DOING THIS IF HE DOESN'T TAKE IT SERIOUSLY?

FRANKLY, ALLEN, YOUR POINTS ARE WEAK.

YOU NEED TO PICK OUT A SPECIFIC PERSON AND TELL THEM TO THEIR FACE WHAT THEY'RE DOING WRONG.

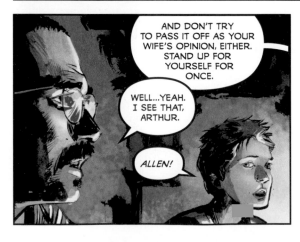

AND DON'T TRY TO PASS IT OFF AS YOUR WIFE'S OPINION, EITHER. STAND UP FOR YOURSELF FOR ONCE.

WELL...YEAH. I SEE THAT, ARTHUR.

ALLEN!

DON'T INTERRUPT HIM.

WE'RE BUILDING SOMETHING HERE. ARE YOU PREPARED TO BE THE REASON WE FAIL, JULIET?

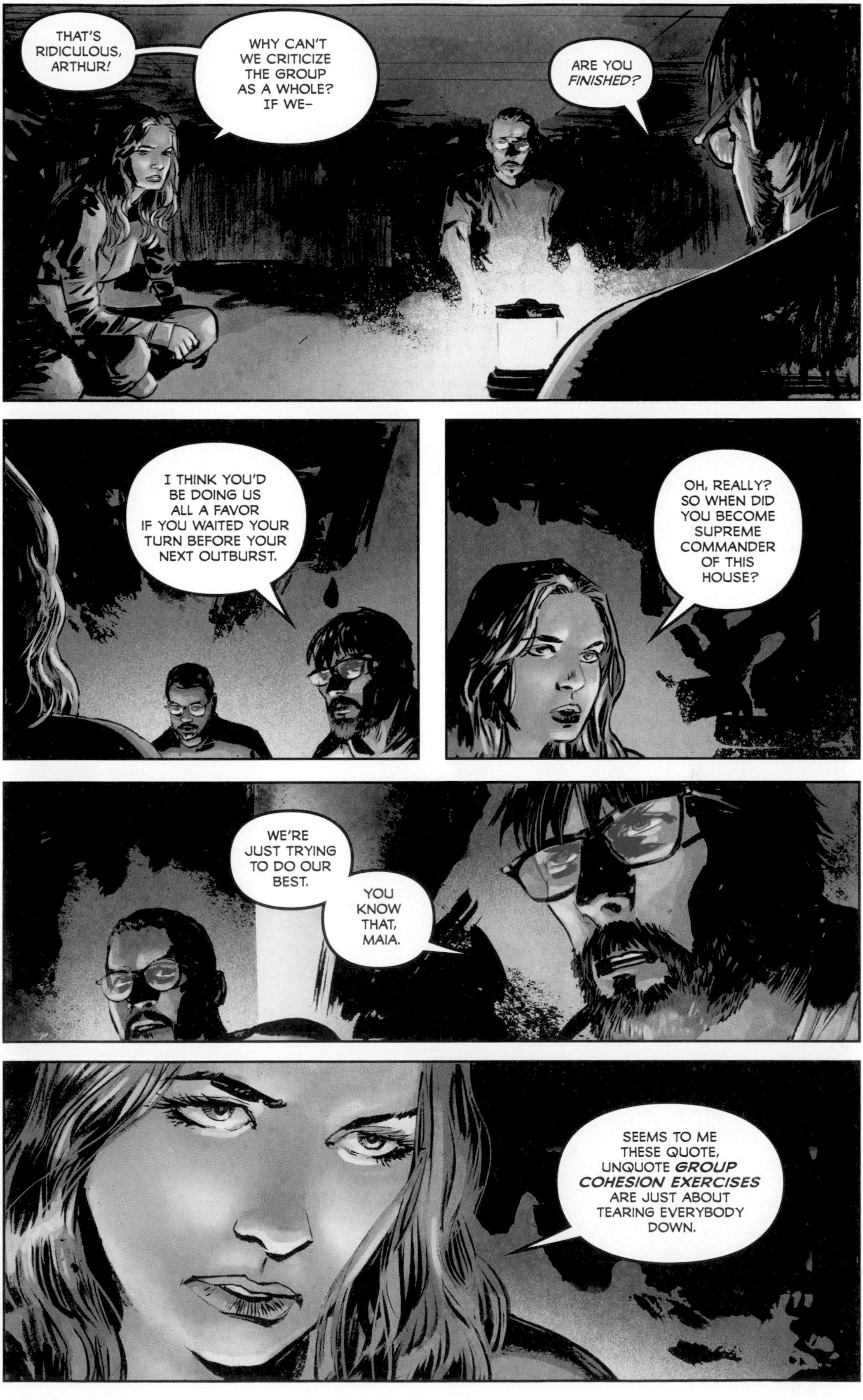
THAT'S RIDICULOUS, ARTHUR!
WHY CAN'T WE CRITICIZE THE GROUP AS A WHOLE? IF WE–
ARE YOU *FINISHED?*
I THINK YOU'D BE DOING US ALL A FAVOR IF YOU WAITED YOUR TURN BEFORE YOUR NEXT OUTBURST.
OH, REALLY? SO WHEN DID YOU BECOME SUPREME COMMANDER OF THIS HOUSE?
WE'RE JUST TRYING TO DO OUR BEST.
YOU KNOW THAT, MAIA.
SEEMS TO ME THESE QUOTE, UNQUOTE ***GROUP COHESION EXERCISES*** ARE JUST ABOUT TEARING EVERYBODY DOWN.

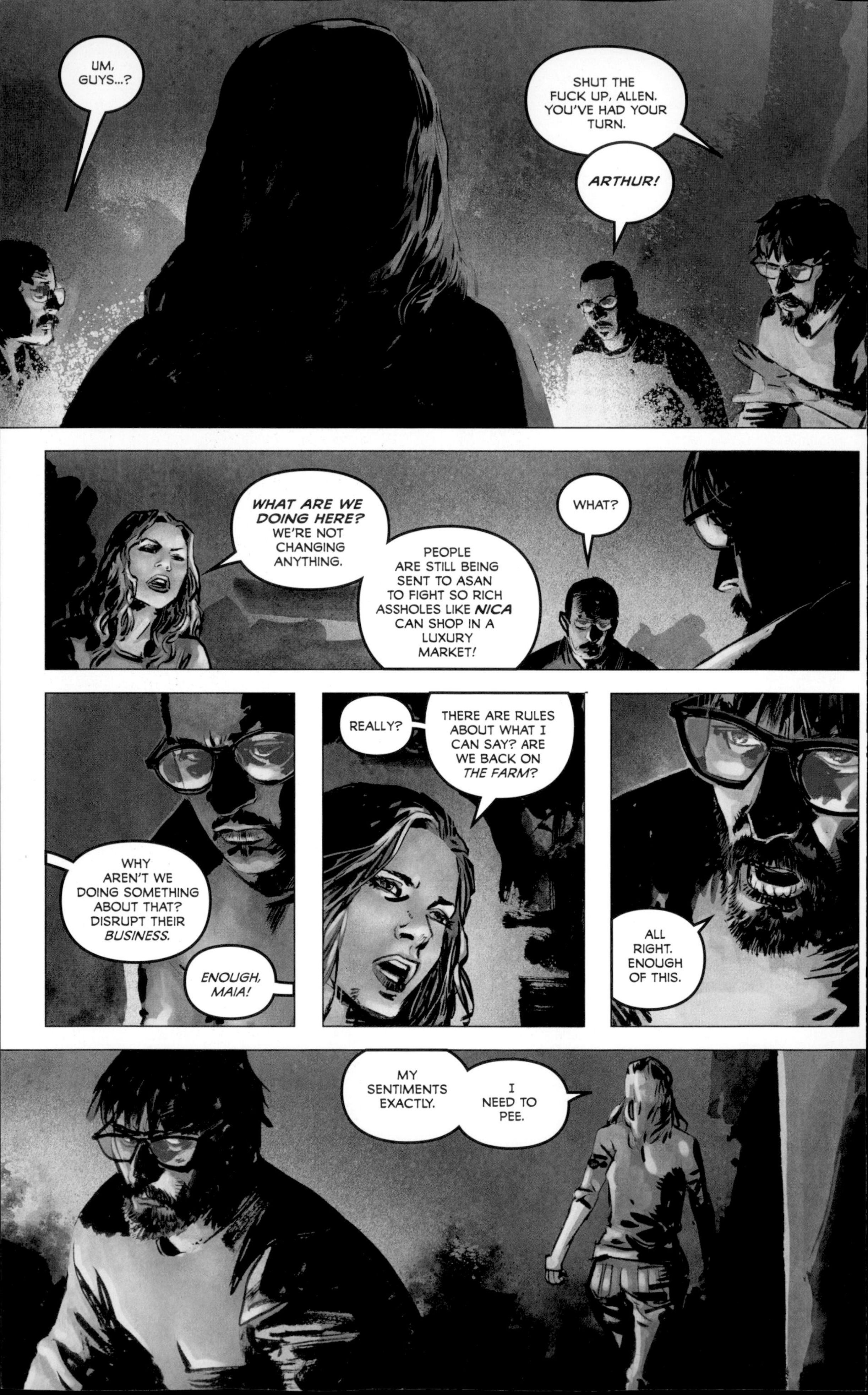
UM, GUYS...?
SHUT THE FUCK UP, ALLEN. YOU'VE HAD YOUR TURN.
ARTHUR!
WHAT ARE WE DOING HERE? WE'RE NOT CHANGING ANYTHING.
PEOPLE ARE STILL BEING SENT TO ASAN TO FIGHT SO RICH ASSHOLES LIKE NICA CAN SHOP IN A LUXURY MARKET!
WHAT?
WHY AREN'T WE DOING SOMETHING ABOUT THAT? DISRUPT THEIR BUSINESS.
ENOUGH, MAIA!
REALLY?
THERE ARE RULES ABOUT WHAT I CAN SAY? ARE WE BACK ON THE FARM?
ALL RIGHT. ENOUGH OF THIS.
MY SENTIMENTS EXACTLY.
I NEED TO PEE.

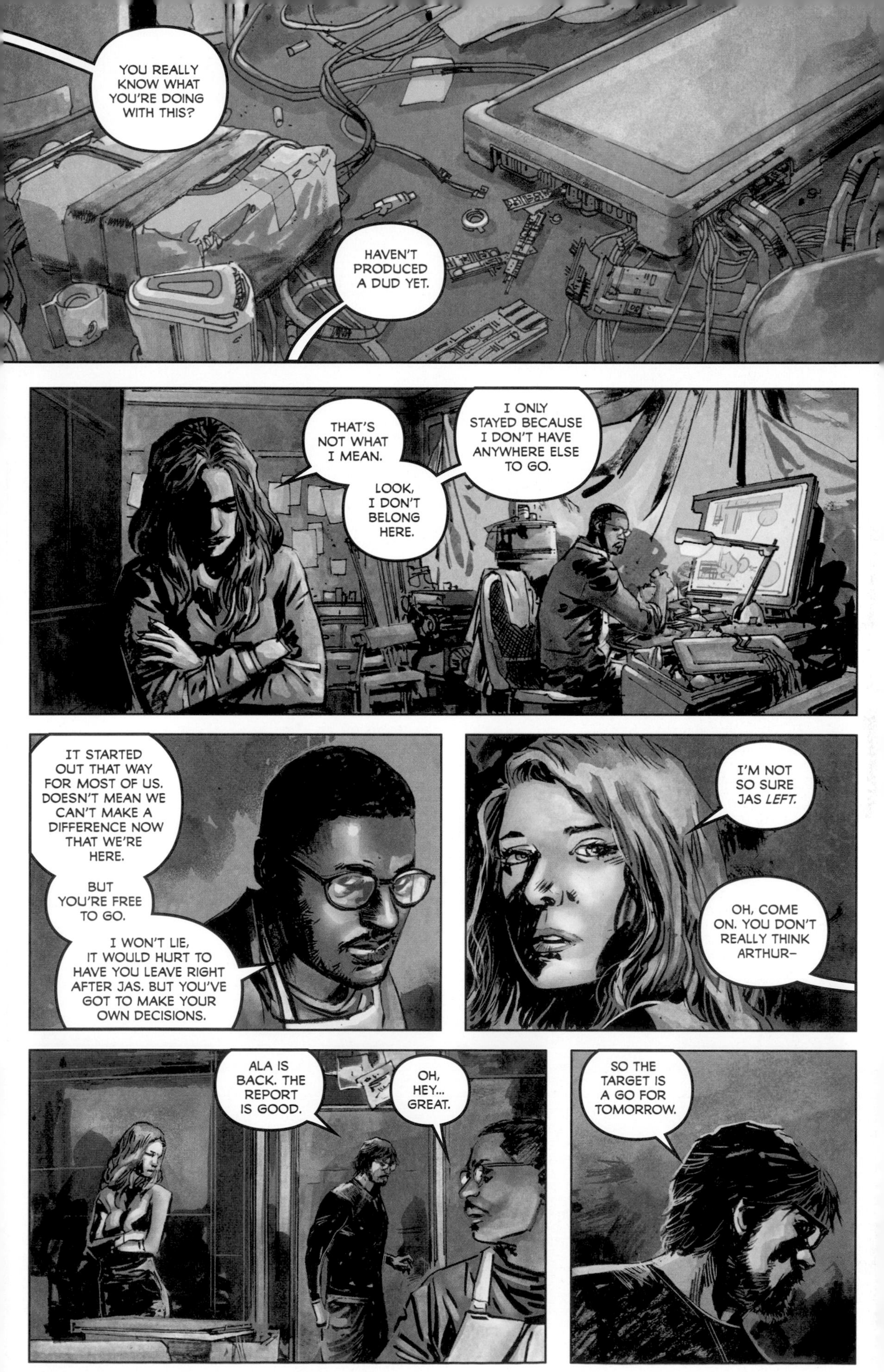
YOU REALLY KNOW WHAT YOU'RE DOING WITH THIS?
HAVEN'T PRODUCED A DUD YET.
THAT'S NOT WHAT I MEAN.
LOOK, I DON'T BELONG HERE.
I ONLY STAYED BECAUSE I DON'T HAVE ANYWHERE ELSE TO GO.
IT STARTED OUT THAT WAY FOR MOST OF US. DOESN'T MEAN WE CAN'T MAKE A DIFFERENCE NOW THAT WE'RE HERE.
BUT YOU'RE FREE TO GO.
I WON'T LIE, IT WOULD HURT TO HAVE YOU LEAVE RIGHT AFTER JAS. BUT YOU'VE GOT TO MAKE YOUR OWN DECISIONS.
I'M NOT SO SURE JAS *LEFT.*
OH, COME ON. YOU DON'T REALLY THINK ARTHUR–
ALA IS BACK. THE REPORT IS GOOD.
OH, HEY... GREAT.
SO THE TARGET IS A GO FOR TOMORROW.

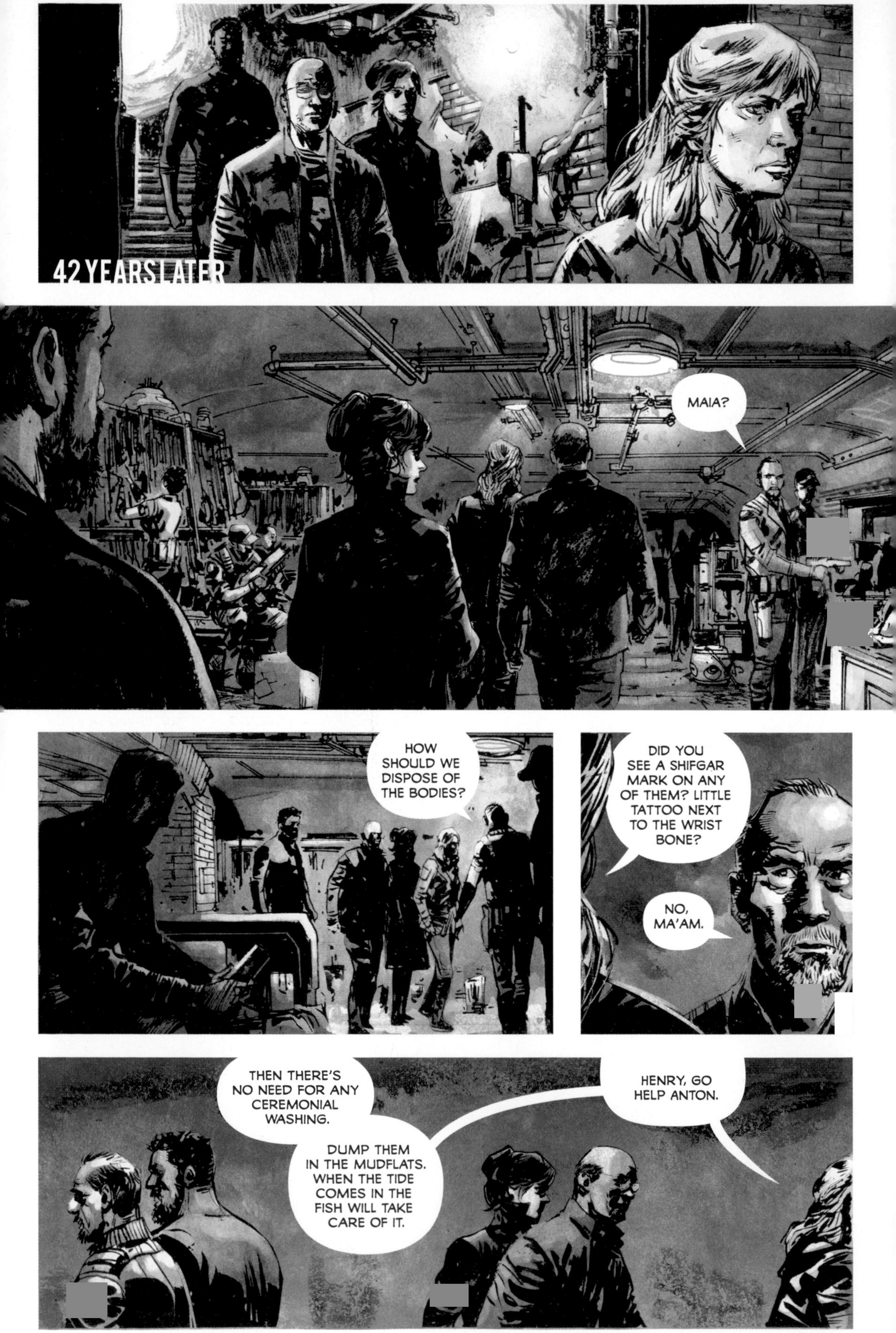
42 YEARS LATER
MAIA?
HOW SHOULD WE DISPOSE OF THE BODIES?
DID YOU SEE A SHIFGAR MARK ON ANY OF THEM? LITTLE TATTOO NEXT TO THE WRIST BONE?
NO, MA'AM.
THEN THERE'S NO NEED FOR ANY CEREMONIAL WASHING.
DUMP THEM IN THE MUDFLATS. WHEN THE TIDE COMES IN THE FISH WILL TAKE CARE OF IT.
HENRY, GO HELP ANTON.

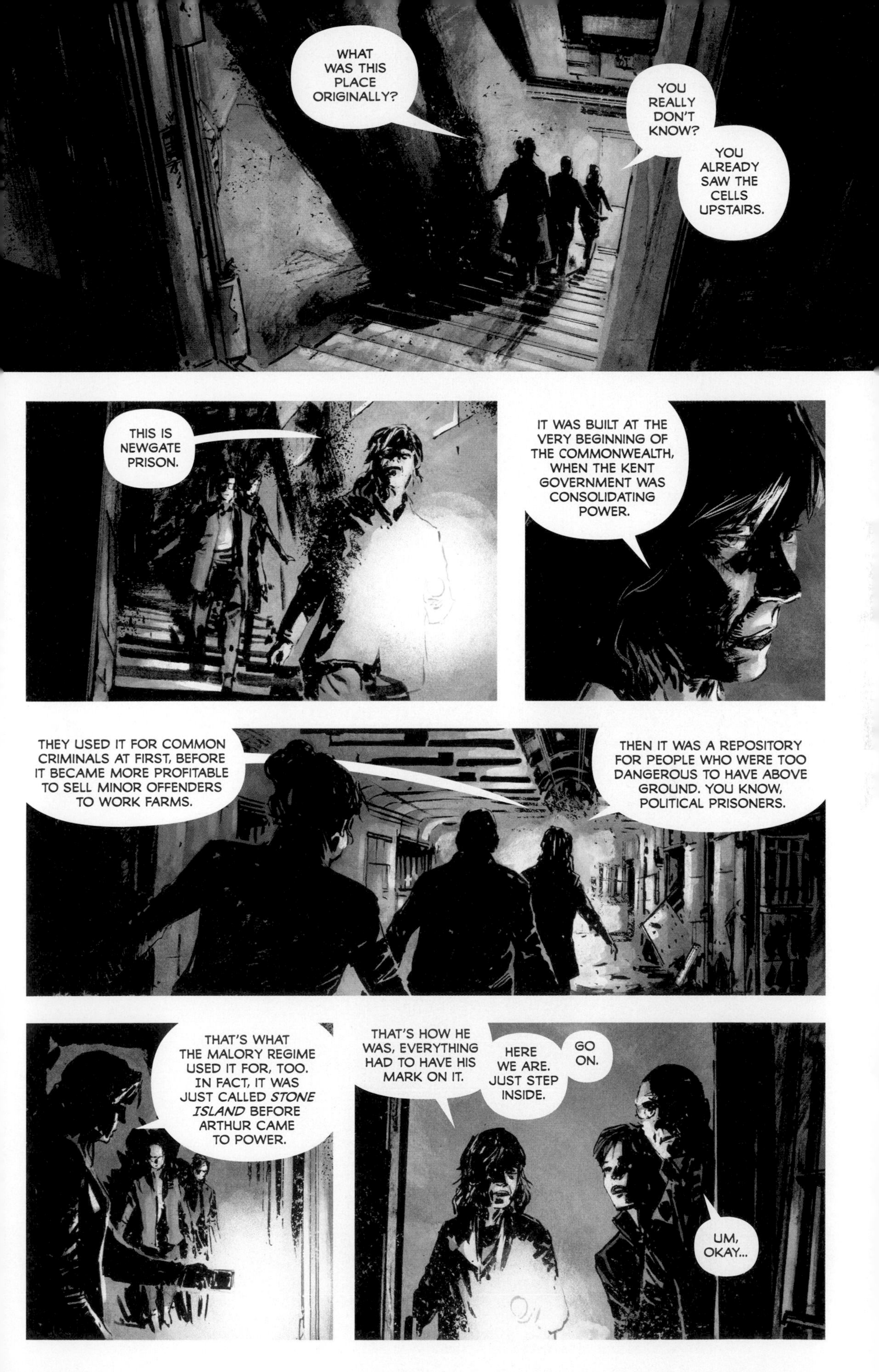
WHAT WAS THIS PLACE ORIGINALLY?
YOU REALLY DON'T KNOW?
YOU ALREADY SAW THE CELLS UPSTAIRS.
THIS IS NEWGATE PRISON.
IT WAS BUILT AT THE VERY BEGINNING OF THE COMMONWEALTH, WHEN THE KENT GOVERNMENT WAS CONSOLIDATING POWER.
THEY USED IT FOR COMMON CRIMINALS AT FIRST, BEFORE IT BECAME MORE PROFITABLE TO SELL MINOR OFFENDERS TO WORK FARMS.
THEN IT WAS A REPOSITORY FOR PEOPLE WHO WERE TOO DANGEROUS TO HAVE ABOVE GROUND. YOU KNOW, POLITICAL PRISONERS.
THAT'S WHAT THE MALORY REGIME USED IT FOR, TOO. IN FACT, IT WAS JUST CALLED *STONE ISLAND* BEFORE ARTHUR CAME TO POWER.
THAT'S HOW HE WAS, EVERYTHING HAD TO HAVE HIS MARK ON IT.
HERE WE ARE. JUST STEP INSIDE.
GO ON.
UM, OKAY...

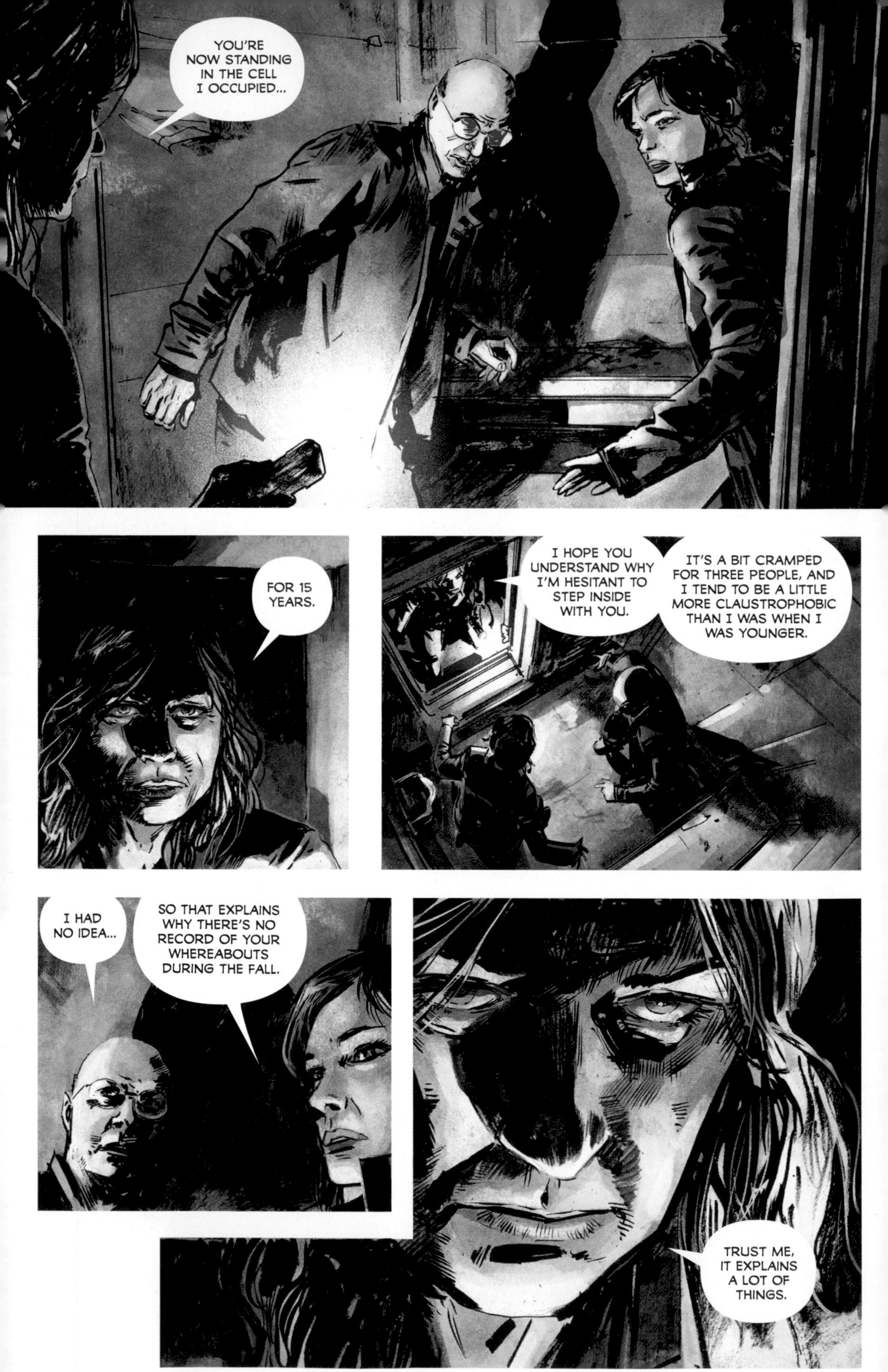
YOU'RE NOW STANDING IN THE CELL I OCCUPIED...
FOR 15 YEARS.
I HOPE YOU UNDERSTAND WHY I'M HESITANT TO STEP INSIDE WITH YOU.
IT'S A BIT CRAMPED FOR THREE PEOPLE, AND I TEND TO BE A LITTLE MORE CLAUSTROPHOBIC THAN I WAS WHEN I WAS YOUNGER.
I HAD NO IDEA...
SO THAT EXPLAINS WHY THERE'S NO RECORD OF YOUR WHEREABOUTS DURING THE FALL.
TRUST ME, IT EXPLAINS A LOT OF THINGS.

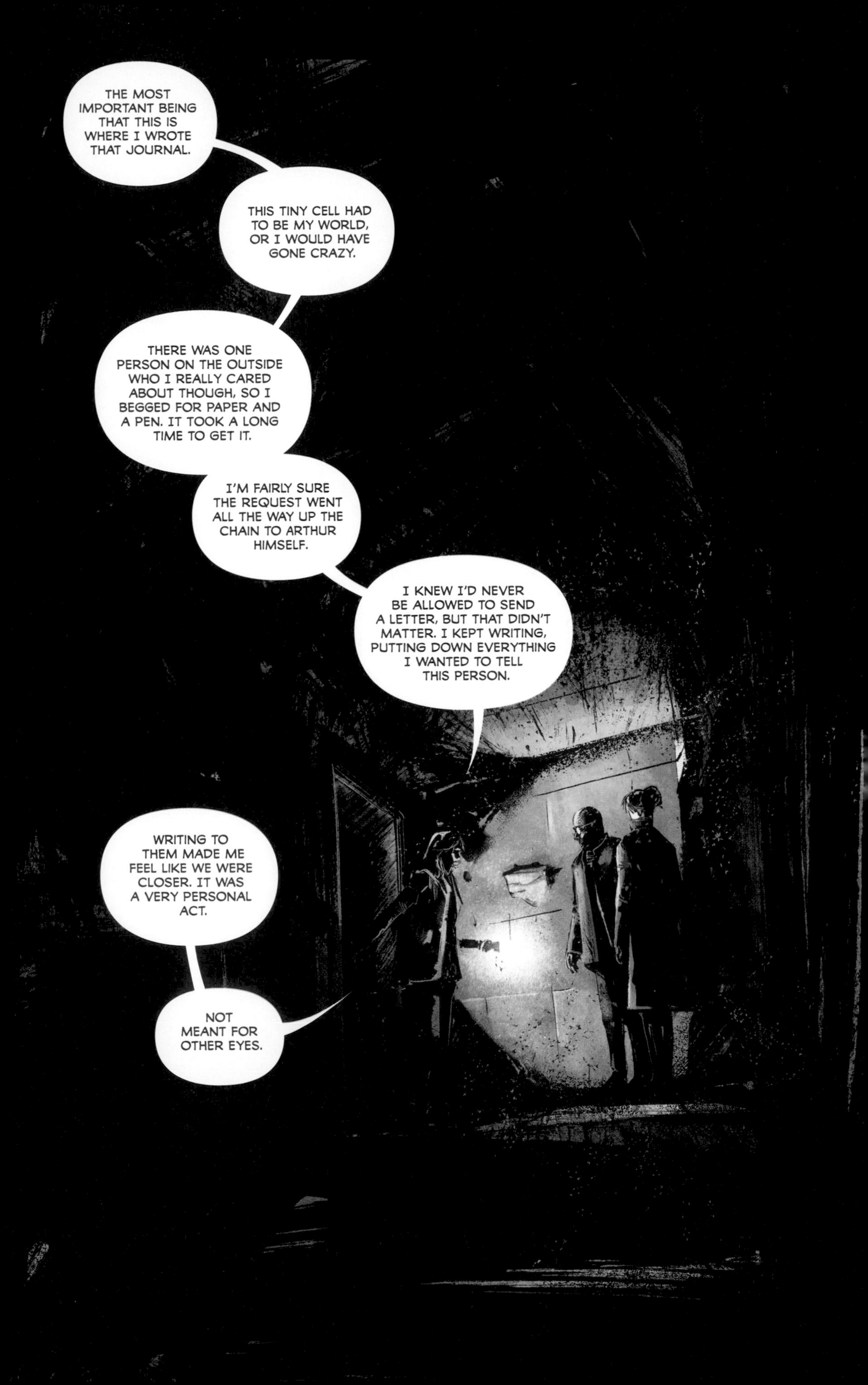
THE MOST IMPORTANT BEING THAT THIS IS WHERE I WROTE THAT JOURNAL.
THIS TINY CELL HAD TO BE MY WORLD, OR I WOULD HAVE GONE CRAZY.
THERE WAS ONE PERSON ON THE OUTSIDE WHO I REALLY CARED ABOUT THOUGH, SO I BEGGED FOR PAPER AND A PEN. IT TOOK A LONG TIME TO GET IT.
I'M FAIRLY SURE THE REQUEST WENT ALL THE WAY UP THE CHAIN TO ARTHUR HIMSELF.
I KNEW I'D NEVER BE ALLOWED TO SEND A LETTER, BUT THAT DIDN'T MATTER. I KEPT WRITING, PUTTING DOWN EVERYTHING I WANTED TO TELL THIS PERSON.
WRITING TO THEM MADE ME FEEL LIKE WE WERE CLOSER. IT WAS A VERY PERSONAL ACT.
NOT MEANT FOR OTHER EYES.

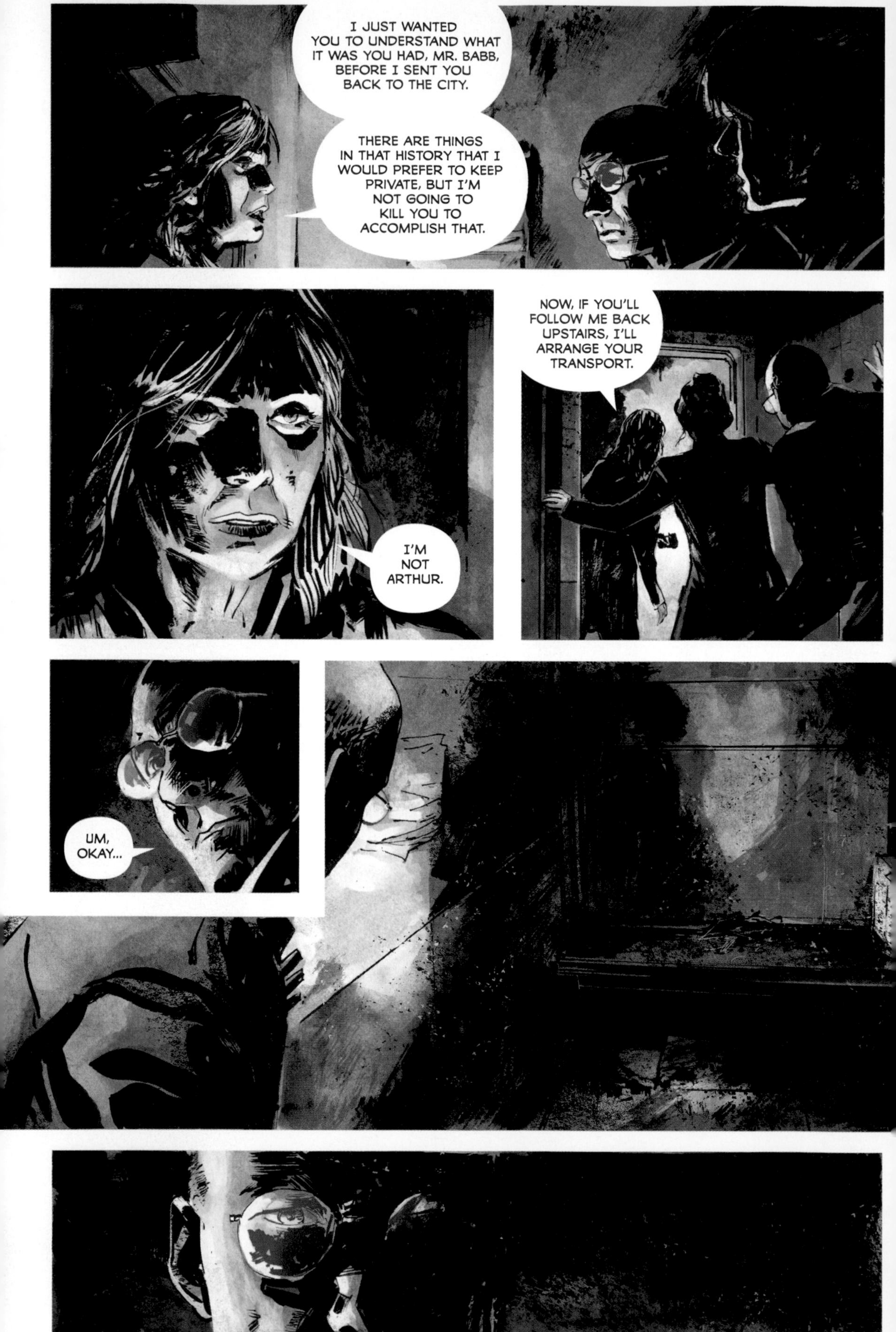
I JUST WANTED YOU TO UNDERSTAND WHAT IT WAS YOU HAD, MR. BABB, BEFORE I SENT YOU BACK TO THE CITY.
THERE ARE THINGS IN THAT HISTORY THAT I WOULD PREFER TO KEEP PRIVATE, BUT I'M NOT GOING TO KILL YOU TO ACCOMPLISH THAT.
I'M NOT ARTHUR.
NOW, IF YOU'LL FOLLOW ME BACK UPSTAIRS, I'LL ARRANGE YOUR TRANSPORT.
UM, OKAY...

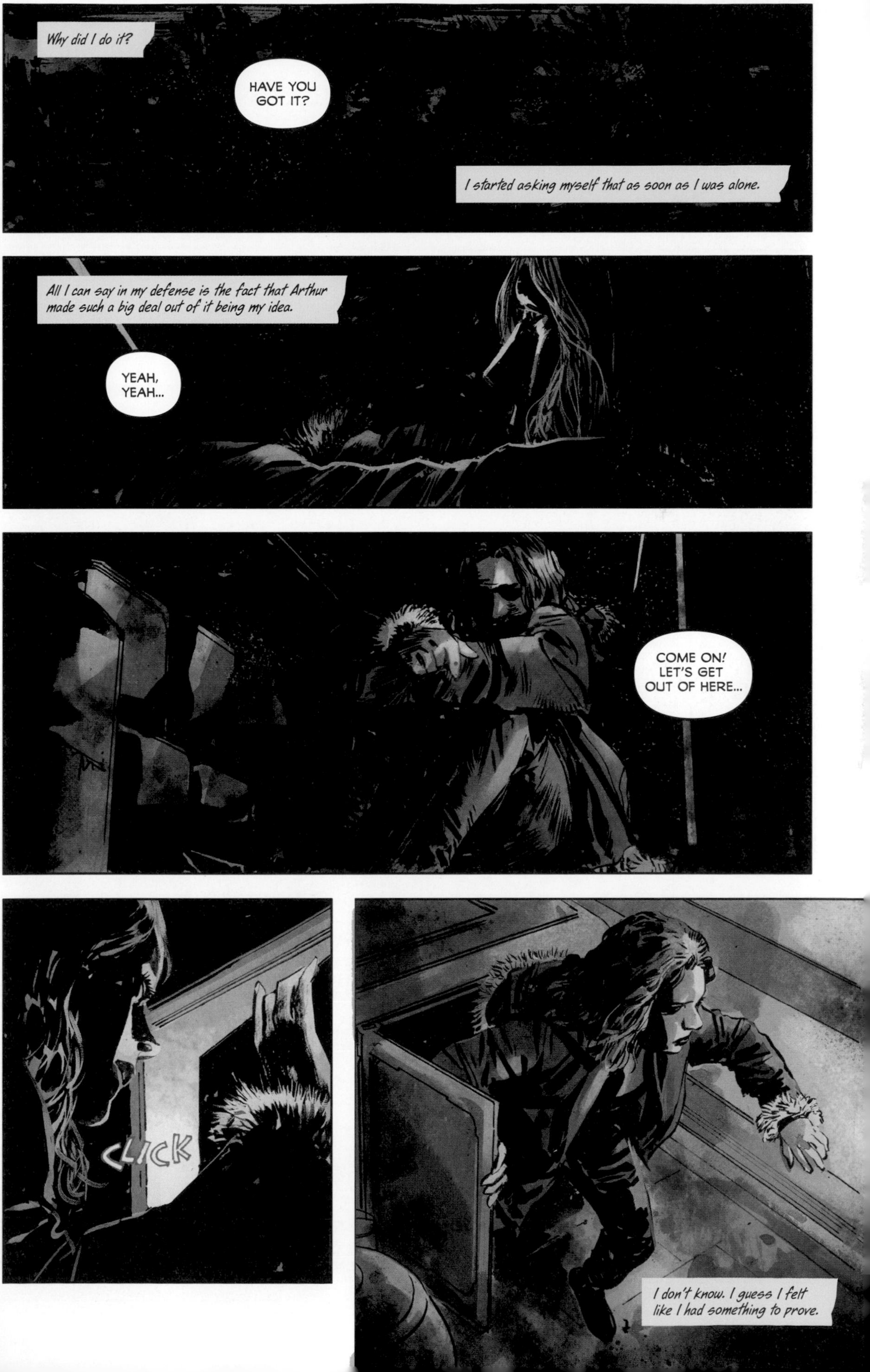
Why did I do it?
HAVE YOU GOT IT?
I started asking myself that as soon as I was alone.
All I can say in my defense is the fact that Arthur made such a big deal out of it being my idea.
YEAH, YEAH...
COME ON! LET'S GET OUT OF HERE...
CLICK
I don't know. I guess I felt like I had something to prove.

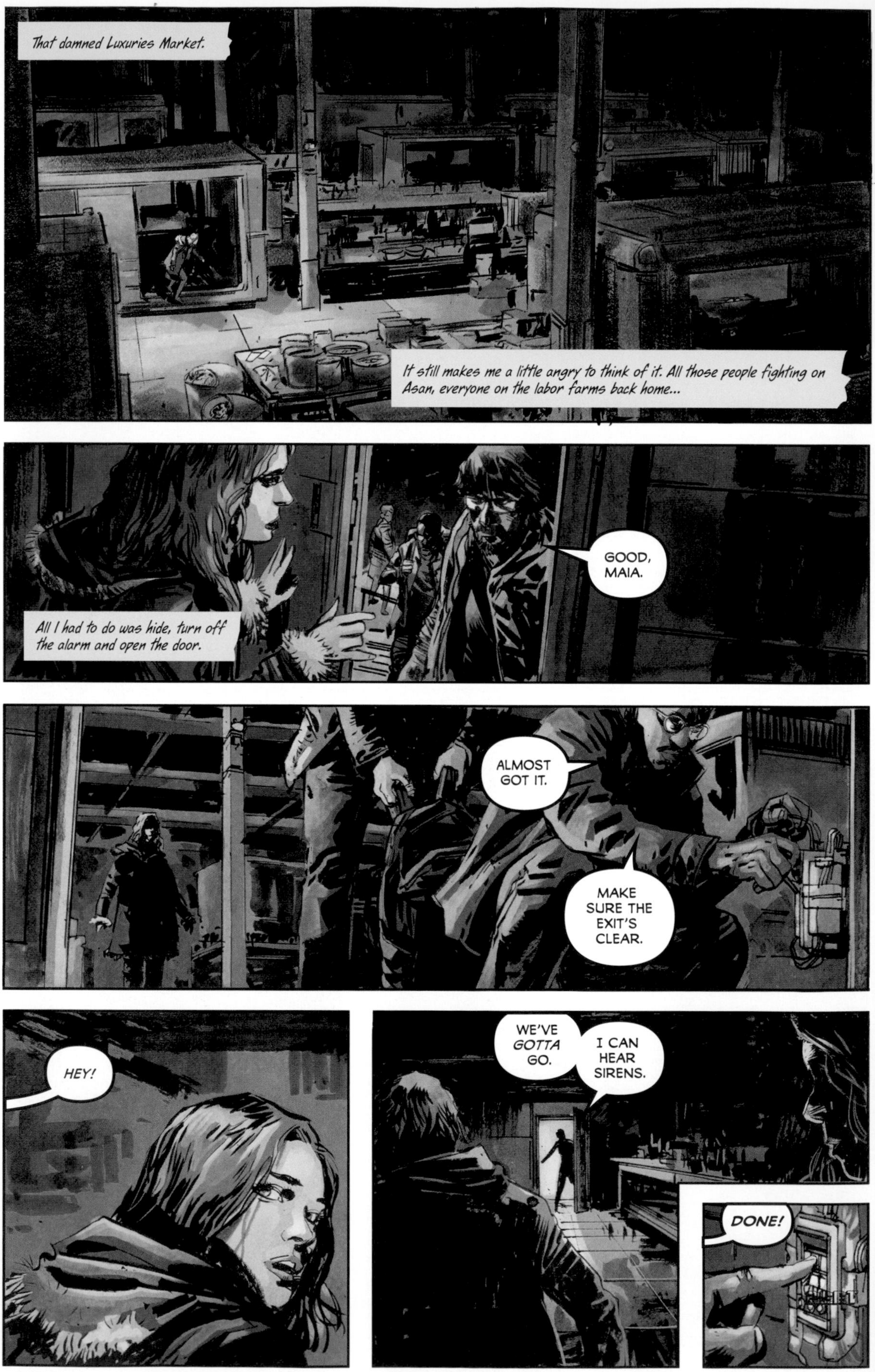
That damned Luxuries Market.
It still makes me a little angry to think of it. All those people fighting on Asan, everyone on the labor farms back home...
All I had to do was hide, turn off the alarm and open the door.
GOOD, MAIA.
ALMOST GOT IT.
MAKE SURE THE EXIT'S CLEAR.
HEY!
WE'VE *GOTTA* GO.
I CAN HEAR SIRENS.
DONE!

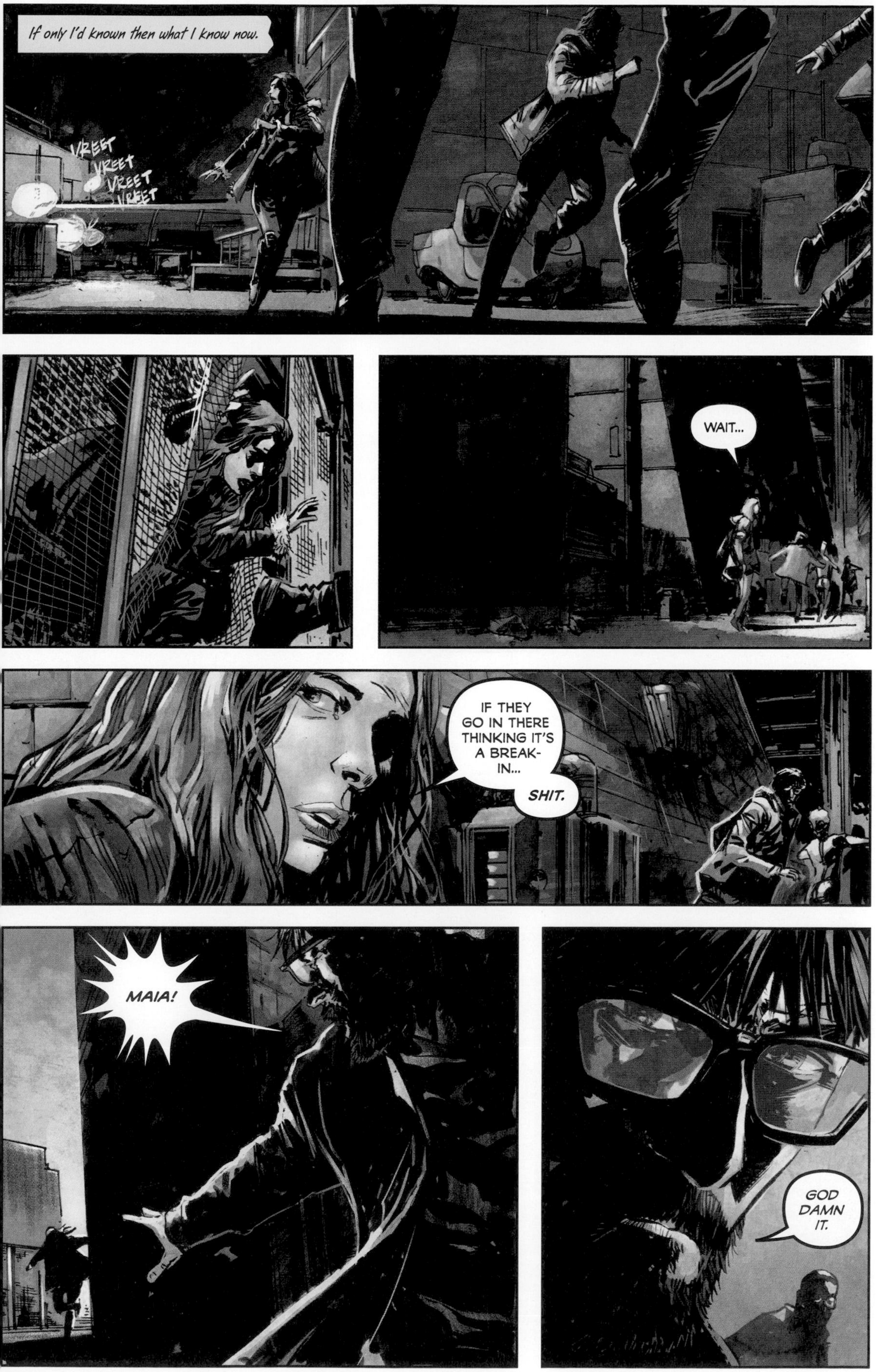
If only I'd known then what I know now.
VREET VREET VREET VREET
WAIT...
IF THEY GO IN THERE THINKING IT'S A BREAK-IN...
SHIT.
MAIA!
GOD DAMN IT.

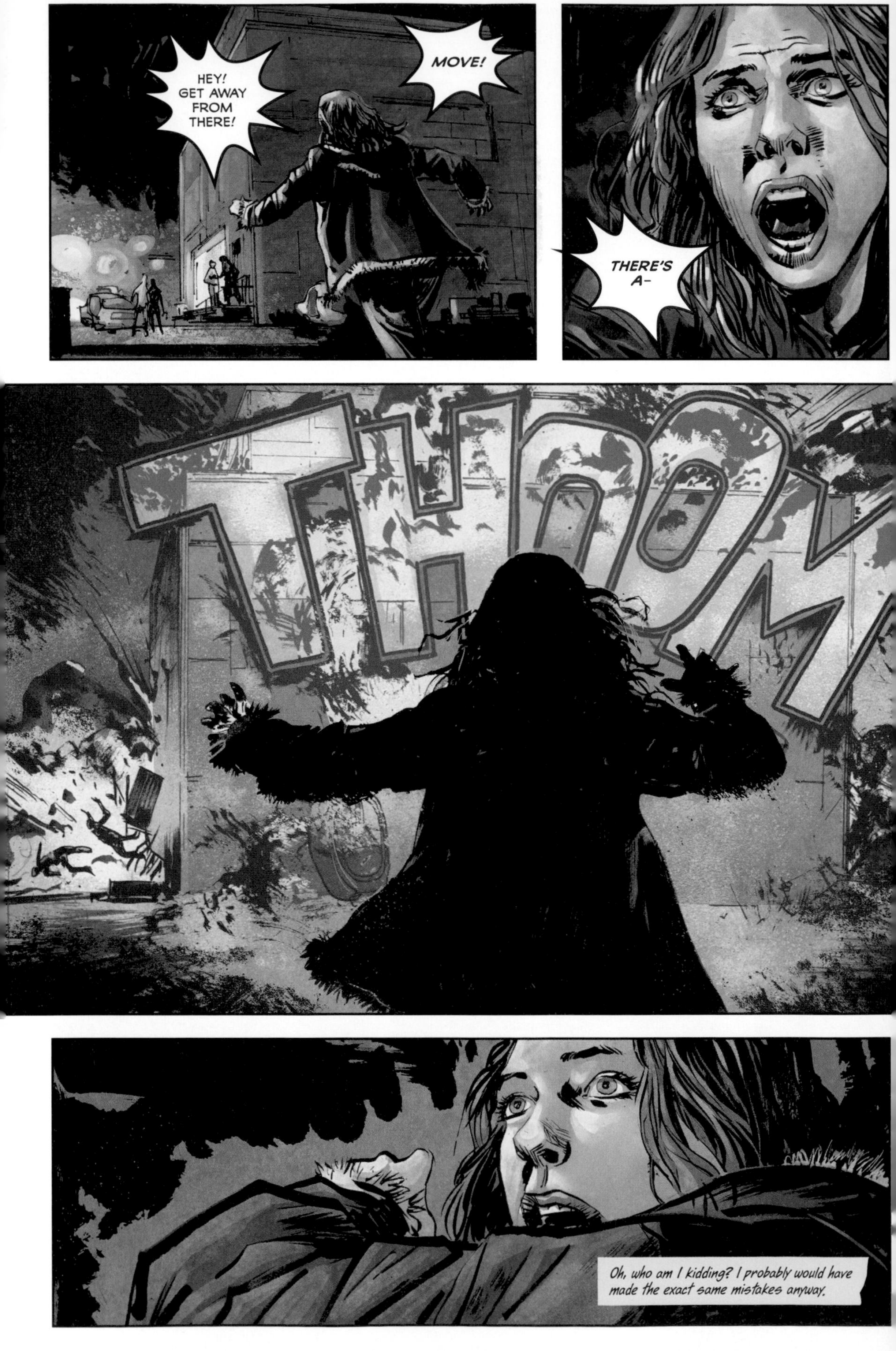
HEY! GET AWAY FROM THERE!
MOVE!
THERE'S A-
THOOM
Oh, who am I kidding? I probably would have made the exact same mistakes anyway.

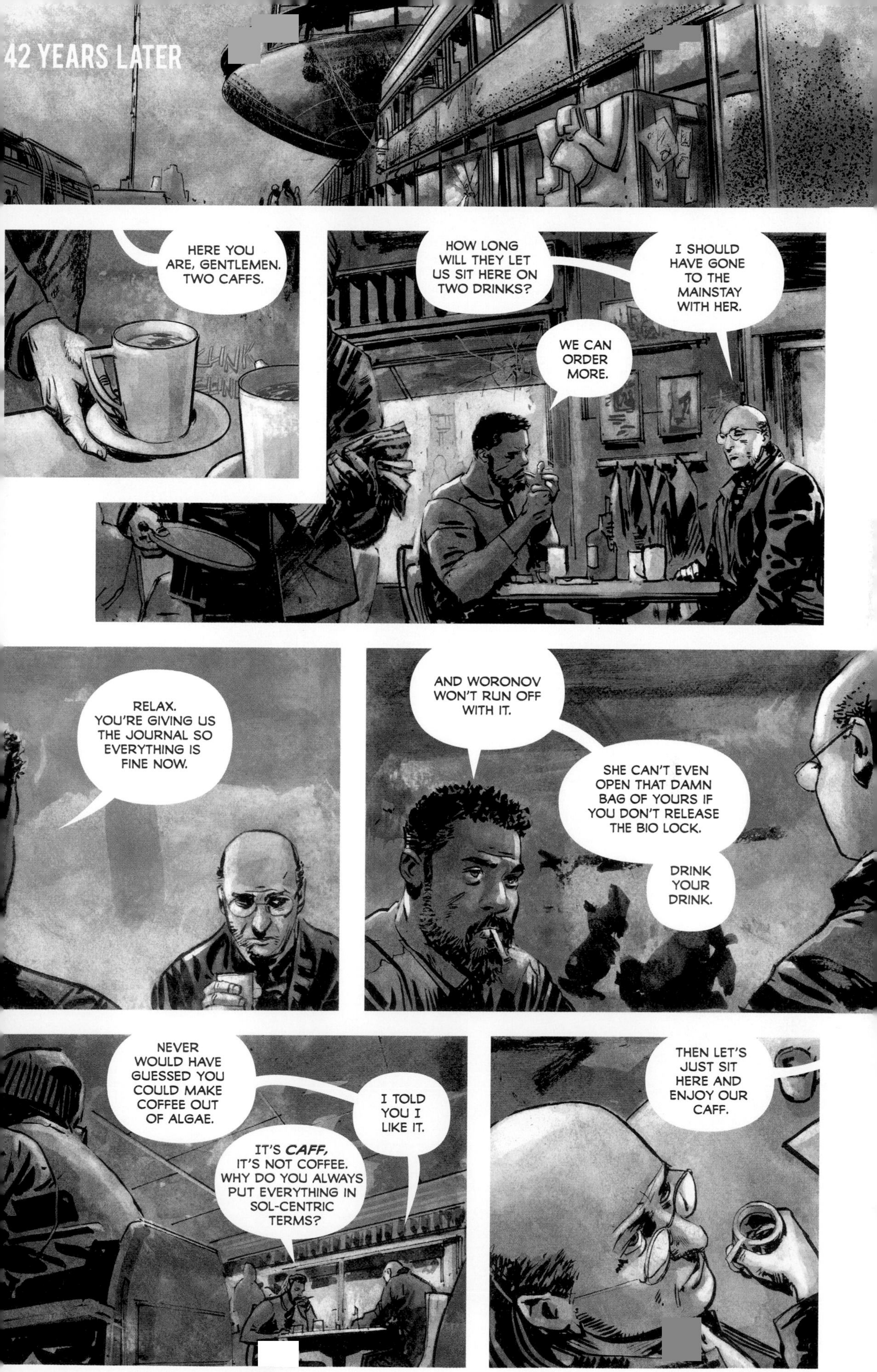
42 YEARS LATER
HERE YOU ARE, GENTLEMEN. TWO CAFFS.
HOW LONG WILL THEY LET US SIT HERE ON TWO DRINKS?
I SHOULD HAVE GONE TO THE MAINSTAY WITH HER.
WE CAN ORDER MORE.
RELAX. YOU'RE GIVING US THE JOURNAL SO EVERYTHING IS FINE NOW.
AND WORONOV WON'T RUN OFF WITH IT.
SHE CAN'T EVEN OPEN THAT DAMN BAG OF YOURS IF YOU DON'T RELEASE THE BIO LOCK.
DRINK YOUR DRINK.
NEVER WOULD HAVE GUESSED YOU COULD MAKE COFFEE OUT OF ALGAE.
I TOLD YOU I LIKE IT.
IT'S *CAFF,* IT'S NOT COFFEE. WHY DO YOU ALWAYS PUT EVERYTHING IN SOL-CENTRIC TERMS?
THEN LET'S JUST SIT HERE AND ENJOY OUR CAFF.

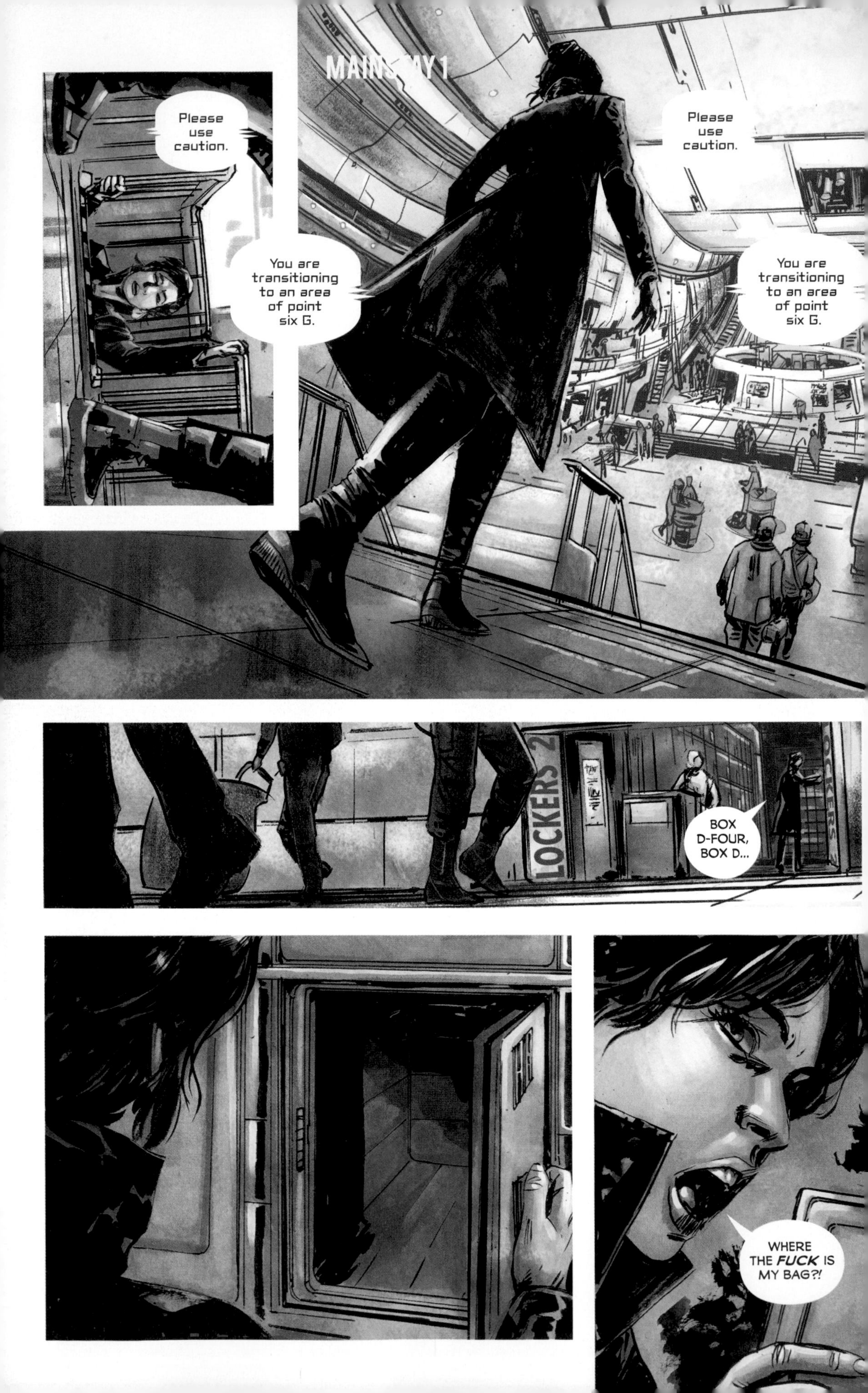

Please use caution.
You are transitioning to an area of point six G.
Please use caution.
You are transitioning to an area of point six G.
LOCKERS 2
BOX D-FOUR, BOX D...
LOCKERS
WHERE THE *FUCK* IS MY BAG?!

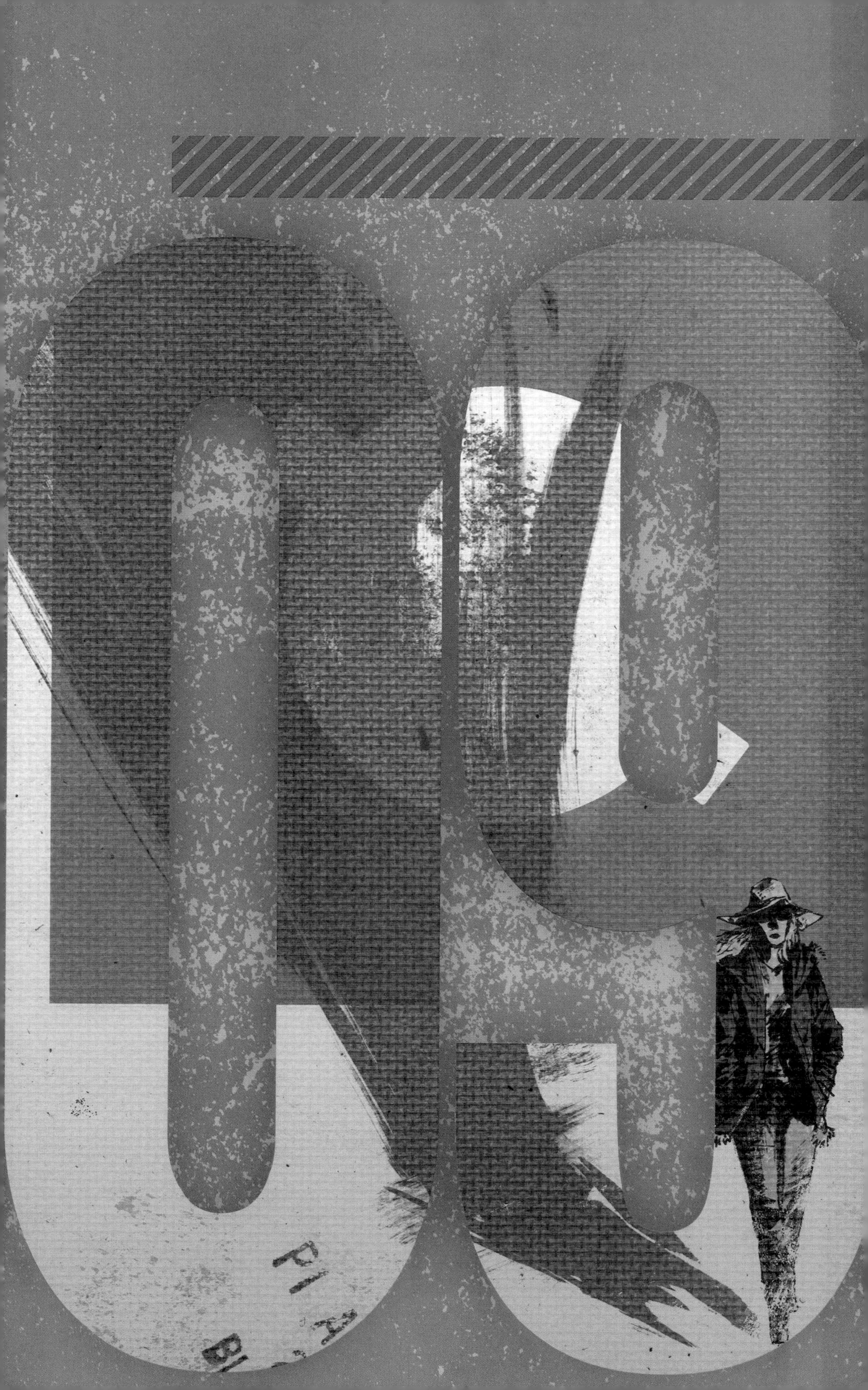

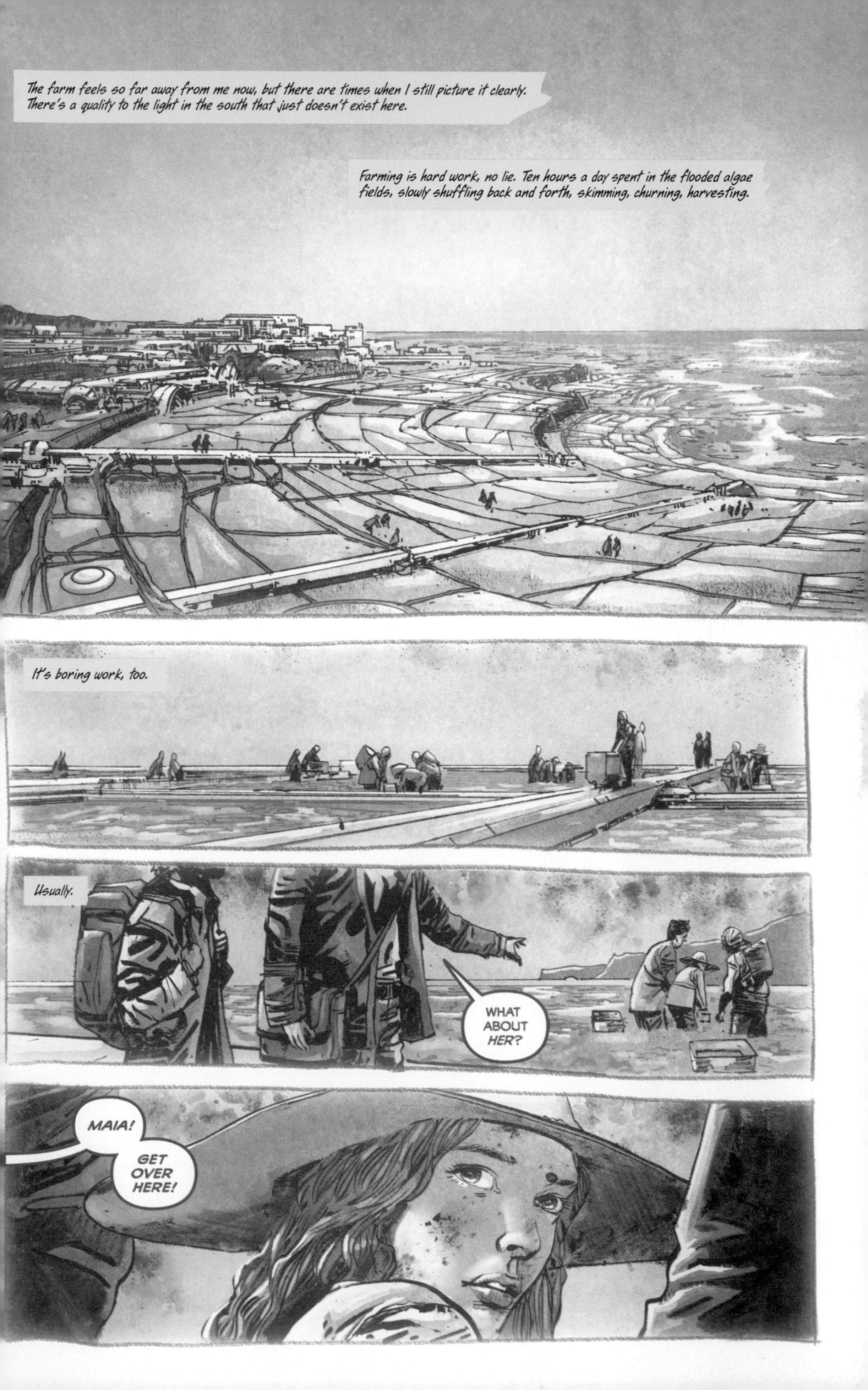
The farm feels so far away from me now, but there are times when I still picture it clearly. There's a quality to the light in the south that just doesn't exist here.
Farming is hard work, no lie. Ten hours a day spent in the flooded algae fields, slowly shuffling back and forth, skimming, churning, harvesting.
It's boring work, too.
Usually.
WHAT ABOUT HER?
MAIA!
GET OVER HERE!

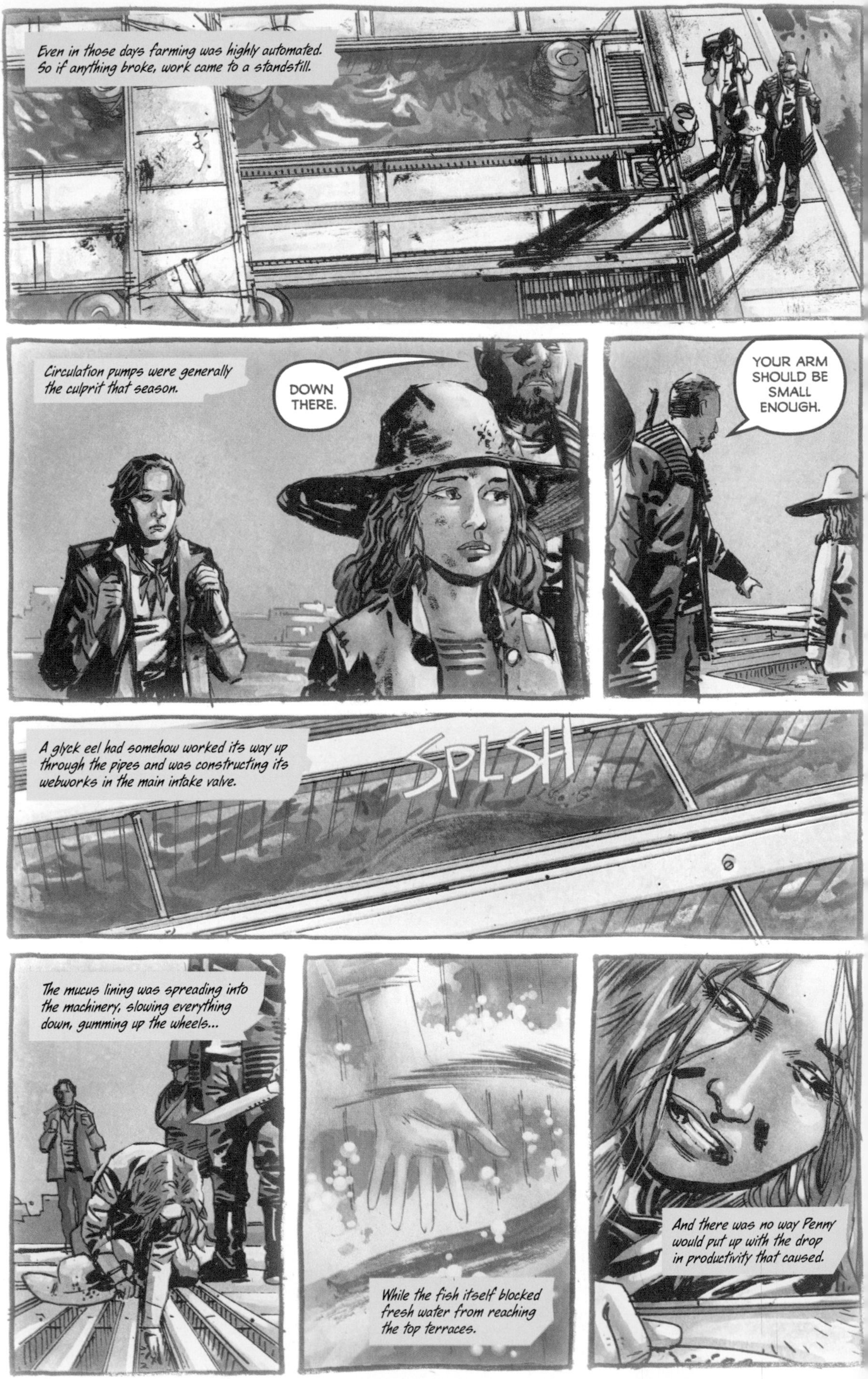
Even in those days farming was highly automated. So if anything broke, work came to a standstill.
Circulation pumps were generally the culprit that season.
DOWN THERE.
YOUR ARM SHOULD BE SMALL ENOUGH.
A glyck eel had somehow worked its way up through the pipes and was constructing its webworks in the main intake valve.
SPLSH
The mucus lining was spreading into the machinery, slowing everything down, gumming up the wheels...
While the fish itself blocked fresh water from reaching the top terraces.
And there was no way Penny would put up with the drop in productivity that caused.

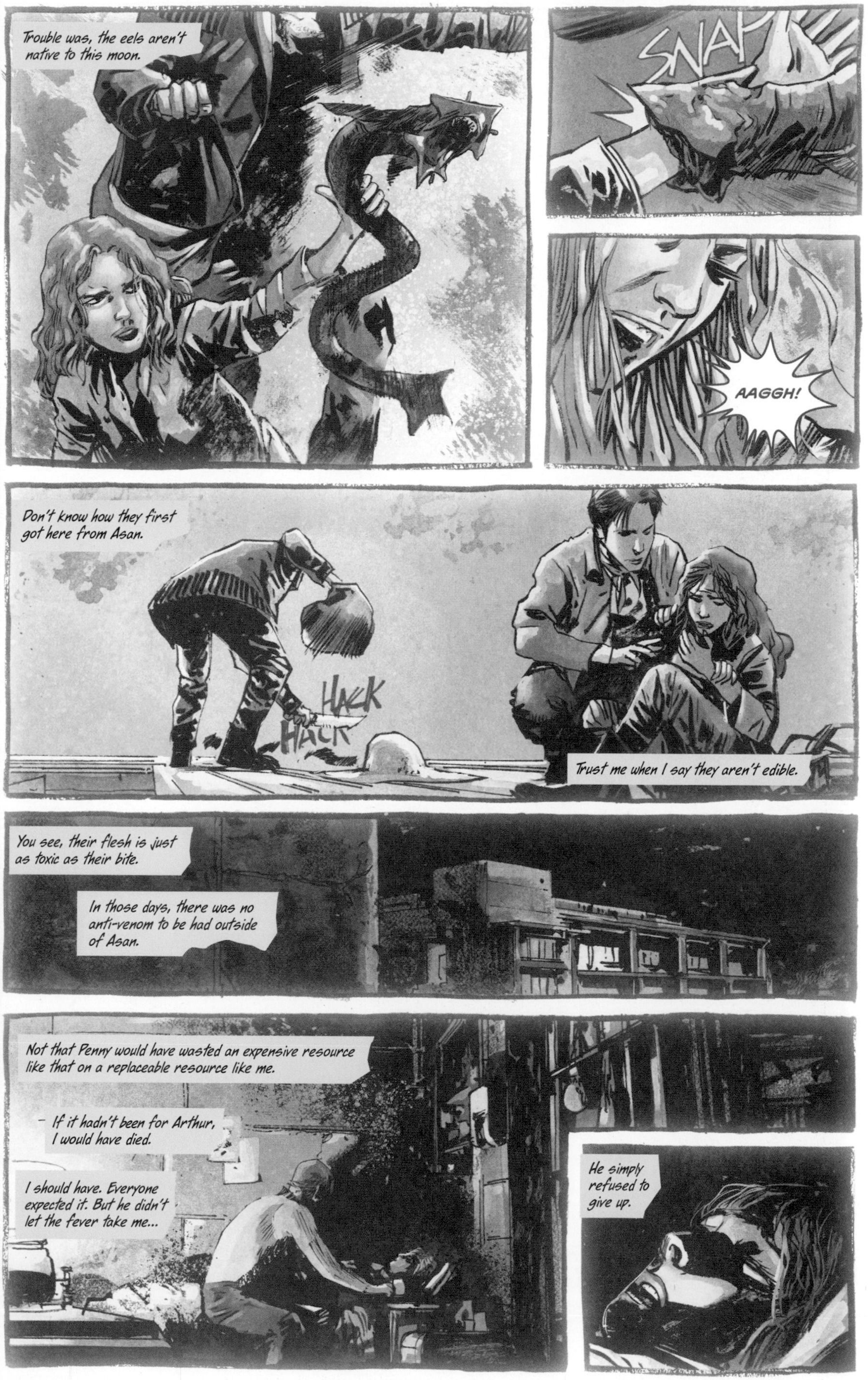
Trouble was, the eels aren't native to this moon.
SNAP
AAGGH!
Don't know how they first got here from Asan.
HACK
HACK
Trust me when I say they aren't edible.
You see, their flesh is just as toxic as their bite.
In those days, there was no anti-venom to be had outside of Asan.
Not that Penny would have wasted an expensive resource like that on a replaceable resource like me.
– If it hadn't been for Arthur, I would have died.
I should have. Everyone expected it. But he didn't let the fever take me...
He simply refused to give up.

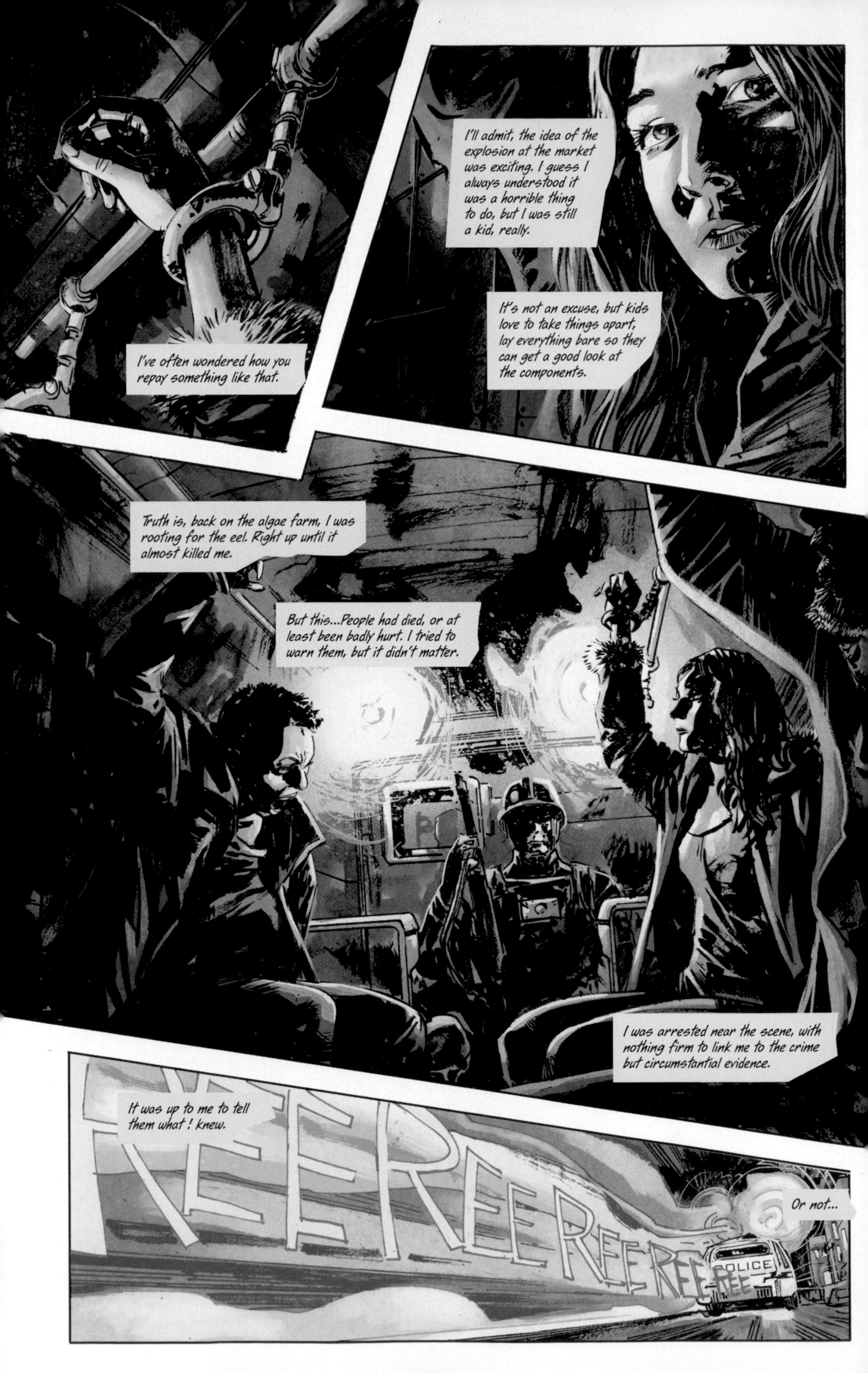
I've often wondered how you repay something like that.
I'll admit, the idea of the explosion at the market was exciting. I guess I always understood it was a horrible thing to do, but I was still a kid, really.
It's not an excuse, but kids love to take things apart, lay everything bare so they can get a good look at the components.
Truth is, back on the algae farm, I was rooting for the eel. Right up until it almost killed me.
But this...People had died, or at least been badly hurt. I tried to warn them, but it didn't matter.
I was arrested near the scene, with nothing firm to link me to the crime but circumstantial evidence.
It was up to me to tell them what I knew.
REEREEREEREEREE
POLICE
Or not...

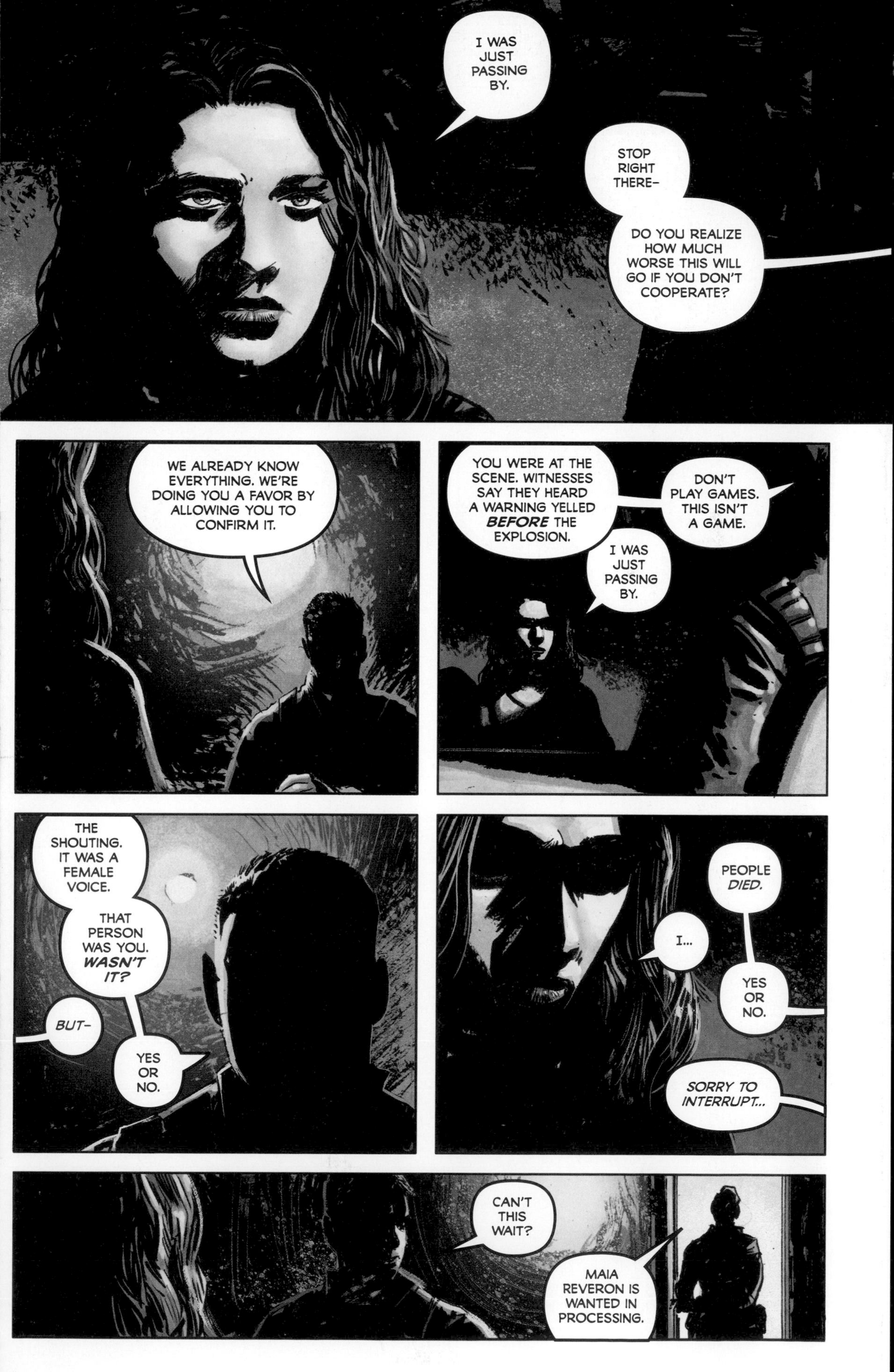
I WAS JUST PASSING BY.
STOP RIGHT THERE–
DO YOU REALIZE HOW MUCH WORSE THIS WILL GO IF YOU DON'T COOPERATE?
WE ALREADY KNOW EVERYTHING. WE'RE DOING YOU A FAVOR BY ALLOWING YOU TO CONFIRM IT.
YOU WERE AT THE SCENE. WITNESSES SAY THEY HEARD A WARNING YELLED ***BEFORE*** THE EXPLOSION.
DON'T PLAY GAMES. THIS ISN'T A GAME.
I WAS JUST PASSING BY.
THE SHOUTING. IT WAS A FEMALE VOICE.
THAT PERSON WAS YOU. ***WASN'T IT?***
BUT–
YES OR NO.
PEOPLE *DIED.*
I...
YES OR NO.
SORRY TO INTERRUPT...
CAN'T THIS WAIT?
MAIA REVERON IS WANTED IN PROCESSING.

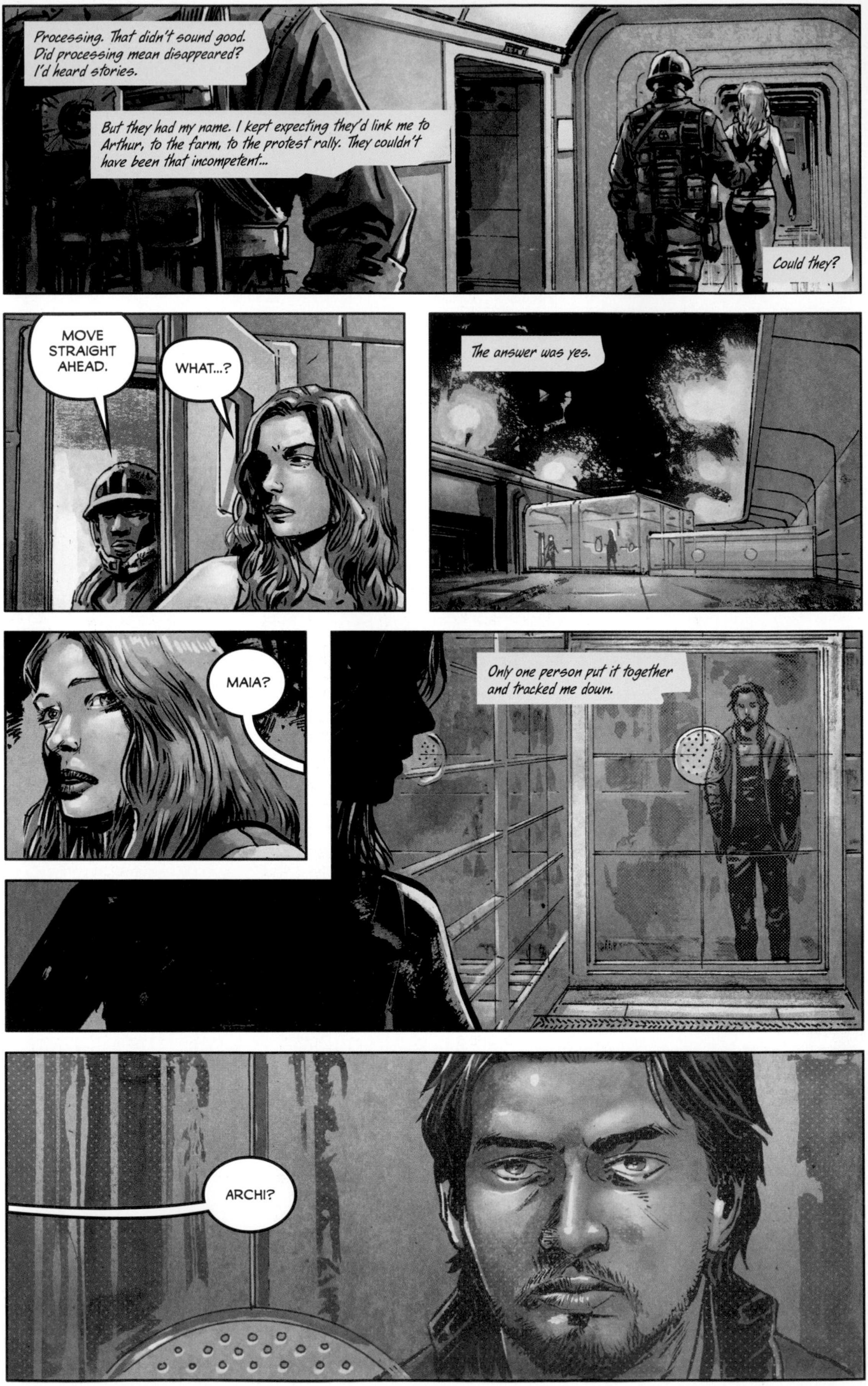
Processing. That didn't sound good. Did processing mean disappeared? I'd heard stories.
But they had my name. I kept expecting they'd link me to Arthur, to the farm, to the protest rally. They couldn't have been that incompetent...
Could they?
MOVE STRAIGHT AHEAD.
WHAT...?
The answer was yes.
MAIA?
Only one person put it together and tracked me down.
ARCHI?

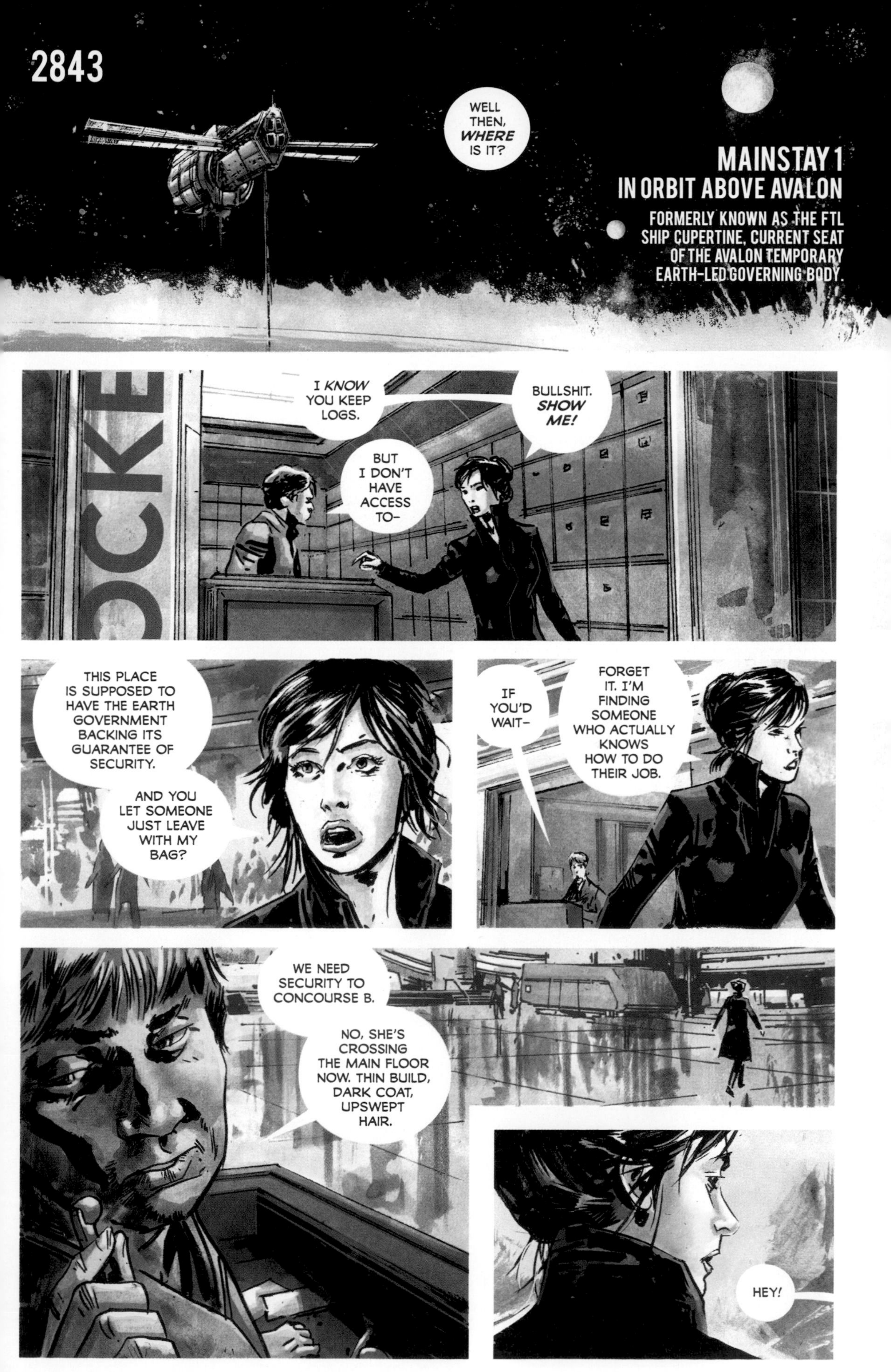
2843
WELL THEN, *WHERE* IS IT?
MAINSTAY 1
IN ORBIT ABOVE AVALON
FORMERLY KNOWN AS THE FTL SHIP CUPERTINE, CURRENT SEAT OF THE AVALON TEMPORARY EARTH-LED GOVERNING BODY.
I *KNOW* YOU KEEP LOGS.
BUT I DON'T HAVE ACCESS TO–
BULLSHIT. *SHOW ME!*
THIS PLACE IS SUPPOSED TO HAVE THE EARTH GOVERNMENT BACKING ITS GUARANTEE OF SECURITY.
AND YOU LET SOMEONE JUST LEAVE WITH MY BAG?
IF YOU'D WAIT–
FORGET IT. I'M FINDING SOMEONE WHO ACTUALLY KNOWS HOW TO DO THEIR JOB.
WE NEED SECURITY TO CONCOURSE B.
NO, SHE'S CROSSING THE MAIN FLOOR NOW. THIN BUILD, DARK COAT, UPSWEPT HAIR.
HEY!

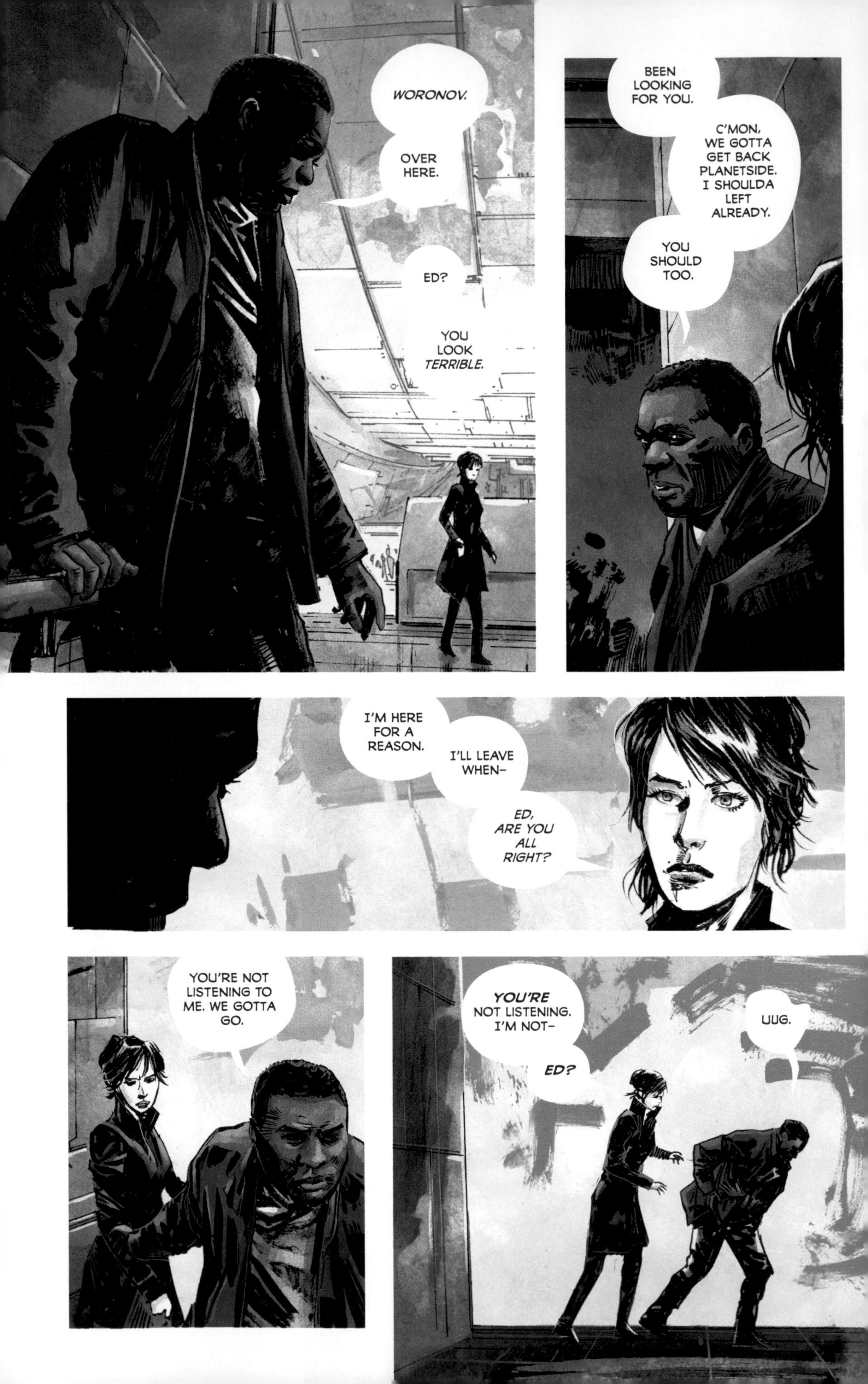
WORONOV.
OVER HERE.
ED?
YOU LOOK TERRIBLE.
BEEN LOOKING FOR YOU.
C'MON, WE GOTTA GET BACK PLANETSIDE. I SHOULDA LEFT ALREADY.
YOU SHOULD TOO.
I'M HERE FOR A REASON.
I'LL LEAVE WHEN–
ED, ARE YOU ALL RIGHT?
YOU'RE NOT LISTENING TO ME. WE GOTTA GO.
YOU'RE NOT LISTENING. I'M NOT–
ED?
UUG.

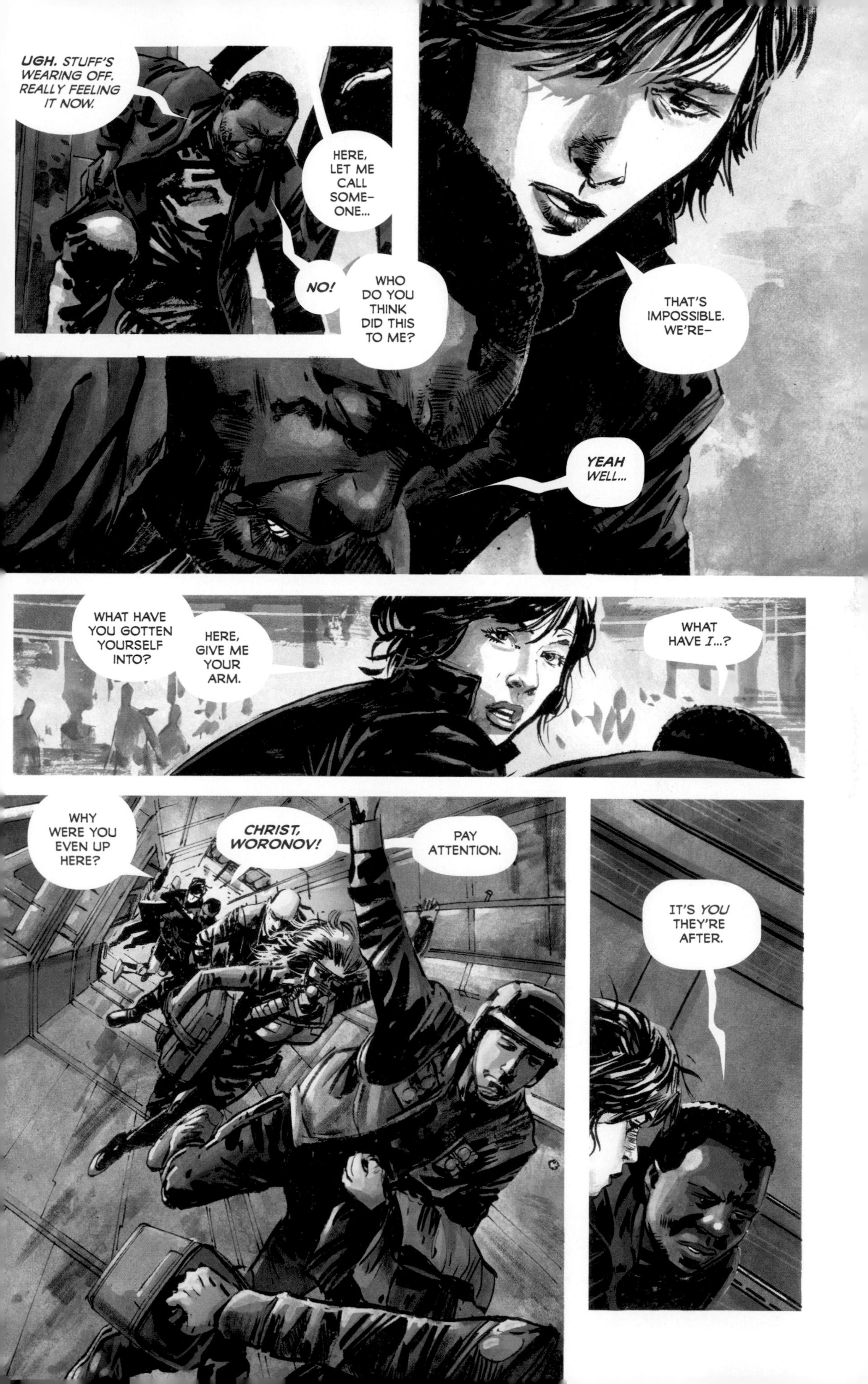

UGH. STUFF'S WEARING OFF. REALLY FEELING IT NOW.
HERE, LET ME CALL SOME-ONE...
NO!
WHO DO YOU THINK DID THIS TO ME?
THAT'S IMPOSSIBLE. WE'RE–
YEAH WELL...
WHAT HAVE YOU GOTTEN YOURSELF INTO?
HERE, GIVE ME YOUR ARM.
WHAT HAVE I...?
WHY WERE YOU EVEN UP HERE?
CHRIST, WORONOV!
PAY ATTENTION.
IT'S YOU THEY'RE AFTER.

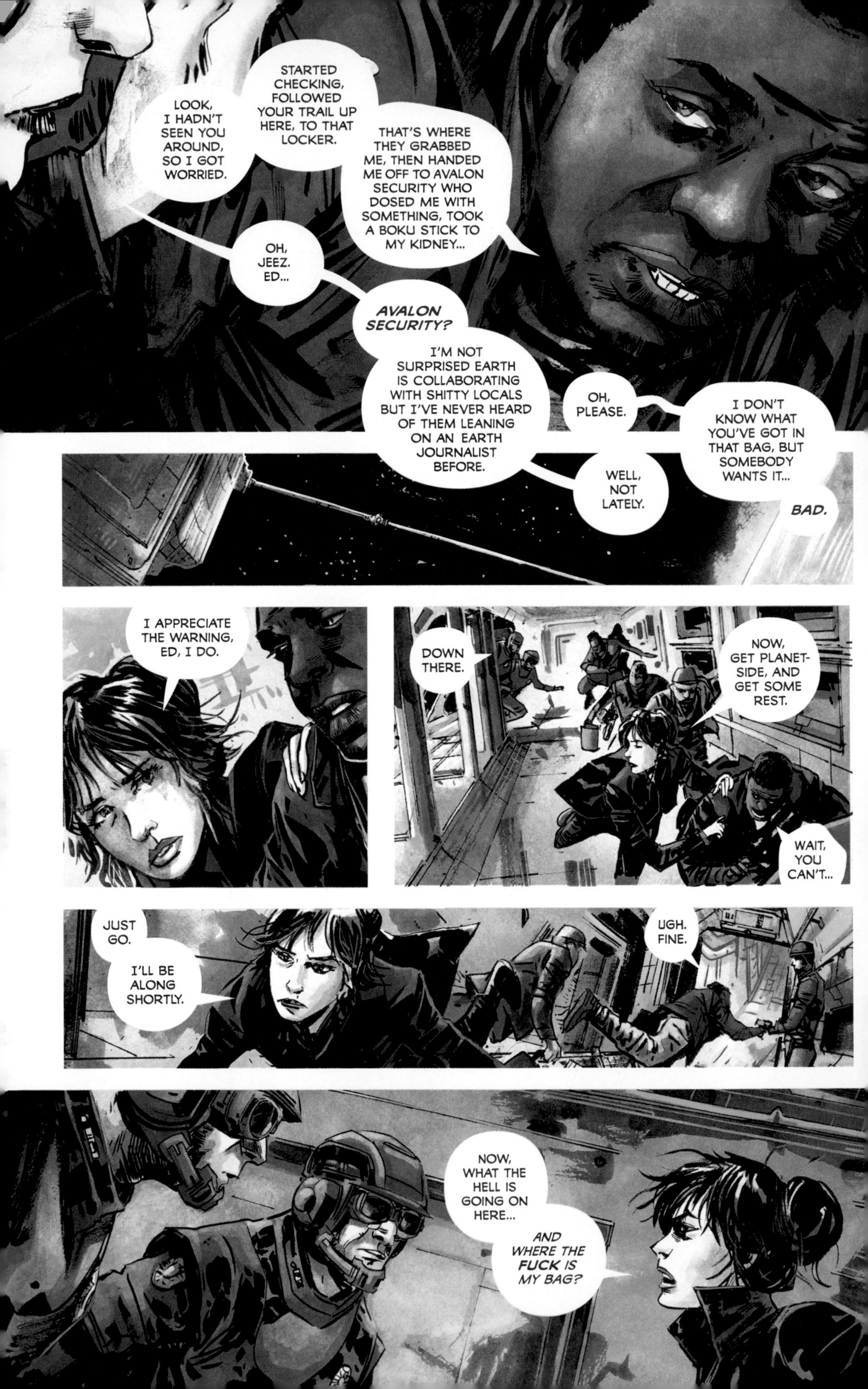
LOOK, I HADN'T SEEN YOU AROUND, SO I GOT WORRIED.
STARTED CHECKING, FOLLOWED YOUR TRAIL UP HERE, TO THAT LOCKER.
THAT'S WHERE THEY GRABBED ME, THEN HANDED ME OFF TO AVALON SECURITY WHO DOSED ME WITH SOMETHING, TOOK A BOKU STICK TO MY KIDNEY...
OH, JEEZ. ED...
AVALON SECURITY?
I'M NOT SURPRISED EARTH IS COLLABORATING WITH SHITTY LOCALS BUT I'VE NEVER HEARD OF THEM LEANING ON AN EARTH JOURNALIST BEFORE.
OH, PLEASE.
WELL, NOT LATELY.
I DON'T KNOW WHAT YOU'VE GOT IN THAT BAG, BUT SOMEBODY WANTS IT...
BAD.
I APPRECIATE THE WARNING, ED, I DO.
DOWN THERE.
NOW, GET PLANET-SIDE, AND GET SOME REST.
WAIT, YOU CAN'T...
JUST GO.
I'LL BE ALONG SHORTLY.
UGH. FINE.
NOW, WHAT THE HELL IS GOING ON HERE...
AND WHERE THE FUCK IS MY BAG?

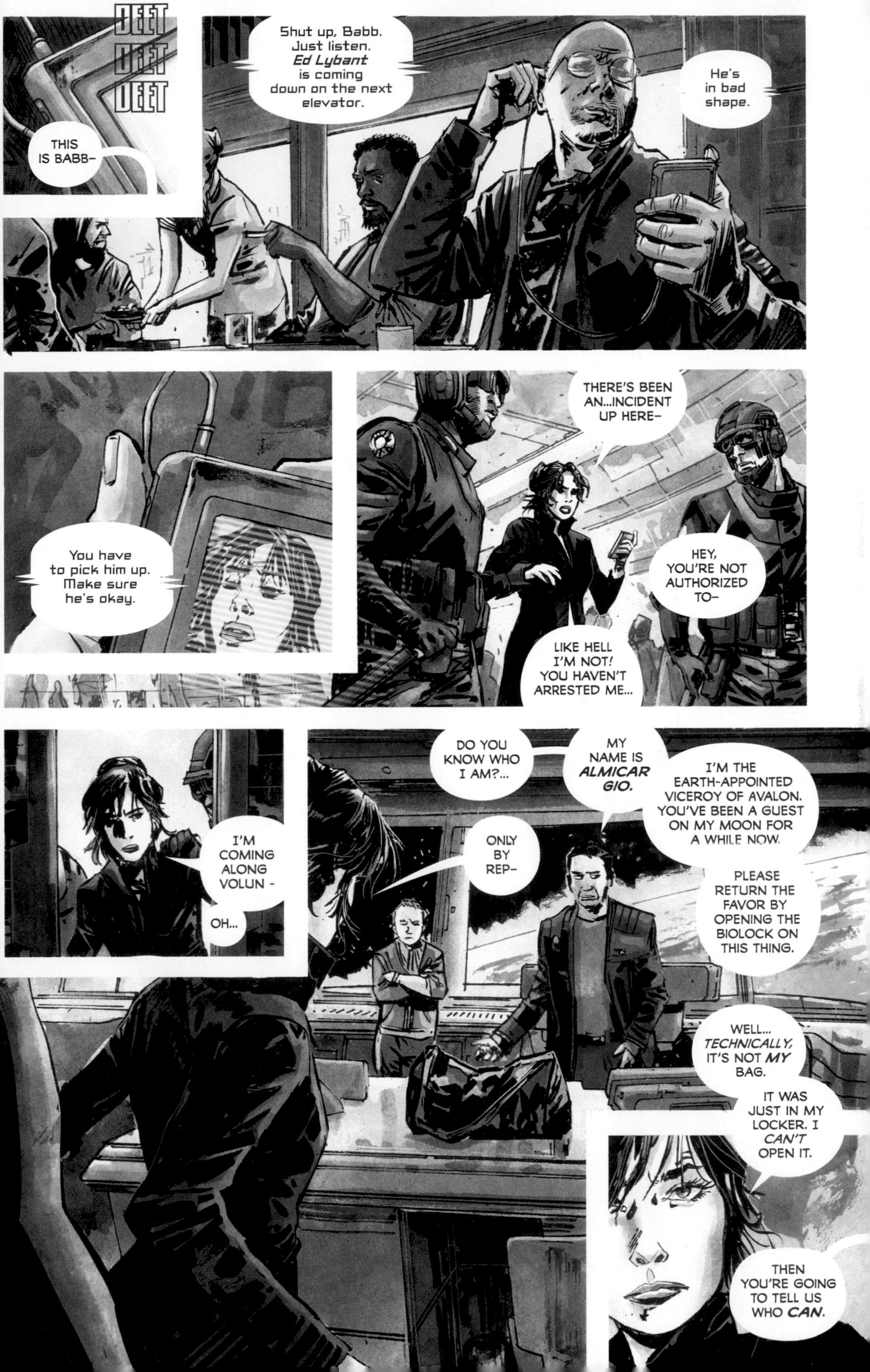
DEET DEET DEET
THIS IS BABB–
Shut up, Babb. Just listen. *Ed Lybant* is coming down on the next elevator.
He's in bad shape.
You have to pick him up. Make sure he's okay.
THERE'S BEEN AN...INCIDENT UP HERE–
HEY, YOU'RE NOT AUTHORIZED TO–
LIKE HELL I'M NOT! YOU HAVEN'T ARRESTED ME...
I'M COMING ALONG VOLUN -
OH...
DO YOU KNOW WHO I AM?...
MY NAME IS ***ALMICAR GIO.***
ONLY BY REP–
I'M THE EARTH-APPOINTED VICEROY OF AVALON. YOU'VE BEEN A GUEST ON MY MOON FOR A WHILE NOW.
PLEASE RETURN THE FAVOR BY OPENING THE BIOLOCK ON THIS THING.
WELL... *TECHNICALLY,* IT'S NOT ***MY*** BAG.
IT WAS JUST IN MY LOCKER. I *CAN'T* OPEN IT.
THEN YOU'RE GOING TO TELL US WHO ***CAN.***

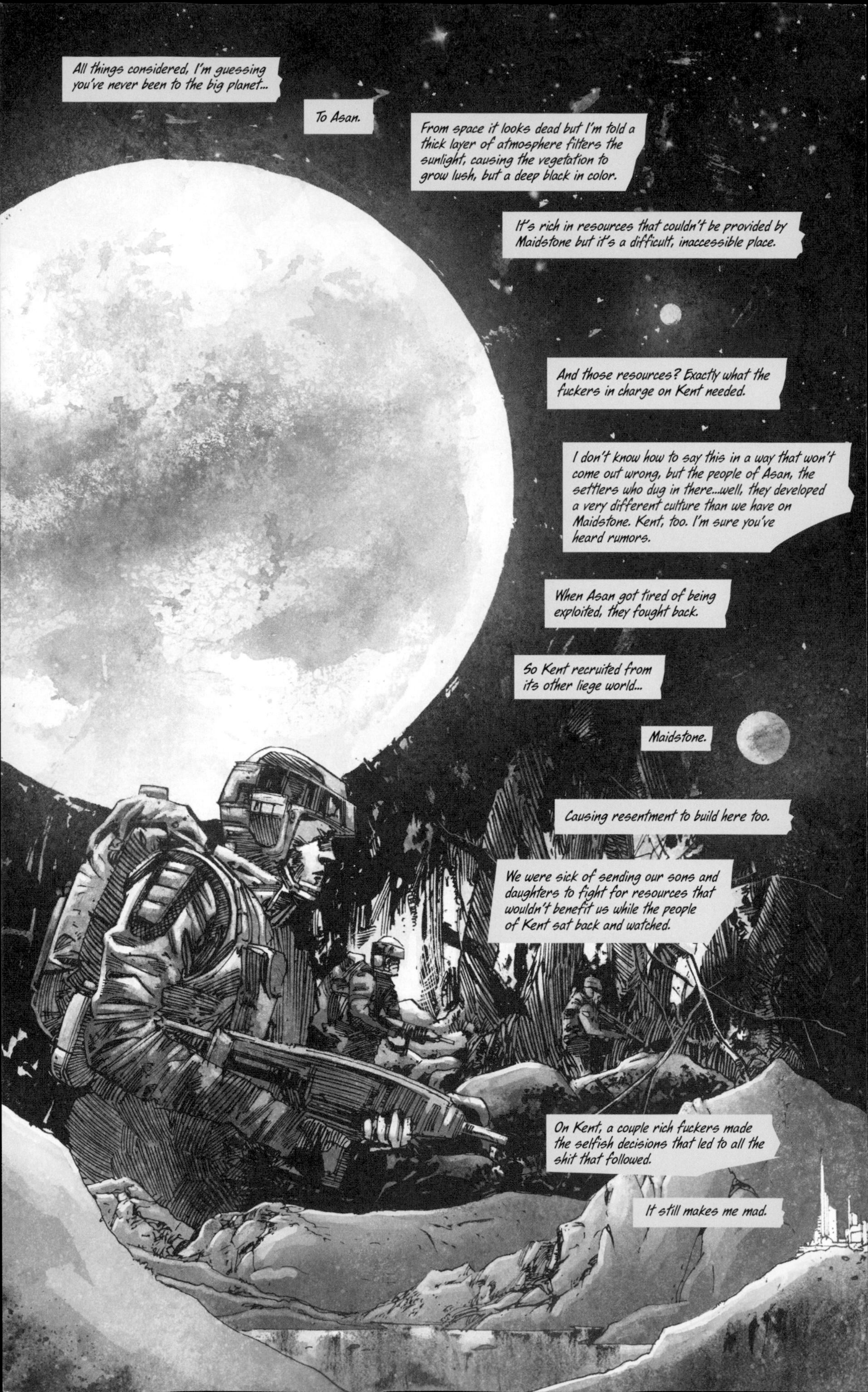
All things considered, I'm guessing you've never been to the big planet...
To Asan.
From space it looks dead but I'm told a thick layer of atmosphere filters the sunlight, causing the vegetation to grow lush, but a deep black in color.
It's rich in resources that couldn't be provided by Maidstone but it's a difficult, inaccessible place.
And those resources? Exactly what the fuckers in charge on Kent needed.
I don't know how to say this in a way that won't come out wrong, but the people of Asan, the settlers who dug in there...well, they developed a very different culture than we have on Maidstone. Kent, too. I'm sure you've heard rumors.
When Asan got tired of being exploited, they fought back.
So Kent recruited from its other liege world...
Maidstone.
Causing resentment to build here too.
We were sick of sending our sons and daughters to fight for resources that wouldn't benefit us while the people of Kent sat back and watched.
On Kent, a couple rich fuckers made the selfish decisions that led to all the shit that followed.
It still makes me mad.

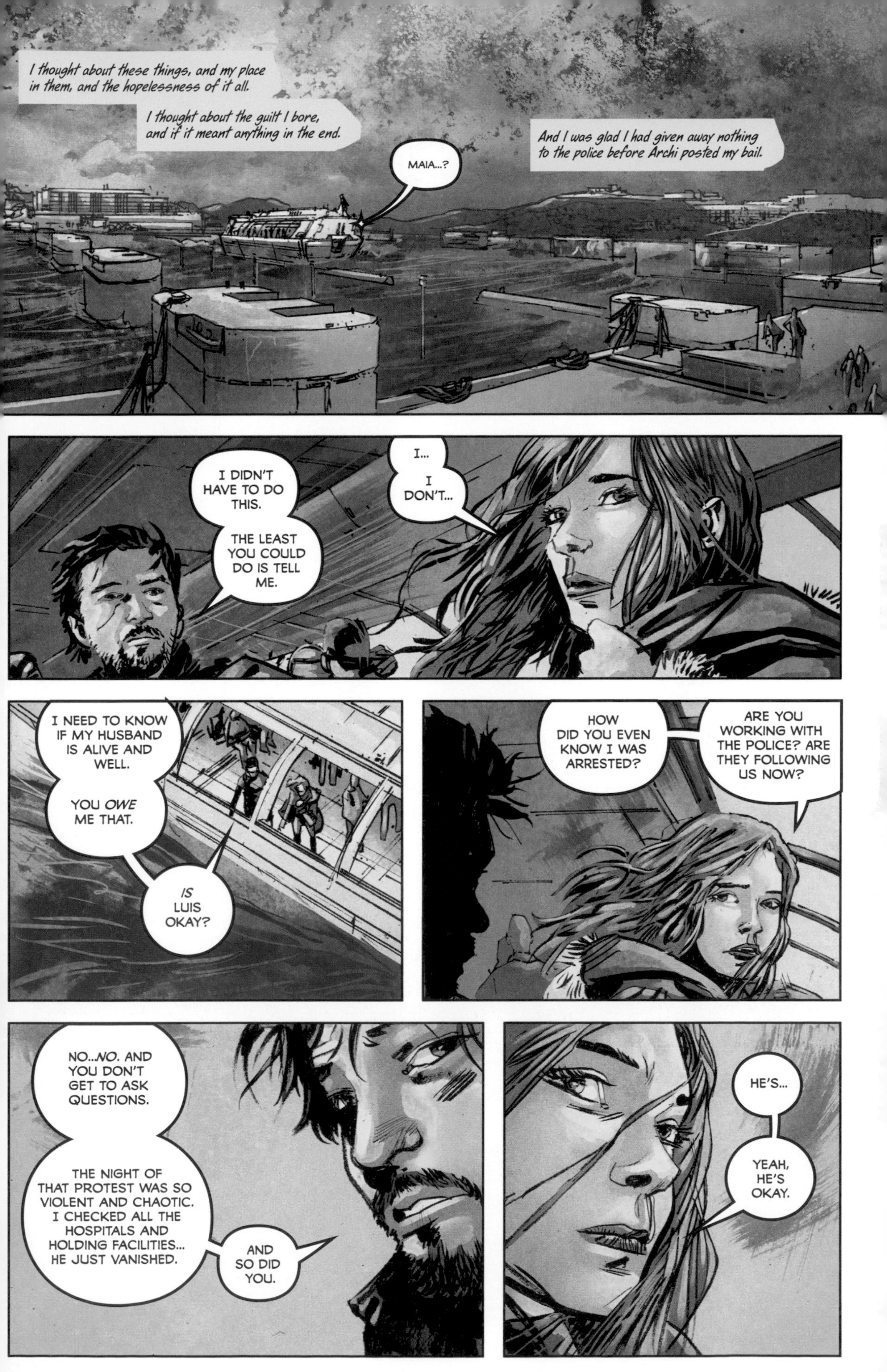
I thought about these things, and my place in them, and the hopelessness of it all.
I thought about the guilt I bore, and if it meant anything in the end.
MAIA...?
And I was glad I had given away nothing to the police before Archi posted my bail.
I DIDN'T HAVE TO DO THIS.
THE LEAST YOU COULD DO IS TELL ME.
I...
I DON'T...
I NEED TO KNOW IF MY HUSBAND IS ALIVE AND WELL.
YOU *OWE* ME THAT.
IS LUIS OKAY?
HOW DID YOU EVEN KNOW I WAS ARRESTED?
ARE YOU WORKING WITH THE POLICE? ARE THEY FOLLOWING US NOW?
NO...*NO*. AND YOU DON'T GET TO ASK QUESTIONS.
THE NIGHT OF THAT PROTEST WAS SO VIOLENT AND CHAOTIC. I CHECKED ALL THE HOSPITALS AND HOLDING FACILITIES... HE JUST VANISHED.
AND SO DID YOU.
HE'S...
YEAH, HE'S OKAY.

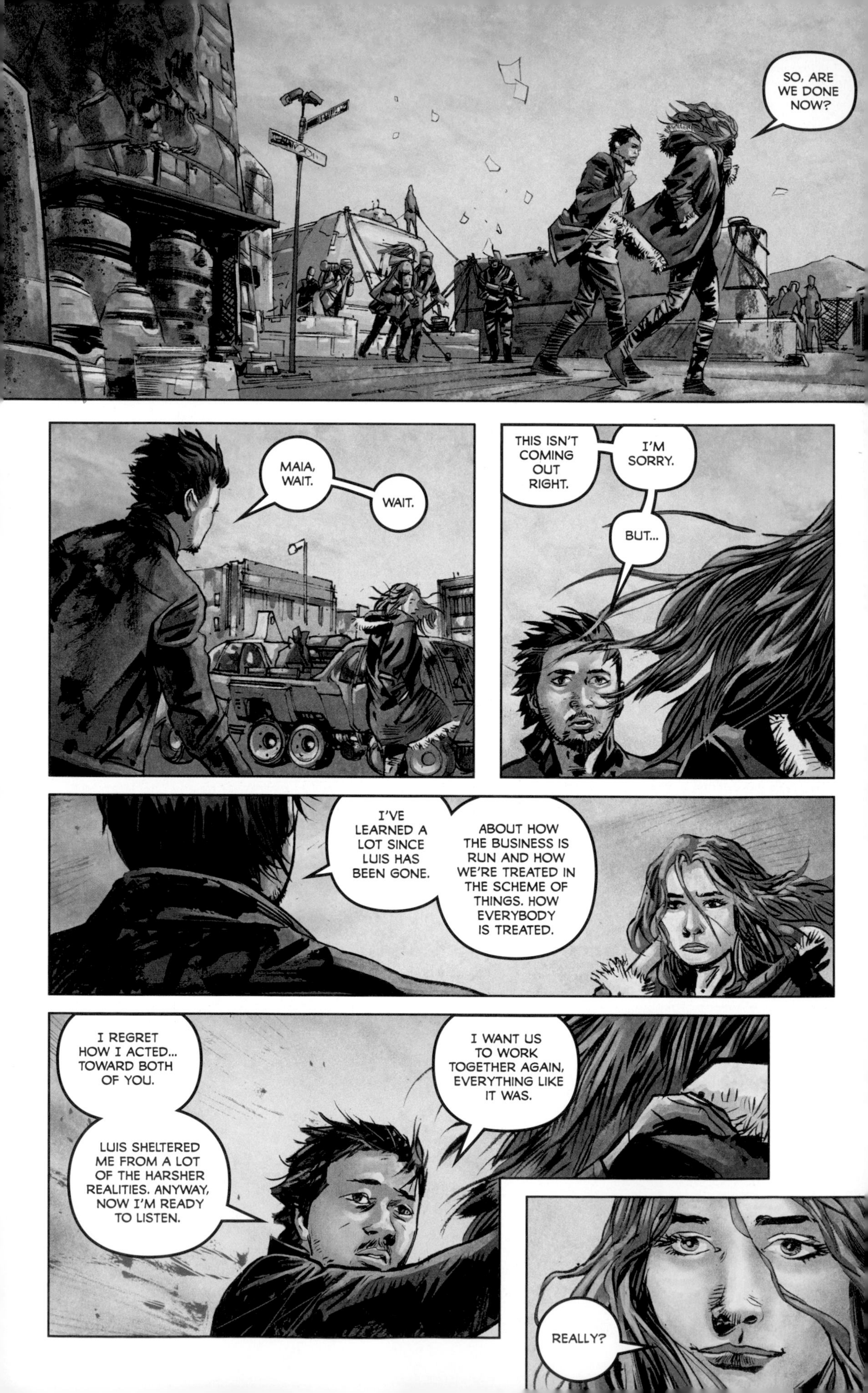
SO, ARE WE DONE NOW?
MAIA, WAIT.
WAIT.
THIS ISN'T COMING OUT RIGHT.
I'M SORRY.
BUT...
I'VE LEARNED A LOT SINCE LUIS HAS BEEN GONE.
ABOUT HOW THE BUSINESS IS RUN AND HOW WE'RE TREATED IN THE SCHEME OF THINGS. HOW EVERYBODY IS TREATED.
I REGRET HOW I ACTED... TOWARD BOTH OF YOU.
LUIS SHELTERED ME FROM A LOT OF THE HARSHER REALITIES. ANYWAY, NOW I'M READY TO LISTEN.
I WANT US TO WORK TOGETHER AGAIN, EVERYTHING LIKE IT WAS.
REALLY?

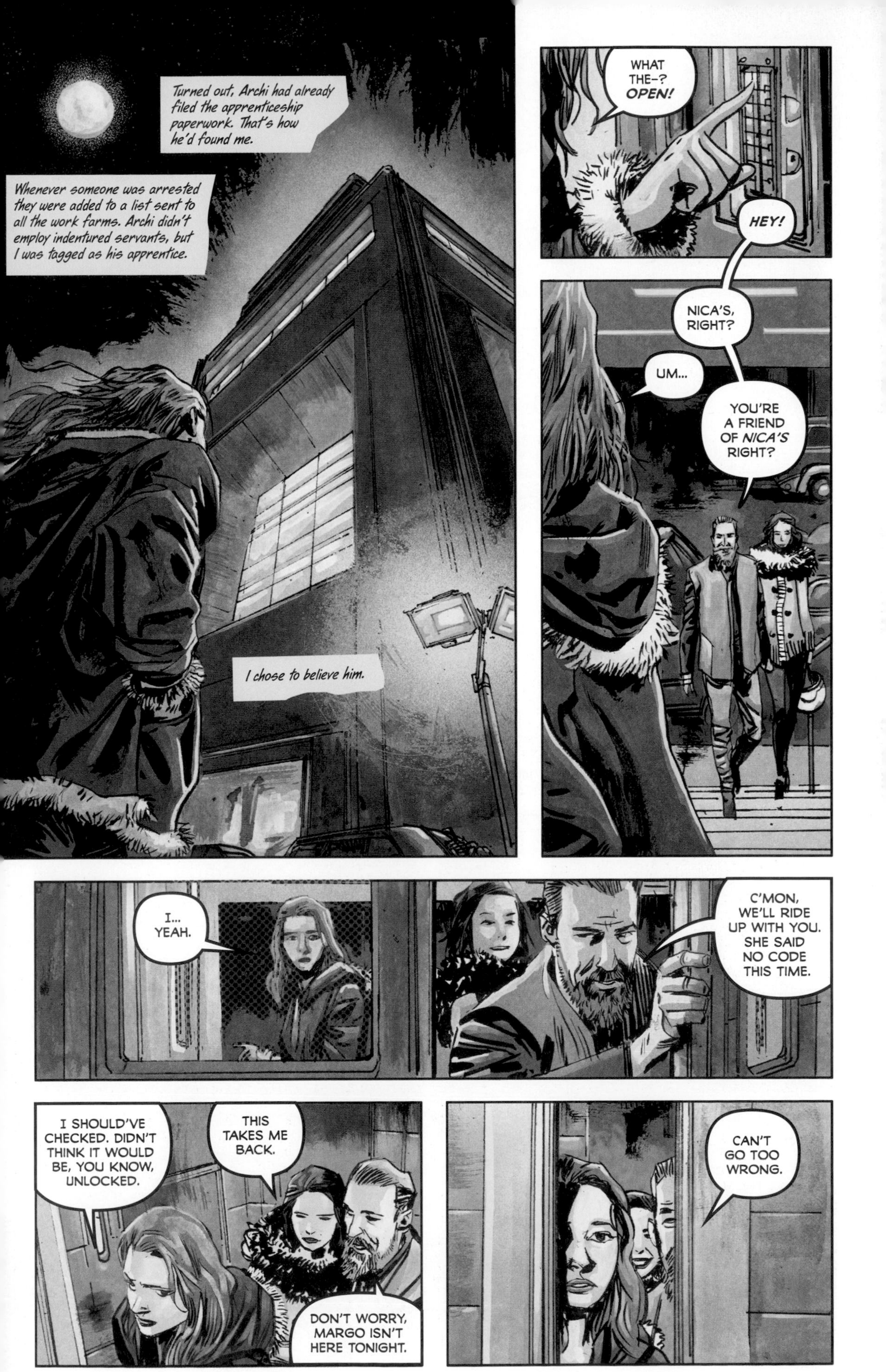
Turned out, Archi had already filed the apprenticeship paperwork. That's how he'd found me.
Whenever someone was arrested they were added to a list sent to all the work farms. Archi didn't employ indentured servants, but I was tagged as his apprentice.
I chose to believe him.
WHAT THE–? OPEN!
HEY!
NICA'S, RIGHT?
UM...
YOU'RE A FRIEND OF NICA'S RIGHT?
I... YEAH.
C'MON, WE'LL RIDE UP WITH YOU. SHE SAID NO CODE THIS TIME.
I SHOULD'VE CHECKED. DIDN'T THINK IT WOULD BE, YOU KNOW, UNLOCKED.
THIS TAKES ME BACK.
DON'T WORRY, MARGO ISN'T HERE TONIGHT.
CAN'T GO TOO WRONG.

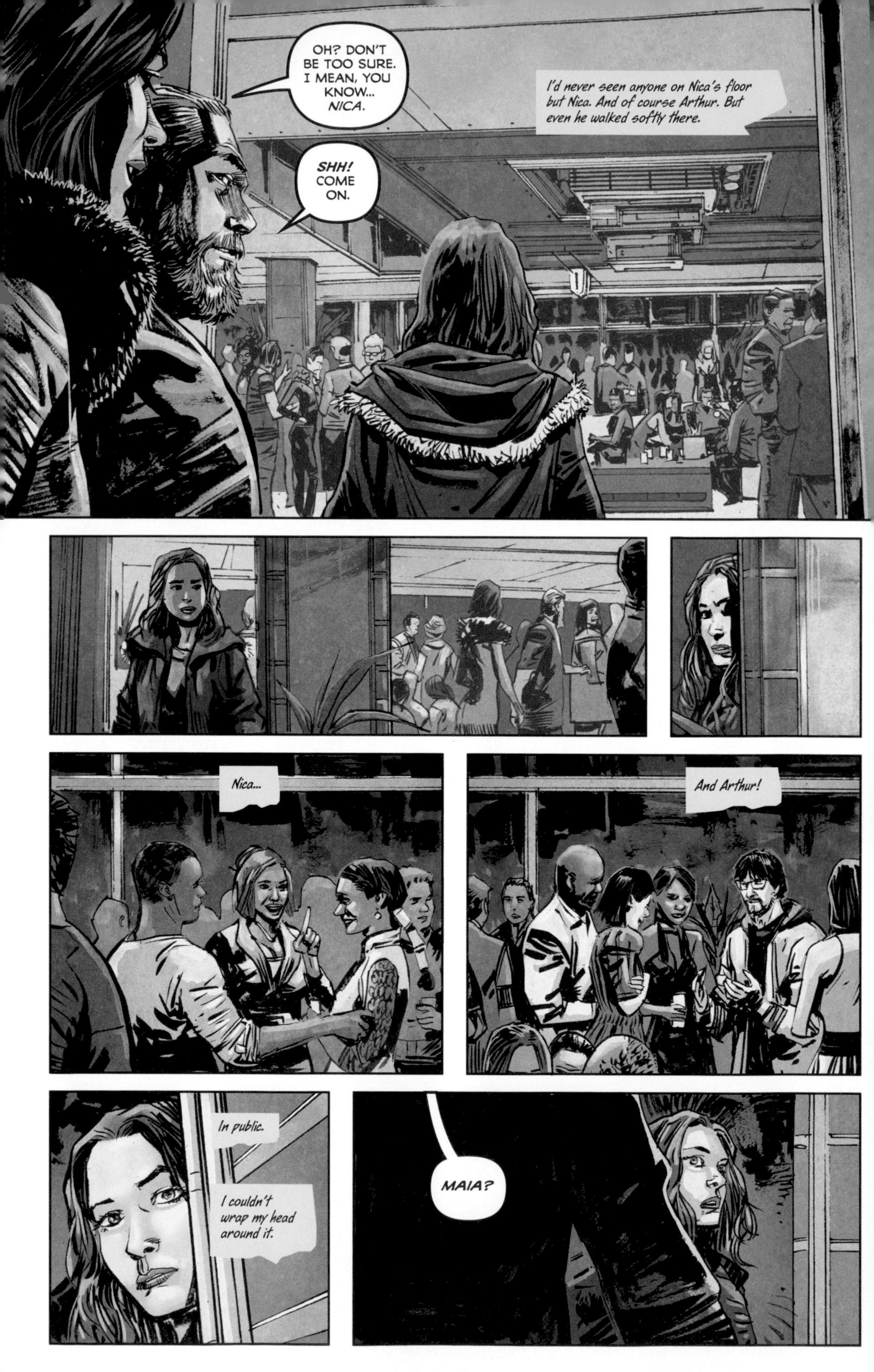
OH? DON'T BE TOO SURE. I MEAN, YOU KNOW... NICA.
SHH! COME ON.
I'd never seen anyone on Nica's floor but Nica. And of course Arthur. But even he walked softly there.
Nica...
And Arthur!
In public.
I couldn't wrap my head around it.
MAIA?

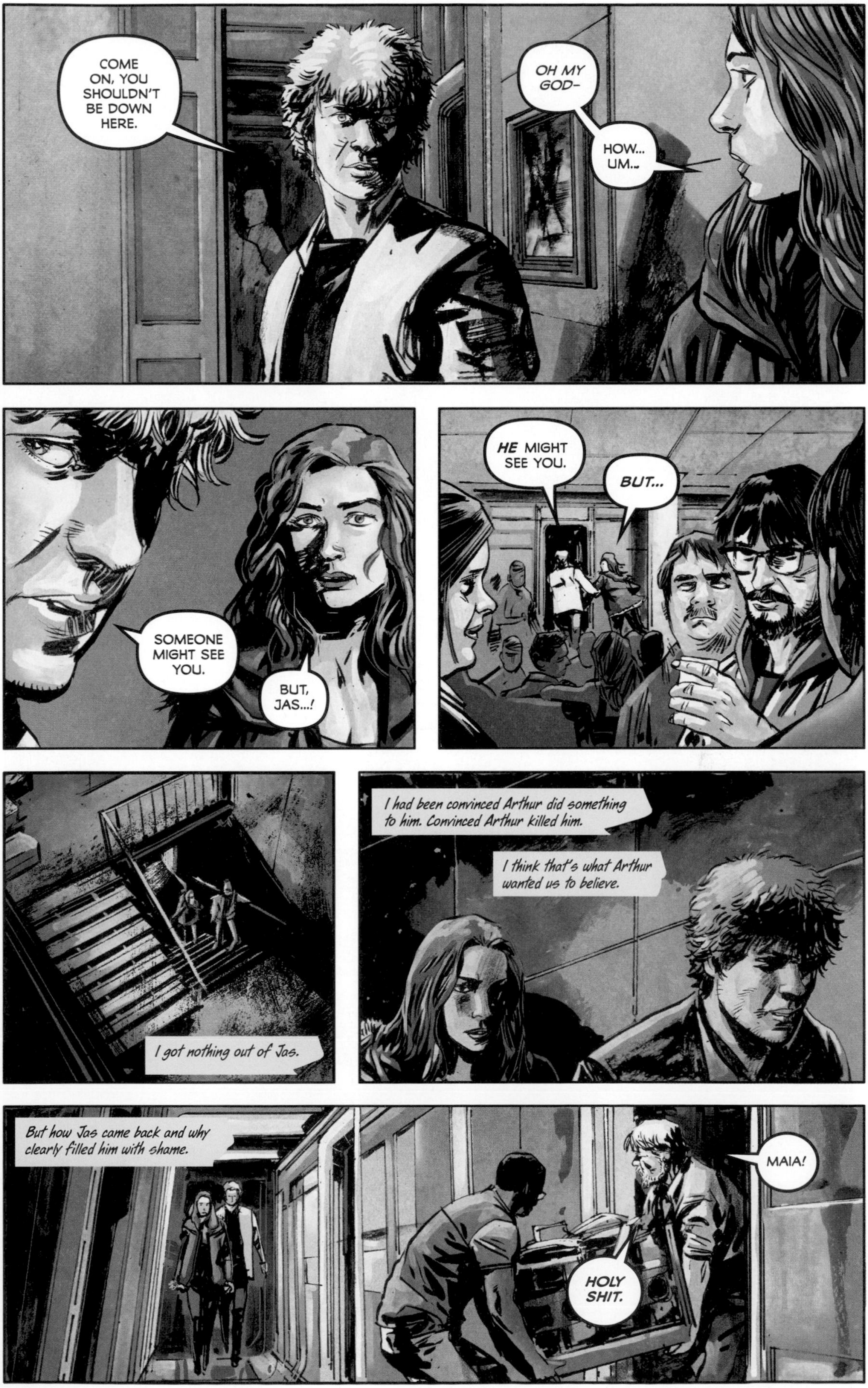
COME ON, YOU SHOULDN'T BE DOWN HERE.
OH MY GOD–
HOW... UM...
SOMEONE MIGHT SEE YOU.
BUT, JAS...!
HE MIGHT SEE YOU.
BUT...
I got nothing out of Jas.
I had been convinced Arthur did something to him. Convinced Arthur killed him.
I think that's what Arthur wanted us to believe.
But how Jas came back and why clearly filled him with shame.
MAIA!
HOLY SHIT.

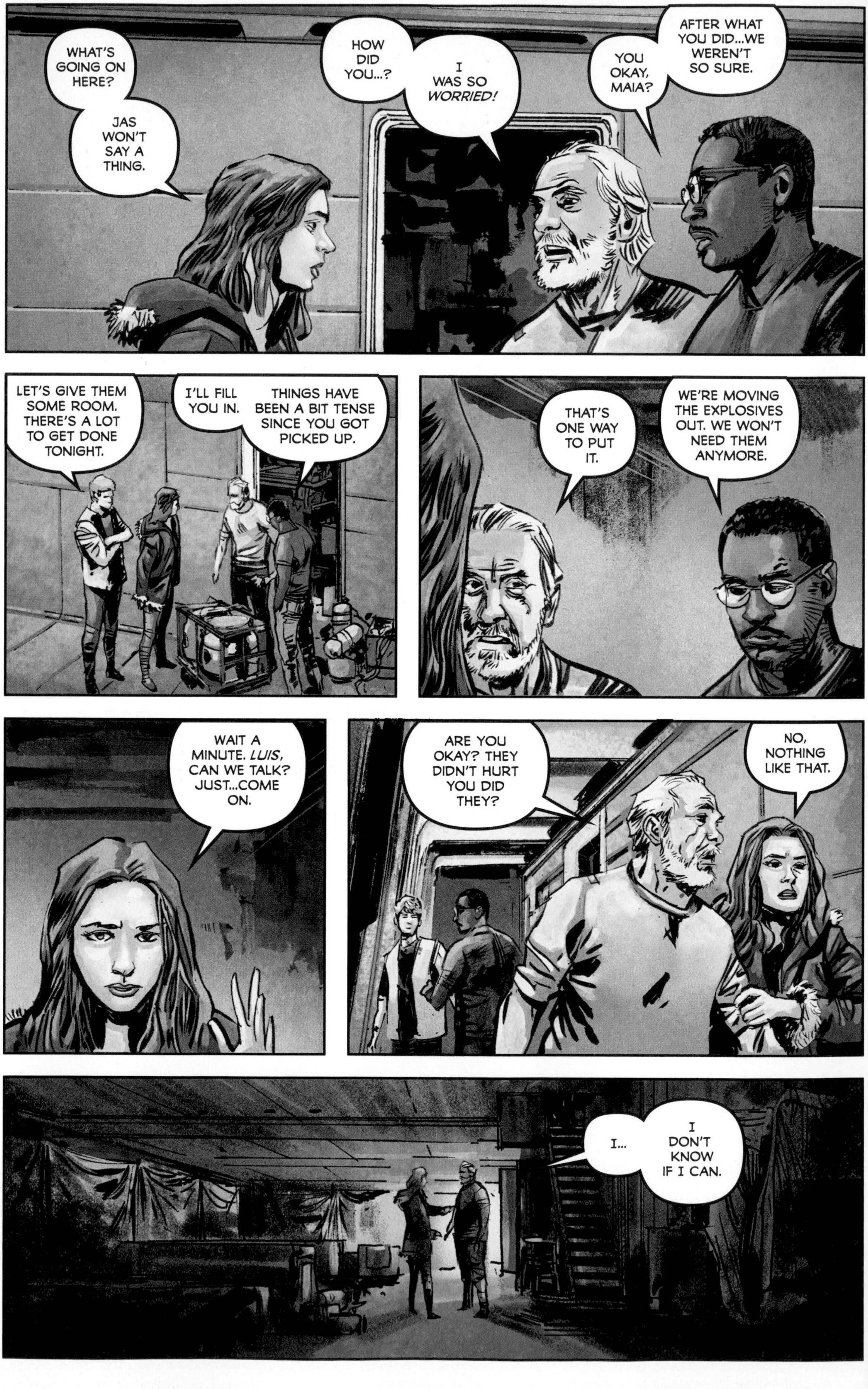
WHAT'S GOING ON HERE?
JAS WON'T SAY A THING.
HOW DID YOU...?
I WAS SO *WORRIED!*
YOU OKAY, MAIA?
AFTER WHAT YOU DID...WE WEREN'T SO SURE.
LET'S GIVE THEM SOME ROOM. THERE'S A LOT TO GET DONE TONIGHT.
I'LL FILL YOU IN.
THINGS HAVE BEEN A BIT TENSE SINCE YOU GOT PICKED UP.
THAT'S ONE WAY TO PUT IT.
WE'RE MOVING THE EXPLOSIVES OUT. WE WON'T NEED THEM ANYMORE.
WAIT A MINUTE. *LUIS*, CAN WE TALK? JUST...COME ON.
ARE YOU OKAY? THEY DIDN'T HURT YOU DID THEY?
NO, NOTHING LIKE THAT.
I...
I DON'T KNOW IF I CAN.

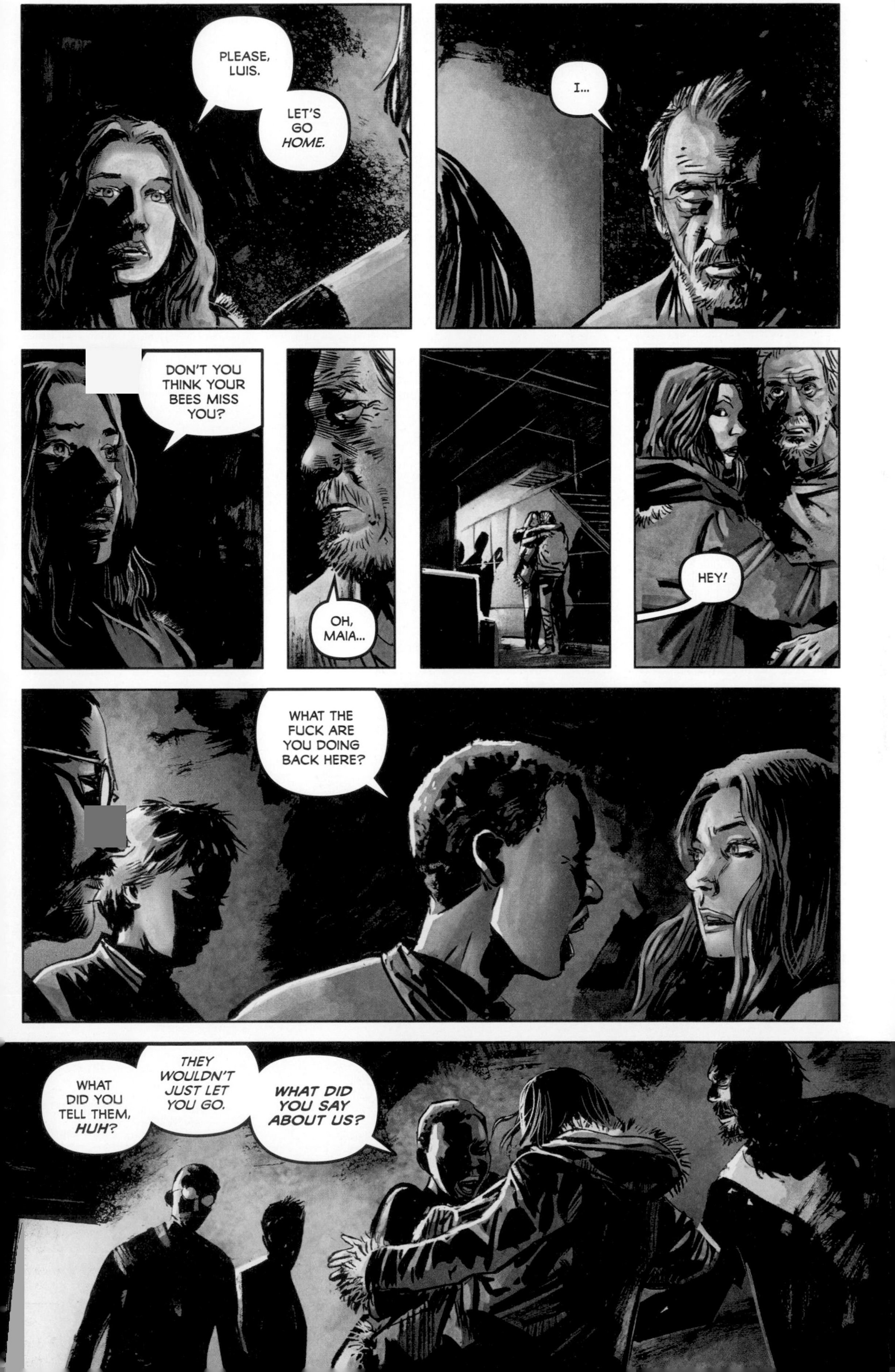
PLEASE, LUIS.
LET'S GO *HOME.*
I...
DON'T YOU THINK YOUR BEES MISS YOU?
OH, MAIA...
HEY!
WHAT THE FUCK ARE YOU DOING BACK HERE?
WHAT DID YOU TELL THEM, ***HUH?***
THEY WOULDN'T JUST LET YOU GO.
WHAT DID YOU SAY ABOUT US?

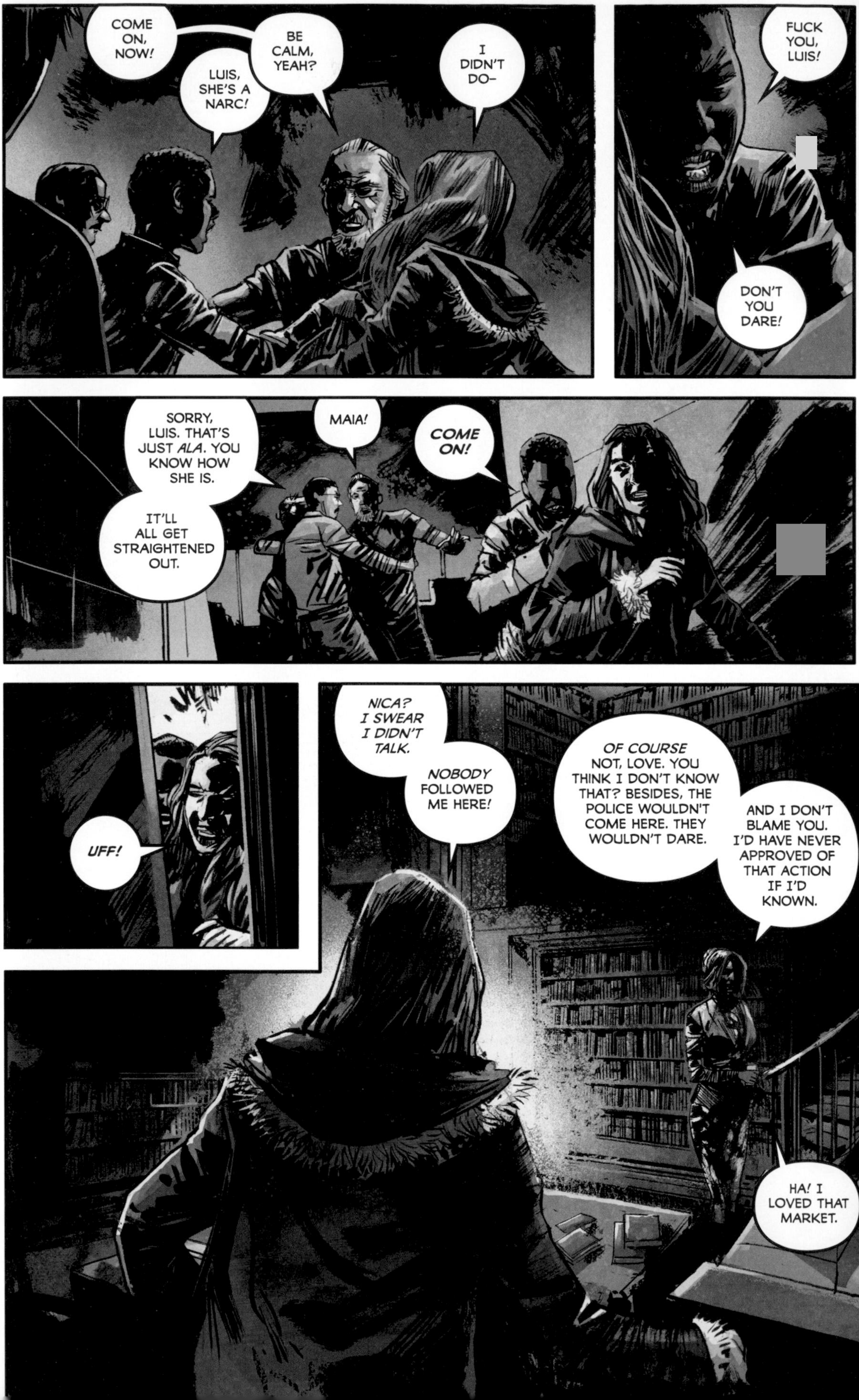
COME ON, NOW!
LUIS, SHE'S A NARC!
BE CALM, YEAH?
I DIDN'T DO–
FUCK YOU, LUIS!
DON'T YOU DARE!
SORRY, LUIS. THAT'S JUST *ALA*. YOU KNOW HOW SHE IS.
IT'LL ALL GET STRAIGHTENED OUT.
MAIA!
COME ON!
UFF!
NICA? I SWEAR I DIDN'T TALK.
NOBODY FOLLOWED ME HERE!
OF COURSE NOT, LOVE. YOU THINK I DON'T KNOW THAT? BESIDES, THE POLICE WOULDN'T COME HERE. THEY WOULDN'T DARE.
AND I DON'T BLAME YOU. I'D HAVE NEVER APPROVED OF THAT ACTION IF I'D KNOWN.
HA! I LOVED THAT MARKET.

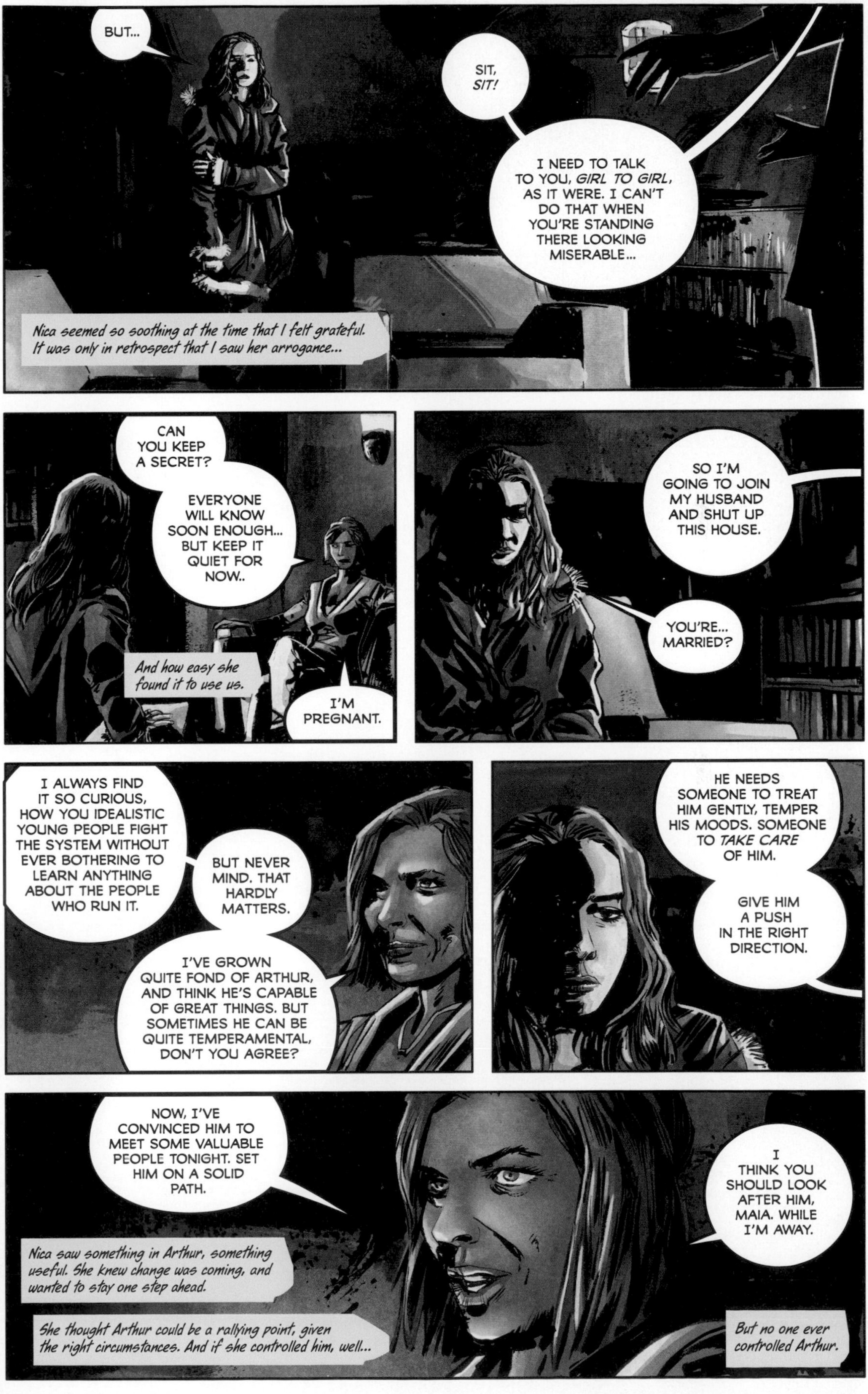
BUT...
SIT, SIT!
I NEED TO TALK TO YOU, GIRL TO GIRL, AS IT WERE. I CAN'T DO THAT WHEN YOU'RE STANDING THERE LOOKING MISERABLE...
Nica seemed so soothing at the time that I felt grateful. It was only in retrospect that I saw her arrogance...
CAN YOU KEEP A SECRET?
EVERYONE WILL KNOW SOON ENOUGH... BUT KEEP IT QUIET FOR NOW..
And how easy she found it to use us.
I'M PREGNANT.
SO I'M GOING TO JOIN MY HUSBAND AND SHUT UP THIS HOUSE.
YOU'RE... MARRIED?
I ALWAYS FIND IT SO CURIOUS, HOW YOU IDEALISTIC YOUNG PEOPLE FIGHT THE SYSTEM WITHOUT EVER BOTHERING TO LEARN ANYTHING ABOUT THE PEOPLE WHO RUN IT.
BUT NEVER MIND. THAT HARDLY MATTERS.
I'VE GROWN QUITE FOND OF ARTHUR, AND THINK HE'S CAPABLE OF GREAT THINGS. BUT SOMETIMES HE CAN BE QUITE TEMPERAMENTAL, DON'T YOU AGREE?
HE NEEDS SOMEONE TO TREAT HIM GENTLY, TEMPER HIS MOODS. SOMEONE TO TAKE CARE OF HIM.
GIVE HIM A PUSH IN THE RIGHT DIRECTION.
NOW, I'VE CONVINCED HIM TO MEET SOME VALUABLE PEOPLE TONIGHT. SET HIM ON A SOLID PATH.
Nica saw something in Arthur, something useful. She knew change was coming, and wanted to stay one step ahead.
She thought Arthur could be a rallying point, given the right circumstances. And if she controlled him, well...
I THINK YOU SHOULD LOOK AFTER HIM, MAIA. WHILE I'M AWAY.
But no one ever controlled Arthur.

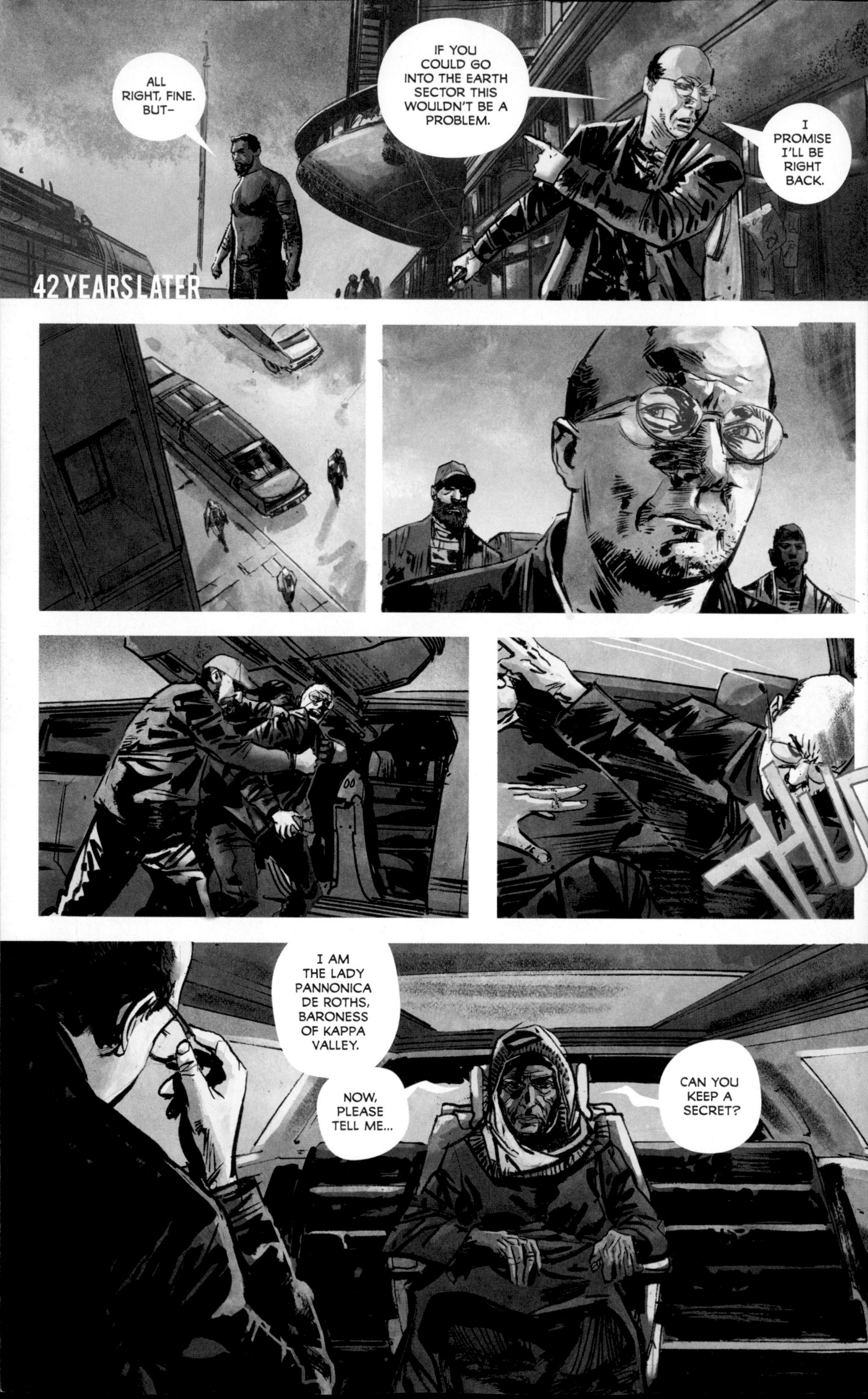
ALL RIGHT, FINE. BUT–
IF YOU COULD GO INTO THE EARTH SECTOR THIS WOULDN'T BE A PROBLEM.
I PROMISE I'LL BE RIGHT BACK.
42 YEARS LATER
THU
I AM THE LADY PANNONICA DE ROTHS, BARONESS OF KAPPA VALLEY.
NOW, PLEASE TELL ME...
CAN YOU KEEP A SECRET?

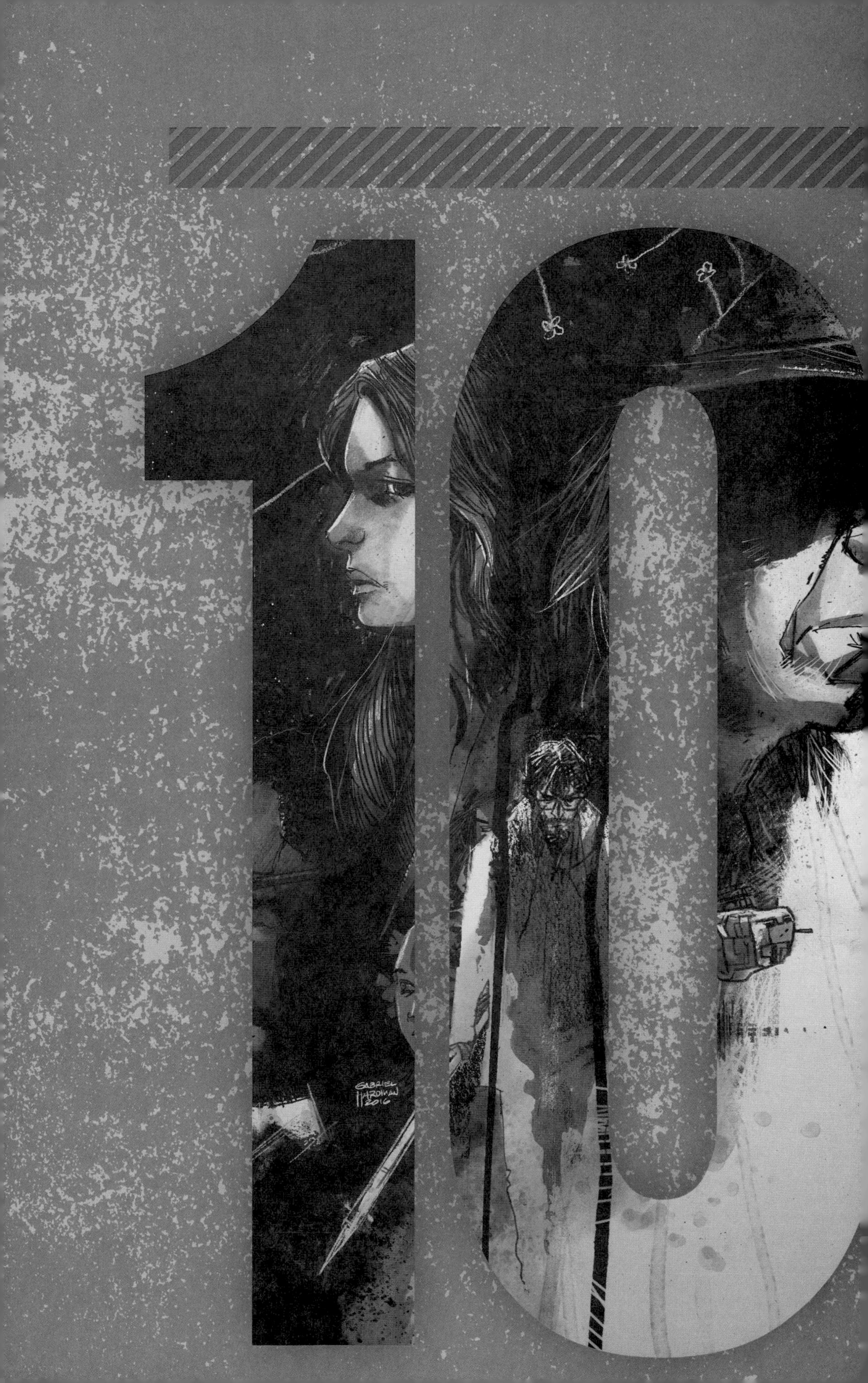
10
GABRIEL HARDMAN 2016

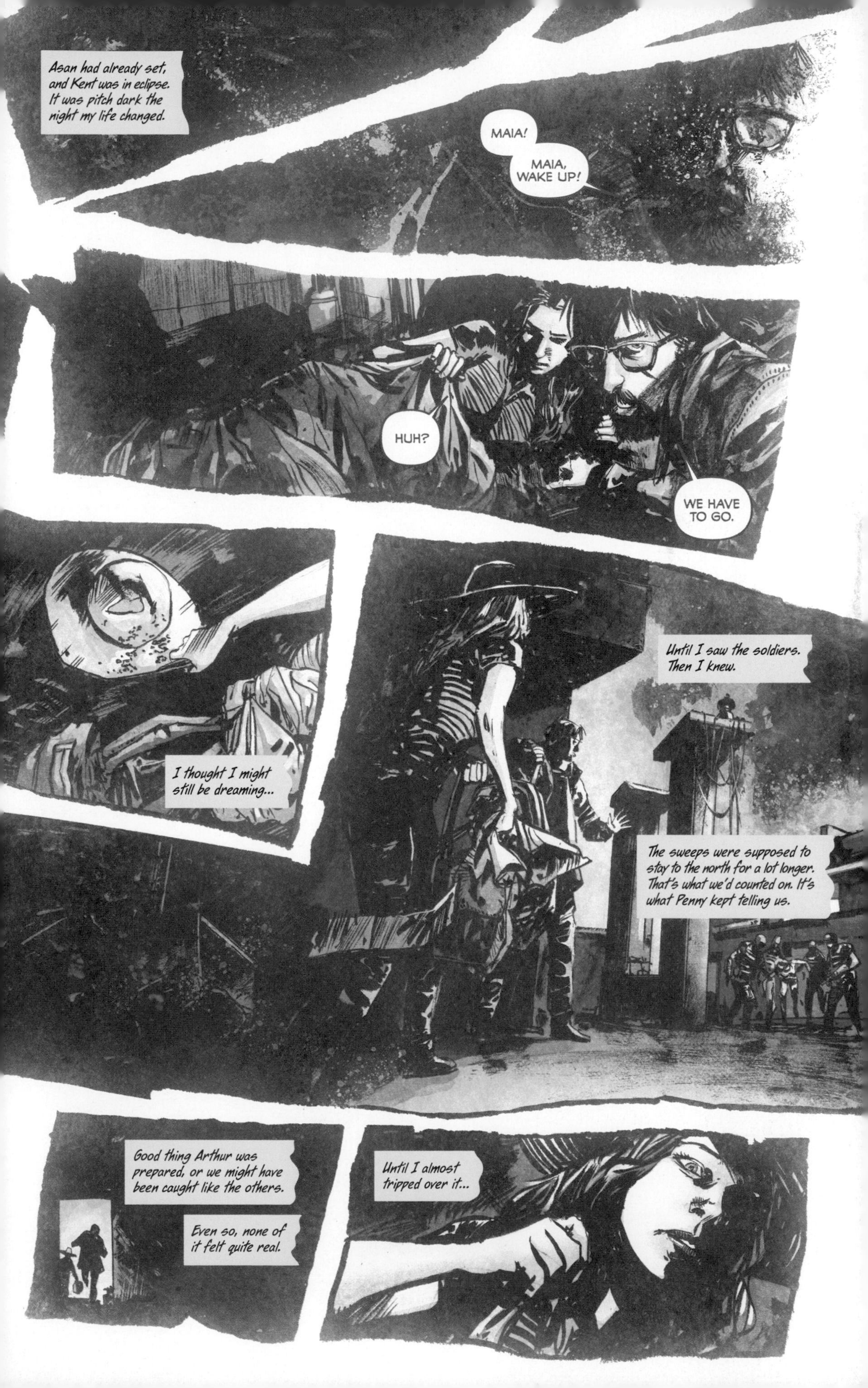

Asan had already set, and Kent was in eclipse. It was pitch dark the night my life changed.
MAIA!
MAIA, WAKE UP!
HUH?
WE HAVE TO GO.
I thought I might still be dreaming...
Until I saw the soldiers. Then I knew.
The sweeps were supposed to stay to the north for a lot longer. That's what we'd counted on. It's what Penny kept telling us.
Good thing Arthur was prepared, or we might have been caught like the others.
Even so, none of it felt quite real.
Until I almost tripped over it...

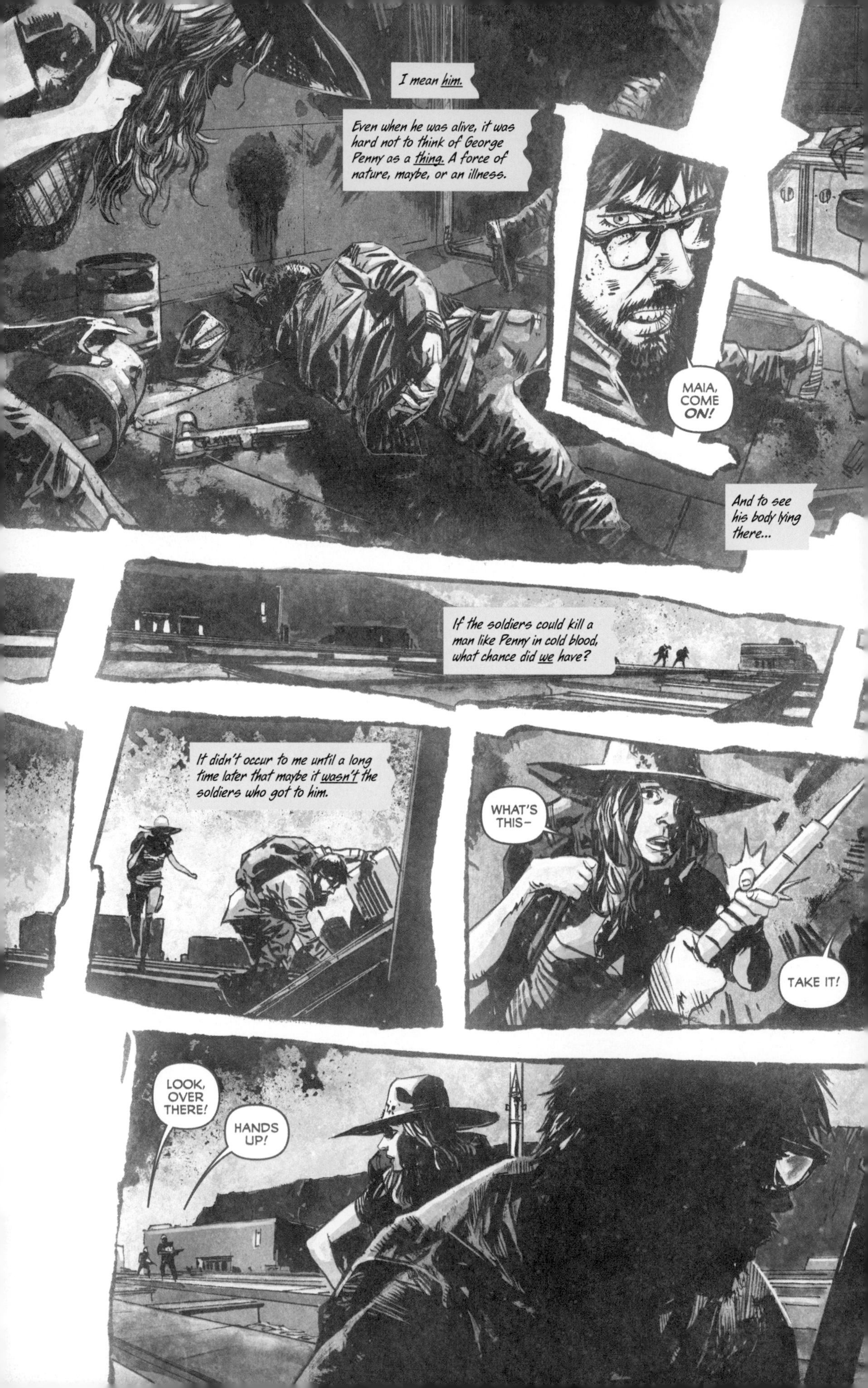
I mean him.
Even when he was alive, it was hard not to think of George Penny as a thing. A force of nature, maybe, or an illness.
MAIA, COME ON!
And to see his body lying there...
If the soldiers could kill a man like Penny in cold blood, what chance did we have?
It didn't occur to me until a long time later that maybe it wasn't the soldiers who got to him.
WHAT'S THIS–
TAKE IT!
LOOK, OVER THERE!
HANDS UP!

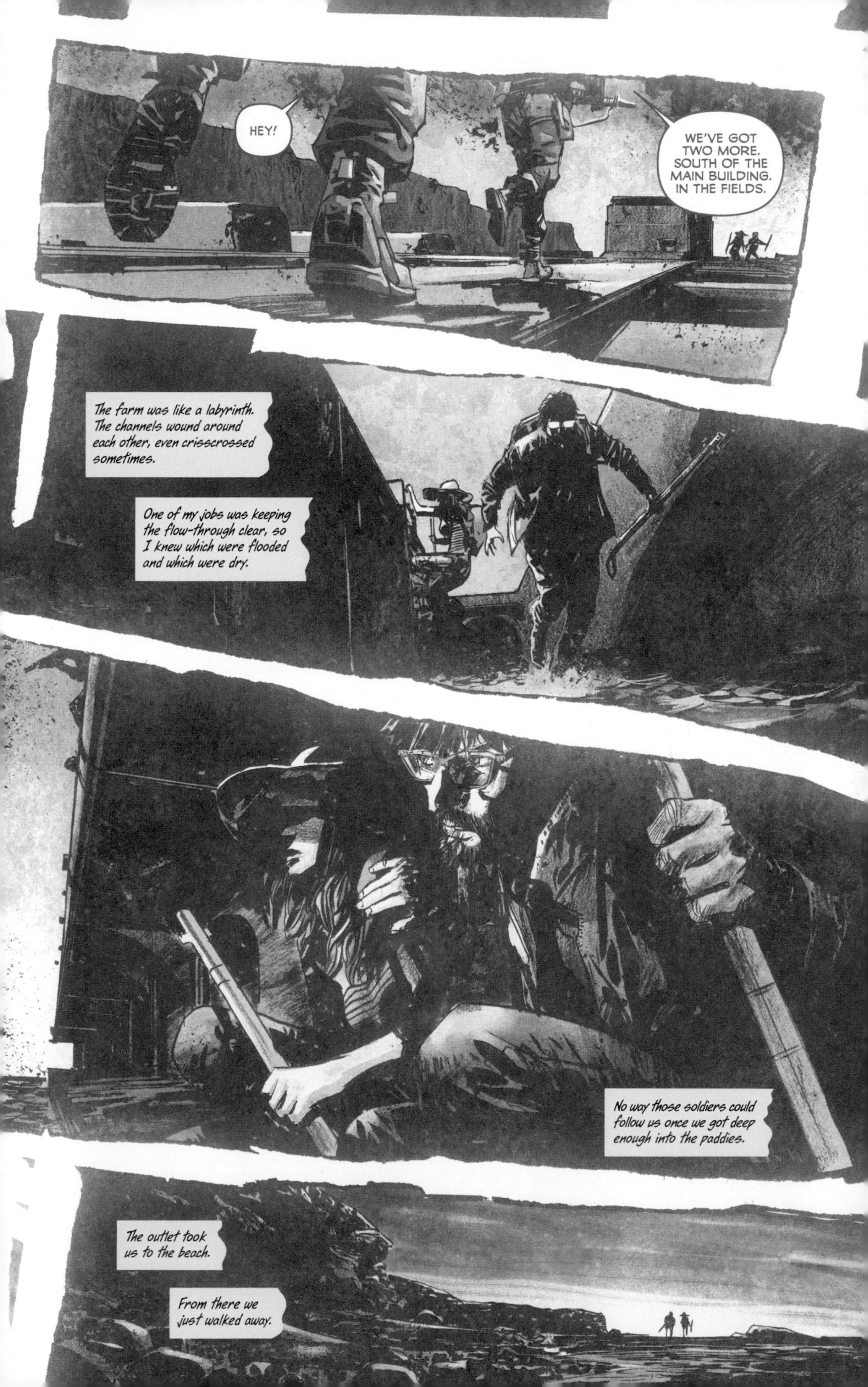
HEY!
WE'VE GOT TWO MORE. SOUTH OF THE MAIN BUILDING. IN THE FIELDS.
The farm was like a labyrinth. The channels wound around each other, even crisscrossed sometimes.
One of my jobs was keeping the flow-through clear, so I knew which were flooded and which were dry.
No way those soldiers could follow us once we got deep enough into the paddies.
The outlet took us to the beach.
From there we just walked away.

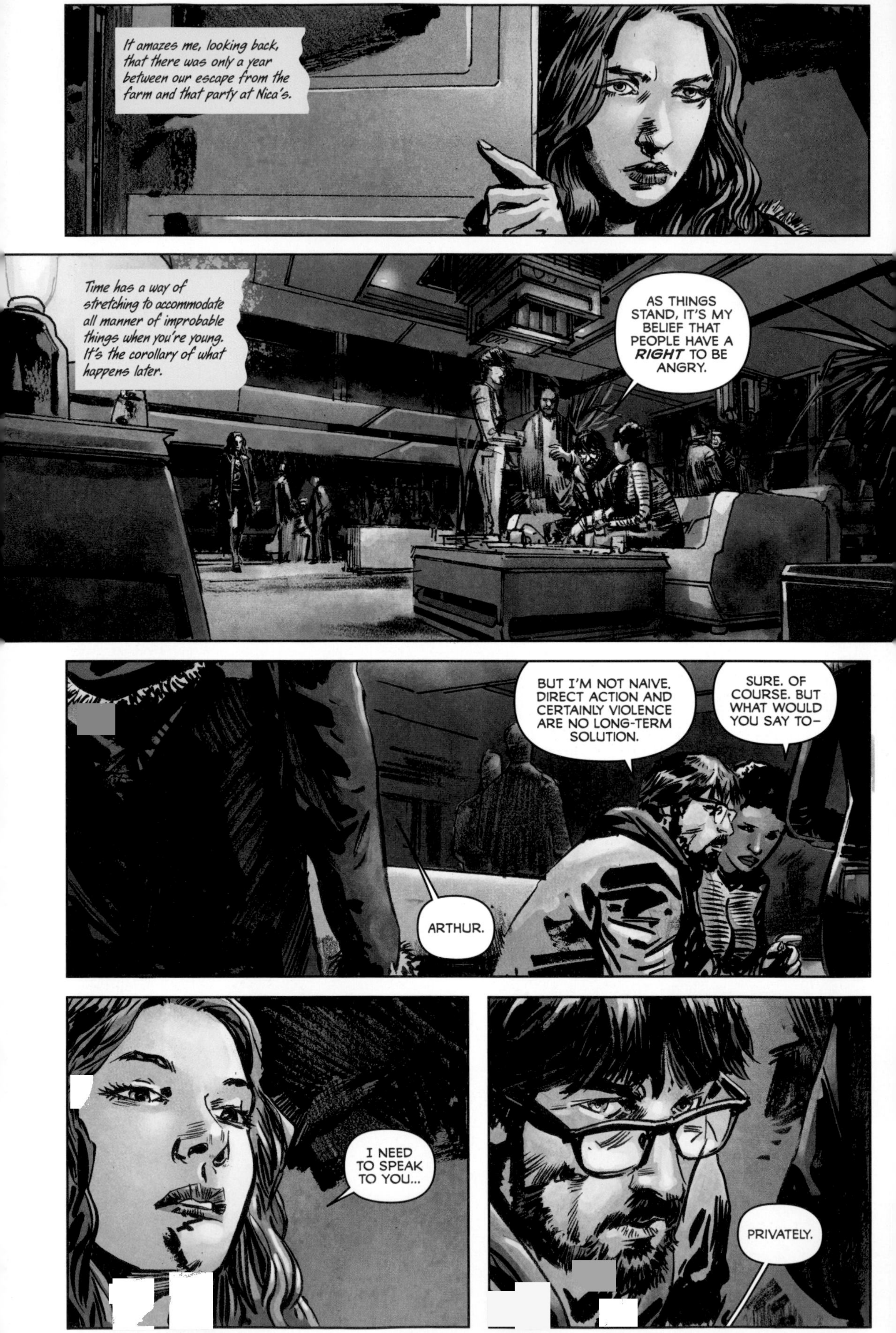
It amazes me, looking back, that there was only a year between our escape from the farm and that party at Nica's.
Time has a way of stretching to accommodate all manner of improbable things when you're young. It's the corollary of what happens later.
AS THINGS STAND, IT'S MY BELIEF THAT PEOPLE HAVE A ***RIGHT*** TO BE ANGRY.
BUT I'M NOT NAIVE. DIRECT ACTION AND CERTAINLY VIOLENCE ARE NO LONG-TERM SOLUTION.
SURE. OF COURSE. BUT WHAT WOULD YOU SAY TO–
ARTHUR.
I NEED TO SPEAK TO YOU...
PRIVATELY.

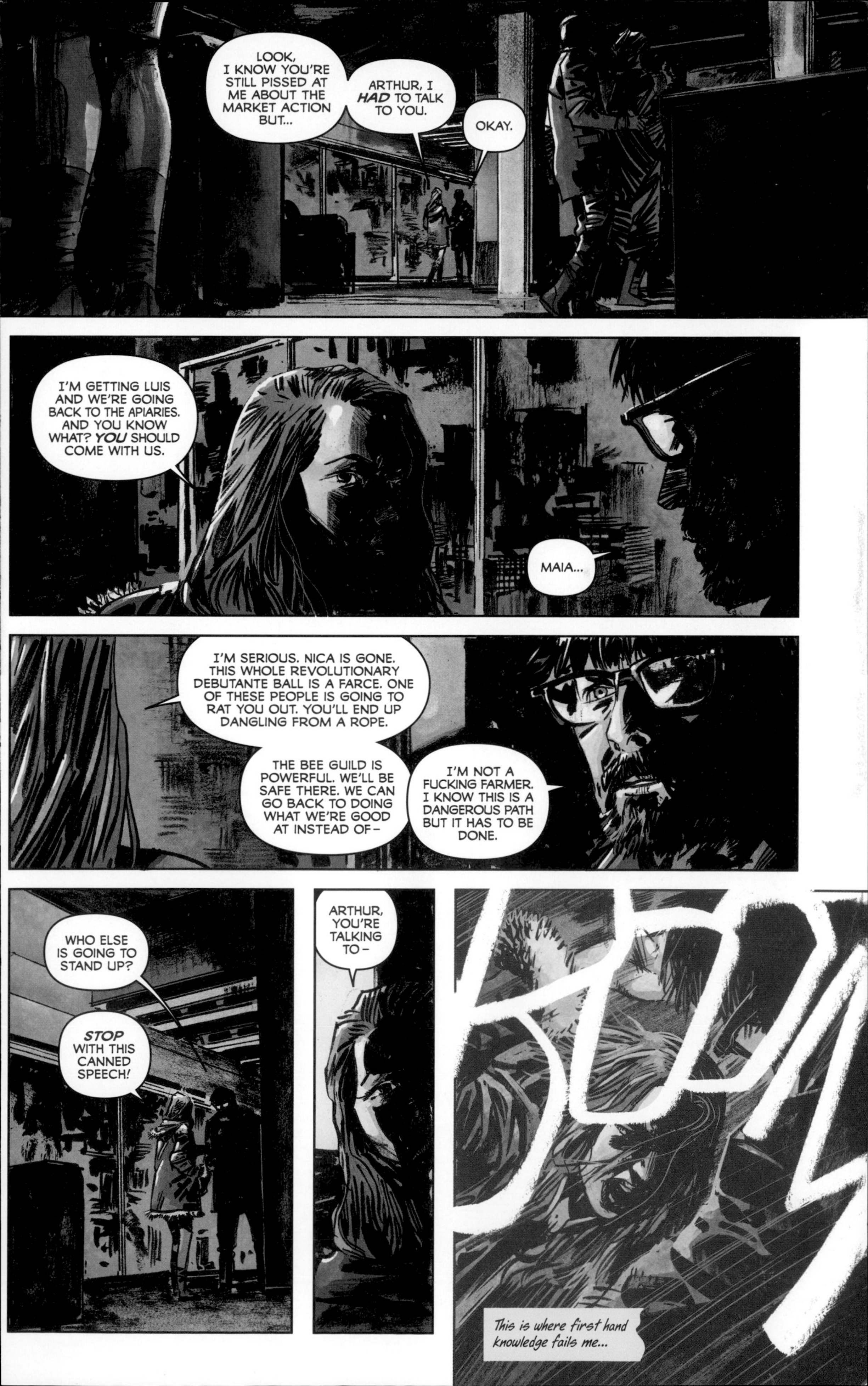
LOOK, I KNOW YOU'RE STILL PISSED AT ME ABOUT THE MARKET ACTION BUT...
ARTHUR, I *HAD* TO TALK TO YOU.
OKAY.
I'M GETTING LUIS AND WE'RE GOING BACK TO THE APIARIES. AND YOU KNOW WHAT? *YOU* SHOULD COME WITH US.
MAIA...
I'M SERIOUS. NICA IS GONE. THIS WHOLE REVOLUTIONARY DEBUTANTE BALL IS A FARCE. ONE OF THESE PEOPLE IS GOING TO RAT YOU OUT. YOU'LL END UP DANGLING FROM A ROPE.
THE BEE GUILD IS POWERFUL. WE'LL BE SAFE THERE. WE CAN GO BACK TO DOING WHAT WE'RE GOOD AT INSTEAD OF–
I'M NOT A FUCKING FARMER. I KNOW THIS IS A DANGEROUS PATH BUT IT HAS TO BE DONE.
WHO ELSE IS GOING TO STAND UP?
STOP WITH THIS CANNED SPEECH!
ARTHUR, YOU'RE TALKING TO–
This is where first hand knowledge fails me...

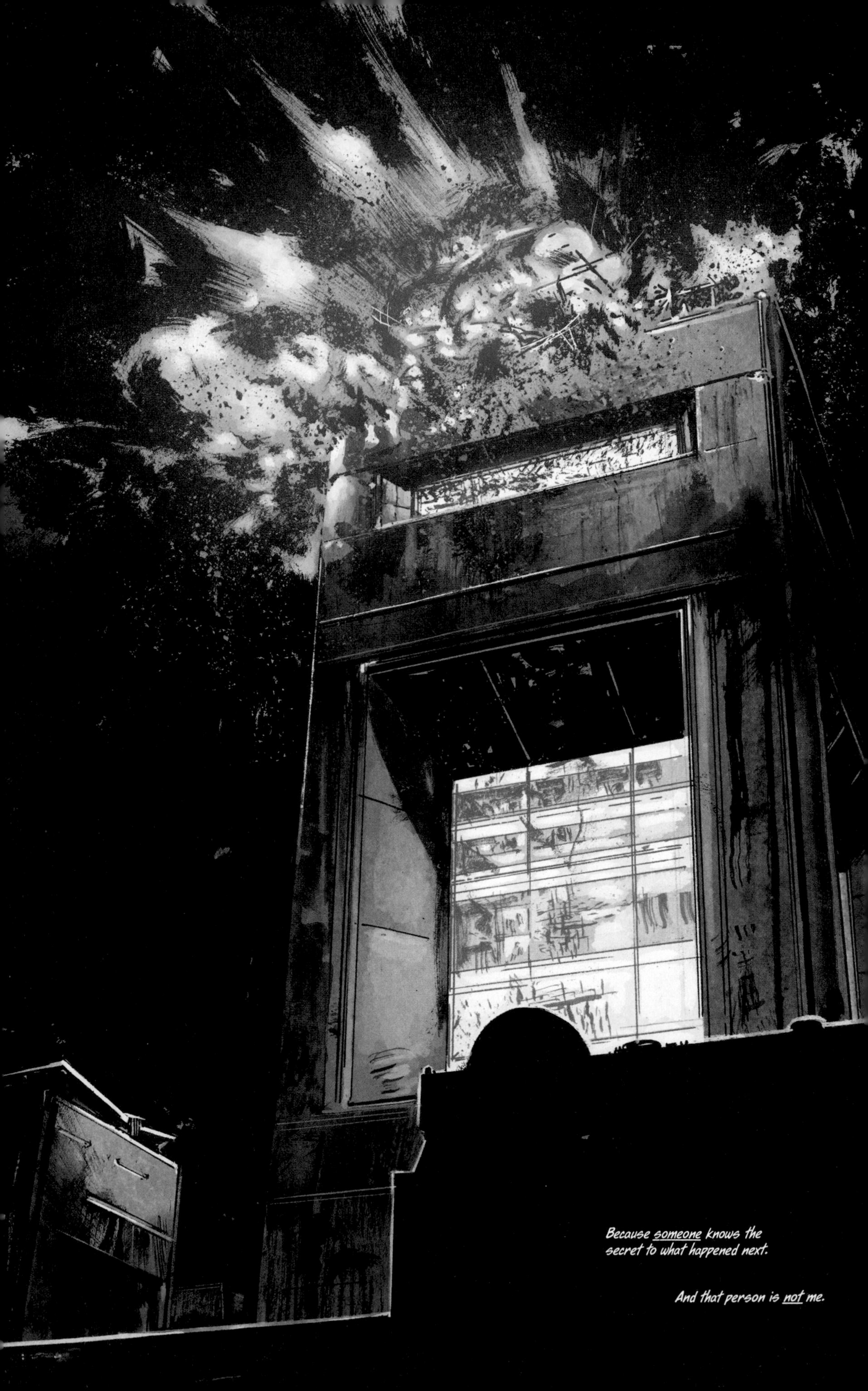
Because someone knows the secret to what happened next.
And that person is not me.

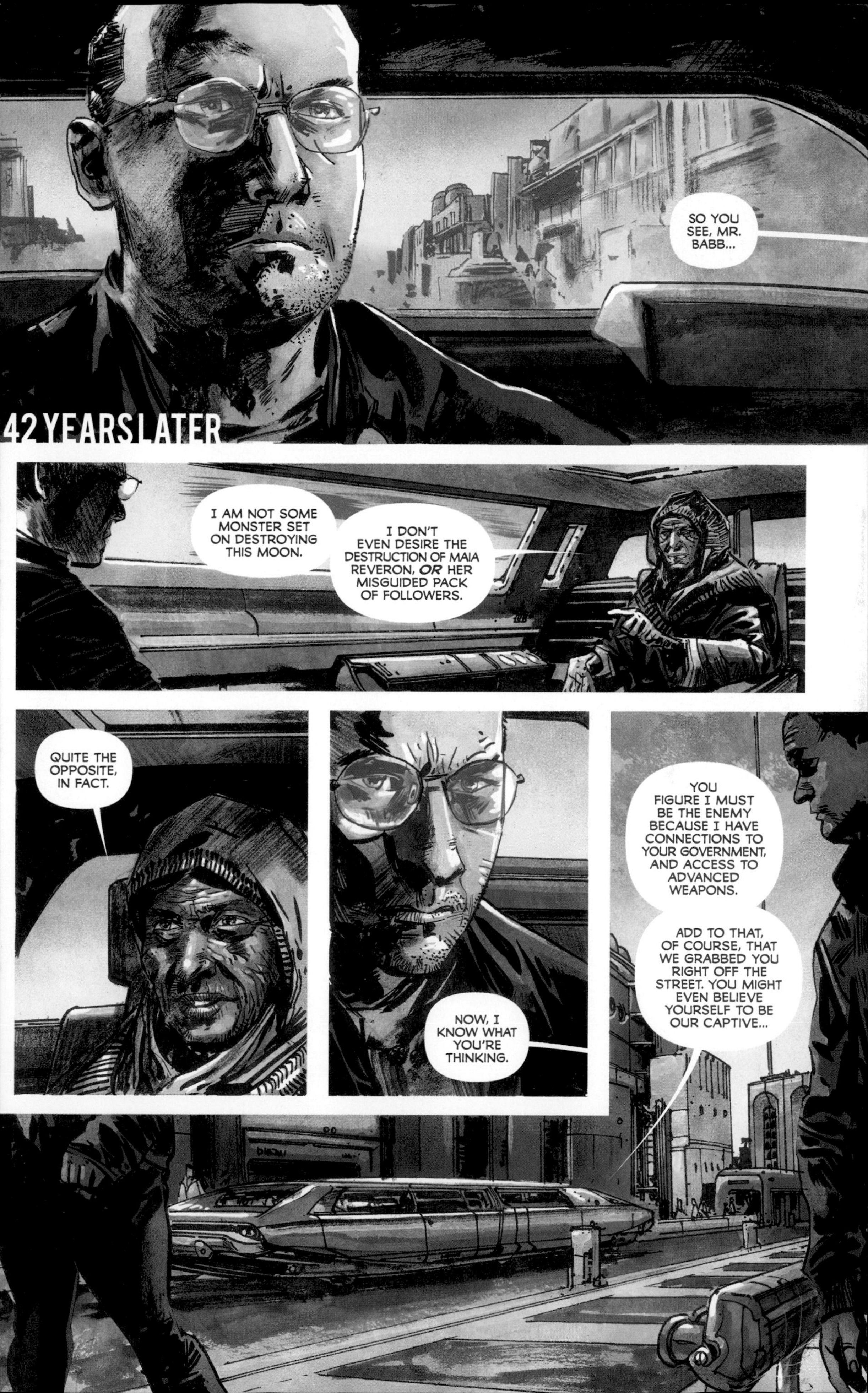
SO YOU SEE, MR. BABB...
42 YEARS LATER
I AM NOT SOME MONSTER SET ON DESTROYING THIS MOON.
I DON'T EVEN DESIRE THE DESTRUCTION OF MAIA REVERON, **OR** HER MISGUIDED PACK OF FOLLOWERS.
QUITE THE OPPOSITE, IN FACT.
NOW, I KNOW WHAT YOU'RE THINKING.
YOU FIGURE I MUST BE THE ENEMY BECAUSE I HAVE CONNECTIONS TO YOUR GOVERNMENT, AND ACCESS TO ADVANCED WEAPONS.
ADD TO THAT, OF COURSE, THAT WE GRABBED YOU RIGHT OFF THE STREET. YOU MIGHT EVEN BELIEVE YOURSELF TO BE OUR CAPTIVE...

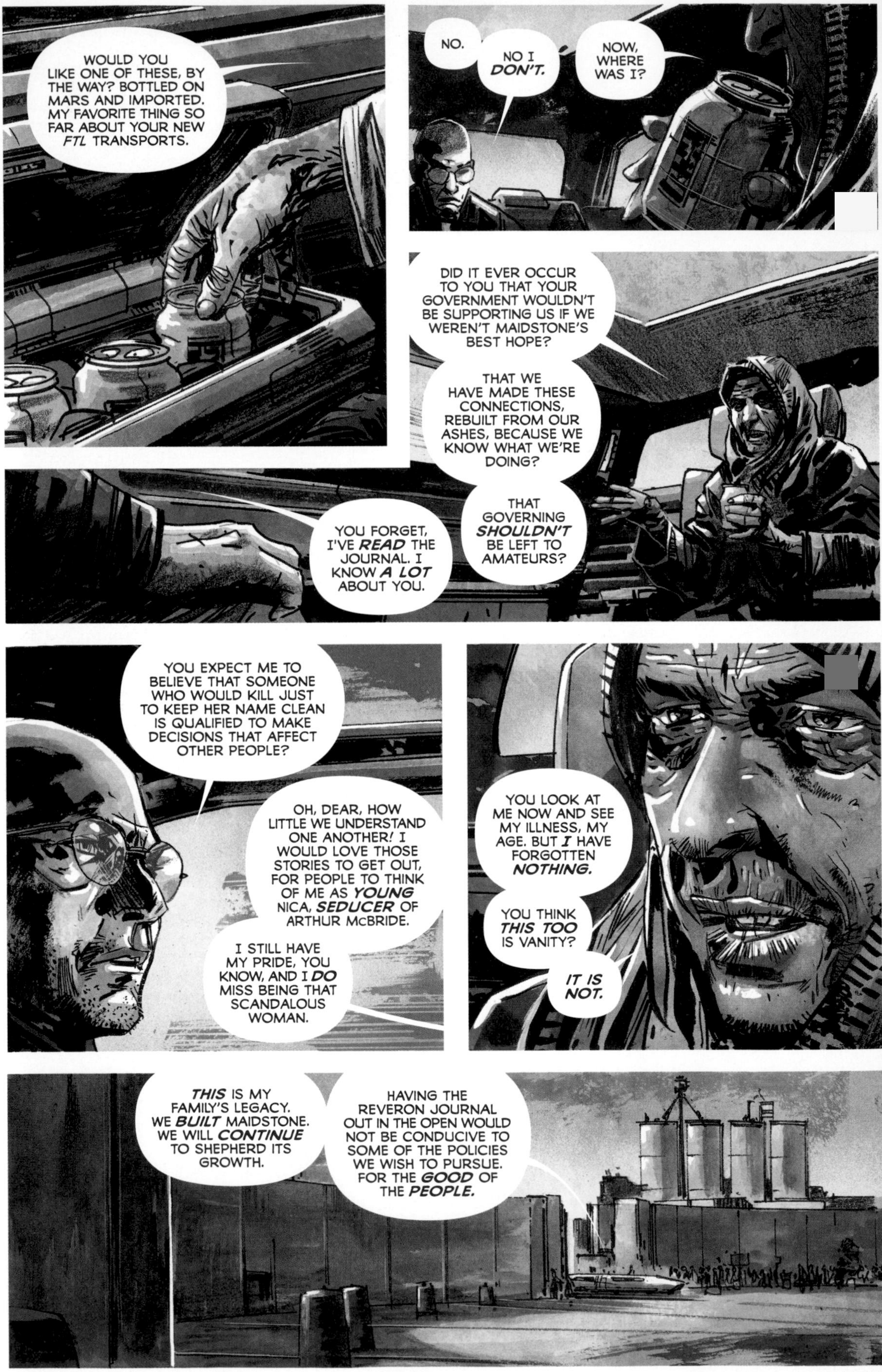
WOULD YOU LIKE ONE OF THESE, BY THE WAY? BOTTLED ON MARS AND IMPORTED. MY FAVORITE THING SO FAR ABOUT YOUR NEW *FTL* TRANSPORTS.
NO.
NO I ***DON'T.***
NOW, WHERE WAS I?
DID IT EVER OCCUR TO YOU THAT YOUR GOVERNMENT WOULDN'T BE SUPPORTING US IF WE WEREN'T MAIDSTONE'S BEST HOPE?
THAT WE HAVE MADE THESE CONNECTIONS, REBUILT FROM OUR ASHES, BECAUSE WE KNOW WHAT WE'RE DOING?
THAT GOVERNING ***SHOULDN'T*** BE LEFT TO AMATEURS?
YOU FORGET, I'VE ***READ*** THE JOURNAL. I KNOW ***A LOT*** ABOUT YOU.
YOU EXPECT ME TO BELIEVE THAT SOMEONE WHO WOULD KILL JUST TO KEEP HER NAME CLEAN IS QUALIFIED TO MAKE DECISIONS THAT AFFECT OTHER PEOPLE?
OH, DEAR, HOW LITTLE WE UNDERSTAND ONE ANOTHER*!* I WOULD LOVE THOSE STORIES TO GET OUT, FOR PEOPLE TO THINK OF ME AS ***YOUNG*** NICA, ***SEDUCER*** OF ARTHUR McBRIDE.
I STILL HAVE MY PRIDE, YOU KNOW, AND I ***DO*** MISS BEING THAT SCANDALOUS WOMAN.
YOU LOOK AT ME NOW AND SEE MY ILLNESS, MY AGE. BUT ***I*** HAVE FORGOTTEN ***NOTHING.***
YOU THINK ***THIS TOO*** IS VANITY?
IT IS NOT.
THIS IS MY FAMILY'S LEGACY. WE ***BUILT*** MAIDSTONE. WE WILL ***CONTINUE*** TO SHEPHERD ITS GROWTH.
HAVING THE REVERON JOURNAL OUT IN THE OPEN WOULD NOT BE CONDUCIVE TO SOME OF THE POLICIES WE WISH TO PURSUE. FOR THE ***GOOD*** OF THE ***PEOPLE.***

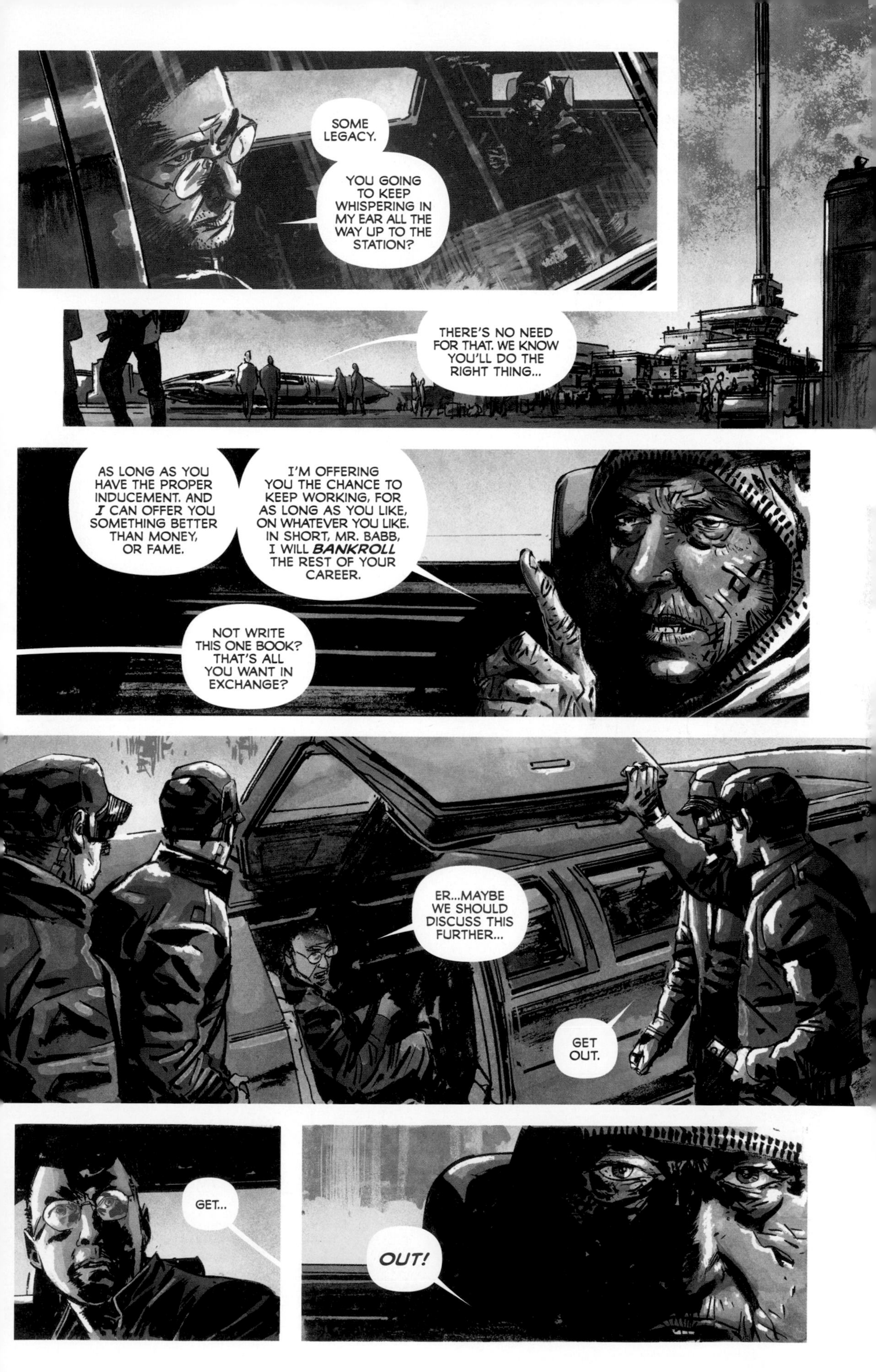
SOME LEGACY.
YOU GOING TO KEEP WHISPERING IN MY EAR ALL THE WAY UP TO THE STATION?
THERE'S NO NEED FOR THAT. WE KNOW YOU'LL DO THE RIGHT THING...
AS LONG AS YOU HAVE THE PROPER INDUCEMENT. AND *I* CAN OFFER YOU SOMETHING BETTER THAN MONEY, OR FAME.
I'M OFFERING YOU THE CHANCE TO KEEP WORKING, FOR AS LONG AS YOU LIKE, ON WHATEVER YOU LIKE. IN SHORT, MR. BABB, I WILL ***BANKROLL*** THE REST OF YOUR CAREER.
NOT WRITE THIS ONE BOOK? THAT'S ALL YOU WANT IN EXCHANGE?
ER...MAYBE WE SHOULD DISCUSS THIS FURTHER...
GET OUT.
GET...
OUT!

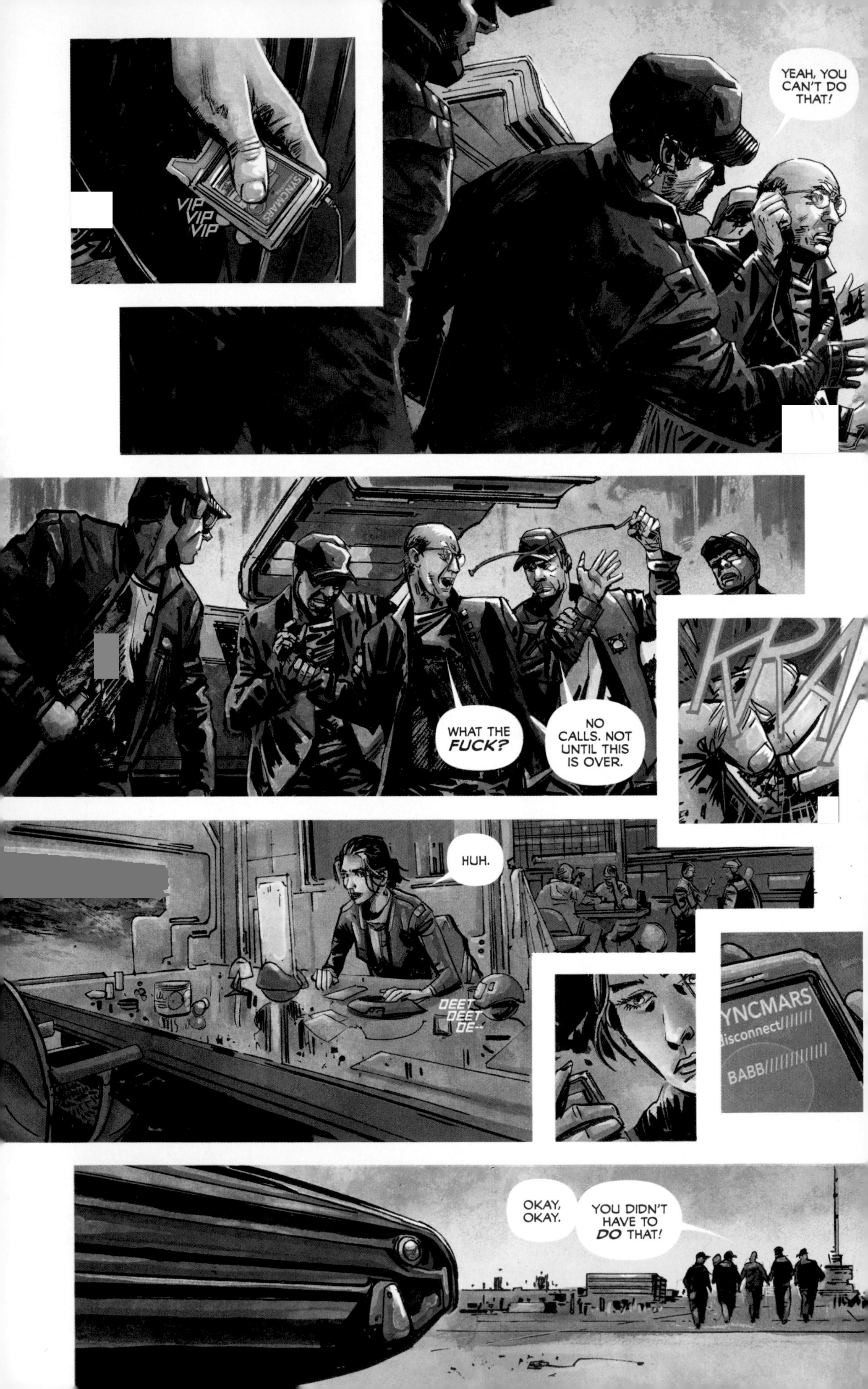
SYNCMARS
VIP VIP VIP
YEAH, YOU CAN'T DO THAT!
WHAT THE *FUCK?*
NO CALLS. NOT UNTIL THIS IS OVER.
HUH.
DEET DEET DE--
YNCMARS
disconnect///////
BABB//////////
OKAY, OKAY.
YOU DIDN'T HAVE TO *DO* THAT!

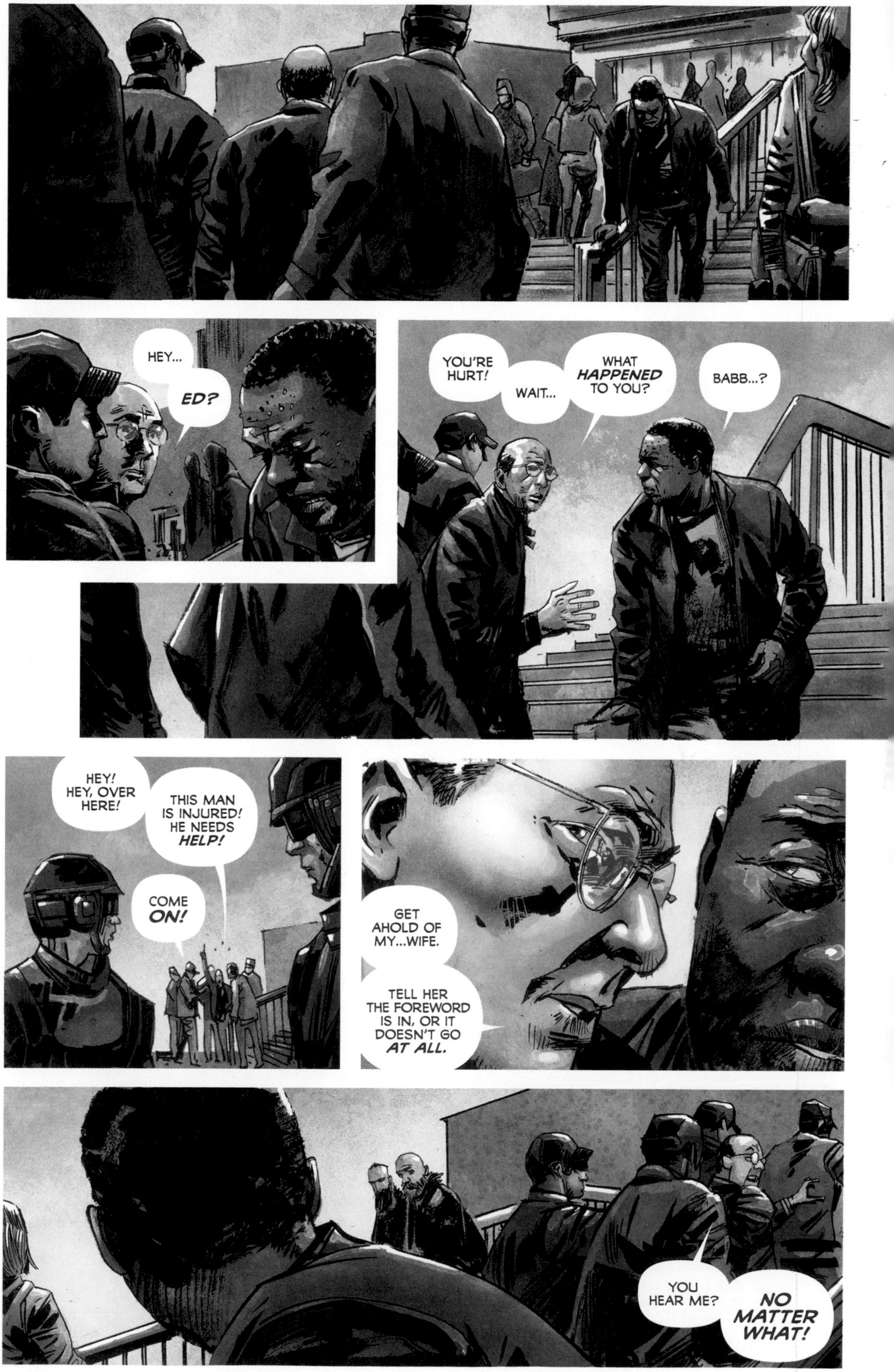
HEY...
ED?
YOU'RE HURT!
WAIT...
WHAT *HAPPENED* TO YOU?
BABB...?
HEY! HEY, OVER HERE!
THIS MAN IS INJURED! HE NEEDS *HELP!*
COME *ON!*
GET AHOLD OF MY...WIFE.
TELL HER THE FOREWORD IS IN, OR IT DOESN'T GO *AT ALL.*
YOU HEAR ME?
NO MATTER WHAT!

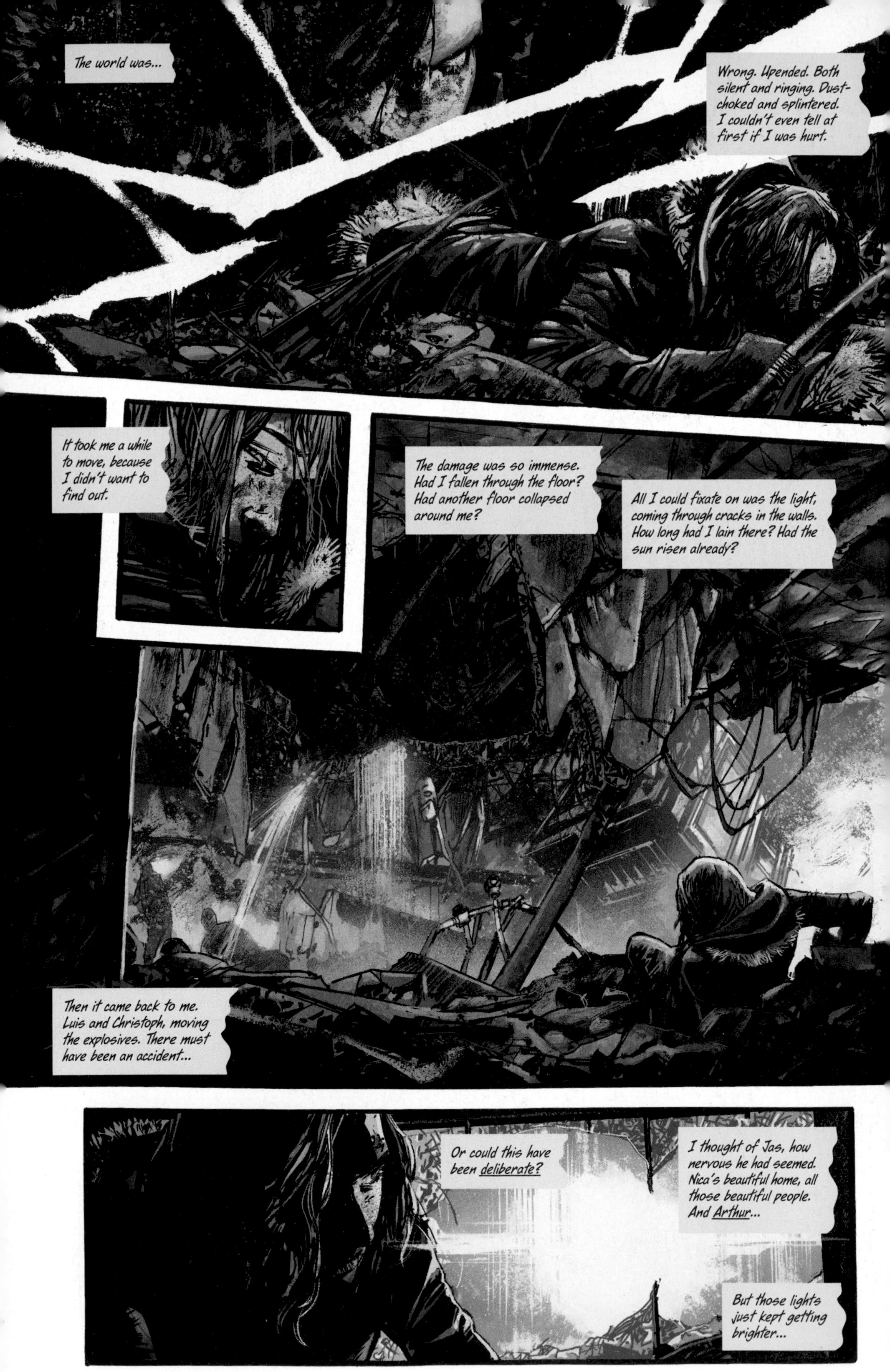
The world was...
Wrong. Upended. Both silent and ringing. Dust-choked and splintered. I couldn't even tell at first if I was hurt.
It took me a while to move, because I didn't want to find out.
The damage was so immense. Had I fallen through the floor? Had another floor collapsed around me?
All I could fixate on was the light, coming through cracks in the walls. How long had I lain there? Had the sun risen already?
Then it came back to me. Luis and Christoph, moving the explosives. There must have been an accident...
Or could this have been deliberate?
I thought of Jas, how nervous he had seemed. Nica's beautiful home, all those beautiful people. And Arthur...
But those lights just kept getting brighter...

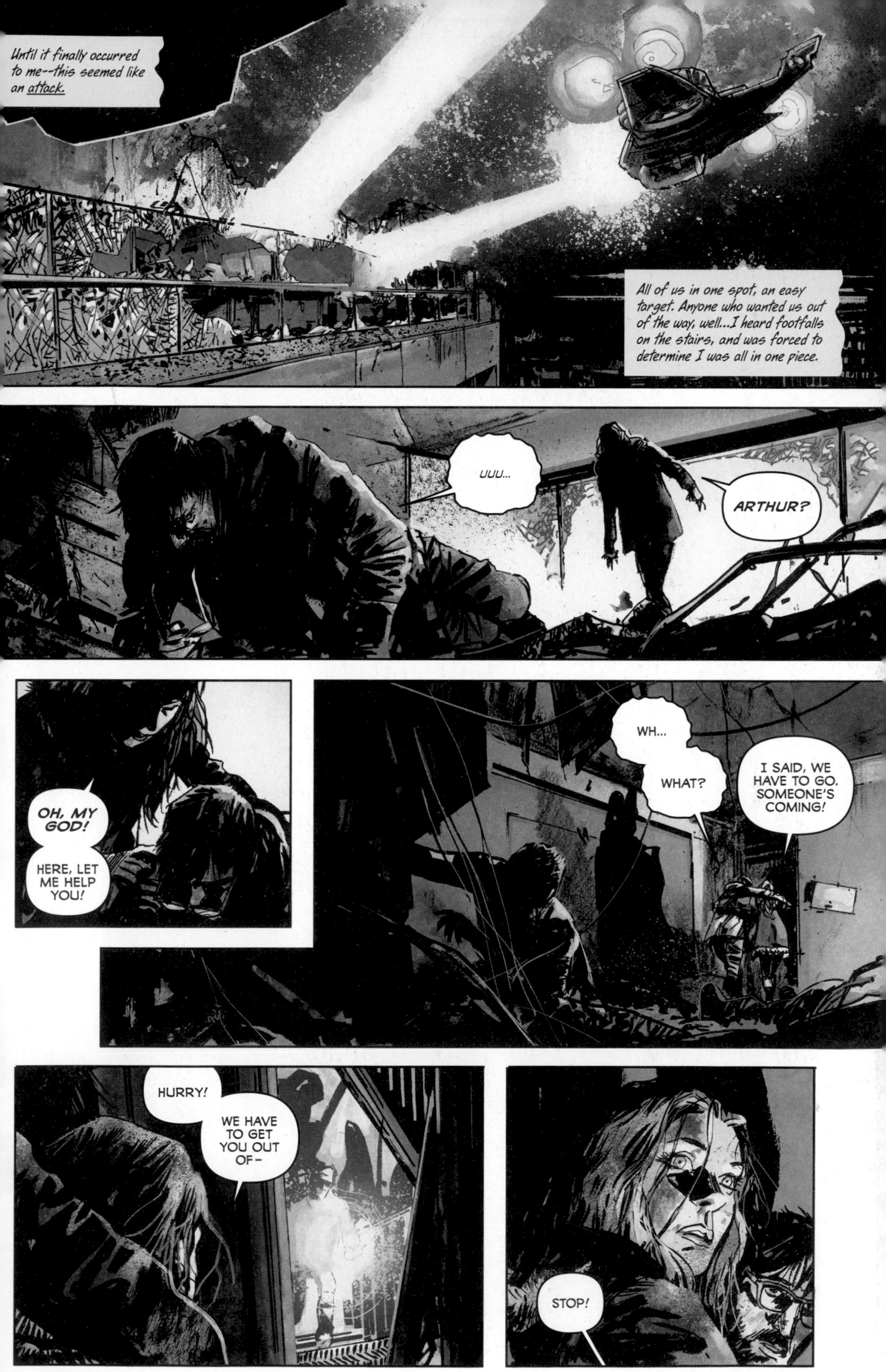
Until it finally occurred to me--this seemed like an attack.
All of us in one spot, an easy target. Anyone who wanted us out of the way, well...I heard footfalls on the stairs, and was forced to determine I was all in one piece.
UUU...
ARTHUR?
OH, MY GOD!
HERE, LET ME HELP YOU!
WH...
WHAT?
I SAID, WE HAVE TO GO. SOMEONE'S COMING!
HURRY!
WE HAVE TO GET YOU OUT OF-
STOP!

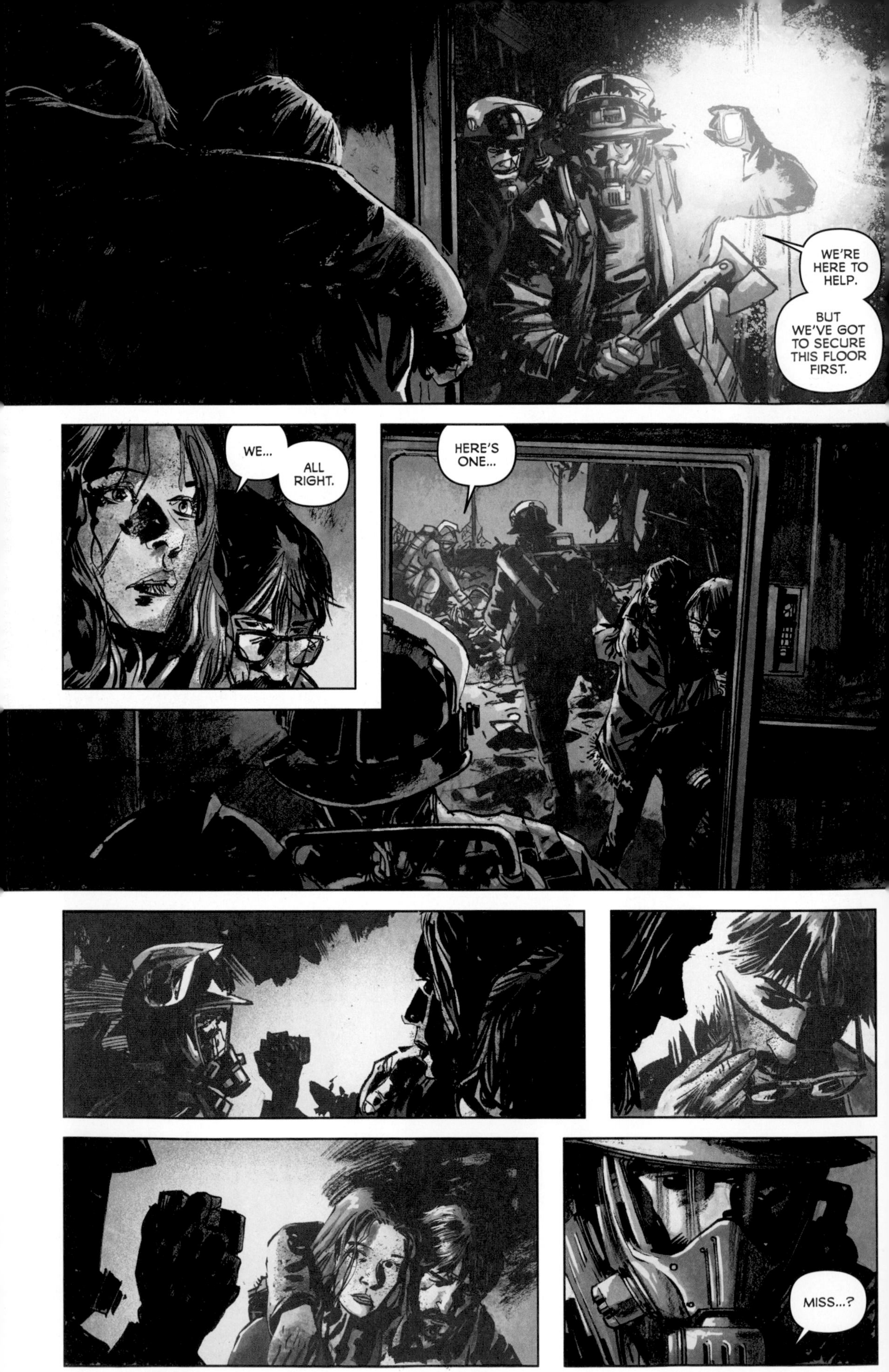
WE'RE HERE TO HELP.
BUT WE'VE GOT TO SECURE THIS FLOOR FIRST.
WE... ALL RIGHT.
HERE'S ONE...
MISS...?

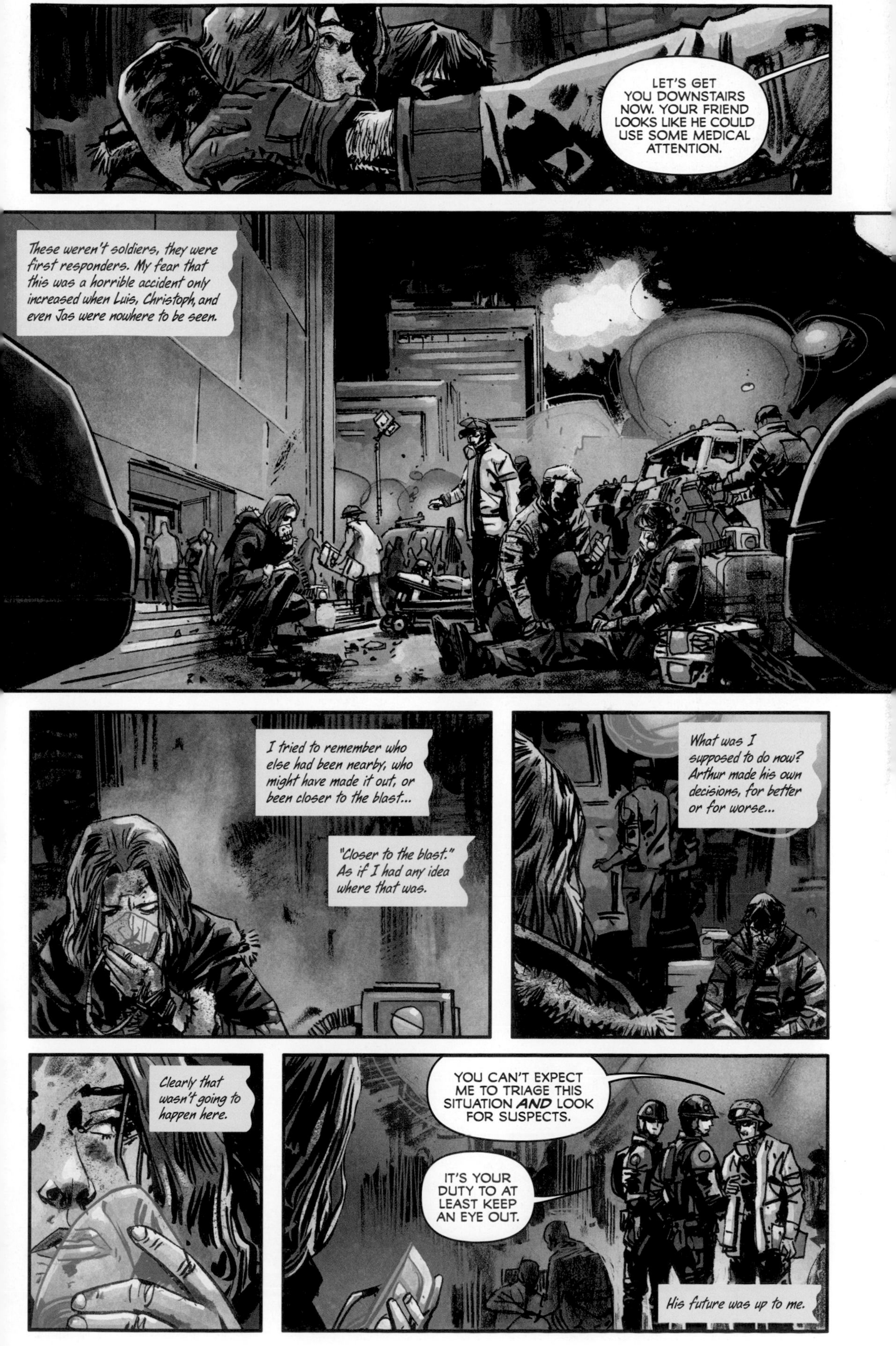
LET'S GET YOU DOWNSTAIRS NOW. YOUR FRIEND LOOKS LIKE HE COULD USE SOME MEDICAL ATTENTION.
These weren't soldiers, they were first responders. My fear that this was a horrible accident only increased when Luis, Christoph, and even Jas were nowhere to be seen.
I tried to remember who else had been nearby, who might have made it out, or been closer to the blast...
"Closer to the blast." As if I had any idea where that was.
What was I supposed to do now? Arthur made his own decisions, for better or for worse...
Clearly that wasn't going to happen here.
YOU CAN'T EXPECT ME TO TRIAGE THIS SITUATION ***AND*** LOOK FOR SUSPECTS.
IT'S YOUR DUTY TO AT LEAST KEEP AN EYE OUT.
His future was up to me.

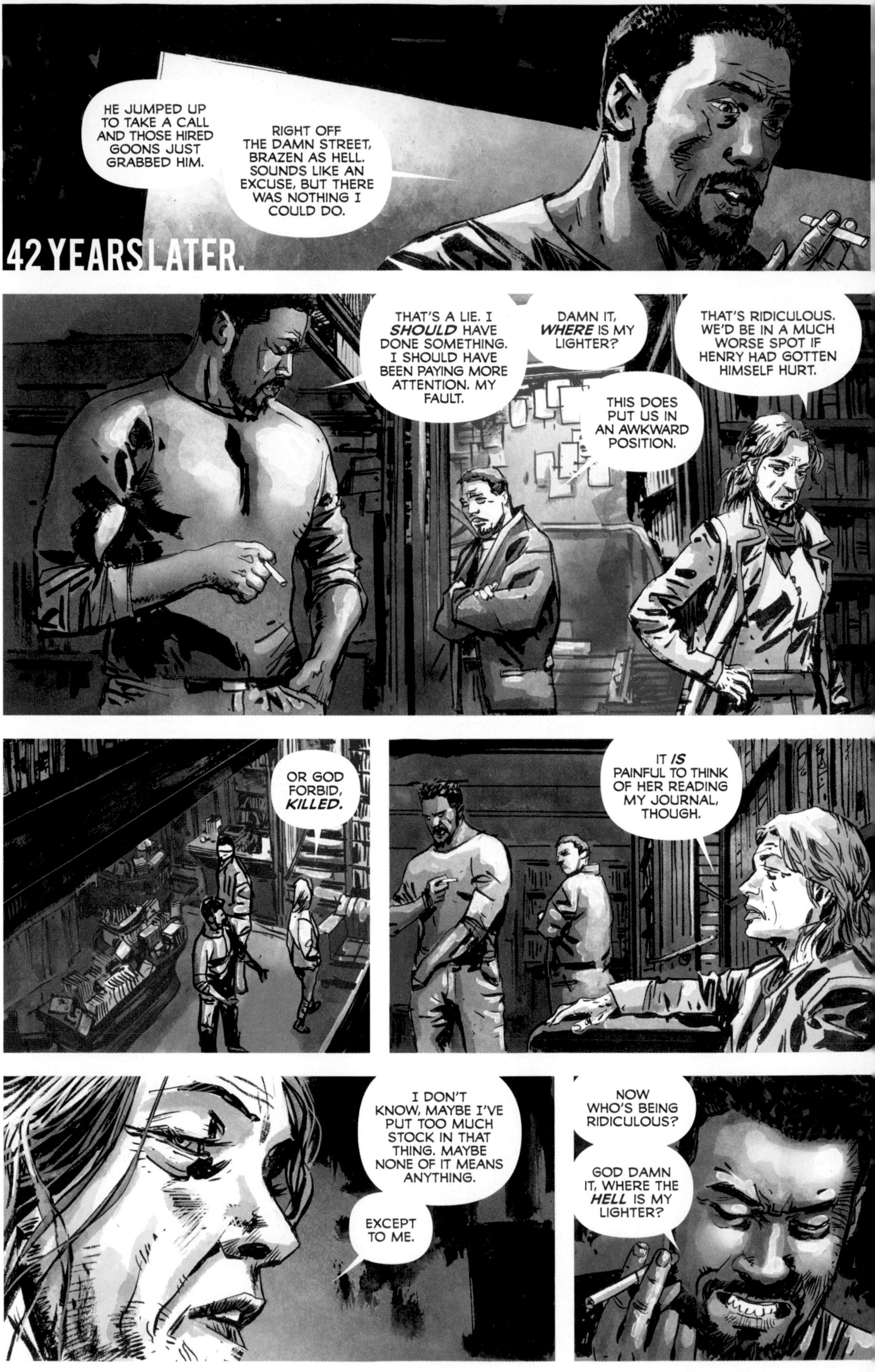
HE JUMPED UP TO TAKE A CALL AND THOSE HIRED GOONS JUST GRABBED HIM.
RIGHT OFF THE DAMN STREET, BRAZEN AS HELL. SOUNDS LIKE AN EXCUSE, BUT THERE WAS NOTHING I COULD DO.
42 YEARS LATER.
THAT'S A LIE. I *SHOULD* HAVE DONE SOMETHING. I SHOULD HAVE BEEN PAYING MORE ATTENTION. MY FAULT.
DAMN IT, *WHERE* IS MY LIGHTER?
THIS DOES PUT US IN AN AWKWARD POSITION.
THAT'S RIDICULOUS. WE'D BE IN A MUCH WORSE SPOT IF HENRY HAD GOTTEN HIMSELF HURT.
OR GOD FORBID, *KILLED.*
IT *IS* PAINFUL TO THINK OF HER READING MY JOURNAL, THOUGH.
I DON'T KNOW, MAYBE I'VE PUT TOO MUCH STOCK IN THAT THING. MAYBE NONE OF IT MEANS ANYTHING.
EXCEPT TO ME.
NOW WHO'S BEING RIDICULOUS?
GOD DAMN IT, WHERE THE *HELL* IS MY LIGHTER?

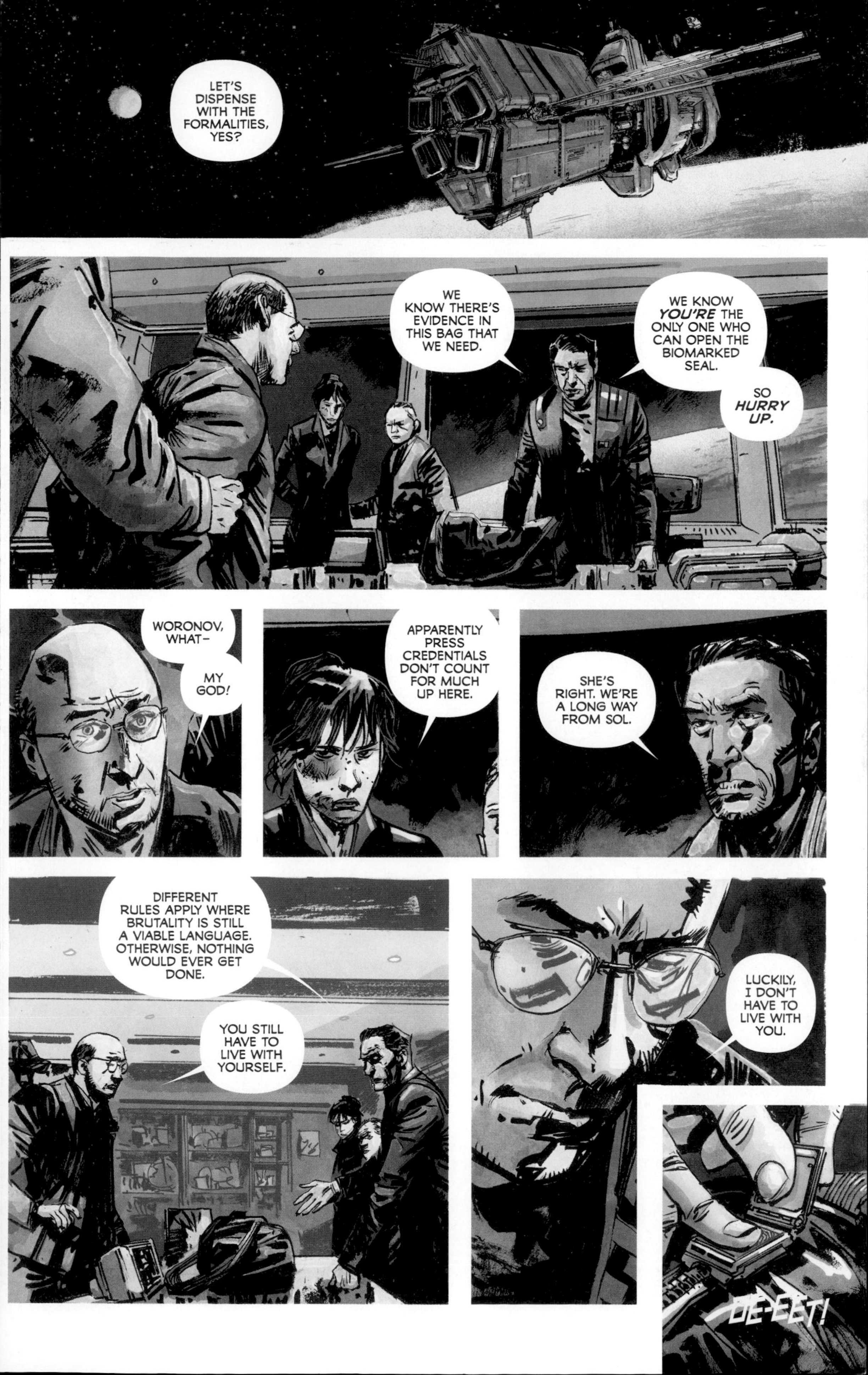
LET'S DISPENSE WITH THE FORMALITIES, YES?
WE KNOW THERE'S EVIDENCE IN THIS BAG THAT WE NEED.
WE KNOW *YOU'RE* THE ONLY ONE WHO CAN OPEN THE BIOMARKED SEAL.
SO *HURRY UP.*
WORONOV, WHAT–
MY GOD!
APPARENTLY PRESS CREDENTIALS DON'T COUNT FOR MUCH UP HERE.
SHE'S RIGHT. WE'RE A LONG WAY FROM SOL.
DIFFERENT RULES APPLY WHERE BRUTALITY IS STILL A VIABLE LANGUAGE. OTHERWISE, NOTHING WOULD EVER GET DONE.
YOU STILL HAVE TO LIVE WITH YOURSELF.
LUCKILY, I DON'T HAVE TO LIVE WITH YOU.
BE-EET!

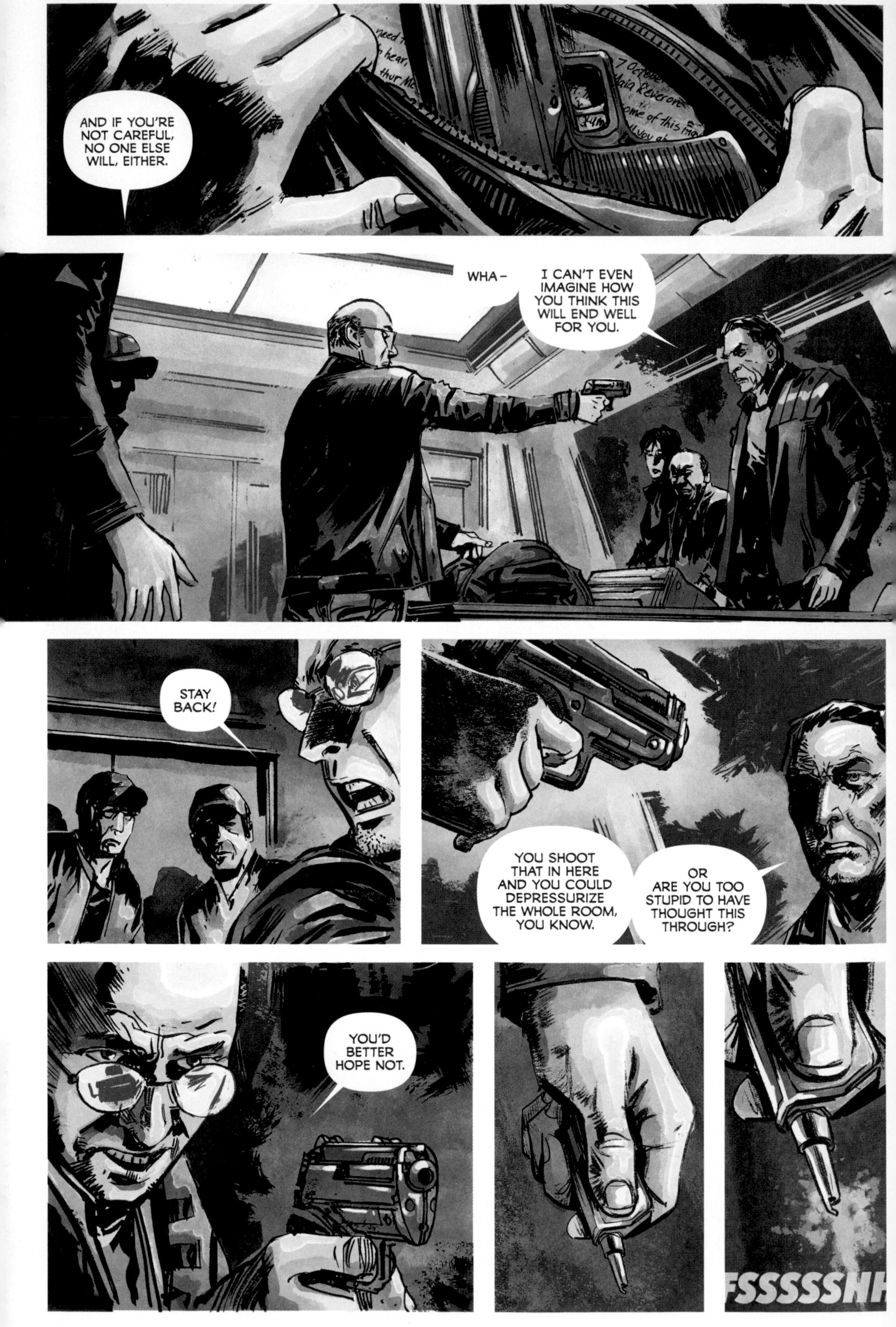
AND IF YOU'RE NOT CAREFUL, NO ONE ELSE WILL, EITHER.
WHA–
I CAN'T EVEN IMAGINE HOW YOU THINK THIS WILL END WELL FOR YOU.
STAY BACK!
YOU SHOOT THAT IN HERE AND YOU COULD DEPRESSURIZE THE WHOLE ROOM, YOU KNOW.
OR ARE YOU TOO STUPID TO HAVE THOUGHT THIS THROUGH?
YOU'D BETTER HOPE NOT.
FSSSSSH

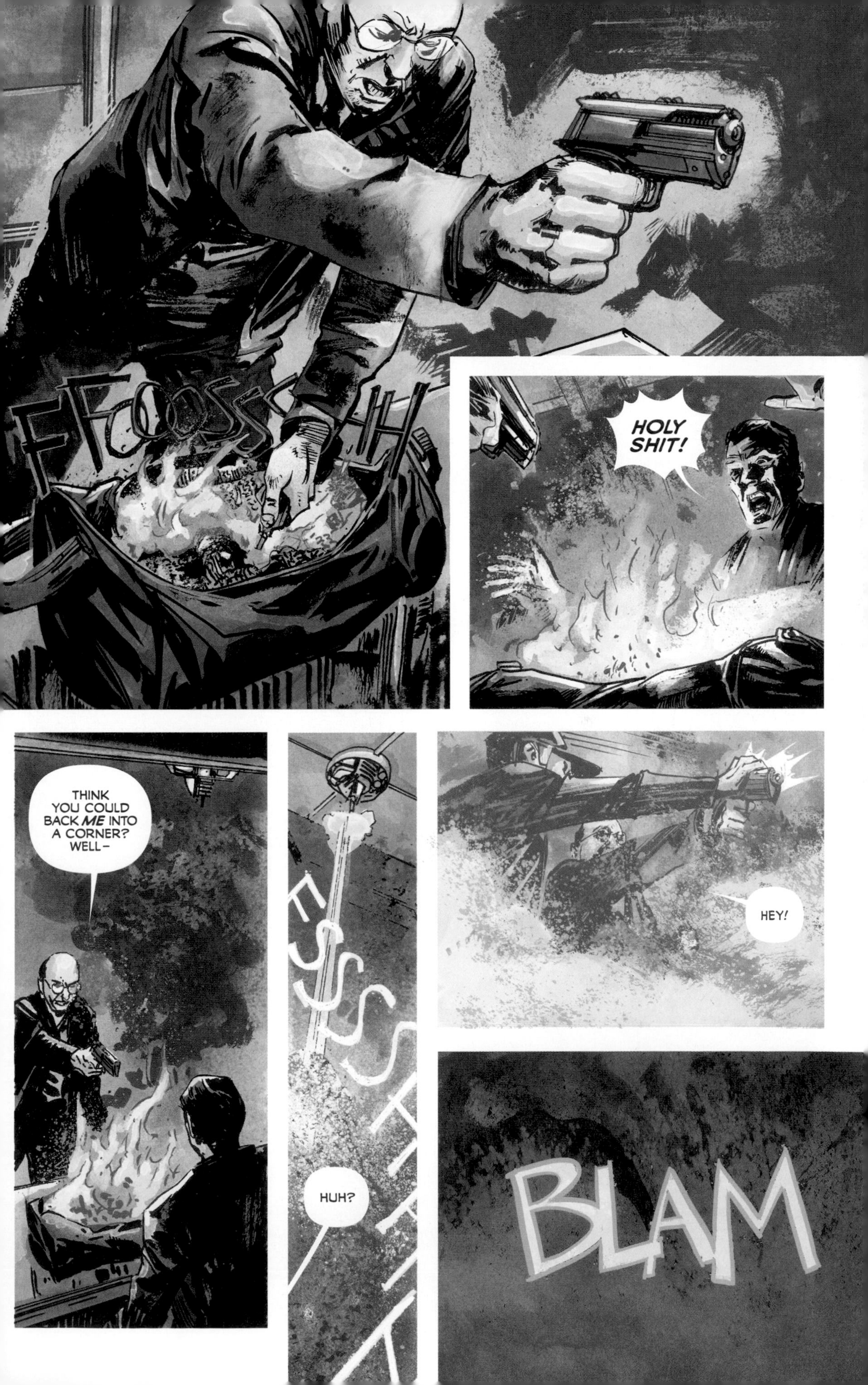
FFOOSSHH
HOLY SHIT!
THINK YOU COULD BACK *ME* INTO A CORNER? WELL–
ESSSHHH
HUH?
HEY!
BLAM

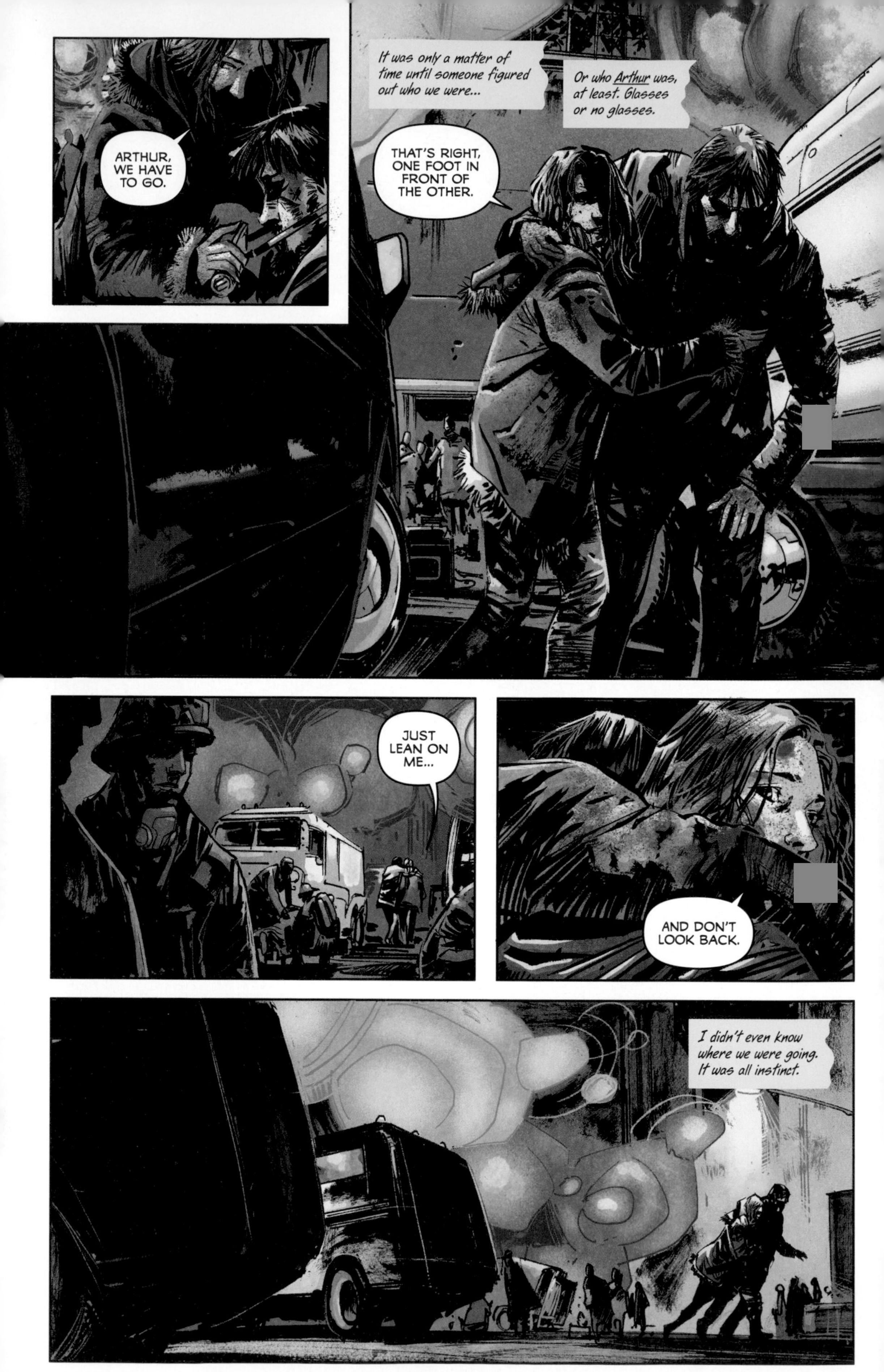
ARTHUR, WE HAVE TO GO.
It was only a matter of time until someone figured out who we were...
Or who Arthur was, at least. Glasses or no glasses.
THAT'S RIGHT, ONE FOOT IN FRONT OF THE OTHER.
JUST LEAN ON ME...
AND DON'T LOOK BACK.
I didn't even know where we were going. It was all instinct.

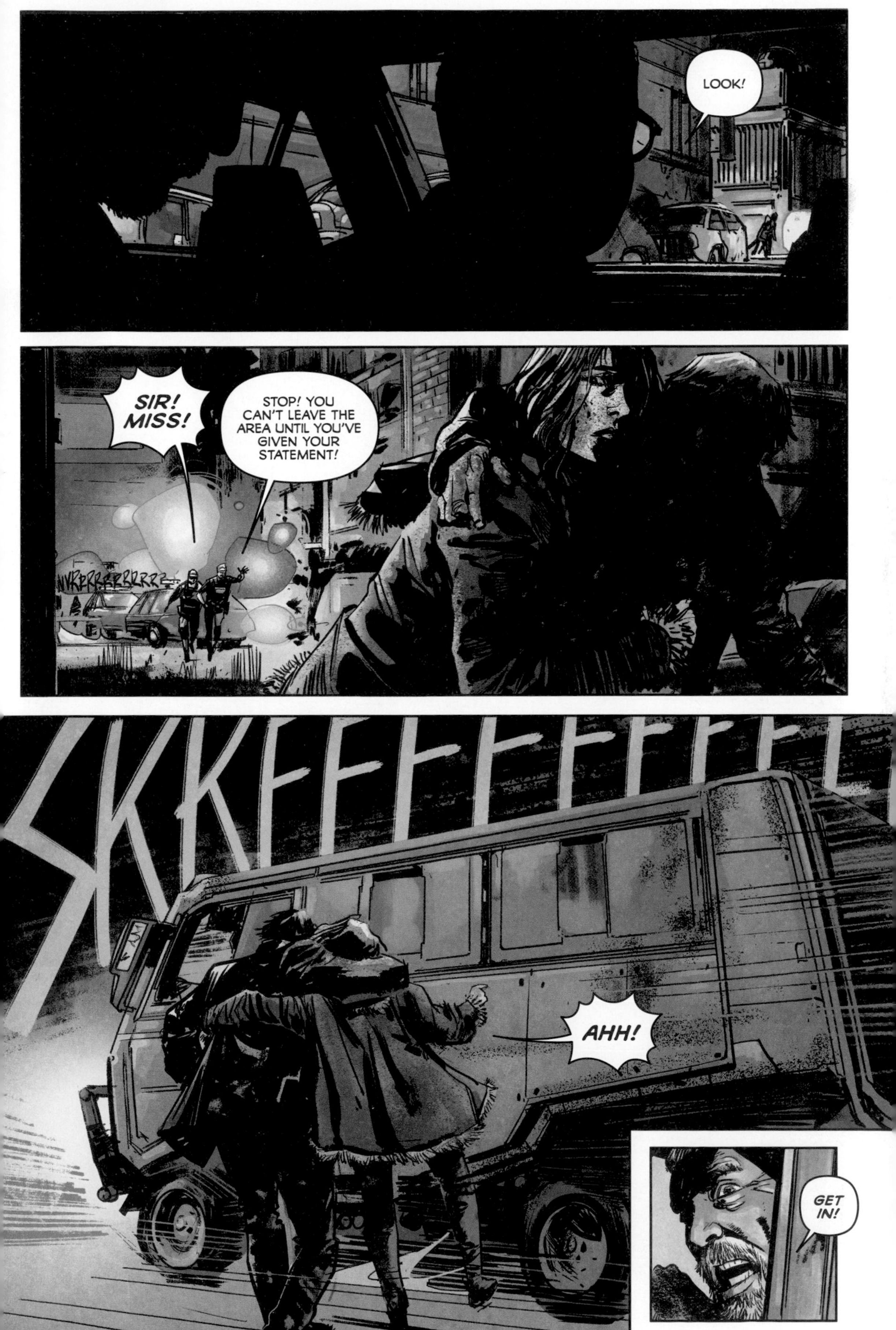
LOOK!
SIR! MISS!
STOP! YOU CAN'T LEAVE THE AREA UNTIL YOU'VE GIVEN YOUR STATEMENT!
NVRRRRRRRRRRR
SKREEEEEEEEEEE
AHH!
GET IN!

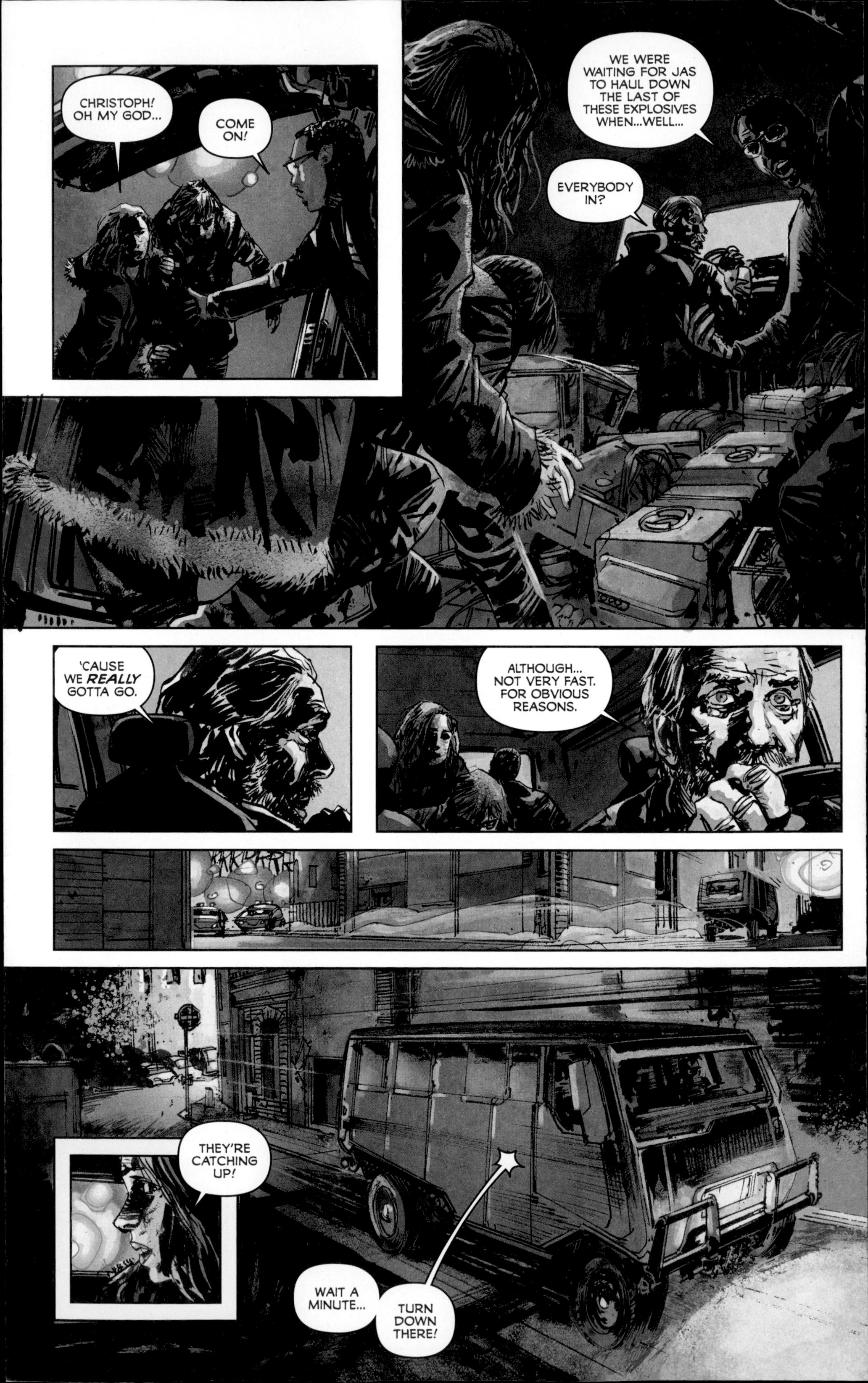
CHRISTOPH! OH MY GOD...
COME ON!
WE WERE WAITING FOR JAS TO HAUL DOWN THE LAST OF THESE EXPLOSIVES WHEN...WELL...
EVERYBODY IN?
'CAUSE WE **REALLY** GOTTA GO.
ALTHOUGH... NOT VERY FAST. FOR OBVIOUS REASONS.
THEY'RE CATCHING UP!
WAIT A MINUTE...
TURN DOWN THERE!

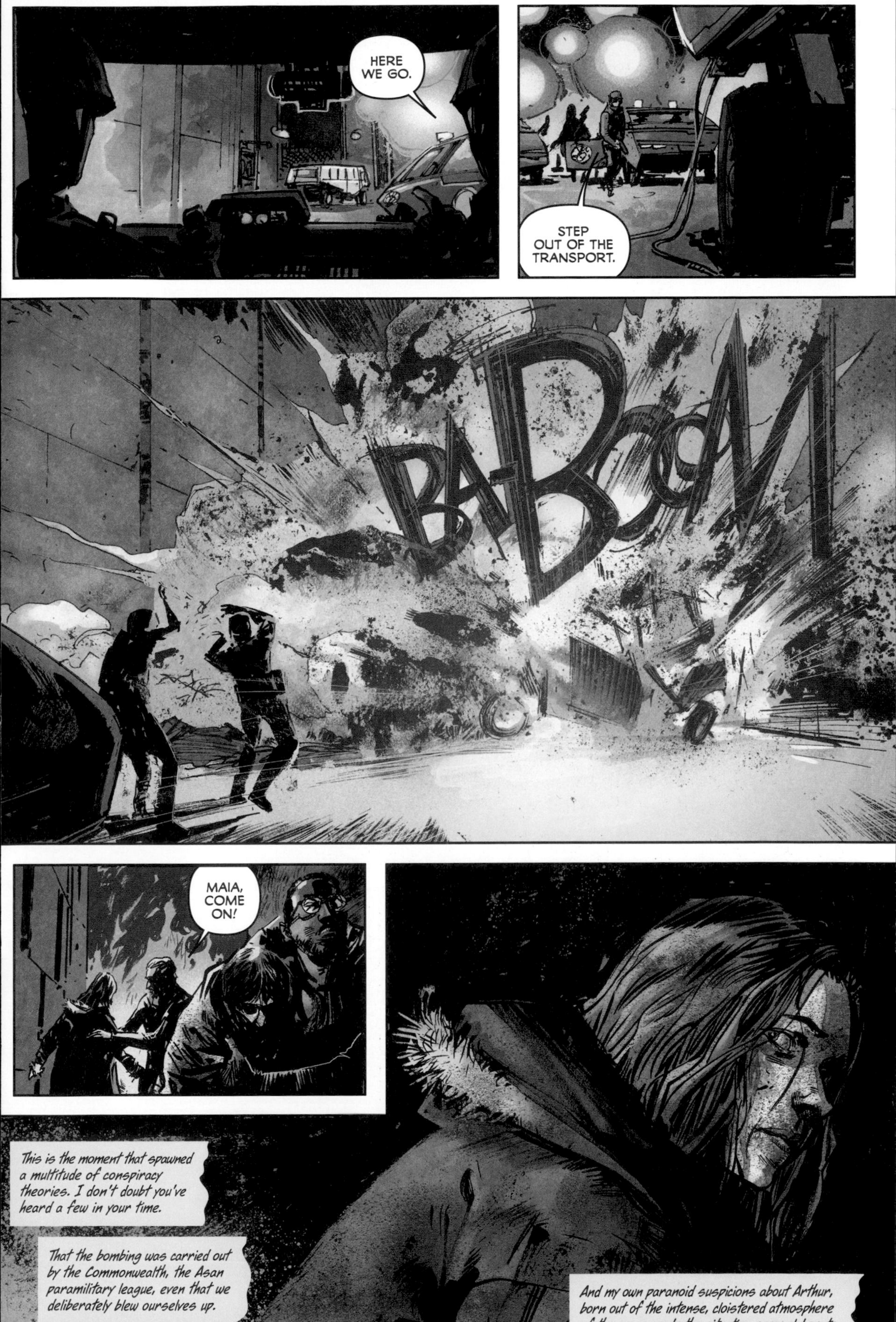
HERE WE GO.
STEP OUT OF THE TRANSPORT.
BA-BOOM
MAIA, COME ON!
This is the moment that spawned a multitude of conspiracy theories. I don't doubt you've heard a few in your time.
That the bombing was carried out by the Commonwealth, the Asan paramilitary league, even that we deliberately blew ourselves up.
And my own paranoid suspicions about Arthur, born out of the intense, cloistered atmosphere of the group, made the situation seem elaborate, when in the end it was so simple.

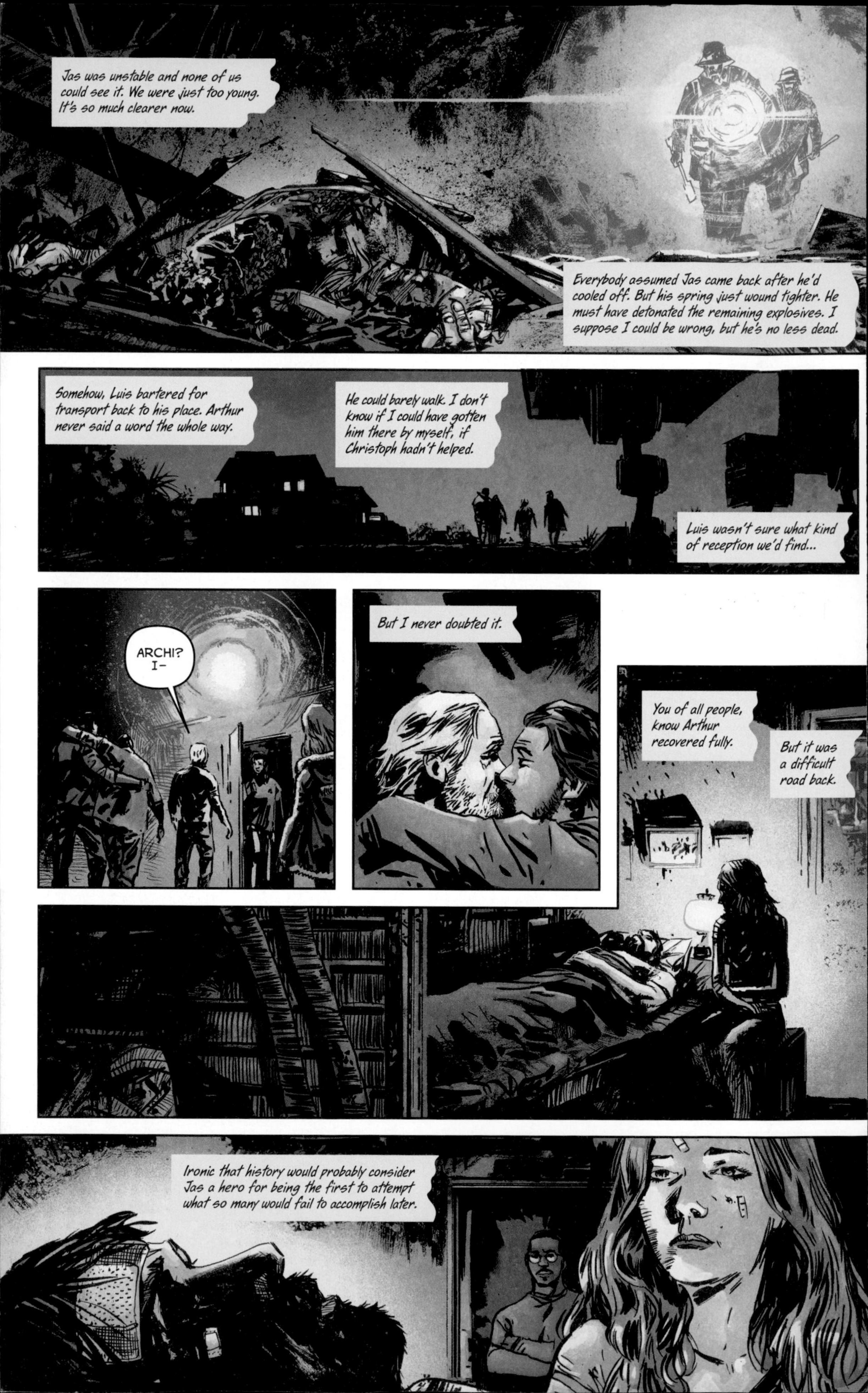

Jas was unstable and none of us could see it. We were just too young. It's so much clearer now.
Everybody assumed Jas came back after he'd cooled off. But his spring just wound tighter. He must have detonated the remaining explosives. I suppose I could be wrong, but he's no less dead.
Somehow, Luis bartered for transport back to his place. Arthur never said a word the whole way.
He could barely walk. I don't know if I could have gotten him there by myself, if Christoph hadn't helped.
Luis wasn't sure what kind of reception we'd find...
ARCHI? I–
But I never doubted it.
You of all people, know Arthur recovered fully.
But it was a difficult road back.
Ironic that history would probably consider Jas a hero for being the first to attempt what so many would fail to accomplish later.

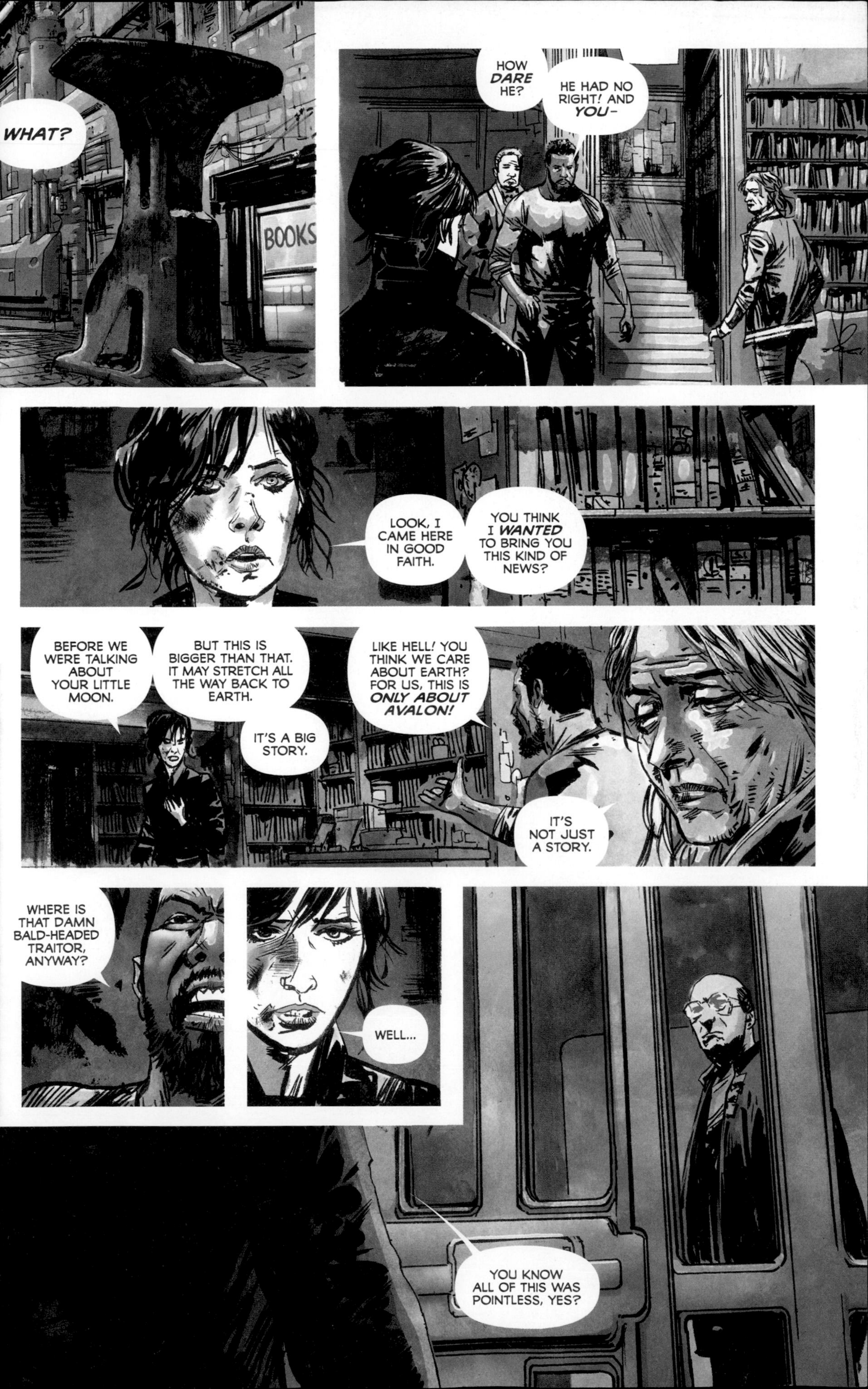
WHAT?
BOOKS
HOW *DARE* HE?
HE HAD NO RIGHT! AND *YOU*–
LOOK, I CAME HERE IN GOOD FAITH.
YOU THINK I *WANTED* TO BRING YOU THIS KIND OF NEWS?
BEFORE WE WERE TALKING ABOUT YOUR LITTLE MOON.
BUT THIS IS BIGGER THAN THAT. IT MAY STRETCH ALL THE WAY BACK TO EARTH.
IT'S A BIG STORY.
LIKE HELL! YOU THINK WE CARE ABOUT EARTH? FOR US, THIS IS ***ONLY ABOUT AVALON!***
IT'S NOT JUST A STORY.
WHERE IS THAT DAMN BALD-HEADED TRAITOR, ANYWAY?
WELL...
YOU KNOW ALL OF THIS WAS POINTLESS, YES?

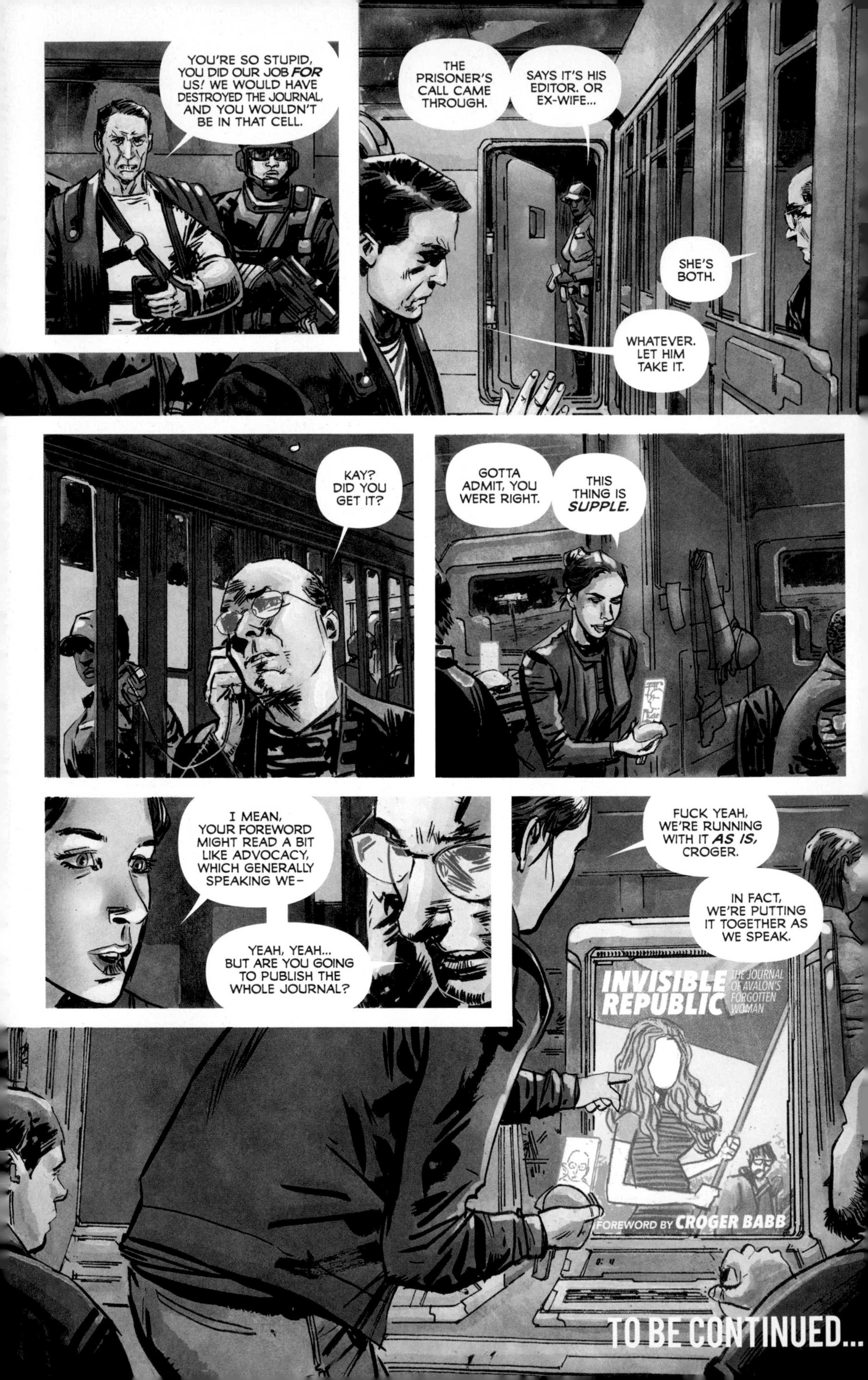
YOU'RE SO STUPID, YOU DID OUR JOB *FOR* US! WE WOULD HAVE DESTROYED THE JOURNAL, AND YOU WOULDN'T BE IN THAT CELL.
THE PRISONER'S CALL CAME THROUGH.
SAYS IT'S HIS EDITOR. OR EX-WIFE...
SHE'S BOTH.
WHATEVER. LET HIM TAKE IT.
KAY? DID YOU GET IT?
GOTTA ADMIT, YOU WERE RIGHT.
THIS THING IS *SUPPLE.*
I MEAN, YOUR FOREWORD MIGHT READ A BIT LIKE ADVOCACY, WHICH GENERALLY SPEAKING WE–
YEAH, YEAH... BUT ARE YOU GOING TO PUBLISH THE WHOLE JOURNAL?
FUCK YEAH, WE'RE RUNNING WITH IT *AS IS,* CROGER.
IN FACT, WE'RE PUTTING IT TOGETHER AS WE SPEAK.
INVISIBLE REPUBLIC
THE JOURNAL OF AVALON'S FORGOTTEN WOMAN
FOREWORD BY CROGER BABB
TO BE CONTINUED...

END OF CHAPTER 02

WELCOME TO AVALON

If this is your first time visiting Asan's largest moon, you are in for a surprise. Avalon retains its reputation as a barren planet of little interest to the tourist, an idea that persists from the days this system was first settled. Even then it was unfounded, as Avalon was a place of stark natural beauty before the many changes that humanity wrought upon its surface.

Still, it must be said that in those early days, when this moon was still known as Maidstone, there was little enough to lure a lover of wildlife away from the lush forests of Asan or the limited though bizarre life forms on Kent. And so the myth of a sterile Avalon, barren of everything not actively cultivated by humans, has persisted. Don't believe the hype. With the help of this guide, you, too, might be lucky enough to catch sight of a slimpet, or even a crackle. Look closely, for even those animals that you recognize as common at home have undergone changes in both behavior and appearance since their introduction here.

For ease of identification all names will appear both as they are known locally and as they commonly appear on their home planets. The scientific names are still contested in most cases due to the paucity of communication with Earth, but since this is a detail usually unappreciated by the general reader, we have decided to leave them out of this guide. HAPPY WILDLIFE SPOTTING!

GREEN (AVALON) / **GREEN ALGAE** (ASAN AND KENT)

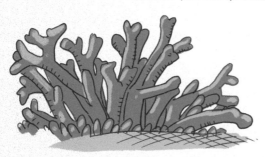

As the only truly endemic life form on Avalon, this strange plant deserves a book all its own. When humanity first explored this moon the algae covered nearly every inch of open salt water, and some forms had even evolved to colonize brackish and fresh water. It is something of a puzzle that nothing else (as far as we know, since the depths of Avalon's seas and some of its remoter regions remain unexplored) has evolved to take advantage of the moon's mild climate and abundant sunshine.

Fortunately, the algae (not truly an algae, being wholly unrelated to any Earth-based form, of course) proved edible, and to be a rich nutrient base when applied as a fertilizer to otherwise sterile soils. Today, much of

Avalon's algae has been tamed for use on the vast farms that cover much of the southern portion of the largest continent. Its use in the local cuisine is ubiquitous, appearing in cakes, noodles, broths, and even a hot drink known as "caff," which has stimulative properties similar to those found in coffee and tea when brewed in a time-consuming process that known locally as "decanting."

SHARP FISH (AVALON) / KRESS (ASAN)

Often called simply "fish," these omnivorous creatures are the product of a failed aquaculture venture dating from the first wave of colonization. Originally found only on Asan, where they rarely grow to be over 24 cm long, these creatures have become something of a nuisance on much of Avalon, where they often reach lengths of more than a meter. On their home planet they spawn early and often to offset the population crashes that occur every third month, coinciding with the wake cycle of their most prolific predator. On Avalon they have no natural predators, resulting in the population explosion that continues to this day.

Sharp fish are now known to become more carnivorous with age, so it might be supposed that the older, larger kress would suppress the spread of new kress. Unfortunately, the frequency of their spawning combined with their talent for parthenogenesis (so-called "virgin births," which are really a form of self-cloning) means that they will not naturally limit their own numbers. They are considered edible by some groups on Avalon (especially those who have difficulty finding enough protein from other sources), but their somewhat bitter-tasting flesh has limited their use in most quarters. Current campaigns to add them to the menus of fashionable restaurants have met with limited success, possibly due to their supposed status as "working class fare."

Spotting a sharp fish is easy in most southern bays, canals, and seashores. They often congregate in great numbers near the surface, sometimes forming knots so tight they appear to be stepping stones. Such gatherings make for great viewing, but be careful not to get too close. Their teeth and armor are both sharp, and they are indiscriminate feeders.

The Gravity Puzzle

BY CORINNA BECHKO

SPACE CAN BE PRETTY UNCOMFORTABLE.

It's vast, it's empty, there's nothing to breathe and nothing to eat. It's hard to get to, and it's hard to leave without dying in a fiery crash. Every one of these problems is related to gravity.

Gravity is a strange thing. We all know what it does, and it's easy enough to describe, but in many ways it's mysterious. It's extremely weak compared to other forces, for one thing. For another, we don't really understand exactly what it is. What we do know is that it is fundamentally related to mass. That's one of the main reasons that the Earth is such a nice place to live. We, and every single other thing on the planet (including the atmosphere), are all constantly in the process of falling towards the center of the planet. But the force of that pull is so weak that even our puny bodies can counteract it, allowing us to walk upright, jump, and even fly with a little mechanical assistance. Of course, our bodies have mass too, so we are pulling everything towards ourselves as well. But it takes something as big as the Earth to exert enough of a tug to keep us anchored to the ground.

And therein lies the problem with creating gravity in space. Weightlessness might look like fun, but living in zero-G or microgravity is a long series of complicated problems. Eating is hard.

Drinking is worse. Toilet design is a nightmare. The sensation itself makes many people "space sick." And that's just the annoying stuff. Worse are the long-term effects on the human body. It doesn't take long for bones to become less dense, muscles to lose mass, vision to be affected by the flattening of the back of the eyeball and fluid leakage around the optic nerve. Obviously, gravity is necessary for just about every biological process.

This presents a problem for long-term space missions as well as the construction of space stations. It even presents difficulties for colonizing Mars, where gravity is only about 62% of what it is on Earth. We are obviously not going to build anything bigger than Mars, so gravity based on mass is not an option for space travel. Nor is the "artificial gravity" that is such a staple of science fiction. This type of gravity, if it's dealt with at all, is usually presented as some form of magnetism, causing people, furniture, tea cups, and tea to magically act as if they were on Earth, with the ship playing the part of the planet. The force of nature in play here is really the human urge to tell stories, since the creators don't want to spend every single episode dealing with how annoying weightlessness is, preferring to dramatize the human condition instead.

In reality, the only practical solution is to utilize other forces that create the same effect. The most obvious when talking about long-range travel is acceleration. In theory, you could accelerate until you reached the halfway point to wherever you were headed, then decelerate for the other half of the journey. This would cause you to "stick" to the side of the ship opposite the direction of thrust if you were going fast enough. The problem is the expense involved. The faster you go, the heavier you get, and the harder it is to go faster still. The same is true of slowing down. In the absence of friction there's no natural slowing, so a great deal of fuel must be used to stop the vehicle.

That leaves only one real, workable plan: centripedal force. In this scenario it doesn't matter if the ship is traveling or stationary, just that the part of it housing humans rotates. If the spin is fast enough, whatever is inside will "stick" to the surface closest to the hull. The effect is exactly like being in a carnival ride, or a car circling a roundabout too fast.

The problem here is one of basic physics. The smaller the ship, the faster it will have to spin to create anything other than microgravity. In practice, astronauts can receive some benefit to being strapped into to whirling "chairs" that let their bodies experience the effects of gravity for a period each day, but these tend to also create

THE EFFECT IS EXACTLY LIKE BEING IN A CARNIVAL RIDE, OR A CAR CIRCLING A ROUNDABOUT TOO FAST.

vertigo, nausea, and general discomfort. Even a much bigger ship risks these things if there are windows, since motion sickness is not unknown in space. To spin at a more leisurely pace, one that might allow a semblance of normal life, the ship would have to be immense, at least the size of a football field. Still, that's a whole lot smaller than a planet, so designing one would be merely difficult, not impossible.

In the end, counteracting weightlessness aboard long-range spacecraft is probably one of the more tractable problems involved space travel, at least from a design perspective. And that's good news for anyone who values having enough muscle tone to set foot on a new world under their own power.

Isle of Apples

BY CORINNA BECHKO

There's a secret paradise. It's right over that farthest ridge, or just out of sight over the horizon where the sun meets the water when it sets. It's on top of a mountain, barricaded against prying eyes by a scrim of mist, or perhaps it's a little out of step with our world, existing next to us but invisible to all but the most gifted. It's an area where humanity and nature exist in perfect harmony, where crops flourish of their own accord, where even the most grievous wounds heal given enough time. It's utterly impossible, often explicitly mystical, and yet almost every culture on Earth has similar legends. Sometimes this perfect garden was lost due to human carelessness and vice, but sometimes it's merely very, very hard to find.

The island of Avalon, famously the last retreat of King Arthur, is such a place. The name itself echoes its primary attributes of preservation and magical abundance, probably deriving from the Welsh word *afal*, meaning apple. Its earliest linkage with the Arthurian canon occurs in Geoffrey of Monmouth's Historia Regum Britannaie (The History of the Kings of Britain), in 1136 ACE, where it is called Insula Avallonis. It's quite possible that Geoffrey was inspired by the older Celtic story about an island called Emhain Abhlach, the "Emhain of the Apple Trees." Both islands are mysterious and not quite of this world, and both boast connections with an older, wilder magic despite their connotations of bountiful cultivation.

It is through Geoffrey's history that we learn of Avalon's healing powers, and that it is the place where King Arthur's sword was forged. This is no unpeopled paradise, though. In almost every story it boasts at least one charismatic resident, a strong feminine presence to counter Arthur's equally masculine one. For Avalon is also the home of Morgan le Fay, Arthur's half-sister, sometimes thought of as his healer and sometimes as one of his most dangerous adversaries.

As the myth of Avalon spread it became entwined with the real Glastonbury Abbey, due in no small part to the supposed discovery of the remains of Arthur and Gwenevere there in the twelfth century. It might seem that moving this mystical stronghold from an island to the mainland is an odd thing to do, but in fact this marshy area of the English countryside used to flood every summer, creating a shallow lake interspersed with hilltops poking above the waterline. This pattern no longer holds, but to this day the Abbey remains firmly linked in most people's minds with the Arthurian tradition.

As early as the late twelfth century, Gerald of Wales was already trying to debunk some of the most fantastical King Arthur stories, saying "...the British peoples even now conten[d] foolishly that he is still alive" despite the fact that "his body was discovered at Glastonbury..." In actuality, the remains there were probably nothing more than a stunt fabricated to raise funds to repair the abbey, which had been badly damaged by fire in 1184.

Regardless of where Arthur actually lies, or even if he ever existed, his legend continues to

fascinate. It has surged into the popular culture over and over throughout the centuries, but experienced a particularly fruitful resurgence during the late 1800s. The island of Avalon held particular appeal for artists such as William Morris at the time, creators who countered the rush to industrial progress they saw around them by highlighting the beauty of the natural world. Today that trend continues, but the message has changed somewhat. The notion of an ethereal yet fertile landscape remains, but the ties to feminine strength have intensified while the Arthurian connection has

IT'S UTTERLY IMPOSSIBLE, OFTEN EXPLICITLY MYSTICAL, AND YET ALMOST EVERY CULTURE ON EARTH HAS SIMILAR LEGENDS.

waned to some extent. Often references to Avalon evoke a mysterious, unobtainable place without benefit of any context whatsoever, having shed everything but the notion of beauty and otherworldliness.

In the end, it's this idea of Avalon that counts, because of what it can tell us about our own desires for an unspoiled paradise. That idea has changed a great deal over the last 1,000 years, but the fact that it persists in our culture proves how powerful the basic concept is. Avalon itself may be illusory, but if we can imagine it, we can aspire to it. And that alone gives this particular mystical garden real value.

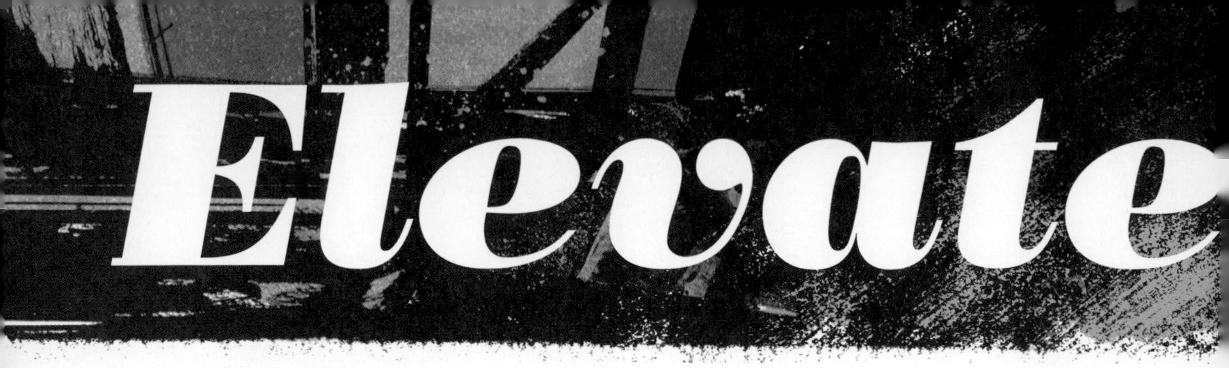

Elevate

BY CORINNA BECHKO

Getting stuff into space is hard, not to mention expensive. Gravity is proportionally a very weak force, but planets and moons are big and they exert a lot of it. To counteract that pull takes a lot of thrust. It's a vicious cycle: the more fuel needed to propel the rocket, the more fuel it has to initially lift–and the stronger the pull of gravity on the vehicle. If we're ever going to explore more of the universe we're going to have to figure a way around this problem or we'll spend all our time (and resources) flinging things out of our atmosphere instead of journeying between worlds. Orbital platforms are one answer (chalk up a win for humans here since we've already got one, sort of. The International Space Station may not be an interstellar launch pad, but it does at least prove that humans can live in space for longer than a few days at a stretch). Still, by themselves they don't solve the problem. Materials still need to be moved up there, leaving behind a not inconsiderable environmental footprint down here.

There are many ideas about how to solve this conundrum. One of the most venerable is the "space elevator." Initially popularized by Arthur C. Clarke in his sci-fi classic *The Fountains of Paradise*, the notion of a large satellite above geostationary orbit–much, much higher than our atmosphere but linked to the planet below by what amounts to a long cable–seems almost too simple to work. Such a system would move freight up and down the cable, like, well, an elevator. And the whole system could run on electricity (maybe even produced with renewable resources) that would be much, much cheaper than rocket fuel.

What keeps the cable, which would have to be about 22,000 miles (35,400 km) long, from crashing back to Earth? The answer is no more complicated than centrifugal repulsion. As long as the orbital platform provides a counterweight, the fact that it's got rotational velocity will keep it aloft. It's the same force that keeps the space station up there, and the same that keeps a tether ball spinning straight out around a pole if

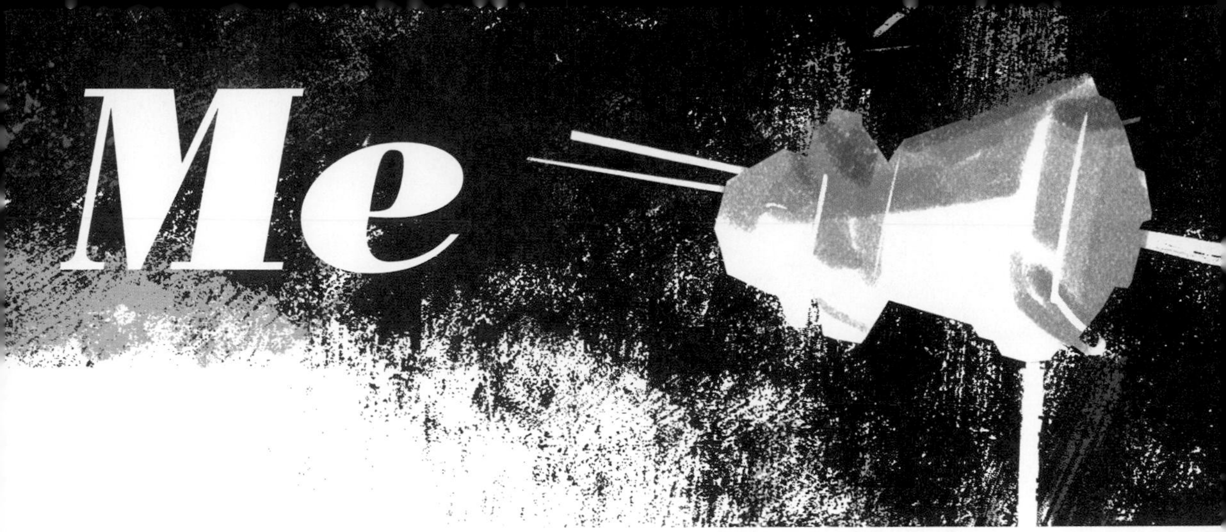
Me

you give it a good thump. Another way to think of it is to imagine a skyscraper. Each floor pushes the one above it up, against the pull of gravity. A space elevator would do exactly the opposite. The cable wouldn't be pushed up by the material below it, but rather pulled up from above. In fact, it wouldn't even have to touch the ground, but could simply float, appearing to be tethered by magic but really just demonstrating how the various physical forces can balance each other out.

Another way to think of it is to imagine a skyscraper. Each floor pushes the one above it up, against the pull of gravity.

A SPACE ELEVATOR WOULD DO EXACTLY THE OPPOSITE.

Of course, in practice it's a lot harder than that. We haven't yet got the proper materials to build a cable that long and strong, although we're working on it. Then there's the same old problem of getting the building materials up there to begin with. Not to mention how vulnerable it could be to space debris at the far end as well as to sabotage on the near end. It's a sad fact that we probably won't be seeing a space elevator on Earth any time soon, despite optimistic announcements to the contrary.

But what about on other planets, or the moon? If we started building from the space end (maybe even with materials mined from asteroids) and worked our way down, the formula suddenly becomes quite a bit more practical. There are even pie-in-the-sky ideas about mining energy from around black holes using a similar system. (Spoiler: this one really would fail. The physics preclude it.) The problem is the same in each instance. How to escape a gravity well with as little fuss as possible? It's easy to imagine a time in the far future when one of the tools available for colonizing distant worlds is a collapsible box that can be deployed along with a really, really long ribbon made of carbon nanotubes while the transport vehicle stays parked safely in orbit. Get ready for one hell of an elevator ride!

Want to read more about that black hole space elevator? Check out Adam Brown's article in the February 2015 issue of Scientific American.

Vegetables Without Borders

BY CORINNA BECHKO

CULTURE IS A CURIOUS THING. So much of our identity is tied up in the culture bequeathed to us by our parents, the dominant culture into which we are born, and the subcultures we adopt. Each has its own signifiers and shorthand, its inclusions and exclusions. A lot of it can be seen as superficial, like the fact that I, hailing from the Southern US, love okra. As a child, this set me apart from the "snowbirds," tourist who would descend on my hometown every winter. Most of them, not having eaten it as children, found the texture to be off-putting. This preference for one vegetable over another is a minor difference, but it says something deep about the histories of our native regions. The derivation of okra is hazy, with roots going back to South Asia, West Africa, and Ethiopia, all places with a tradition of using it in a wide variety of dishes.

We do know how it got to the Americas over 300 hundred years ago, and that story isn't pretty. It arrived on the same ships that plied the Atlantic in service to the slave trade, a tragic fact that I didn't learn until I was living far from my own Floridian origins.

My new knowledge didn't make me dislike okra. After all, it wasn't because of the plant that these crimes were committed. But I do think about it now whenever I eat it. Okra is part of my cultural heritage (for good or for ill) as someone born in the South, but it's also part of very different cultures half a world away. Nearly everything we see, hear, and consume is the same. No modern human exists in a vacuum, and "cultural purity" in the modern world is a concept with no basis in reality.

Surely though, in the past, there were distinct cultures that grew and changed on their own? It isn't likely, for humans love to borrow and repurpose, building different traditions and meanings around everything from food to fashion.

In the case of okra, we can chart its path back through time from the United States (where even Thomas Jefferson was known to cultivate it) to Brazil, where it first arrived on slave ships, to Africa and the Mediterranean. Before that it was known to the Egyptians, who may have eaten it fried, as I usually did.

On its own the history of a single food item may seem insignificant. But dig a little, and every preference we have reveals a story about what it means to be human, and why we do ourselves no favors when we ignore the historical implications of the cultures we embrace without question.

MY NEW KNOWLEDGE DIDN'T MAKE ME DISLIKE OKRA. AFTER ALL, IT WASN'T BECAUSE OF THE PLANT THAT THESE CRIMES WERE COMMITTED. BUT I DO THINK ABOUT IT NOW WHENEVER I EAT IT.

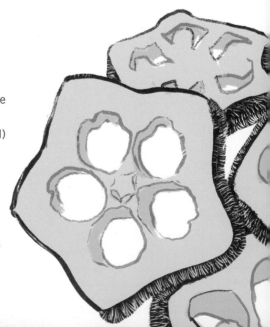

COVERS

BY **GABRIEL HARDMAN**

ISSUE SIX

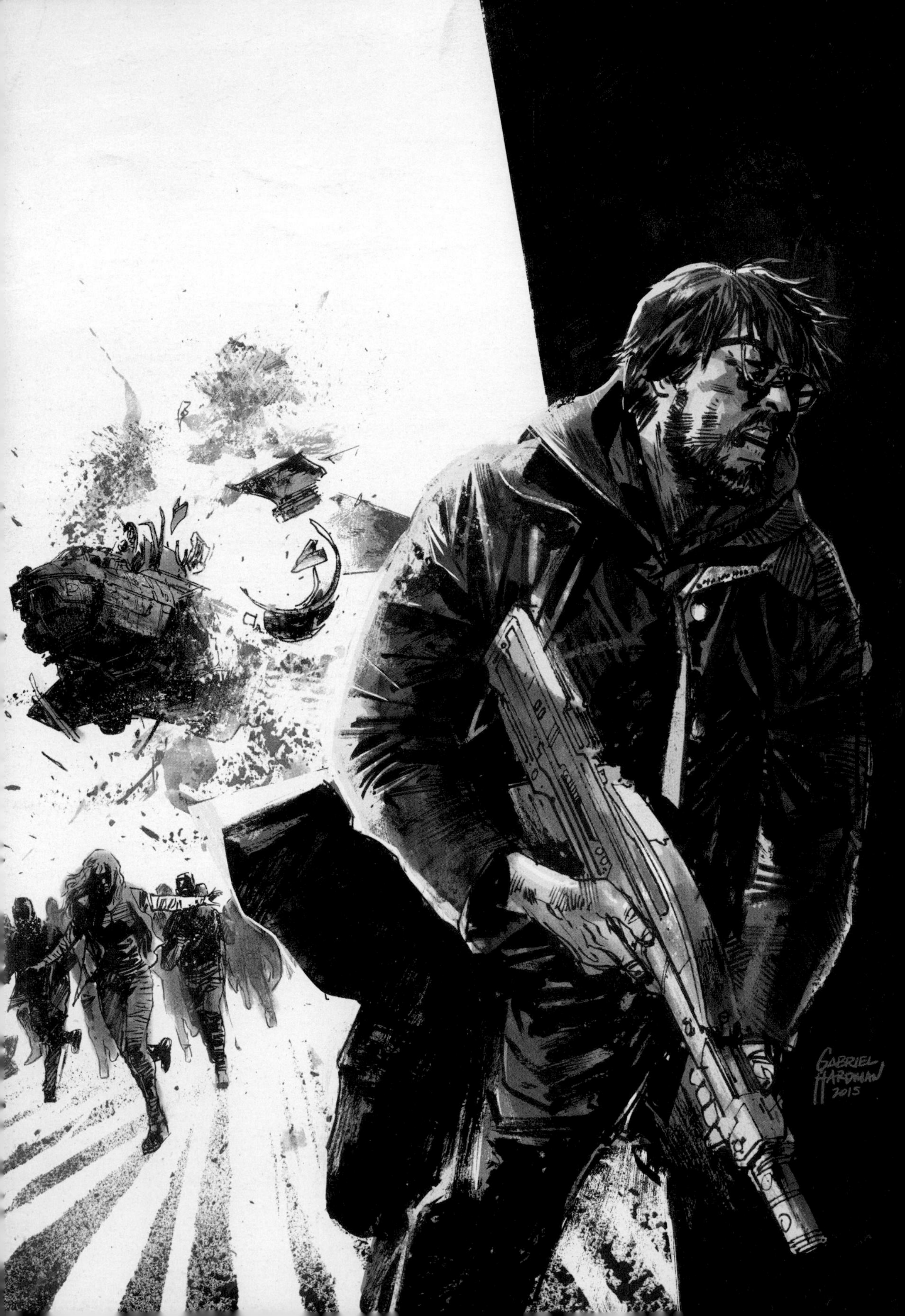
GABRIEL HARDMAN 2015

ISSUE SEVEN

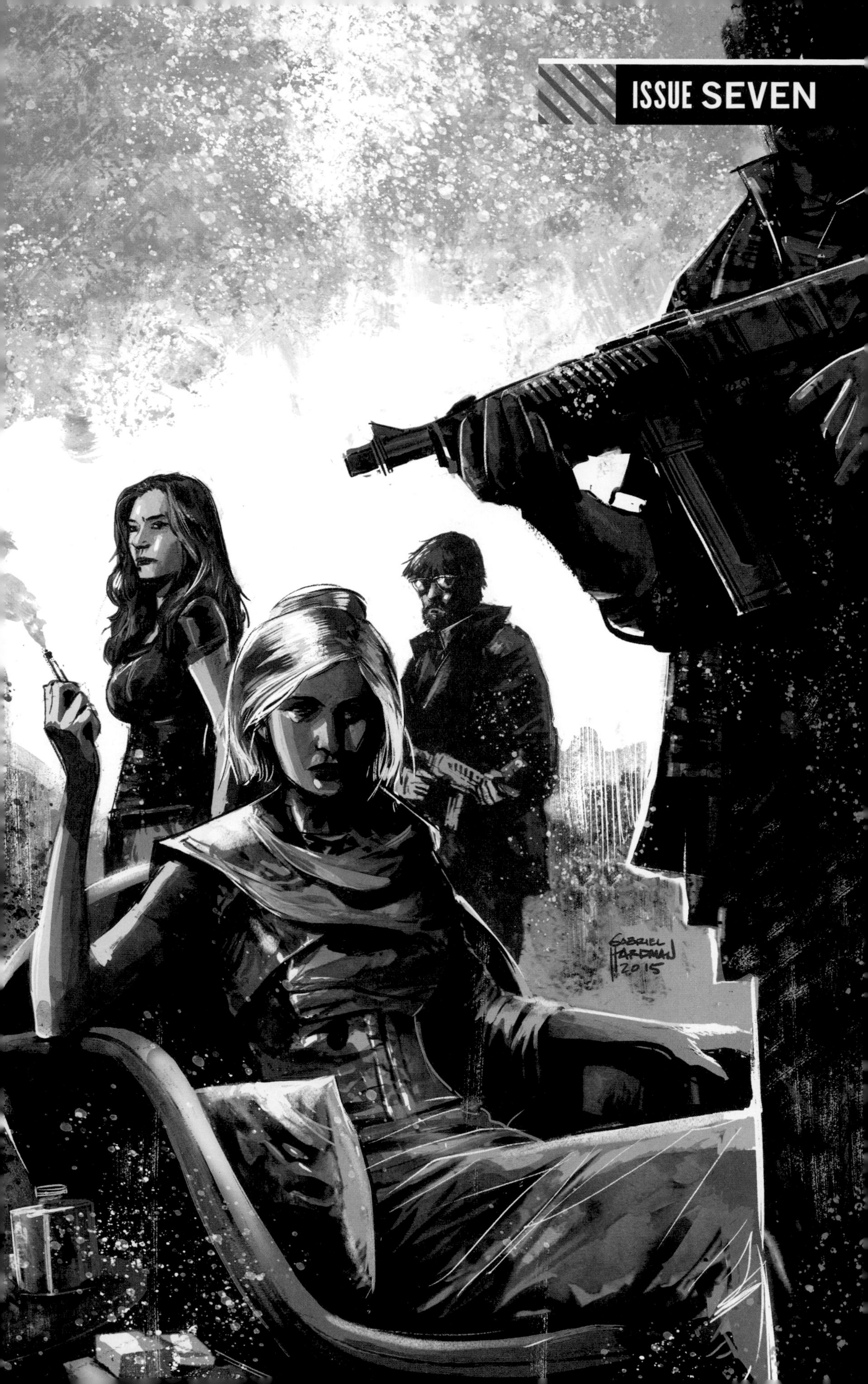
GABRIEL HARDMAN 2015

ISSUE EIGHT

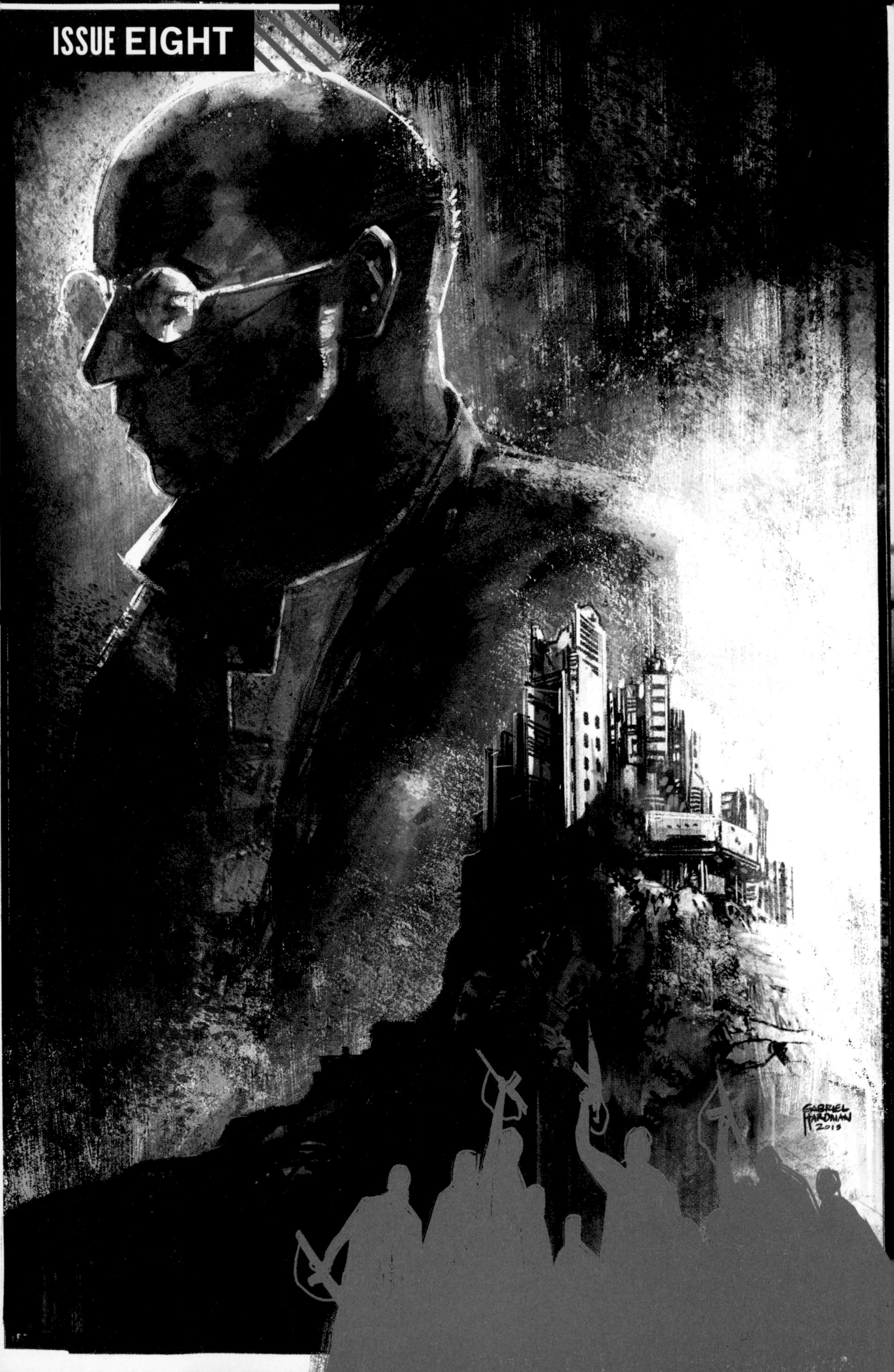
GABRIEL HARDMAN 2015

ISSUE NINE

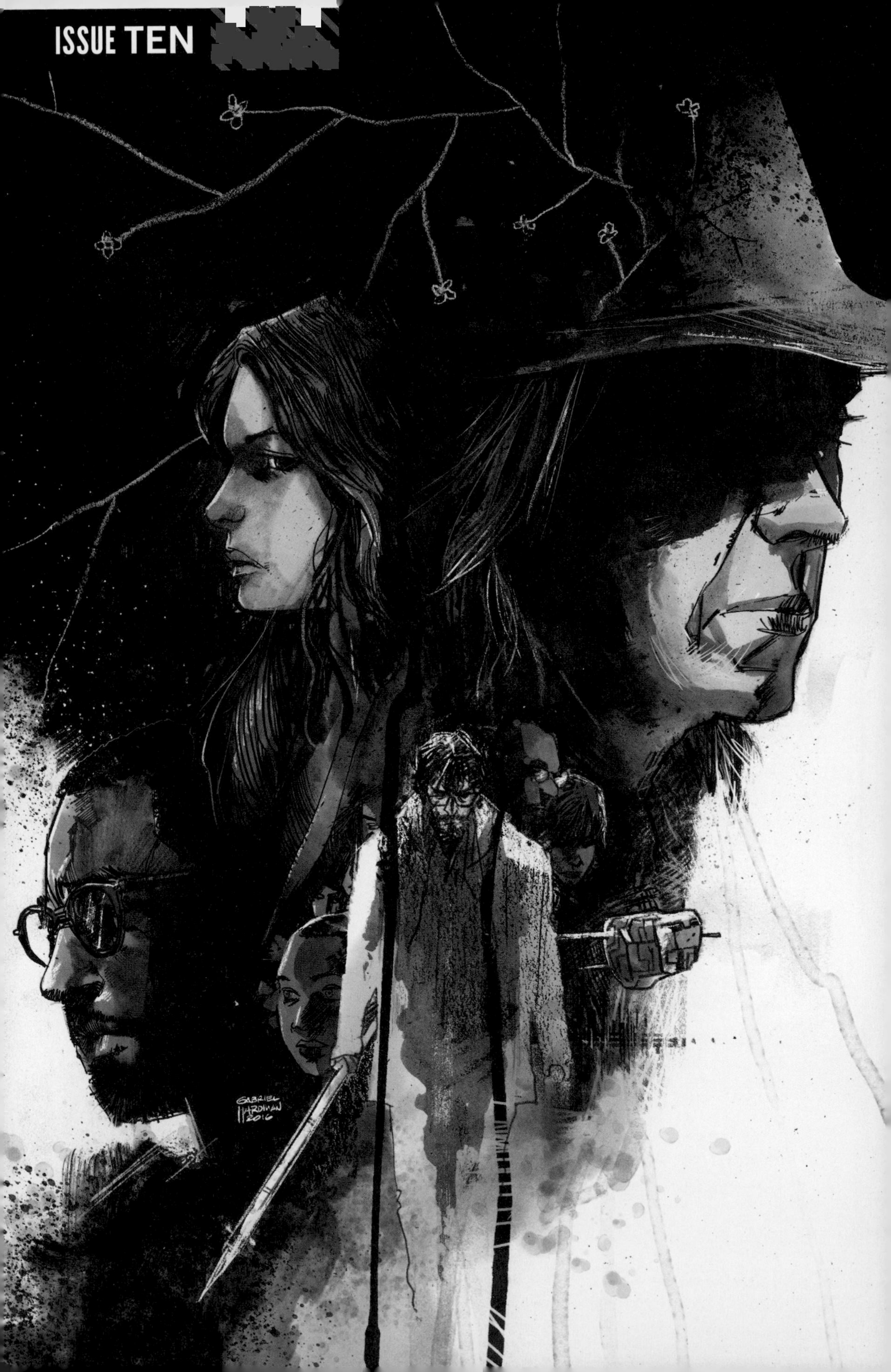
ISSUE TEN [redacted]
GABRIEL HARDMAN 2016

GABRIEL HARDMAN is the writer/artist of *Kinski,* published digitally by Monkeybrain Comics and collected in print by Image Comics. He also co-wrote (with Corinna Bechko) and drew *Savage Hulk* for Marvel Comics, *Sensation Comics* for DC Comics, *Star Wars: Legacy* for Dark Horse Comics, and *Planet Of The Apes* for Boom! Studios. He has drawn *Hulk*, *Secret Avengers* and *Agents of Atlas* for Marvel as well as the OGN *Heathentown* for Image/Shadowline. He's worked as a storyboard artist on movies such as *Interstellar*, *Inception*, *Tropic Thunder,* and *X2*. He lives with his wife, writer Corinna Bechko, in Los Angeles.

gabrielhardman.tumblr.com   @gabrielhardman

CORINNA BECHKO has been writing comics since her horror graphic novel *Heathentown* was published by Image/Shadowline in 2009. Since then she has worked for numerous publishers including Marvel, DC, Boom!, Dynamite, and Dark Horse on titles that include *Aliens/Vampirella* and *Lara Croft and the Frozen Omen*, as well as co-writing *Star Wars: Legacy Volume II, Savage Hulk,* and *Sensation Comics featuring Wonder Woman.* She is a zoologist by training and shares her home with co-creator/husband Gabriel Hardman, three cats, a lovebird, a farm dog, and a fancy street rabbit.

corinnabechko.tumblr.com   @corinnabechko

JORDAN BOYD

Despite nearly flunking kindergarten for his exclusive use of black crayons, Jordan has moved on to become an increasingly prolific comic book colorist. Some of his most recent credits include *Planet Hulk* and *Ant-Man* for Marvel, and *Deadly Class* for Image. He and his family reside in Norman, OK.

boydcolors.tumblr.com   @jordantboyd

DYLAN TODD is an art director and graphic designer. You might have seen his work on comics like *Sacrifice*, *Five Ghosts*, *Edison Rex*, *POP*, or *Avengers A.I.* Sometimes he writes comics and sometimes he writes about comics. Despite the fact that they don't show up in pictures, he actually does have eyebrows. His life's ambition is to meet an actual ewok.

bigredrobot.net   @bigredrobot

ALSO BY THE AUTHORS

HEATHENTOWN
WRITTEN BY CORINNA BECHKO
ART BY GABRIEL HARDMAN

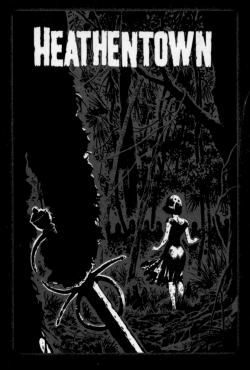

When Anna travels deep within the Florida Everglades to attend her closest friend's funeral she finds herself in an eerie, small town where death might not be the end. To discover the truth she unearths a coffin, starting a chain reaction and bringing an ancient malevolence into the town bent on Anna's destruction!

"An unorthodox horror story, equal parts hidden worlds, lost love and mammoths, Heathentown is that rarest of things—a genuinely unusual take on the undead... Bechko and Hardman are a perfectly matched team as Hardman's beautiful, highly cinematic art captures the excitement and complex emotions of Bechko's memorable and nuanced story."
–Publishers Weekly

FROM IMAGE COMICS/SHADOWLINE

KINSKI
WRITTEN AND DRAWN BY GABRIEL HARDMAN

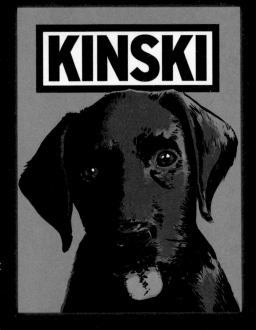

Kinski. The story of a boy and his dog. Only the boy is a traveling salesman and the dog doesn't belong to him.

Joe's self-styled mission to save a puppy from its neglectful owners escalates into a righteous crusade in this quirky crime thriller written and drawn by Gabriel Hardman (*Hulk, Heathentown, Planet of the Apes*).

"Hardman...creates a tense atmosphere that makes *Kinski* the *Breaking Bad* of dognapping tales." –A.V. Club

"[Gabriel] Hardman doesn't waste one line here, and the work is strong, iconic, and just plain awesome...This one is a true winner. You need this comic."–Bag and Board

FROM IMAGE COMICS